ALONE AT LAST

"Let's stop here for a few minutes," Bryce said, indicating a grove of cottonwood and peach leaf willow.

"What would people think if they found us alone so far from the fort?" Abby's tone was sarcastic.

He put his hands around her waist and lifted her from the saddle before he let himself answer. "I don't know what they might think about you, but they would know the only reason I would be out here would be to rescue a stubborn, hardheaded female from the folly of her own actions."

Abby looked angry, but the fact that she could be angry at being called to book for such a crazy stunt only increased his frustration.

"Did you think I was just trying to scare you when I told you how dangerous it could be out here, or did you think I was trying to make you think I was a big, brave soldier who would take care of the little, helpless woman?"

Abby backed away from him. "I never thought that. I thought—"

"That's the problem. You never thought!"

The Independent Bride

LEIGH GREENWOOD

LEISURE BOOKS NEW YORK CITY

To Pat and Nancy,
for all those Thursday mornings around the dining room table.

A LEISURE BOOK®

March 2004

Published by

Dorchester Publishing Co., Inc.
200 Madison Avenue
New York, NY 10016

ISBN 0-8439-5235-0

Visit us on the web at www.dorchesterpub.com.

The Independent Bride

Chapter One

Colorado Territory, 1868

Abby Pierce stared in disbelief at the building that was supposed to house her father's store. It didn't look like the stores she was used to in St. Louis. It was a squat, broad-fronted building of adobe and rough-hewn logs that didn't have all the knots shaved off. It did have glass windows, but each appeared to be covered with enough dirt to support a small plant. A pair of sturdy iron hinges held the door in place, and a boardwalk kept customers' feet out of the mud, but neither did anything to improve the looks of the building.

"Surely they've directed us to the wrong place," Moriah said. Abby's sister looked even more dazed than Abby felt. "It's hardly better than a dog kennel."

"I suspect dogs have to do with a good deal less in the Territories than in St. Louis," Abby said. "The sign would hardly say Pierce's Supplies if it wasn't Father's store."

1

"But surely—"

"The Colorado Territory isn't like St. Louis, Moriah. The trip out here should have convinced you of that."

The stage journey had been long and harrowing. Abby had dreamed of going west ever since her father left them with his sister in St. Louis fourteen years earlier. Mile by weary mile, her bright expectations had been jolted out of her by roads rutted from winter rain and snow, and frozen out of her by the bitter winds that howled across the plains and worked their way inside the stagecoach. Mud that splashed up from the flat, empty prairie had spattered her from head to foot. Later it dried, turned to dust, and infiltrated every pore in her body. Denver had sparked a brief resurgence of her hopes for a few comforts. The wagon trip to Fort Look-out had bludgeoned them into extinction.

Discovering that her father had worked in a place like this to send money to his two daughters so they could continue to live in comfort made her feel like a selfish woman. If she'd had any notion, she'd have come out to help him years ago. From the time she was a little girl, she'd always wanted to be with him wherever he went. Following him west wouldn't have been what her mother would have wanted, but if she'd gone, at least Abby wouldn't now be suspected of embezzlement.

"We can't stay here," Moriah said. "I'll see about making arrangements to return to St. Louis."

"You can go back if you wish. I'll stay," Abby said.

"You can't even be sure of your safety. I've seen nothing but men since we arrived, half of whom wouldn't be allowed on the streets in St. Louis."

Abby looked around. What she saw made her feel small and insignificant. To the west, a range of mountains rose like a wall, their peaks towering thousands of feet above the plain. They looked so immense, dwarfed the distance so completely, she almost felt she could reach out and touch them. To the north and south lay a narrow band of hills and canyons created by streams that tumbled out of the mountains, their waters still icy from mountain snow. To the east lay the bleak plain that stretched all the way back to Missouri.

In the middle of this wilderness sat Fort Lookout. Whether she liked it or not, this unfamiliar, hostile land would be her new home, her father's store her means of support. She didn't know anything about running a store, but she would learn. She had always worked in a bank, but there wasn't a bank at the fort. Even if there had been, no one would have hired her.

Not after St. Louis.

As for the men . . . well, it didn't matter what they looked like. After Albert, she'd never trust a man again.

"I'm going inside," Abby said. "You stay here. There may be mice."

"I'm sure there will be," Moriah said. "Rats and snakes, too. Just because people move into their territory, you can't expect all God's creatures to leave."

Abby took her sister's hand and gave it a squeeze. Moriah had an almost phobic fear of mice. "You really shouldn't have come."

"Don't be silly. I don't like mice, but they're probably more suited to inhabit this earth than you or I. It'll be up to me to make peace with them."

"But you don't like the West, either. You hate everything about it."

"What kind of sister would I be if I let you stay here and do all the work while I went back East and lived in comfort? Now let's not talk of it again. It's time we had a look at Father's store."

Hand in hand, they entered the building.

Abby felt like she was entering a cave. Two kerosene

lamps suspended from the ceiling did little to relieve the darkness. She was used to brightly lighted stores with well-swept floors, neatly stacked shelves, candies and valuables under pilfer-proof glass. She was also used to clerks in vests and rolled-up sleeves hurrying to wait on her.

Her father's store looked more like a warehouse, with barrels of pork, vinegar, and flour hard by bags of beans, boxes of soap, candles, and salt. Abby wasn't the least bit encouraged by the large quantity of merchandise she saw on the shelves or stacked on tables or in piles. She couldn't imagine anyone wanting to buy in such a depressing atmosphere. Any merchant in St. Louis who dared open such a store would have gone out of business in less than a week.

"It's not very appealing," Moriah said.

Abby had expected someone to come out of the back to wait on them, but no one appeared. A survey of the stock told her that however unattractive the layout of the store and the disposition of its goods, it contained just about everything a person would need to survive. Guns, ammunition, cloth, kettles, axes, sugar, tobacco, coffee, molasses, and alcohol were only a few of the items her father had sold. There were even luxury items such as butter crackers, cotton hose in six shades, Berlin gloves, silk handkerchiefs, and many kinds of canned goods, including table fruit, oysters, honey, and olives. Clearly not all aspects of life at the fort had been reduced to essentials.

"I wonder who buys lobster?" Moriah said, holding up a can.

"At seventy-five cents each, not many people."

"How can you tell?"

"It's marked on the bottom," Abby said, turning the can upside down.

"I suppose we'll have to learn how much everything costs. I'll see what's through that door," Moriah said, indicating a sagging door beyond a counter and the pot-bellied stove that was likely their only source of heat during the winter. "Maybe the clerk is having his noon meal."

"No matter what he's doing, I'll want to know why he isn't watching the store. Anyone could drive away with a loaded wagon and he'd be none the wiser."

The sound of footsteps behind them caused both women to turn. Three men had entered the store, men unlike any of Abby and Moriah's acquaintance. Two were tall and thin, one shorter and broad with muscle. All three wore sturdy boots caked with mud, dirty pants, and heavy coats. Three very dissimilar hats covered heads of unkempt hair and shaded faces obscured by shaggy beards.

Abby's first impulse was to escape through the back door. These men looked wild and dangerous. And drunk. But she told herself not to be foolish, that most westerners would probably look wild and dangerous compared to men in St. Louis.

The men moved slowly, apparently letting their eyes gradually become accustomed to the dark interior. Instinctively Abby and Moriah moved closer together behind a counter that displayed stacks of men's checked shirts and heavy wool pants. Abby started to offer to help them, but these men had no reason to know she owned the store or that she had the authority to accept money for purchases. Furthermore, she didn't know anything about the stock, and probably wouldn't know the price of what they wanted or where to find it. Any attempt to help them would probably just create confusion.

"I'll see if there's someone in the back who can help you," she said.

5

"No need," the broad-shouldered man said. "You'll do just fine."

"I've only just arrived and don't know the stock," Abby said.

As the man approached, Abby's first impression was confirmed. He was big and frightening. Her instincts told her to be wary; her brain said he was a customer who needed help.

"You can do everything I want," the man said.

Since Abby felt incapable of doing anything, that was not a comforting thought.

"I'll do the best I can," Abby said. "Do you need supplies?"

"Yeah, we need grub," one of the tall men said. They had come up behind their friend, standing a little to each side of him. They looked even bigger and more fearsome up close.

"That ain't all we need," the big man said.

"I imagine you would appreciate a bath and a shave," Abby said, "along with new clothes. We can help you with the clothes, but you'll have to seek out a hotel for the rest."

"You shouldn't be talking to strangers in such a familiar manner," Moriah whispered to her sister.

"I like it when gals is friendly," the man said. "All three of us likes it a lot."

The men grinned at Abby, but she was sure their interpretation of friendly behavior differed from hers by a considerable degree.

"It's my intention to be as friendly as possibly to all customers," Abby said. "It's good business."

The grins grew even broader. "Sure is," the man said. "I wish more ladies felt that way."

"Are you sure you wouldn't prefer to take a bath and

have your dinner before you do your shopping?" Moriah asked.

"We done our shopping," the big man said. "Now we're ready to buy."

Abby said, "Just tell us what you want. We'll try to find it, but you'll have to carry it out to the wagon yourselves."

One of the tall men stepped forward and swept Moriah up into his arms. "This is what I want. I'll carry her out to the wagon."

"Put me down," Moriah cried. She underlined the urgency of her request by beating the man about the face. She might as well have saved her energy. The man appeared completely unaffected by her blows.

Abby realized these men had misinterpreted everything she'd said. "Put my sister down immediately," she ordered. "We're the owners of this store, not doxies selling our virtue for a few dollars. If you wish to buy supplies, we'll try to help you. Otherwise, I must ask you to leave. Not before you release my sister, however," she said, when the one man started to turn.

He acted as though she hadn't spoken. Having captured his prize, he seemed determined to hold on to it.

"You can't have one to yourself," the other tall man said. "There's not enough to go around."

"You can share with Larson."

"I ain't sharing with nobody." The barrel-chested man pointed straight at Abby. "She's my woman."

"I'm nobody's woman," Abby declared. "Neither is my sister. Tell your friend to put her down immediately."

Larson just laughed. "Orman ain't had a woman in more than six months. Now he's caught himself one, you can't expect him to let her go."

Moriah continued her futile struggle.

"That's exactly what I expect," Abby stated as she walked past Larson. "Put her down this instant," she ordered Orman. She pulled ineffectively on his arm. "If you don't, I'll summon the police."

"Do I have to?" Orman said, turning to Larson.

"Yeah, you do," the third man said. "There's not enough for you to have no woman to yourself."

"Shut up, Hobie," Larson said. "You got another female around here?" he asked Abby.

"I thought you were here to buy supplies. It never occurred to me that you'd . . . well, it never occurred to me. Tell that man to put my sister down."

Abby didn't like the way Larson eyed her, like she was a piece of meat he was checking for excess fat. Neither did she like it that Orman didn't set Moriah down. She was unused to such men, and she was becoming afraid.

Larson turned to Orman. "You and Hobie share that one. I'm taking the mouthy one for myself."

Before Abby could utter the outraged protest on the tip of her tongue, Hobie pulled a knife from his belt.

"Put her down, Orman. You're going to have to cut me to keep her."

Moriah hit the floor with a thud as Orman pulled his own knife. She was up in an instant and clutching Abby with both arms. Abby gaped at the two men. Their knives had twelve-inch blades and looked as sharp as razors.

"We could share like Larson said," Orman said.

"I ain't sharing."

"This is absurd," Abby said. "Leave my store immediately."

Larson turned his drunken, leering gaze on her. "You two stay still while Orman and Hobie settle who gets the quiet one."

Abby couldn't have moved if she'd wanted to. There were only two routes of escape. Orman and Hobie filled one. Larson blocked the other.

Abby watched in fearful fascination while Orman and Hobie circled one another, feinting, lunging forward, backing away from a flashing blade that could easily have severed a finger, maybe even a hand. As they maneuvered, trying to find an opening, they backed Abby and Moriah closer to the side of the store that had neither door nor windows. Larson's attention was focused on the combatants. Taking what she feared might be her only chance, Abby grabbed Moriah's hand, and the two of them made a run to get round him.

Larson took a quick step forward and his huge arm swung up and out, trapping them against the wall. "Stay put."

"They mean to rape us," Moriah whispered after they'd retreated beyond Larson's reach.

"Not if I have anything to say about it."

Much to her surprise, Abby was so mad, she almost forgot to be afraid. "This place is full of weapons and ammunition," Abby said. "All we have to do is get our hands on it."

"But that would mean we'd have to shoot them."

"Better that than let ourselves be raped."

It shouldn't be difficult to reach the weapons. They were so far from the door, Larson probably wouldn't pay attention if she eased away from him. Being careful not to move too quickly, Abby edged toward the guns. Her fearful looks, while not entirely false, were intended to make Larson think they were merely trying to get as far away from him and the fight as possible.

The last, at least, was true. Orman had drawn blood. It ran down Hobie's cheek and dripped onto his coat.

"I don't want to kill you," Orman said. "Say we can share."

Hobie responded by throwing himself at Orman. Both men were bleeding when they separated.

"Go easy," Larson cautioned. "You'll be soft pickings for some grizzly if you get cut real bad."

"Do you know anything about pistols?" Abby whispered to her sister.

"Of course not. How could I? I never went hunting with Father every chance I got."

Abby knew almost nothing about pistols or shotguns—her father had taught her to shoot with a small rifle—but she wasn't going to let that stop her. She picked up a pistol and a box of shells. But as soon as she opened the box, she could tell the shells were the wrong size.

A shout caused her to look up. Orman had cut Hobie again.

"That's enough," Larson said. "I don't want you crippled. You share with Orman or find your own woman."

Realizing Hobie's wound would occupy them for only a few minutes, Abby searched frantically for the correct shells. Her movements became so agitated, she dropped the pistol. The clatter caused Larson to look her way. He was on her in a flash. Moriah tried to stop him, but he pushed her aside. He looked at the shells in her hand and the pistol on the floor.

"Them's rifle shells," he said as he knocked the box from her hand. The shells rolled noisily about the floor. "You'd better stick to things a woman knows how to do. Get your woman, Orman. We can come back for the supplies later."

"Where can we take 'em?"

"Through that door," Larson said, pointing to the door through which Abby had once hoped a clerk would materialize. "Old man Pierce lived here. There must be beds back there."

Abby was determined she wasn't going to be dragged anywhere if she could help it. Several knives lay next to the pistols. She snatched up two and handed one to her sister. Moriah stared at it as if she didn't know what to do with it.

"Use it on them," Abby said as she grabbed up a second knife for herself. Larson could grab one hand but maybe not two. She'd make him sorry he'd ever laid a hand on her.

Larson looked more menacing than before. "Put the knife down before I have to hurt you."

"You're going to hurt us anyway," Abby said. "I mean to hurt you, too."

"Stop fooling with Hobie's arm and get around behind them," Larson said to Orman.

"The other one's got a knife, too."

"You've got a knife, you fool. Use it."

Orman's relief was short-lived. "If I cut her, she can't be my woman."

"You don't have to kill her, you idiot."

"Don't take your eyes off Orman," Abby said to Moriah as she kept her own gaze glued to Larson. "If he comes close, go for his throat."

The four of them stood there, staring at each other, frozen in a tableau for mere seconds that seemed like much longer. Then Larson pounced. Abby didn't know how a big man who'd drunk too much could move so quickly. One moment he was standing there, glaring angrily at her, the next he had grabbed both her wrists.

Abby didn't know what came over her. After a life of perfect ladylike behavior, she was kicking, screaming, and biting like an alley cat. Larson was too strong for her. She couldn't break his hold.

Then suddenly she found herself free. Larson had released her and slumped to the floor. Next thing she knew, Orman hit the floor and didn't move.

A man in a blue uniform turned to Hobie. "Touch that knife and you'll join your friends."

Hobie, his arm clumsily bandaged and his face still bleeding, backed into two soldiers, who immediately took hold of him. The man who'd issued the threat turned toward Abby. She found herself staring up into the face of a very tall military officer. She knew nothing about the bars and ribbons that signified rank and decorations, but she could tell this man had been rewarded with a generous measure of both.

"Did he hurt you?" he asked.

"No, but he scared me very badly."

He smiled and pointed at the knives. "It looks like you were ready to give a good account of yourself."

Abby stared down at her clenched hands. She still held a knife in each. She told herself she was safe, that Larson couldn't hurt her anymore. For a moment her muscles wouldn't respond. Then her strength left her in a rush and the knives clattered to the floor. She put out a hand to keep her balance as she slumped against the counter.

He reached out and touched her arm. "Are you all right?"

"Yes."

But she wasn't. She was weak from shock. She still found it difficult to believe the last few minutes had actually happened. If Larson and Orman hadn't been lying on the floor in front of her, she could've believed she'd imagined everything.

But she certainly hadn't imagined this army man or the effect his touch had on her. Her reaction to him wasn't at all what she would have expected, even for a man who'd just saved her from a terrible fate. A feeling of excitement caused her pulse to quicken, her breath to come in snatches. Maybe it was his size. He was as big as Larson, taller than Orman. Maybe it was the way he looked down at her with his sky-blue eyes. Maybe it was the warmth of sincere interest in his voice. Maybe it was the feeling that as long as this man was around, nothing really bad could happen to her.

Abby pulled her galloping thoughts to an abrupt halt. Brought face-to-face with a handsome man in uniform, she was behaving like a silly girl. He was just a man. There were lots of them around.

"How about you, ma'am?"

He had turned to Moriah. Abby was ashamed to admit that for a moment she'd forgotten her sister. He might be *just* a man, but no other man had ever caused her to forget Moriah.

The soldier introduced himself. "I'm Colonel Bryce McGregor, commander of Fort Lookout," he said. "I heard these three were here. I'm sorry they found you before I found them."

"Did you kill them?" Moriah asked. Neither Larson nor Orman had moved.

"I'm surprised you care what happens to them."

"My sister doesn't believe in killing," Abby said.

"These men are little better than animals. Lock them up," he told his men. "I'll deal with them later." He turned back to Abby. "You ladies are new out here. Let me escort you to where you're going."

"Thank you, but we're already there," Abby said.

"If it's shopping you have in mind, you'll have to go to Boulder Gap. Better still, Denver."

"Why? This store seems well supplied."

"Maybe, but since Abner Pierce died, you can't find anybody to serve you. Half the time the clerk's drunk

13

or gone. Abner held the lease on the store, but now that he's dead, I'll have to find someone else to take it."

"You can't do that," Abby said.

"I have to, ma'am. There's no one to run the place."

"There is now," Abby said. "I'm Abigail Pierce. This is my sister, Moriah. We're Abner Pierce's daughters."

Chapter Two

"Women can't run this store," Bryce said.

"We can and we will," Abby declared. "Since you're the authority out here, I expect you to make sure no one interferes with us."

Bryce knew he was staring at Abby as if he'd never seen a woman before. He *felt* as if he'd never seen one like her. She was everything a man should avoid—a figure made for temptation, thick brown hair, big hazel eyes, a face of beauty, and an expression of stubborn determination. At the same time she was exactly what no man could resist. It was easy to see how Orman and his friends had gone a little crazy. He didn't feel too normal himself. There was nothing weak or shy about Abby. It was her intensity that drew him. She wasn't a woman to sap a man's strength. She would fill him with the courage to face danger without flinching, drive him to do without thinking what a wise man would think twice about.

"Where do you want us to put them?" one of the soldiers asked Bryce.

"The stable will be fine until I decide what to do with them."

He warned himself to get a grip on his emotions. The one time a woman had affected him like this had led to a disastrous marriage. His father had warned Bryce that a man in his position should never let his heart rule his head. He'd made that mistake once. He didn't intend to make it again.

The men staggered to their feet. The Pierce sisters watched nervously as they were dragged from the store.

Bryce didn't have anything against women engaging in business as long as it didn't affect him. But anything that happened in the trader's store would affect him and the men under his command. It could also affect the situation with the Indians on the reservation. That was where the problem got personal.

Bryce had been breveted a general during the Civil War. But like so many officers who were promoted on the battlefield, his rank had been temporary and had been reduced with the advent of peace. Also, like so many other officers, he found that the cessation of war meant the army's only theater of activity was the West. That meant fighting Indians. Bryce had nothing against the Indians. In fact, he'd have been perfectly happy to leave them in possession of this vast wasteland, but hundreds of thousands of people had come west looking for gold, their own land, a chance to start over, a chance to make their fortune in a land they saw as free for the taking. That was where things got complicated. The Indians were already in possession of the land, but it was a kind of possession the white invaders didn't recognize.

Settlers plowed up the sod and killed the buffalo. In an attempt to solve the Indian problem, the government made treaties that guaranteed the Indians their own land and food supply as long as they stayed on a reservation. But the settlers didn't honor the boundaries, especially when gold was found, and the Indian agents didn't deliver food and supplies as guaranteed. So conflict between Indians and settlers continued, and it became the army's job to solve the problem.

With the reduction of the army in peacetime, assignments out West were virtually permanent. Bryce knew he would have little chance of being posted back East if he had trouble with the Indians or complaints from the civilian population. Avoiding both would be difficult under the best circumstances. It could become impossible with a woman untutored in the ways of the West thrust into the middle of everything. The fact that she was extremely pretty would only make things worse. He had to find a way to convince her to go back where she came from. For her benefit as much as his.

"I take it you've just arrived," Bryce said to Abby once the men had been hauled away.

"What has that to do with anything?"

"You're unfamiliar with the West, this fort, how to run a trading post. And that doesn't touch on the problems of fulfilling your contract to deliver beef to the Indians."

"What contract to deliver beef?"

He had to get his mind off her eyes. They were huge, dominating her face. The way she looked at him—eyes wide and inquiring—made him feel she was innocent, in need of protection. "The federal government has made treaties with several Indian tribes. In exchange for the Indians staying on their reservation, the government provides them with basic necessities. The most important is beef. Just before his death, your father won the contract to supply the beef. The last herd was stolen, but the Indians found the cattle somehow."

"How much? How often? Where does the beef come from?"

Bryce cursed silently. She was indeed innocent and in need of more protection than he could give her. If she didn't know what the contract required, how could she possibly fulfill it? "You'll have to talk to the Indian agent. The Indian Bureau is part of the Department of the Interior. The army has no jurisdiction over them."

"But wouldn't you bear responsibility if the Indian Bureau fails to achieve its goal of keeping the Indians pacified?"

Bryce was relieved to see Abby was quick to understand the situation. It made him more hopeful she would see the wisdom of selling the trading post. "We're also called on to protect miners, ranchers, farmers, townsmen, freighters, even rail layers when there's trouble."

"That's what the army is here for, isn't it?"

"For real danger, not for fools," Bryce said. It was almost a relief to let his mounting frustration surge to the surface. It made him less aware that Abby Pierce was a disturbingly attractive woman. "Let a man lose a single cow and he starts demanding that every Indian from here to Wyoming be wiped out. Many a disgusted cavalry troop has marched for hours seeking Indian cow thieves, only to find the cows have merely strayed."

"They need better fences," Abby said.

"Ranchers don't use fences. Cows roam free."

"How do they get them to come back? How do they know which cows are whose?"

She obviously knew absolutely nothing about the West. From the silence of her sister, he assumed Moriah didn't know any more. If Bryce could have legitimately done so, he'd have picked Abby Pierce up and bodily put her on the first wagon out of Fort Lookout. From the way his body reacted to the thought, he decided the notion of touching Abby in any manner wasn't a good idea.

"Cows are branded with their owner's mark. During spring and fall roundups ranchers cut out beeves for sale, brand the new calves, and castrate the males. That's fundamental knowledge. Surely you can't expect to survive out here if you don't know things like that."

Abby raised her chin defiantly. "Thousands of people come West knowing as little as I do, but they manage to learn. I will, too."

"You don't know enough to sell the items before you." He knew he'd hit on a weak point, but Abby didn't back down.

"We just got here. We haven't even had time to see where Father lived."

Bryce was ready to tie them up and force them to leave, but he figured they'd make that decision on their own once they saw their living quarters. Abner hadn't been noted for being particular about his surroundings. Bryce couldn't understand how such a rough man could have fathered two such lovely daughters. They must take after their mother. He could certainly understand why their father had kept them safely back East.

"He lived through there," Bryce said, pointing to the door at the back of the room.

Just as the women turned their attention to the door, two enlisted men burst into the trading post. They came to an abrupt halt when they saw Bryce.

"What are you doing here?" he asked.

"We heard there were two women in the store," one of the men said, apparently too agitated by the sight of Abby and her sister to think of some evasive explanation. "We wanted to be the first to ask them to marry us."

Abby and Moriah looked at the two soldiers as if they'd lost their minds.

"Women are rare at Fort Lookout," Bryce explained. "You and your sister will probably receive proposals from every single man at the fort inside a week." Once the men got a good look at them, they'd be fighting to see who asked first. Bryce had to stifle an impulse to throw both men out on their backsides.

"Why?" Abby asked. "They don't even know us."

Didn't the woman have a mirror? Didn't she know she was pretty enough to make even a sensible man forget himself? "A man whose wife becomes a laundress gets to move out of the barracks into a shanty. An industrious wife can earn two or three times what he earns a month, as well as providing him with home-cooked meals and other creature comforts. Women are in such high demand, no one can keep female servants."

Abby's look of astonishment turned to indignation. "You can tell all your soldiers they'll be wasting their time. Neither of us has any interest in getting married. We certainly aren't interested in doing so to enable our husbands to live better while we slave to support them."

"They'd have to have my permission to marry," Bryce said. "I won't give it."

"A free-born man has to have your permission to marry?" Abby asked, looking at him in amazement.

"It's regulations. The army allows only as many enlisted men to marry as we have need for laundresses. At the moment we have enough."

Abby looked as though she would explode. "I've never heard anything so medieval in my life. You would never actually deny a man the right to marry, would you?"

"It's my responsibility to think of the good of all the men, not just of one or two. Yes, I would deny permission to marry."

"I expect you're married, with a house full of kids and servants."

"I'm a widower with a young daughter. I have only one servant, and he's a man. The two women I hired are both married now."

That was another reason he needed to be posted back East. His parents thought he should have left his daughter with them, but he hadn't wanted to be separated from her. There was the question of proper schooling and, later, a suitable husband. He needed a post back East to build his career, and with his family connections, he had a good chance of getting one soon if there were no troubles with his command. That was where he needed to be if he ever wanted to find a wife who could step into the social and political roles that had been traditional in his family for generations.

"Thank you for arresting the men who attacked us," Abby said. "I also appreciate your sharing information about the way people live out here."

She spoke as though people in the West were a different breed from those back East, and he had no intention of trying to disabuse her of that notion. The stranger she thought the people and the more uncomfortable their way of life, the sooner she'd go back where she came from.

In a way it was a shame she couldn't stay. He hadn't seen such an attractive woman—single or married—in three years. It would be a relief and a pleasure to spend some time in female company. But even though Abby Pierce was lovely enough to make him wish he could forget his duty, she seemed very prickly, very determined, even aggressive. Her sister looked more amiable.

He liked his women soft and pliable, but he did prefer that they speak.

"If you would ask these two men to bring our trunks in, I'd be grateful," Abby said.

Bryce didn't have to say a word. The request was barely out of Abby's mouth before the soldiers darted outside and dragged two enormous trunks into the store.

"Put them through there," Abby said, indicating the door at the back of the store. The trunks made an unpleasant grating noise as they were dragged over a floor covered with grit. "I think we'll close the store for the rest of the day," Abby said to Bryce. "That will give us a little time to get settled and become familiar with the merchandise."

"I'd advise you to consider selling. I'll send some people over who're interested. At least listen to their offers," Bryce said when she appeared ready to launch a protest. "If nothing else, you'll know what your business is worth. That will be important when you decide to go back East to get married."

"Neither of us is interested in marriage," Abby said.

He'd heard that before from women who'd been treated badly, but they all jumped at the first chance to make a good marriage. He didn't expect Abby and her sister to be any different. "One can never have too much information," Bryce said. "Now, if there's nothing else I can do for you, the men and I will leave you to take stock of your situation."

Despite his irrational attraction to Abby, Bryce hoped the Pierce sisters would decide Fort Lookout wasn't the place for them. As much for his peace of mind as theirs.

Abby watched Bryce leave the store with mixed emotions. The fact he wanted them to leave as soon as possible didn't endear him to her, but she was coming to the conclusion he might be the only person who didn't want to use her and her sister for his own personal advantage. It was very hard not to ask him to stay, not to want to get to know him better. Since he'd saved them, his mere presence was a comfort, but Abby suspected her desire to keep him close had as much to do with being attracted to a handsome man as it did with thankfulness. After Albert, the last thing she needed was to become involved with a man.

"We ought to take the colonel's suggestion," Moriah said. "This isn't what we expected."

So far nothing had been what Abby expected, including the fort commander. She was having a difficult time fighting down the fear that danced wildly in the back of her mind. She'd expected danger from wild animals, not from wild men. She was still shaking from the encounter with those men. She still hadn't assimilated the reality of how close they'd come to being raped. If Colonel McGregor hadn't arrived when he did—

It didn't bear thinking of.

"I admit my first inclination is to turn tail and run," Abby said, "but I can't go back to St. Louis. The police might arrest me."

"They said they had no evidence against you," her sister said.

"It doesn't matter as long as Albert keeps telling them I did it. My only choice is to build a future elsewhere, and this is the only place I can go."

"You could get married."

"It was hoping to get married that got me into trouble in the first place. From now on I want nothing to do with men."

"I don't see how you can do that if you're going to be surrounded by them."

"You know what I mean."

"I'd rather be suspected of being a thief than murdered in my bed."

"I don't intend to be murdered in my bed. But speaking of beds, it's time we had a look at where we're going to live."

That look almost convinced Abby to return to St. Louis. Everything in the room was coated with grease or soot—walls, furniture, windows, the dirty dishes and pots that covered the table and stove. The air smelled of rank grease and acrid soot. The low ceiling and clutter of the room made it feel small, claustrophobic. Abby crossed the room and tried to open a window, finding it nailed shut.

"It's worse than a pigpen," Moriah said.

Abby wasn't ready to go that far, but the rooms where her father had lived were filthy. She wasn't entirely certain she couldn't detect the smell of urine. At least the room had a wooden floor.

"I can't believe Father lived like this," Abby said. "You heard the colonel say the store was closed half the time because the operator was drunk. I'm sure that man was responsible for this."

"I don't care who's responsible—we can't live here," Moriah declared. She opened the door to a bedroom. The situation there was no better. "I couldn't touch that bed. Sleeping in it would be impossible."

Abby had to agree with her sister. She was certain the mattress was infested with lice and bugs. It made her skin crawl to think of it. "We'll think of something," she said. "In the meantime, we might as well begin to clean up this place."

"You can't mean to stay here," Moriah said in disbelief.

"Tubs of hot, soapy water will soon put everything to

rights," Abby said with a show of bravery she didn't entirely feel.

"Not that bed."

"We can see about getting another mattress until that one can be aired out."

"It will never be aired sufficiently for me to sleep on it."

"Then I'll sleep there."

"I can't stay here. I won't live like an animal."

Abby felt a sinking feeling in her stomach, but she refused to give in without a fight. "I told you to stay in St. Louis with Aunt Emma."

"You can't mean to stay after seeing this," Moriah said, her hand sweeping the room. "I'm sure there are rats."

Abby knew there were. She'd seen one. "There won't be rats or any other vermin once we've cleaned the place up."

"I can't touch anything here," Moriah said. "I'd feel contaminated."

"Then I'll do the cleaning. You can make an inventory of the stock. Please write everything down so I won't have to do it all over again after you leave."

"I'm not leaving without you."

"I've already told you, I won't go back to St. Louis."

"We can go somewhere else."

"This is the only place I can support myself."

"Then I'll stay, too."

"Moriah, you're scared to death of this place. You'll faint if a mouse crosses your path."

"I won't leave you alone in this horrible place."

"There's no point in both of us suffering."

"You're the only sister I have. I couldn't live with myself if I left and heard you'd been raped or killed by some savage."

"There's no point in both of us being subject to danger."

"I'll learn to use a gun."

Moriah couldn't have said anything that would have shocked Abby more. "You don't believe in killing anything, even bugs."

"Maybe if people think I'll shoot, it would achieve the same thing."

Abby doubted men willing to be cut up in a knifefight would be intimidated by a woman brandishing a gun. "You're going back on the first wagon out of here," Abby said, "and that's the end of it. But you're here now, so you might as well give me a hand. I wonder where Father kept the soap."

"I doubt any has been used on this place since it was built."

"We must have some for sale."

"You'll also need wood and water and a tub to heat it in."

"Wood and water have to be here somewhere, and we must have tubs in the store."

But as Abby surveyed the magnitude of her task, she wasn't so sure she shouldn't be on the next wagon out with Moriah.

Bryce wasn't entirely surprised to open his door and find Abby and her sister, but his reaction to seeing her extinguished any hope he'd had of being able to put her out of his mind. Abby simply wasn't the kind of woman you forgot. "What can I do for you?" he asked.

"I want you to teach us about guns."

Bryce just barely stopped himself from jumping aside when she raised a pistol and pointed it at him.

"It's not loaded," Abby said. "I can't find the shells that go in it."

"I'd rather show you how to make arrangements to return home."

"My sister will be leaving soon. I'm staying."

"I'm not leaving unless Abby does," Moriah said.

Okay, he'd lost the first skirmish, but he had plenty of time. There ought to be at least a half dozen things a day that would make them long to go back East. He couldn't take a chance on their making a shambles of the store. It was too important to the post. "I can't have you using a gun at the fort. That could be dangerous."

"I don't want to shoot anyone. I just want to know enough to sell the guns in my store."

Bryce couldn't imagine a man buying a gun, much less a rifle, from a woman who couldn't load it, but he was certain saying that would only encourage Abby to stay and prove him wrong. He decided to let her discover it for herself.

"The first thing you need to know is, never point a pistol at anyone unless you mean to use it," Bryce said as he ushered them into the house. "The other person will be sure it's loaded and expect you intend to use it on him. He'll try to shoot before you do."

"So much for your idea of pointing an empty gun at people to intimidate them," Abby said to Moriah.

"Nobody out here is intimidated by guns," Bryce said. "Even kids live with them constantly." He couldn't imagine women surviving in the Colorado Territory thinking they had only to brandish a pistol and whoever was threatening them would scamper away. They'd be dead before the end of the summer if he didn't do something to prevent it.

"Lay the guns out on my desk," Bryce said. They had brought pistols, rifles, and shotguns. Moriah dropped a sack on the desk. Ammunition. From the looks of it,

Bryce figured they'd brought some of everything they had.

"I'll tell you which ammunition goes with which weapon," Bryce said, "but you shouldn't attempt to use any weapon without proper instruction."

Reluctantly, Bryce spent the next twenty minutes explaining each weapon's use, how it worked, and the kinds of ammunition it used. He didn't attempt to explain that there were dozens of makes of these three kinds of weapons, each with its own strengths and drawbacks. He hoped they'd be gone before they needed that kind of knowledge. But he'd underestimated Abby Pierce.

"My sister made a list of all the firearms we found in the shop," she said, handing him the paper. "How will we know which one to recommend to a customer?"

Moriah Pierce had apparently written down everything she found on each weapon—name, style, model number, manufacturer, even the city where it had been made.

"There are too many for you to learn about," he said.

"There are only fourteen," Abby said. "I can easily master that many in a week."

"You can't really understand these guns until you've used them," Bryce said.

"I expect to hire someone to teach me how to use each of them as soon as I get the store organized and operating smoothly."

"Didn't you like any of the offers for your store?"

"We didn't answer the door," Abby said. "We were busy cleaning and in no fit condition to receive visitors."

"Is that why your hands are so red?" He didn't know why he'd noticed that. He never noticed the hands of any of the laundresses, and they were much worse than Abby's. He'd never noticed their eyes, either. Something about Abby was different . . . and dangerous.

"I've had to scrub the kitchen stove from top to bottom, wash every plate, cup, and pot. I used to work in a bank. My hands aren't used to hot, soapy water."

"The living quarters are uninhabitable," Moriah said. "I can't believe you would expect any human to live like that."

"No one is requiring you to live like that or any other way," Bryce said, taking umbrage that these women seemed to believe the condition of their father's living quarters was his responsibility. "The trading post was your father's home. What you found is what he left."

"I'm convinced the man who has occupied those rooms since my father's death is responsible for their miserable condition," Abby said. "I would prefer to hire only women in the future."

"There are no women at the fort to hire," Bryce said. "Every woman who's not an officer's wife is employed as a laundress."

"Then I will speak to the officers' wives," Abby said.

"You won't find any of them willing to take employment."

"Why not? Surely at least one or two of them could use some extra income."

"They probably could, but there's a strict separation on the base between enlisted men and officers. Officers communicate with sergeants, who communicate with the enlisted men. No enlisted man is allowed to speak to an officer without his sergeant's permission. The same separation exists between the officers' wives and the wives of the enlisted men. That's why no officer's wife would work in your store."

"Who's responsible for that piece of nonsense?" Abby asked. "This is a democratic country."

"It's the way it has been since I entered the army."

The look of outraged disbelief on Abby's face was comical at first. Then he found himself feeling embarrassed. He'd accepted the system without question because everyone else had accepted it. During combat, all separations of rank fell away. To stay alive, every man did what he had to do, shouted at anyone he needed to shout at.

"That's immoral," Moriah said. "And unchristian."

"It flies in the face of all our forefathers fought for," Abby said. "I can't imagine a man of honor bowing to such a system."

Bryce was willing to forgive these women a lot. They were suffering from the loss of their father and the shock of finding themselves in a situation as frightening as it was beyond their experience, but they had gone too far.

"Let me suggest that you moderate your language until you have a better understanding of the conditions under which we live at this fort," Bryce said, trying hard to keep his voice level, his expression neutral. "Not every man will take kindly to being told he's immoral, unchristian, and without honor."

"I didn't say that of you," Abby said.

"It sounded like it to me."

"Then I apologize. But I don't under—"

"That's just it. You *don't* understand, which is why you should turn around and go home."

"My sister is going home, but I intend to stay."

"I will not leave without Abby," Moriah said.

"Now, Moriah, I've told you—"

"There's no point to discussing it," Moriah said. "If you say, I stay."

Wonderful! Now he had two impossibly stubborn, totally inexperienced women on his hands. They would probably be more trouble than the Indians. How could he be crazy enough to be attracted to Abby? Apparently part of him didn't respond to common sense. He desired this woman more strongly than any he'd ever met.

"I have one further request to make of you," Abby said, turning back to Bryce. "Where can I find two mattresses? Those in the trading post are infested with lice and bedbugs."

"I doubt you can find any tonight, but I'll see what I can do for you tomorrow."

"I appreciate that, but my immediate concern is for tonight. It's impossible for us to sleep on those mattresses until they've been cleaned and aired."

"They can stay with us, Daddy."

Chapter Three

Bryce turned at the sound of his daughter's voice. "You're supposed to be in bed, Pamela."

"I couldn't sleep with you talking."

His daughter had an irrepressible curiosity, much more than was good for her at a place like Fort Lookout.

"They can use Miss Wallace's room," she said.

Pamela entered the room, her bare feet showing under the hem of her embroidered nightgown, a redheaded doll held tightly in the crook of her left arm. "How do you do?" she said, stepping forward with her hand held out to Abby. "I'm Pamela McGregor. I'm seven."

Bryce saw Abby's lips twitch, but with suitable gravity, she took Pamela's hand and shook it. "I'm Abby Pierce and this is my sister, Moriah. We've come to run the trading post."

"Was Mr. Pierce your daddy?"

"Yes, he was."

"I liked him. He smiled at me."

"He also gave you candy behind my back," Bryce said.

"He said it was our secret."

"Everybody on the post knew he spoiled you."

"I liked him," Pamela insisted.

"It's nice to know my father was liked by such a sweet child as you," Abby said.

"I'm not a sweet child," Pamela declared. "Daddy says everybody spoils me rotten. He says I'll grow up to be a termagant. Did I say it right this time?" she asked her father.

Unfortunately she'd pronounced it with such accuracy and clarity that Abby knew exactly what she'd said.

"I don't think you need to tell Miss Pierce everything I say."

"She said her name was Abby."

"I heard her."

"Then why don't you call her Abby?"

"Because it's much too familiar."

"Is it all right for me to call you Abby?" Pamela asked Abby.

Abby said yes at the same moment Pamela's father said no. "It's very kind of Miss Pierce to invite you to call her by her first name," Bryce said, "but you know I don't allow you to address adults except by their surnames."

"She said I could."

"I said you couldn't."

"Is that fair?" Pamela asked Abby.

"Colonel McGregor is your father," Abby said. "You have to do what he says."

"I don't see why I can't call you Abby if you don't mind."

Abby looked up at Bryce, but he shook his head. They

wouldn't be here long. He didn't want them undermining his daughter's manners.

"You have to do what your father wants," Abby said.

"Did you do what your father wanted?"

"Always."

"But he was nice."

"I'm sure your father is nice, too."

Pamela looked doubtful. "He's very strict."

"A father can't be too careful with his daughter," Abby said.

"Do you think she's right?" Pamela asked Moriah.

"Without question," Moriah answered.

Bryce figured that of the two, Moriah was the one with the better understanding of how to deal with people. Her sister seemed too headstrong.

"But if I have to call each of them Miss Pierce, how can they tell which one I'm talking to?" Pamela asked.

"We can worry about that another time," Bryce said. "It's time for you to get back into bed."

"Are you going to let them say in Miss Wallace's room?"

Bryce had nothing against Abby or her sister, but he'd have let them sit up all night fending off bugs and chasing mice if it would have made them take the first opportunity to leave. However, his daughter had put him in the position of being forced to offer hospitality. He did have an extra room, and he was certain Abner Pierce's mattress wasn't fit for anything but burning.

"There's only one bed in the room," he said, "but you're welcome to use it." He hoped he didn't sound insincere, but it made him very uncomfortable to think of Abby sleeping under his roof. His reaction was completely nonsensical, but there was a kind of physical closeness about the situation that made him overly aware of her as a woman. It was out of the question that he

34

show an interest in a woman at the fort. It would undermine discipline and cause gossip.

"Thank you for the offer," Abby said. "Under the circumstances we'll gladly accept your hospitality."

"Since she made the offer, I'll let Pamela show you the room."

"We didn't come prepared to stay."

"You can return when it's convenient. I'll be up working for several hours yet."

"Follow me, please," Pamela said in a charming attempt to act grown-up.

"You can show my sister the room," Abby said to Pamela. "I need to speak to your father."

"Can I offer you something to drink?" Bryce asked Abby. "It won't take long to make coffee."

"No, thank you."

"If you'll excuse me for a moment, I feel like a brandy."

As Abby watched Bryce leave the room, she tried to organize her thoughts. During the several hours she'd spent in her future living quarters trying to scrub away some of the accumulated grime, she'd had plenty of time to consider her present situation. It was abundantly clear that Bryce McGregor didn't want her here and didn't think she could handle the trading post. Abby didn't want to stay here, but she didn't have a choice. Therefore, she had to make the best of things. But it didn't take much pondering to know she had a lot to learn. She could become familiar with her stock, learn what people needed and how much to charge for it, but she didn't understand anything about living in this brutal place. She had no idea what she was supposed to do about the contract to provide the Indians with beef, and she had no idea how to keep herself and her sister safe from men like the three she'd already encountered.

She'd decided Bryce McGregor, his prejudice not withstanding, would have the honor of helping her learn to survive in this new and unfriendly environment.

She realized the attraction she felt for him would make that uncomfortable, but she expected it would fade quickly. It had to rest on the fact that he was the most handsome man she'd ever seen, and that he'd saved her from a terrible fate. It was only natural she should be attracted to him. She took comfort in knowing he was too cold and forbidding for her to like for long.

The style of furnishing in his house gave her a different impression of him from the stern commander she'd seen. The house was neat, uncluttered, and minus the little touches that indicated the presence of a female, but the furnishings were comfortable, stylish, expensive, and showed just enough feminine influence to indicate he'd been married. A thick carpet covered the floor and velvet curtains hung at the windows. One table was covered by lace of an intricate design, another with the neatly organized evidence of his work. Pictures on the wall were of his daughter and several women, all of whom were heavily jeweled and expensively dressed; there was also a painting of a house that looked like a mansion. Clearly Colonel McGregor came from a wealthy family. All the more reason for her to throttle her absurd attraction to him.

Abby drew back from inspecting an ormolu clock when she heard Bryce returning.

"As you've no doubt guessed, learning about weapons is just the beginning of what I need to know to operate this store successfully," she said when they were seated.

"It's an impossible task," Bryce said. "I can understand why you want to leave."

"I've already told you I don't intend to leave," Abby

said, somewhat irritably. "I wish you could believe I mean it."

"I do believe you mean it. I keep hoping if I mention it often enough, you'll realize you've made a mistake and reconsider."

"I won't, so let's not waste any more time on it. I have lots of questions about the store, and you seem to be the most logical person to answer them." From his strained expression, she knew he was not happy with her conclusion.

"I realize you're newly arrived at Fort Lookout, but it couldn't have escaped your notice that I have a fort to run, two hundred men whose safety and well-being I must be concerned with at all times, an Indian situation to watch carefully, and a civilian population that thinks the army has nothing better to do than solve its problems."

He was trying to show her how unimportant she and her sister were. "In other words, you don't have time to waste on two females who own and will operate the store at your fort."

"Obviously I have to be concerned with your store. It's badly understocked at present, but it's our only source of supplies without going into Boulder Gap, which is off limits to the enlisted men. If you can't restock quickly, I'll have to look for someone else to take over the lease."

"I just got here. You can't expect me to work miracles overnight."

"I don't have the time to give you all the help you'll need. I suggest you contact the man who worked for your father."

"Why? He's the one who was too drunk to mind the store."

"Whom you hire is up to you. I'm only interested in

who can do the best job as quickly as possible and most dependably over a period of time."

"I can," Abby stated with more confidence than she felt.

"That has yet to be seen."

She had believed he was a little bit attracted to her, but maybe she was wrong. "You don't approve of women, do you, Colonel McGregor?"

His smile was quick and disarming. It would be easy to become infatuated with this man. Dangerous, too.

"Whatever gave you that idea? I certainly do approve of women. I like them and enjoy their company. Nevertheless, I can't let the fact that you're a woman, and a very attractive one, interfere with the running of the fort. While you're a guest under my roof, I'll treat you with all the deference you deserve. But my only concern about you as the store owner is that you fulfill the requirements of your lease."

"I haven't had time to go through my father's papers."

"There's not much in the lease you need worry about. Essentially it says you have to supply the fort with everything the army doesn't give us. There's something in there about selling liquor to the Indians and being drunk and disorderly, but I doubt I'll have to worry about that."

Abby saw amusement in his eyes. Maybe he wasn't as cold and forbidding as she thought. She didn't like the tremor that zigzagged through her body. She was relieved when Moriah and Pamela entered the room. "I'll find the contract and read every word," she said.

"This Miss Pierce says it's a very nice room," Pamela announced, pointing to Moriah.

"Thank you very much for letting us use it," Moriah said to Bryce.

"You're welcome. It's back to bed with you," he said to Pamela. "The ladies will return later."

"Can't I stay up?"

"No."

"Did you get to stay up when you were seven?" she asked Abby.

"We were sent to bed promptly after supper."

"It's still light outside then."

"I begged to be allowed to play outside, but I never was."

"Daddy's not that mean."

"Then you're a very fortunate little girl."

Pamela drew herself up. "I was a little girl when I was six. I'm a big girl now."

Abby was certain Colonel McGregor turned his head to hide a smile. It was only with difficulty she was able to keep a straight face. "Of course you are. I would never have made such a mistake, but I'm very tired. Moriah and I have been scrubbing and cleaning all afternoon."

"Daddy said it was worse then a stable yard," Pamela said.

Abby didn't know anything about the colonel's philosophy on rearing children, but in less than five minutes with Pamela, she was certain he had more on his hands than he could handle. You had only to see the way he looked at his daughter to know he adored her.

"I said the man who took over after Abner Pierce died had turned it into a mess worse than a stable yard," Bryce said with an apologetic grin at Abby. "If you're going to get me in trouble, Pamela, at least make sure you quote me exactly."

"Am I getting you in trouble?"

Abby decided the child's look of innocence was genuine. She hadn't reached the age when she realized truth could be dangerous.

39

"No," Abby said, "but if you had, he's more than compensated for it by inviting us to stay here until we can make our living quarters habitable. Now it's time for us to get our bedclothes."

"And time for you to go to bed," her father said.

"I'll see you in the morning," Pamela said. "I get up very early."

"I like those ladies," Pamela said as she allowed her father to pull the covers over her. "I'm glad they're going to stay with us."

"They're not *staying* with us," her father corrected. "They're just spending the night to give them time to get their living quarters cleaned up."

"Is it right for nice ladies to live in the trading post?"

There were times when Bryce wished his daughter hadn't spent virtually her whole life surrounded by adults. He'd have been much happier if she'd been thinking of her dolls instead of the Pierce sisters. But though he was uncomfortable with his daughter's perspicacity, he was also proud of her. "It's not ideal, but they own the store, so it's their home."

"They could live with us."

"That would be even more unsuitable."

"Why?"

Bryce tried to answer all his daughter's questions truthfully, but he often didn't know how much to say or how to say it most effectively. At times like this he wished there was a woman he could turn to for help. "If everyone only thought good things about each other, there wouldn't be a problem. But people aren't all good. When a man and a woman are together too much, people start to think they're doing something they shouldn't."

"Like making babies?"

Somebody had been giving Pamela more information

than she needed at her age. He'd always encouraged her to be open with him, but apparently she'd been open with someone else as well. He sat down on the side of the bed. This might require more than a simple answer.

"Yes, like making babies. But nice people wouldn't think other nice people would do that."

"Why can't everybody be nice?"

A good question for which he had no good answer. "I don't know. Maybe some people aren't made nice to start with."

"You said God was nice. Why would he make bad babies?"

He was in trouble now. He glanced at the picture of her mother Pamela kept on her bedside table, but he knew Margaret wouldn't have known how to answer her daughter's questions any better than he. "I'm sure God doesn't make bad babies. He made you, didn't he?"

"You said I'm a termagant. Miss Wallace said that was bad."

"I was teasing."

"Do you think Miss Pierce—the one who did all the talking—is a termagant?"

"Why would you think that?"

"You said I'm a termagant because I try to tell you what to do. She does, too. I listened on the stairs."

The last thing he needed was Pamela announcing to everyone at the fort that her father thought Abby Pierce was a termagant. That would be almost as bad as an Indian uprising.

"I think both ladies are very nice. They're in a very difficult situation. I think they'll go back home before long."

"I don't want her to go. I like her. Don't you like her?"

If he said he didn't like Abby, Pamela would undoubtedly whisper it to at least five people before noon tomorrow. If he said he liked Abby, she'd announce that to even more listeners. There were times when it would be better if he didn't say anything at all to his daughter.

"I'm certain she and her sister are very nice women."

"Do you think she's pretty?"

Bryce could feel the quicksand under his feet. "It's not suitable for a man in my position to go around saying he thinks women are pretty."

"Why? Will she think you want to make a baby with her?"

"She might, but this isn't something you should talk about with anyone except me."

"Okay, but do you think she's pretty?"

"Yes, I do, but if you breathe a word to a soul, I'll trade you for a little Indian girl who's been brought up not to make trouble for her father." He pinched his daughter's cheek, and she giggled.

"I wish I had a sister."

"I wish you did, too."

"Do you think Miss Pierce—the Abby one—would like to be my momma?"

Something akin to panic coursed through Bryce faster than a rifle bullet could hit its target. "Under no circumstances are you to mention that to anyone. It would be very improper and make Miss Pierce—the Abby one— very unhappy."

"Why? Wouldn't she like to be my momma?"

Bryce wondered why his life had suddenly become so complicated. "If she were your momma, she'd have to marry me. If people thought she wanted to do that, they'd say things that would make her so unhappy she would leave."

"But you said you wanted her to leave."

"I don't think she's suited to run the store, but I

wouldn't want her to leave because of anything you or I had done. That would be unfair."

"I don't want to make her unhappy."

"I know that, so promise you won't tell anybody what we've talked about tonight. It'll be our secret." Pamela liked having secrets because it made her feel grown-up.

"I promise."

"Good, now go to sleep."

Bryce kissed his daughter and left her bedroom, feeling rather unsteady on his feet.

Whatever could have made Pamela think about Abby being her mother? Abby was attractive, intelligent, and kind, but she seemed too independent to want to be a wife, and far too businesslike to want a perpetually curious seven-year-old as a daughter. He wanted a mother for his daughter, but he also wanted a wife who shared his background, was part of his social world, believed in the traditional values and goals of his family. That was why it was essential he be posted back East as soon as possible.

"Colonel McGregor didn't invite us to stay more than one night," Moriah said to Abby as they walked back to the colonel's house from the store. "I doubt he would have suggested even that if his daughter hadn't offered for him."

"I'm well aware of that," Abby replied, "but that room will be vacant if we don't use it. I see no reason to give it up until our living quarters have been thoroughly cleaned, everything washed and aired."

It was a long distance between the store and the colonel's house. The fort was arranged on four sides of a very large open square. Abby didn't know why it had been built with so much open ground. It made everything far apart. She didn't pretend to know anything about fighting, but she would have thought such a layout would make the fort hard to defend. It didn't have a surrounding wall. The fort was set right down on the plain at the foot of the mountains with nothing to keep anyone who wanted to from walking in. The only fortifications were around the store. Abby had been informed that was more to protect her supplies from theft than from any danger to herself or her sister.

The Rocky Mountains looked magnificent against the backdrop of the western sky. The peaks were snow covered, the rough-looking slate-gray flanks covered in a few places with the green of trees. Abby had marveled anew at them each day of her trip from Denver, especially in the evening, when the setting sun changed the sky from red to orange to pink to purple and every color in between. She'd seen the Appalachian Mountains when they moved from South Carolina to Missouri, but she'd never seen anything like this massive wall of granite that rose from the floor of the plains like a colossal curtain. There was no gradual ascent, no hills preparing the viewer for the mountains. It was like running into a wall that closed off the rest of the world. She liked looking at them. Something about their strength helped shore up her spirits when she felt despondent and on the verge of giving up.

"You can't force your way into a man's home," Moriah protested.

"I won't, but I see no reason to leave until we're ready. We have no other place to go, so stop worrying about it. It'll probably be the best bed we've slept in since we left St. Louis." The journey had been a nightmare she hoped to forget someday. "I've got to remember to give Pamela a special present. Help me think of something."

"I have no idea what a little girl would like."

"She was a *little girl* when she was six. She's seven now."

Moriah didn't smile. "She's still a child."

"And a very sweet one."

"I'm surprised he didn't leave her back East with his family," Moriah said. "This is not a suitable place to bring up a daughter, especially one as quick-witted as Pamela."

"He wouldn't want to leave his only child. Think of what it was like for us to live without Father." She had kept hoping her father would invite them to join him, but he never had.

"We were older."

"I wouldn't want to leave my only child, even if it meant she had to be in a terrible place like this. Apparently Miss Wallace used to take care of Pamela. I'm sure he'll get someone to replace her soon. We may be living in the middle of the Great American Desert, but the colonel has managed to set up a more than adequate household."

"I'm sure his family was anxious to see he was comfortable."

"Moriah, comfortable is having enough food, warm clothes, a decent bed, and a roof that doesn't leak. The colonel's house is better furnished than Aunt Emma's."

"I don't believe fancy furnishings are an adequate substitute for civilized company."

"We don't know anything about his company. I expect the other officers are just as nice as he, and their homes as comfortably appointed."

"We'll see," Moriah muttered as Abby raised the knocker on the colonel's door.

He opened it promptly. Abby knew Bryce was tall, but seeing him standing like a shadow in the doorway, the light coming from his back, made her feel she was facing a giant. Maybe it was the uniform that gave him the appearance of being so powerful and well-muscled. Maybe it was that she was standing on a step below the level of the floor. Whatever the reason, for a moment Abby was breathless.

"I hope we didn't keep you up too late," Moriah said. "I have work to do."

"We won't keep you," Abby said, collecting her wits and stepping inside. "We'll go to bed as soon as we wash up."

"I put a basin and a pitcher of water in your room," Bryce said. "I believe it's already furnished with towels."

"Thank you," Abby said. "You're really very kind."

"It's no trouble," he said.

Maybe it wasn't any trouble, but she got the impression it wasn't something he was happy to do. "We'll do our best not to disturb you in the morning."

"I'm sure you won't."

She stood there feeling foolishly tongue-tied, unable to think of anything else to say, so she murmured a good night and followed Moriah up the stairs and down a short hall to a nicely appointed room. "I wonder what happened to Miss Wallace."

"Pamela said she got married a few months after she arrived." Moriah poured some water into the basin and began to wash. "Pamela said her father has employed two women and both have gotten married. She said he decided to use only enlisted men until he's posted back East."

Abby didn't know why she'd assumed Bryce would always be here. Any sensible person would want to live back East rather than in this remote outpost of civilization. Maybe because she knew she didn't have anywhere else to go, she wanted to feel someone she could depend on would be nearby. That was foolish. He was much more interested in convincing her to return to St. Louis than in helping her.

"Did she say when he expected to return?" Abby asked.

"Soon." Moriah finished washing and moved to give Abby access to the basin. "She said his mother is already picking out ladies for him to marry."

Another unpleasant jolt. Really, she was behaving very foolishly. Naturally a man with a young daughter and a career would want to marry again, for his own satisfaction as much as for his daughter's sake. A wife with the right connections could give his career a powerful boost.

"Pamela says his family has been doing everything possible to get him home ever since he got here."

"Is Pamela looking forward to it?" Abby turned her back to her sister as she washed. She didn't want to have to meet her gaze, to let her know she had more than a passing interest in Colonel McGregor's future.

"I don't think so. She says her grandmother disapproves of everything she does." The bed groaned softly as Moriah got into it and pulled up the covers. "The child is precocious and dangerously curious. The sooner the colonel finds himself a wife, the better. That child needs a woman's supervision."

"I find her self-assurance refreshing," Abby said.

"I find it unfitting in a child so young. However, I'm glad she was forward enough to offer us this room. This is a very comfortable bed."

"Good. We have a lot of work to do tomorrow."

It didn't take long for Abby to finish washing, change her clothes, and climb into bed. It took longer to fall asleep. Despite her exhaustion, stark fear of what might happen in the coming days kept her awake. It would take months to organize the store properly, become familiar with all the merchandise, and stock everything people wanted. She didn't know if Bryce would allow her that much time

Then there was the troubling beef contract. She had no idea where to begin, but she was certain it was crucial. Even inexperienced women from St. Louis knew keeping the Indians quiet and on their reservations was the primary job of the army. If she couldn't deliver the beef, Bryce would certainly see that she lost the store.

Bryce was another problem. Just knowing she was in his house made her acutely aware of the tug of attraction. His behavior with Pamela had convinced her it was only the responsibilities of his position that made him appear cold and forbidding. He was a kind, loving, adoring father, the kind of man every woman hoped to find. Or maybe his attractiveness stemmed from the fact that she felt overwhelmed by her present position and he was willing to let her lean on him. Whatever the reason, she couldn't stop thinking about him. She was relieved to know he'd be leaving before long.

She didn't know when she drifted off to sleep. Her dreams seemed to pick up where conscious thought left off. It seemed no time at all until she was jerked awake by the sound of a trumpet blaring from the square. And the unshakable feeling that there was someone else in the room.

"Good morning," Pamela said when Abby woke with a start. "Will you help me cook breakfast for Daddy?"

Chapter Four

"Doesn't your father have anyone to cook his breakfast?" Abby asked.

Pamela ignored Abby's question. "Good morning," she said to Moriah, who was just waking up. "Did you sleep well?"

"What are you doing up at this hour?" Moriah asked. "It's still dark outside."

"It's five-thirty," Pamela replied. "Everybody is up."

"Why?"

"It's reveille," Pamela said.

That didn't mean anything to Abby. She was sure it didn't mean anything to Moriah, either.

"Everybody has forty-five minutes to get dressed, eat, and be ready for drill."

Abby looked out the window. "How can they see to drill?"

"It'll be light by then. Hurry up," Pamela said. "We don't have much time."

Abby wasn't quite sure how, but she found herself

downstairs with Moriah within ten minutes, facing a stove that had gone cold overnight. On a counter near the stove were eggs, bacon, coffee, bowls, large spoons, plates, everything for the making of a substantial breakfast.

"I put all this stuff out before I went up to wake you," Pamela said, clearly proud of herself. "Daddy's striker will be in soon, but he's a terrible cook."

"Your daddy's striker?" Abby asked. She had given up any idea of resisting this child and was lighting the fire in the stove.

"That's what they call the soldiers who work for the officers in their homes," Pamela informed her. "His name is Zebulon Beecher, but we call him Zeb. The men like to be strikers because they get paid extra, but they're not any fun. They grumble about having to help with children, and they're terrible cooks."

Moriah had already begun to slice bacon. Pamela was breaking eggs into a bowl. Abby ground the coffee. By the time Zeb arrived, they had breakfast well under way.

"We don't need you to cook today," Pamela informed Zeb, "but you can stay and have some breakfast."

Zeb looked utterly confused by the sight of two strange women in the colonel's kitchen. Abby decided that just because he couldn't cook didn't mean he couldn't be useful.

"You can set the table and pour the milk," she said.

"I want coffee," Pamela said.

"What does she normally drink?" Abby asked Zeb.

"Milk."

"Ask your father. Until he gives permission, you'll have milk."

Pamela wanted to argue, but there wasn't time. As near as Abby could figure, Bryce wouldn't have more than fifteen minutes to eat before he had to leave for the drill field, though she wasn't sure if commanders of forts drilled.

"It smells wonderful this morning," Abby heard Bryce telling Zeb in the dining room. Pamela started to dart from the kitchen.

"Let's surprise your father," Abby said. "We'll wait until Zeb has everything on the table; then we'll come in and take our seats like fancy ladies who've just come down from getting dressed."

Moriah scowled.

"He'll know Zeb didn't cook," Pamela said.

Nevertheless, they waited while Zeb carried bowls and platters and pitchers from the kitchen into the dining room.

"Can we reach the stairs from here without your father seeing us?" Abby asked.

Pamela grinned. "Follow me."

There was little *following* to be done. They simply went into the hall from the kitchen and then into the dining room. There were only six rooms downstairs.

"You almost missed breakfast," Bryce said when they entered. "I don't know who Zeb got to help him, but everything smells good today."

"We did it!" Pamela exclaimed, unable to contain her excitement any longer.

Bryce went still. When he turned to his daughter, all the geniality had gone out of his expression. "Explain what you mean," he said.

Abby could tell Bryce was unhappy and not about to be cajoled by sweet talk or feigned innocence. "Since you were kind enough to let us use your spare bedroom, we wanted to show our appreciation by cooking breakfast. Pamela said Zeb wasn't a very good cook."

"When did she tell you that?"

"I don't remember."

Pamela had guilt written all over her face. Abby could tell Bryce wasn't happy, but he couldn't chastise his daughter without in essence calling Abby a liar.

"It's not my custom to require guests to cook their own breakfast."

"We're not exactly guests," Abby said, beginning to help herself to eggs and sausage. "We were more or less forced on you."

Bryce glanced at his daughter. "Pamela has a way of doing that."

"Which I greatly appreciate. Now stop looking at your toast as if it's burned and eat your breakfast before it gets cold."

Though there wasn't the variety their aunt used to serve each morning, there was more than enough food, even for a man as big as Bryce.

"It's very good," he said. "The biscuits make everything worthwhile."

"Moriah made the biscuits," Abby said. "Hers are a lot better than mine."

"And the coffee's just right."

"I made that, so you can thank me."

"We thank both of you, don't we, Pamela?"

"She helped," Abby said.

"Abby let me break the eggs, and Moriah let me pour the milk for the biscuits."

Bryce opened his mouth, but Abby forestalled him. "I know what you're going to say, but I don't know how we're to know who she's talking to unless she uses our names. If you have a solution, we'll be happy to hear it."

"Give me some time to think about it," Bryce said. "But in the meantime, you're to refer to them as Miss Abby and Miss Moriah."

"Yes, Daddy."

Pamela looked like the cat who got the cream, but she had enough presence of mind to lower her head.

"What do you plan to do today?" Bryce asked Abby.

"Continue work on the store. I don't want to impose on your hospitality any longer than necessary."

As Abby had expected, Bryce looked shocked at her expectation that she would continue staying with him.

"I'll have a sergeant send some enlisted men to help you," Bryce said. "How many do you need? Six? A dozen?"

Abby nearly laughed at his hurry to get rid of her. "I think three or four would be enough. The storeroom is a mess. I don't see how the clerk could find anything."

"I don't think he tried very hard. Anything else I can do for you?"

"I'll let you know tonight at supper. Speaking of supper, my sister and I would like to cook that, too. It's about the only way we can repay your kindness."

Abby admitted to a slight twinge of guilt over bribing Bryce so blatantly. He couldn't kick them out without looking ungentlemanly. He couldn't refuse their offer to cook without appearing ungrateful. Having accepted their offer, he was even less able to throw them out without seeming mean-spirited.

"Please, Daddy," Pamela pleaded. "I can help."

"That ought to slow them down considerably," Bryce observed dryly.

"Every female needs to learn to be comfortable in the kitchen," Moriah said. "The sooner she begins, the better equipped she is to handle it alone when she marries."

"I usually dine at six-thirty," Bryce said, stiff and very regimental. "Make sure Zeb knows he's to serve and clean up afterward." He changed the subject. "I expect you'll have quite a few visitors today."

"I don't mean to open the store to customers just yet."

"I don't mean customers. I expect every enlisted man without a wife will find a reason to visit the store."

"Then I will keep the doors locked. I have no intention of getting married."

"I worked for Abner," the man said. "You'll need me to run the store."

Abby didn't like Bill Spicer from the moment she set eyes on him. He was slovenly and suffering from a hangover. Knowing he was the man who was often too drunk to wait on customers didn't make her any better disposed toward him.

"Where were you yesterday?" she asked. "The store was unattended when we arrived."

"I wasn't feeling too good, but you don't have to worry. People write down what they take and pay for it when they come back in."

"There was nothing written down."

"Then nobody took anything."

"I doubt that was the case. In any event, I want to see the records of sales since my father died."

"I didn't keep no records."

"How do you know what was sold, or what to reorder?"

"I keep it in my head."

"Since your head is full of at least two months' business, it must be crowded. You'd better write it down before you forget it."

"I can't remember all that stuff now."

"For just how long *can* you remember that stuff?"

"As long as I need to." He had been sullen. He was now becoming surly.

"I'm afraid that won't be adequate for me. I need a record of every transaction that takes place in the store."

"What's she doing messing with men's clothes?" Spicer asked, pointing to Moriah. "She can't wear none of it."

"She's trying to put them in order."

"Won't do no good. People will just mess them up again."

"Then we'll just straighten them again."

"I won't find nobody willing to work for me if I set them to straightening stuff all the livelong day."

"Let's get one thing straight right now," Abby said. "My sister and I own this store. Anybody who works here works for *us*. If they don't want to do what we say, they can look for a job somewhere else."

"Won't no man work for a woman," Spicer said.

"Why not?"

"No man can call hisself a man if he takes orders from a female."

"I guess that means you won't be working here."

Spicer looked startled. Clearly he hadn't made that connection.

"If you work for me," Abby said, "you'll take a bath, put on clean clothes every day, and refrain from drinking spirits until the store closes."

Spicer looked dumbfounded.

"You will also come to work on time, make a written record of every transaction, and straighten the stock before leaving for the day."

"You're crazy," Spicer exclaimed.

"Those are my conditions."

"You won't find nobody to work for you."

"Then we'll manage by ourselves. Good day."

"What about my wages?"

"I'll pay you when you present me with a record of sales and income. The bank in Denver says nothing has been deposited since our father's death. Neither my sister nor I have been able to find any money."

"It's here," Spicer said, drawing a bag from his coat. Abby took it quickly.

"There doesn't seem to be much in it."

"Most everybody buys on credit. They pay up when they get paid."

"And when is that?"

"Every two months."

"When do they get paid next?"

"Next month."

"Where's the money from last payday?"

"In there," he said pointing to the bag.

In other words, there was no money. He'd either drunk it up or simply not collected it. "You're fired," Abby said. "*If* you can produce a record of sales for these last weeks, and *if* anybody pays for purchases, I'll give you a percentage. Otherwise, you get nothing."

Spicer stormed out, making dire threats against them and the store.

The day didn't improve. Abby had hardly gotten the five soldiers Bryce sent her—Zeb was one of them—assigned to their various tasks when a man showed up and introduced himself as Luther Hinson, the Indian agent.

"Who are you little ladies going to get to run the store for you?" he asked as he looked around, walking with a swagger that exuded just enough arrogance to stoke Abby's temper.

"My sister and I will run the store."

He looked at Abby as if she was joking. "You can't run this store."

"Why?"

"You're females," he said, as though that explained everything. "You'd best find Bill Spicer. He's the man you need."

Abby didn't want to make any more enemies the first

day so she rejected the words that rose to her tongue. "I've already met Bill Spicer, and we've decided we can't work together. Despite being females, my sister and I *will* run this store."

"You can't," Hinson said, very much as if he was forbidding her and expected her to obey.

"I'm afraid that's out of your control."

His glance turned angry. "Your father had a contract to deliver fifty beeves a month to me for the Indians on the reservation. There's been trouble the last two times. You have to deliver or the contract will be taken away."

"You'll receive your deliveries."

"I doubt it," he said with so much mockery in his voice Abby wanted to slap him. "No man will do business with a woman."

She didn't know what kind of women the men at Fort Lookout were accustomed to dealing with, but they must be completely lacking in courage as well as common sense. She knew lots of women who owned stores and other businesses who had proved they were as capable as men. The males at Fort Lookout were in for a rude shock if they expected the Pierce sisters to defer to their every wish.

"Do you know who's delivering the beef this month?" Abby asked. It would be a relief to find out so she could talk to the rancher and get that settled in her mind.

"No, I don't, and that's what I want to talk to you about."

"I'll keep working while you talk." She had decided the store, as well as their living quarters, needed to be cleaned from top to bottom. She and two of the enlisted men were in the process of removing everything from the tables and shelves, then scrubbing them thoroughly before putting everything back in neat and carefully organized piles. She'd get to the walls and floors next.

"I don't know if you're aware of this," Hinson said, "but Ray Baucom and his partners used to hold the beef contract. One of his partners died a few months back. Before he could get reorganized, your father put in a bid and won the contract. I think you ought to give it back to Ray."

Abby told herself she had to stop being prejudiced because of the way western men groomed themselves. It was a harsh land, so she supposed they had to dress rough. But even though Hinson had shaved some time in the last month and didn't smell so strong she had to step away from him, there was something about him that smelled rotten.

"Why would I want to do that?" she asked.

"This is rough country," Hinson said. "It's full of rustlers, murderers, and desperate men who have little to lose. A herd of cattle is an irresistible temptation. It was all Baucom and his partners could do to get enough beef through to keep the Indians from going on the warpath. You'd never be able to get fifty beeves to the reservation."

"It would seem pointless to give Mr. Baucom and his partners a contract they've never been able to fulfill. In fact, I would think it might be illegal."

"It wasn't illegal because they were the only ones who bid on it."

"Then you should be thankful my father won the contract. Now you have a chance of getting your whole allotment."

"The last herd was rustled."

"Colonel McGregor told me the Indians found it." She could tell her refusal to back down was making him angry. He didn't seem nearly so eager to sweet-talk her.

"The Indians have been known to steal some of their own beef before."

"Why should they steal what's already theirs?"

He appeared to be trying to control his irritation. "There are a lot of things that won't make sense to an Easterner. It's all the more difficult because you're a female."

Now it was Abby's turn to struggle to keep her temper under control. "What is it that I, being an Easterner and a female, won't understand?"

"Men won't work for a woman. You won't get anybody to sell you beef."

Abby believed ranchers would get over any reluctance to deal with a woman as long as they got paid.

"What else?" Abby asked.

"Your whole herd will be stolen before it gets to the reservation."

"Why will mine be stolen and not Baucom's?"

"There's not much law out here. If you're not strong enough to hold your beef, or take it back from anyone who steals it, you lose out."

"I gather you believe Baucom and his partners are strong enough to go after anybody who tries to steal their beef."

"Yes."

"But not strong enough to keep all the beef they contracted to deliver, just the ones the rustlers let them keep." Hinson's face turned red. "It doesn't seem as if they're particularly strong at all. I think I'll hold on to the contract."

"Your father stole that contract from Baucom when his back was turned, and I want him to have it back."

"I haven't had time to read the contract, but I'm sure it only runs for a year. He'll be able to submit a bid when it comes up for renewal."

"That contract ought to be Baucom's," Hinson nearly

shouted. "Your father knew he couldn't deliver what he promised."

"How many deliveries are left on the contract?"

"Ten."

"Did he deliver on the first one?"

"No. Rustlers ran off every head."

"Did he recover any?"

"He was dead by then. Spicer got some men together, but they couldn't find the herd."

"Why didn't he ask Colonel McGregor to help? I'm sure he's just as interested in seeing the Indians get their beef as anybody else."

"He did, but the colonel has a lot of territory to cover and not enough men."

If Bryce could afford to offer as many as a dozen men to work in the store, Abby was sure he would have sent even more after the missing beef.

"Well, Mr. Hinson, I appreciate your concern for me and for the Indians. I don't understand why you want to give the contract to a man who didn't deliver what he promised, but I've been here little more than a day. I have no intention of making decisions of such importance until I know more about all the issues you've mentioned."

"I can understand your concern, little lady," Hinson said more calmly. "I know it must be a lot for you to try to run this store. It'll probably take months before you get everything figured out. I'm only trying to make things easier for you. If you'd just release the contract, you could get on with your cleaning and straightening."

No one had ever dared patronize Abby in such an insulting manner. It was all she could do not to throw her pail of dirty water in his face. "I don't think you understand, Mr. Hinson. The discussion is over. Good day."

He looked as if he couldn't believe his ears. Apparently no woman had ever refused to do what he wanted.

"I'll come back tomorrow."

"You won't talk to me about this for at least a month."

His temper snapped. "You'll talk to me before then whether you want to or not. The next shipment is due in a week. When it doesn't arrive, I will be down on you like a swarm of bees. And if the Indians leave their reservation and steal from the ranchers, you'll have Colonel McGregor to deal with."

"Thank you for the warning," she said and turned her back on him.

"You are a stupid and hardheaded woman," Hinson shouted. "I've tried to talk some sense into you, but you're too dumb to know what's good for you. I'm not having my position here wrecked by some tenderfoot female. The first time you fail to deliver, I'll snatch that contract from you so fast you won't know what hit you. If you'd take my advice, you'd head back East where people like you don't put sensible men in danger."

"That man is a liar," Zeb said after Hinson slammed out. "Spicer never said a word to the colonel. Neither did Hinson. The colonel only heard about it when some of the Indians left the reservation to find the herd themselves."

"What happened?"

"They found it, all right. They found the rustlers, too. The only reason we didn't have every white man for fifty miles around clamoring for us to murder the Indians who left the reservation is, they had enough sense to bring the rustlers to the fort. A few of them had bullets in them, but they were still alive."

"What did Bryce—I mean Colonel McGregor—do?"

"Shipped them off to Boulder Gap to let the law there deal with them."

"Do you think anybody will try to steal the herd this time?"

"Seems half the people out here are stealing cows from the ranchers, gold from the miners, or land from the Indians."

"What do you think of Hinson?"

"I think he'd as soon steal from his mother as the Indians. Everybody knows he don't give the Indians what's promised. If he does, it's spoiled, broken, or the wrong thing."

"And Baucom?"

"He says rustlers kept stealing his cows, but he seems to have plenty of money just the same."

"Do you think Baucom and Hinson are working together?"

"I wouldn't be surprised. Baucom was plenty mad when your pa won that beef contract. He swore he'd get it back one way or the other."

Chapter Five

"We came to see how you're doing," Pamela announced as she burst into the trading post followed by her father. "Daddy said I couldn't come by myself."

Abby looked up from where she'd been sorting through stock that had been piled randomly in one corner. She'd already decided she needed more shelves so that she and Moriah could see what they had and the customers could find what they wanted.

"You should have warned me you were coming," she said to Bryce. "I don't normally greet visitors sitting on the floor."

"We can fix that easily enough," he said.

He extended both hands in the obvious expectation that she would let him help her up. She wasn't sure of the etiquette that prevailed on isolated army posts, but this would have been considered a familiar gesture in St. Louis. However, greeting a guest while sitting on the floor was probably even worse, so she cast aside her doubts and let him help her to her feet.

Help wasn't the right word. *Lift* was. Bryce wasn't merely big and tall. He was strong. Having her hands in his firm grasp made Abby keenly aware of herself as a woman, but she was determined she wouldn't let herself be carried away again by a handsome face and impressive strength . . . or a warm smile. She'd let herself be fooled by a man's outward appearance in St. Louis, and she had almost ended up in jail.

"It looks as if you've made some good progress," Bryce said.

"Only on the surface," Abby said. "I don't know how Father managed to make any money with everything in such disorder."

"He seemed to know what everybody wanted and where to find it. I remember people saying as soon as they walked in the door he would start pulling down things for their order."

"It will take a while before Moriah and I know our customers that well, but we hope to compensate by being more organized. As soon as I'm able, I'll have shelves built on all the walls. It's hard to keep things organized when they're stacked on tables or piled in the corner."

She was talking too much. She was sure Bryce didn't want to hear about her plans. Most likely he wouldn't have come if Pamela hadn't dragged him. If he was interested at all—except in trying to convince them to return to St. Louis—he probably wanted only to make sure she could supply the needs of his soldiers and their families.

"Let me know when you're ready for the shelves," Bryce said. "I've got a couple of men who're very good carpenters, but they'll each cost you thirty-five cents a day."

"I don't know that I can pay them. Bill Spicer handed over almost no money from the last few weeks."

"I imagine he drank up a good bit of it."

"He said he left the store unattended because people would write down what they took and pay for it later."

"That's a bigger lie than I thought even Spicer would try to pull off. Your father gave credit, but he would never have allowed such a practice."

"Why would Spicer do it?"

"I imagine he expected the lease to lapse and someone else to take over. He was just taking care of himself while he could."

"He's a thief."

"Nobody doubts that, but you'll have a hard time proving it. I advise you to chalk it up to experience and forget it. Even if you could prove Spicer stole from the store, there'll be nothing to recover."

That was what she'd expected, but she wasn't happy to have her suspicions confirmed.

"You'd be well advised to look for a buyer. I'm sure it wouldn't be hard to—"

"Do you think my sister and I would be doing all this work if we intended to sell the store? You've been very kind to us, but your constant effort to get rid of us is beginning to make me angry."

"I haven't been trying to *get rid* of you," Bryce said. "I admire your courage and determination. I was just giving you the advice I believe is in your best interest."

"Thank you, but my sister and I will decide what's in our best interest." She was irritated at herself for being even the slightest bit attracted to a man who was doing his best to make her think she was incapable of running a store. She would have been livid at anyone else, but she seemed to have an irrational attraction to this man. The sooner he got his appointment back East the better.

"Where's Pamela?" Bryce asked, breaking the strained silence. "I have to be going."

"I expect she's gone to see what Moriah's doing," Abby said, leading the way from the store to the living quarters.

Moriah had made good use of the three enlisted men at her disposal. The room had been scrubbed from floor to ceiling, removing thick layers of smoke, grease, and dirt. Once the walls were whitewashed, the room wouldn't be so gloomy. Abby hoped to find a way to cut out a window to let in more light. Even clean, the room gave her the feeling of being in a cave.

"I'm helping," Pamela said to her father. She was pushing a wet cloth over the top of the table.

"I'm sure they appreciate it," her father said, "but it's time for us to go. I have to get back to work."

"Can't I stay?"

"Not today. They still have a lot of work to do."

"I can help."

"You have your own work. Remember your lessons?" Pamela made a face. "Do I have to do them?"

"You know you do. Now say good-bye."

"You can help us cook dinner," Abby said to Pamela.

"That's not necessary," Bryce said.

"Of course it is. It's all decided."

After he left, Abby realized he hadn't protested a second time. In fact, he looked relieved. She wondered if it was just the food, or whether he might actually enjoy their company. They weren't the most brilliant conversationalists, but it had to be a change from talking to a seven-year-old and discussing military matters all day. And while she and her sister were no beauties, they weren't ugly. He had to like looking at them better than at Zeb.

Abby told herself to stop imagining things. If Bryce was still trying to get them to go back to St. Louis, he couldn't be that enthralled with their company.

* * *

Abby's day was completed by the appearance of Ray Baucom in the late afternoon. She was tired, dirty, and disheveled. She was short of temper, angry that Spicer had stolen the proceeds of the last months and indignant that Hinson thought she was incapable of managing the store. She tried to convince Baucom to come back the next day, but he said he was the one responsible for the beef shipment and needed to talk to her. He was the third person to whom Abby had taken an instant dislike.

"What do you mean you're responsible for the beef shipment? You lost that contract," Abby said, too tired and angry to mince words. Moriah had found some of their father's recordbooks. The stock on the books didn't match what was on the shelves, and there was no income to account for it.

"I was bending the truth a little so you'd let me in," Baucom said.

Abby felt a surge of anger. "I've already had to endure Mr. Hinson's lecture on why I can't possibly manage to live up to my contract and that I ought to turn it over to you. I don't need you telling me the same thing."

"I don't want it back," Baucom said. "I was glad when your father won it."

Abby stopped scrubbing and looked at Baucom. "I was told you were furious when my father got the contract, that you swore to get it back *one way or the other*."

"I may have said something like that," Baucom said, looking slightly embarrassed. "I was very angry at the time, but I've had time to reconsider."

"And just what caused you to change your mind?" Abby didn't know whether to believe him or not. He certainly *seemed* sincere, but she couldn't understand why everyone else would tell her just the opposite.

"The contract looks like a good way to make money.

You buy beef at a low price and sell it to the government at a contracted price, regardless of whether it's above current market price or not. And it always was. The government needs the beef no matter what."

"So what made you decide you didn't want to be rich?"

Baucom laughed. "I wasn't getting rich. Rustlers and Indians attacked so often, I had trouble finding cowhands to work for me. I rarely delivered more than half of my contract. I decided it would be easier to grow the beef and sell it to you."

The fact that everything Baucom said was calculated to make Abby think she couldn't deliver on the contract caused her to distrust the man. But he was telling her what others had already said, and that made her think he might be telling the truth. But Bryce was trying to convince her to go back to St. Louis, and Hinson was a woman-hater.

"I'll do what I can to help you, short of taking on the contract," Baucom said. "I know it's got to be difficult for you, coming in here like this."

At least he didn't say the job was too difficult for a woman. That was a handful of points in his favor. "I might take advantage of your offer," Abby said.

"I know every rancher within two hundred miles," Baucom said. "I'll be glad to recommend you to any of them."

"That's very kind. How can I get in touch with you?"

"Ask anybody in Boulder Gap. I'm easy to find."

"I don't like that man," Moriah said after Baucom had left.

"He didn't tell me anything I haven't heard already," Abby said.

"Don't trust him," Zeb said. "He's a mean, greedy man."

Abby wasn't sure she could hold that against him. It would take a greedy man to choose such a hazardous way of making a living, and a really tough one—maybe even a mean one—to succeed. The real question was whether she would be able to succeed where he hadn't.

"I don't care what he's like as long as he doesn't get in my way."

Abby's words were bold, but she didn't feel nearly so confident. She was beginning to wonder whether it was possible for anyone to handle the beef contract and the trading post. Her father had died before he'd been able to answer that question for himself. She stood up from where she'd been bending over to wash a shelf and stretched to get the knots out of her muscles. "We should start thinking about supper," she said to Moriah. "You ready to go?"

"Give me five minutes."

That would give Abby a chance to clean up herself. "It's time we had a talk with the colonel about this beef contract."

"If you decide to give up the store, you could hire out as cooks," Bryce said as he savored the taste of a prairie chicken cooked with rice and simmered in its own juices. He didn't have to worry about his compliments hurting Zeb's feelings. His striker wasn't the least bit upset about having his kitchen taken over by the Pierce sisters. At this moment he was in the kitchen enjoying his own share of the supper.

"I'll keep that in mind," Abby said. "Maybe someday we can offer a few simple dishes for officers not fortunate enough to have a striker who can cook."

"That will depend upon how much time we have," Moriah said. "Men don't realize how long it takes to cook a meal."

Actually he did know. It was one of the things he'd learned from being the commander of the fort. He had to know everything about everybody's job in order to make sure everything ran smoothly. And Bryce was determined things would go smoothly until he got posted back East.

"Maybe you can find someone who will work with you," Bryce said, "and give you more time."

"I'm more worried about the beef delivery," Abby said. "I haven't found anything about it among my father's papers. Wouldn't he have some sort of written agreement?"

"I would expect so, but I can't be sure. The Indian agent is appointed by and works under the Department of the Interior, not the army. I'm only called on when there's trouble."

Which was a stupid arrangement. The Department of the Interior could make all the half-witted mistakes it wanted, like giving guns and ammunition to Indians who were friendly *at the moment*, but when it came to dealing with those same Indians when they got angry and were no longer friendly, it was the soldiers who had to face up to the guns their own government had provided. And the reason the Indians got angry was because the Indian agents, miners, or settlers ignored the terms of the treaties, something else the army had no control over.

"Who would I ask to find out who's delivering the beef and when?"

"The Indian agent."

"What do I do about payment?"

"What do you mean?"

"I expect the man providing the beef will want his money before he turns the beef over to me."

"Over to the agent. You're only the go-between. Your contract determines how much you're paid. Your arrangement with the rancher determines how much you owe him. The difference is your profit."

"I can figure that much out for myself," Abby said.

Bryce thought she was only being abrupt because she was caught in between and didn't have enough information. It wasn't his job to educate her, but no man could ignore a woman like Abby. Besides, if the beef didn't come, the Indians would get angry and possibly cause trouble, and then it would become his job. Also, several people were trying to take advantage of her father's death to cheat a little. Or a lot. That angered him. He didn't think Abby and her sister ought to stay, but that was no reason to cheat them.

Besides, despite everything, he liked Abby. He had decided he would keep his distance, that she had too many sharp edges to appeal to him, but his brain was in a corner by itself. The rest of him liked everything about her. She had courage. She was in a tough place, but she wasn't running scared. Though she would accept help, she didn't expect it. Bryce didn't mind admitting to himself he enjoyed having her around. She brightened up his dull evenings. He couldn't imagine being married to such a spunky woman—he looked for comfort and support in a wife, not entertainment—but she did make for interesting company.

And Pamela couldn't stop talking about her.

He had still another reason for helping her. He didn't like the circumstances surrounding Abner Pierce's death. Everyone was satisfied it was an accident, but something about the way he'd died—combined with the fact that he'd just won the beef contract—had made Bryce uneasy. He had no facts to support his suspicions, but if he was correct, Abby and her sister could be in danger.

"I will ask around tomorrow," Bryce said. "Someone is bound to know who's delivering the beef, but keep looking for the contract. Your father may have had an oral agreement with the rancher, but I doubt it. He wasn't a trusting soul."

"Unlike his daughters, you mean."

"You've been brought up among people who've lived in the same community most of their lives. You know their histories and their reputations."

"Not everybody you've known for years can be trusted," Abby said. "A man I'd known for some time was arrested and convicted of embezzlement. It came as quite a shock to his family and friends."

"We have a lot of men in the West who've run away to avoid facing up to the consequences of what they've done. It's best to put everything in writing."

"I plan to do that," Abby said.

Bryce could see fear in the back of her eyes but not panic.

"What if Hinson has already paid for the beef and I haven't paid the rancher? Will I lose the contract if he takes his beef back?"

"That could be a blessing in disguise. Then you could concentrate on the store. Your father should have done well with the store, but he never seemed to have more than enough money to keep his head above water."

"That's because he was sending a monthly allowance to support us," Abby said. "He'd been doing so ever since our mother died."

That explained why Abner never seemed to stop working, never drank or gambled—two of the most common activities of western men—never patronized saloons or the women there.

"We told him he didn't need to send as much after I started to work," Abby said, "but he always sent the same amount. That's the money we used to come to Fort Lookout. We don't have much left."

"As long as you've got good references, you can get credit from your suppliers," Bryce said.

Abby didn't know what kind of references people needed to get credit, but she couldn't ask anybody in St. Louis. "I've never tried to run a business before," she said. "I have no references. What can I do?"

Chapter Six

"I can vouch for you."

Bryce had considered his decision carefully, but he still found it hard to believe he would tie his reputation to two women he barely knew. His instincts told him Abby and her sister were honest, but he'd just counseled Abby to get a contract to make sure she was always on firm ground. He should have at least gotten to know these women before agreeing to vouch for their character and fiscal responsibility. What was it about Abby that caused him to keep doing things he'd never done before? It wasn't as if she was helpless and clinging. She had enough vinegar in her personality for two people.

"Why would you do that?" Moriah asked. "You don't know us."

"For goodness sake," Abby said, "we're not going to cheat him."

"I know, but we shouldn't ask him to vouch for strangers."

"I didn't ask. He volunteered."

"That's all the more reason we shouldn't take advantage of his kindness."

"What do you propose we do?"

"I don't know," Moriah admitted.

"Neither do I. Until we figure it out, I say we accept Colonel McGregor's offer."

"Call me Bryce," he said. "I'm called Colonel McGregor all day long."

"I call you Daddy," Pamela reminded him.

"I'm glad I have a daughter to call me Daddy," he said. "You haven't eaten all your dinner. You don't want the ladies to think you didn't like it."

"I'm full."

"I'm afraid she sampled everything with us in the kitchen," Abby said.

Bryce felt warmth flood through him. He remembered doing the same thing as a small boy when he could sneak into the kitchen without his mother knowing. He was pleased his daughter was able to enjoy that important part of childhood. She had missed so much as a result of her mother's untimely death.

"You'll have to go to bed early if you don't eat all your dinner," Bryce said.

"But I ate an awful lot."

"I didn't see you."

"Miss Abby and Miss Moriah did."

"Do you think they'll vouch for you?" Bryce winked at Abby.

Pamela turned to Abby. "Will you vouch for me?"

"Of course we will," Abby said.

"Maybe I should ask Zeb."

"He tasted everything, too. Miss Abby kept asking him if he thought you would like it or if she ought to make something else."

Out of the corner of his eye, Bryce saw Abby looking

very self-conscious. He could have told her never to depend on Pamela not to say the one thing you wished she wouldn't.

"It would have been foolish to prepare something you didn't like," Abby said, a bit stiffly, he thought.

"I doubt there's anything you could cook that I wouldn't like."

"Liver."

"I love it."

"Grits."

"If they're anything like hominy, I'll love them with gravy."

"Collards."

"Where in St. Louis would you learn to cook collards?"

"My mother came from South Carolina."

"If we ever end up in South Carolina at the same time, you can fix me some."

He realized what he'd said. There was an awkward silence.

"I want to thank you again for sending the men to help us," Abby said, changing the subject. She smiled. "All of them except Zeb proposed to Moriah and me. Do you think I ought to inquire as to whether they want us singly, or should we take them as a package?"

"We can't continue staying in the colonel's house," Moriah said as they prepared for bed.

"We're not *staying* here," Abby said. She was unpinning her hair and brushing it before going to bed. "We're only here until we can make our living quarters bearable."

"They'll never be fit for decent people," Moriah said.

Abby turned to dispute with her sister, but the words froze on her tongue when she saw tears running down

Moriah's cheeks. She laid her brush aside, sat down on the bed beside her sister, and embraced her. "I know it's not what we're used to, but it won't be so bad after we get everything cleaned and painted."

"It'll always be an awful cave," Moriah said, giving in to the tears now.

"There's no reason for you to stay here if it upsets you so. You ought to go back to St. Louis as soon as you can."

"I'll do no such thing! I may hate it here, but if you stay, I stay."

"But I wanted to come here. You didn't."

"You'd never have come if that horrible Albert hadn't stolen money from the bank, then tried to make them think it was your idea."

"I love Aunt Emma, but it was never the same after Father left."

"That didn't mean you wanted to come here."

"Lots of things have happened that I didn't want, but I have to make the best of it all. Fort Lookout has been a shock to me. I thought there'd be some kind of town, schools, churches, women with their families. It's nothing like what I expected. It's even a bit frightening, but I mean to stay. I'm never going back to St. Louis, but that doesn't mean you have to stay here just because I'm too full of pride to put up with distrustful looks and whispering behind my back."

Moriah stopped crying. "I couldn't live with myself knowing you were out here alone, facing God only knows what horrors. What kind of sister do you think I am?"

"The very best," Abby said as she hugged Moriah.

"Not if you think I'd stay back in St. Louis. Despite the horrible place we have to live, I'd rather be here than with those wretched people who suspected you had anything to do with stealing that money."

Abby gave her sister a heartfelt hug, grateful Moriah had come with her, guilty for being the reason she was so miserable. "Things are going to be all right," Abby assured her. "I have a feeling Bryce will make sure of it."

Moriah broke the embrace. "Abigail Emmeline Pierce! Don't tell me you're falling in love with that man!"

Abby was so surprised at Moriah's remark, she was momentarily speechless. Then it struck her as so funny she started to laugh. The more she thought about what Bryce's reaction to such a statement would be, the harder she laughed.

"It's not funny," Moriah said.

"Yes, it is," Abby finally managed to say. "You know I have absolutely no intention of getting married. Albert soured me on men forever."

"That's not the impression I got watching you with the colonel."

"I'll act as sweet as can be as long as he helps us." She suddenly felt less amused. "How could I fall in love with a man who thinks we're ignorant about everything and incapable of learning anything? He's only helping us because it's his duty—and because he's afraid something will go wrong and he'll be stuck here forever. Zeb told me he has an important family with lots of connections trying to secure him an appointment. An Indian uprising is the worst thing that could happen. Why else do you think he's so willing to help us?"

"He's letting us stay in his house."

"Only because his daughter offered and he couldn't think of a way to refuse."

"You're making him sound mean-spirited and selfish."

"I expect he's really quite nice. He doesn't mind helping us as long as he's helping himself, but Zeb said he'll wait to marry until he's back East and can choose a wife from among the wealthy and influential families."

"You're making him sound even worse."

"That's the smart way to do things: Don't let your heart get in the way of your head. I forgot that with Albert."

"I don't think you ever loved Albert. I never trusted him."

Moriah never trusted any man, especially one as handsome and charming as Albert. She always thought they were up to something. In that instance she had been right.

"I intend to behave exactly like Bryce," Abby said. "If I ever do consider marriage, you can be certain it will be to my advantage."

But as Abby drifted toward sleep, her attitude softened and her attraction to Bryce reasserted itself. He really didn't seem angry with them or resentful of their presence in his house. She was sure he would have offered them his extra bedroom if Pamela had given him a chance to think of it himself. And he didn't have to help them. If he was only worried they would cause trouble that would endanger his promotion, he could have canceled their lease and ordered them to leave the fort. He really was trying to help in spite of the possibility of danger to himself. He really was kind. She had known he was. No mean-spirited or selfish man could love his daughter the way he obviously loved Pamela. Abby was sure he would love his wife just as wholeheartedly.

She drifted off to sleep with a smile on her lips and that thought in her heart.

*　　*　　*

"I've found the beef contract," Abby announced, striding into the store, where Moriah was explaining to the carpenters exactly how she wanted the shelves built. They had decided Moriah would run the store and stock merchandise, while Abby handled the accounts and the beef contract.

"Does it say how much we owe the rancher?" Moriah asked. She pulled Abby back into the living quarters and closed the door so they could have some privacy.

"Yes. I also found the agreement with the rancher, a Mr. Lavater. We'll make twelve dollars on each head of beef that's delivered to the reservation. That's six hundred dollars, enough to resupply the store without having to depend on Bryce to vouch for us."

This was the first good news she'd had since coming to Fort Lookout. She was still overwhelmed with the whole idea of running the store, but it would be a lot easier with money. Now she only had to find where her father had purchased his goods, decide what she needed, and place the order.

"Start making up a list of what we need," Abby said. "I'll ask Bryce if we can use his telegraph to send the order. In the meantime, I'll look for father's records of what he bought and from whom. I can't believe everything is in such disorder."

"I've been thinking about that," Moriah said. "Our money was never late and was always exactly what he said it would be. That's not the sign of a man who'd run his business the way this seems to have been run, or keep records in such a sporadic way. I think somebody has been through everything looking for something. Where did you find that beef contract?"

"At the bottom of a sugar tin."

"I think Father hid it because he didn't want anyone to find it."

Abby had been thinking the same thing, but she kept telling herself she was imagining things, that she didn't know how people in the West did things, that she hadn't even really known her father. She'd been nine when her mother died. A year later her father had moved to St. Louis from South Carolina, left them with his sister, and disappeared into the West. They had gotten letters and money regularly, but they'd never seen him again.

Still, everything had felt wrong from the moment she arrived here. Their father's death had been a shock but not a surprise. Aunt Emma had been predicting it for years. According to her, the West was a death sentence just waiting to happen. If the savage Indians didn't get you, you would be eaten by vicious mountain lions, torn to bits by huge bears, die a terrible death from freezing or thirst, or be shot by a sinister criminal gone West to escape punishment for some bloodcurdling crime.

Abby had assumed her father had gone West because he couldn't stand to live without their mother, not because he was a misfit looking to run a store at a United States Army fort. Nor did she believe Bryce would have trusted a shiftless and irresponsible man.

"Why would anyone want to steal a contract?"

"I don't know. Maybe this person wasn't after the contract. Maybe he wanted something else."

"What?"

"It couldn't have been money. Spicer saw to that. Let's see what else we can find." A knock sounded at the door. "Come in," Abby called.

"There's a lady in the shop," one of the carpenters said.

"Tell her we're not open."

"I did, but she wants to see you."

Abby was reluctant to invite anyone into their living quarters, even though the room was now clean, but she told herself she had to get over expecting things would be as they had been in St. Louis. She'd probably never again live in a house as nice as Aunt Emma's. "Tell her to come on back."

A moment later a very pretty young woman came through the door. "I'm Dorrie Spaugh," she said. "My husband is Captain Ronald Spaugh. I heard two women had taken over the trading post and had to come over right away."

"We've been here three days now."

"Everybody expected you to turn around and leave. When my husband told me Colonel McGregor had lent you the fort carpenters, I knew you were here to stay."

Abby waited for her to say why she'd come, but Dorrie was more interested in looking around. "I can't believe what you've done to this room," she said. "It was never like this when your father was alive."

"Forgive me if my question seems rude, but what were you doing in this room?"

Dorrie laughed. It was a high-pitched, giggly laugh.

"I helped your father in the store occasionally," Dorrie said. "There's nothing to do here if you aren't a laundry woman and don't have children. My husband didn't like for me to work here, but I was so bored, I'd have mucked out the stables."

"Maybe you can tell me where my father kept his business records," Abby said. "I haven't been able to find them."

"He kept them in the top drawer of the chest against that wall," Dorrie said, pointing to an old, badly scarred chest with five deep drawers.

"I've emptied everything out of that chest," Abby said. "I didn't find any records."

"Then Bill Spicer must have moved them. Of course,

he might have thrown them out with the rest of the mess."

"What mess?"

"Somebody broke in after your father died, threw everything all over the room. I offered to help Spicer put things back in order, but he was too drunk to care."

"Did anybody have any idea what the thief was looking for?"

"What would anybody want with old records? Now, if stuff from the store was missing, I would have understood. Abner wouldn't let anybody in the store unless he was here, too. Locked this place tight as a drum at night. Even had a dog at one time, but somebody poisoned it. Mean thing to do."

"My father's letters never mentioned anything about that," Abby said.

"It wasn't always that way. Things went really smoothly until he decided he wanted to bid for that beef contract. I told him he was asking for trouble, but he said he could handle it. Maybe he could, but he got killed before he had a chance to prove it."

"Killed?" Moriah said. "We were told our father died."

"I didn't mean to upset you. It was an accident, though it didn't make sense. Nobody could remember Abner ever losing control of his horses."

"What happened?"

"Nobody knows. He was found with the wagon smashed. He must have hit his head on a rock when he got thrown out."

Her father loved horses. He used to ride all across the county when they lived in South Carolina, jumping anything in his path. He never once fell that Abby could remember.

"When do you plan to open the store again?" Dorrie asked.

"I'm not sure. We want to get the shelves finished, the merchandise organized, and reorder what's missing."

"That sounds like a long time. People here have no-where to buy things unless they ride fifteen miles to Boulder Gap. My husband won't let me go without him. It's a rough town."

"We're working as fast as we can," Moriah said.

"Maybe I can help," Dorrie said. "I know what your father charged for things. I know the suppliers he or-dered from."

"You're a lifesaver," Abby said. "Can you start right now? I can't pay you until we make some sales because Spicer drank up whatever profits were made since my father's death."

"I don't know why your father put up with him. I wouldn't have let him in the store."

Abby felt the same way.

"I can do the pricing," Dorrie said. "Your father marked everything, but Spicer was too lazy to keep it up."

"That would be perfect. I don't see a great deal here for women. Don't they buy from this store?"

"Your father never carried much for us. He said there weren't enough women at the fort to make it worth-while."

"Well, there are two more women here now," Abby said, "and we definitely consider it worthwhile."

"You really don't have to keep cooking for me. It's no trouble to have you here. The room would be empty if you weren't using it." Bryce tried to sound sincere, but he hoped they wouldn't listen. Aside from the fact that he now looked forward to meals, he enjoyed Abby's company. She was a little prickly, but it made her more interesting than the other women he met. Most of them were anxious to agree with everything he said or defer to his opinion. Though that was a desirable trait in a wife, it made for boring company. Abby Pierce was anything but boring.

Pamela had taken Moriah off to discuss making new clothes for her favorite doll. It probably wasn't a good idea for him to be alone with Abby, but his mother had hammered into his head that a gentleman never left a lady to entertain herself.

"Moriah and I have to eat, too," Abby said. "If we're going to cook for ourselves, it's no trouble to cook for two more."

"Three," he said. "Zeb said he's never going to eat in the mess hall as long as you cook."

"As long as he cleans up, we'll cook enough for him, too."

"You realize you're making it nearly impossible for us to go back to Zeb's cooking when you leave," Bryce said.

It startled him to realize he didn't want Abby to leave. He found himself thinking of her during the day, wondering what she was doing, if she was thinking about going back to St. Louis, how she was doing in the store, if the men were respectful, if she liked the work they did. He also wondered if she smiled at them the way she occasionally smiled at him. In short, he was jealous. He wanted to be the one she talked to, the one she thanked, the one she thought about when she needed help.

Of course, this unexpected preoccupation with Abby was foolish. She didn't want to get married, and he had no time or taste for flirtation, but he couldn't stop thinking about her. It played havoc with his concentration. He should send her to stay with one of his married officers, but he was worried about the beef contract. As long as she stayed in his house, he had the excuse he needed to monitor the situation. He had to make certain nothing happened to jeopardize his transfer back East.

Pamela was delighted to have Abby and her sister staying with them. She behaved much better during the day, even applied herself to her lessons so she could be free to spend time with them. Bryce was grateful they seemed happy to include Pamela in everything they did. He knew she suffered from not having a woman she could feel close to, but he couldn't send her back East to his mother. Pamela didn't like the restrictions her grandmother placed on her. His daughter would probably be perfectly happy to live at the fort for the rest of her life.

"Dorrie Spaugh came by today," Abby said. "She said she worked for my father. She's offered to help us get organized and tell us the things we need to order first."

"Her husband doesn't like her working in the trading post, but I'm glad she's helping you."

Bryce stood to refresh his brandy. "Can I bring you something?" he asked. Abby hadn't touched her coffee, but she said she didn't want anything.

"Dorrie said my father was killed in an accident," Abby said when Bryce returned. "Why didn't someone tell me? When I was told he'd died, I thought he'd been sick."

"It's less upsetting to say he died than that he was killed."

"She said Father lost control of his horses, that his wagon crashed and he was killed when his head hit some rocks. I'm not saying it didn't happen, but my father was an excellent horseman. He could drive a buggy in his sleep."

Abby's questions revived Bryce's own feeling that

something wasn't right about the accident. Abner had been known for his skill with horses. Bryce had often had him teach new recruits how to ride, how to control every kind of buggy and wagon, how to handle teams of two, four, even six mules. It was odd that Abner would have been killed by failing to do something he did better than anyone else.

There wasn't a shred of evidence it had been anything other than an accident, but Bryce had never seen the body or been asked to view the scene. He hadn't even known about it until the next day.

"You'll have to talk to the people in Boulder Gap," Bryce said. "Your father wasn't a soldier, so I wasn't called on to investigate the accident."

"Was he alone at the time?"

"I don't know, but Abner always handled the reins. He didn't trust anyone else. I'm sorry I can't tell you more, but I wasn't involved. The accident happened outside of Boulder Gap."

Zeb entered the room. "Can I bring you some fresh coffee, ma'am?" he asked Abby.

"No, thank you. I've had enough."

"Anything I can do for you, Colonel?"

"No. I think that'll be all for the night."

Bryce didn't like the people in Boulder Gap. They were a rough lot of merchants, saloonkeepers, gamblers, and prostitutes whose sole objective seemed to be to separate people from their money as quickly as possible.

"It seems I'll have to travel to Boulder Gap," Abby said.

"You can't go alone," Bryce said.

"Why not?"

"It's a rough town. I recommend that my officers not take their wives there. It leads to trouble."

"Moriah and I will have to go," Abby said. "It's time we knew where our father was buried."

"You're not going to listen to any of my advice, are you?" Bryce asked.

"Not in this instance, but I would like your advice on the beef contract. I found the papers today."

"What do you want to know?"

"First, how the transaction works. The agent owes me money and I owe the rancher money. He will turn the beeves over to the agent before I give him the money, won't he?"

"I'm sure he understands you can't pay him until you get paid."

"Will the agent pay me right then?"

"You'll have to talk to the agent."

"What do I do if the rancher doesn't deliver all the cows I've contracted for?"

"You don't pay for what you don't get."

"Suppose Father paid him already?"

"Did he?"

"I don't know. Dorrie told me someone broke into the store a while back, and that Spicer probably threw the records away when he straightened up."

"It's more likely he shoved them somewhere and forgot them."

"What do I do if the herd is stolen?"

"There's nothing you can do."

"What will *you* do?"

Chapter Seven

"That depends. If you ask me, I'll send a patrol out to investigate. If the agent asks me, I'll send a patrol out. If the Indians ask me, I'll send a patrol."

"What if you don't find anything?"

"The Indians will have been cheated of what the treaty guarantees them, and they will be hungry and angry. It's my job to make sure they stay on the reservation. If they had killed even one white man, rustler or not, when they went after that herd before, we'd have had trouble."

"Why would my father want such a troublesome contract?"

"Because of the money he could make. Once again, if you take my advice, you'll give it up."

"I don't trust Luther Hinson not to cheat the Indians."

"I expect you're right." Bryce didn't like having to stand aside while Hinson had a free hand to do whatever he wished.

"What are you going to do about it?"

"Nothing. As I told you before, that's outside my authority. If I interfere, I could end up court-martialed. You said you worked in St. Louis. What did you do?"

"I worked in a bank."

"If the bank had been cheating the customers and you'd tried to warn them, wouldn't you have lost your job?"

"Yes, but—"

"I have to do what the army tells me or I'll lose my job. If that happens, I'll be in no position to help the Indians at all."

"Do you try to help them?"

"Whenever I can. They've been treated badly."

Abby seemed to jerk her thoughts away from the Indians. She smiled in a way that struck terror into his heart. She had to stop doing that. With a little effort and that smile, she could probably talk him into anything. He'd been a widower too long.

"I have a favor to ask," she said.

With a sinking feeling, Bryce asked, "What is it?"

"I want you to teach me how to ride sidesaddle."

"You don't need me to teach you," Bryce said the following morning. "You ride like you were born on a horse."

"I used to ride all the time when we lived in South Carolina, but I stopped after we moved to St. Louis. Aunt Emma said it was unladylike."

"How old were you when you moved?"

"Nine. I rode bareback." Abby had been affronted when Bryce chose a horse barely able to canter.

"It won't take you long to get used to a sidesaddle. We can ride toward the mountains."

"Why don't you want us to stay here?" Abby asked.

"See those men?"

The parade ground in the middle of the fort measured

more than a thousand feet on each side. It seemed that everywhere she looked, men were standing, watching, but that didn't surprise her. There were more than two hundred men at the fort. "What about them?"

"You're a beautiful woman."

"I'm only pretty."

"Okay, for argument's sake, let's say you're only pretty in St. Louis. Out here, you and your sister are spectacular. Nearly every man at this fort is unmarried. Nearly every one of them is starved for the company of a lovely young woman. Letting you ride around this parade ground would be like holding raw meat under the nose of a starving wolf. Let him look at it too long and he'll go mad enough to do anything to get it."

"You're scaring me."

"It's one of the reasons I urged you to go back to St. Louis. You'll be safe as long as you're careful, but don't forget you never know who may be watching you."

Abby had been viewing the men as a wall of protection against the unknown dangers of the West. She didn't like having to add them to the list of hazards. It left her feeling very vulnerable. "Remind me never to turn to you for reassurance," she said.

Bryce laughed easily, and she felt something go soft inside her. There was something about this man that captivated her against her will, and it wasn't his looks, wonderful though they were. The feeling had started the moment she set eyes on him and hadn't let up since. She could say he was kind, thoughtful, and helpful, that he loved his daughter and was too handsome for words, but none of that reached down to the depths where this attraction was seated. She had thought this was a momentary attraction based on looks and thankfulness for his support. She was beginning to fear it might be more threatening than that.

"I wouldn't have told you if I didn't believe you were strong enough to handle my advice," Bryce said. "Now, let's ride. Ask questions about anything you see."

Abby adjusted quickly to the sidesaddle. It didn't take long for her to remember how to communicate with the horse, but it took a little longer to convince the horse she knew what she was doing.

"Some of these horses know more than the recruits who ride them," Bryce explained. "The recruits find it easier to let the horse make the decisions."

"That won't work for me."

"I didn't think it would."

Abby turned sharply to look at him, but Bryce's expression betrayed nothing. "I will want a horse of my own."

"You'll be safer in a buggy, and you can't leave the fort by yourself."

Abby bridled. "Says who?"

"This is still untamed country. There are wild animals out there; snakes, wolves, bears, mountain lions. But even more dangerous are the two-legged varmints. No woman is safe alone."

"Can you protect me from all these dangers?"

Bryce smiled at her in a way that made her wish she hadn't asked the question so blatantly. She really shouldn't see so much of him. It made it harder to get over this attraction that wouldn't go away.

"Only if you help by doing what I ask."

"Tell me about what your soldiers do."

For a man who'd grown up in the East, Bryce knew an incredible amount about the country he was charged to protect. He had apparently made it a point to get to know as much about the Indians as he could. He made regular visits to the reservation to talk to the chief. He was equally concerned about the civilians—farmers, ranchers, townspeople, miners, trappers—anyone who lived inside the area of his responsibility. He seemed most concerned about his soldiers. So many of them were young, inexperienced, lacking in knowledge and basic skills. He spent most of his time training them.

"They're awfully green when I get them," he said. "If I do the rest of my job right, I'll have time to train them before they face combat."

He told her about the land itself. He showed her that it could be beautiful as well as awe-inspiring and terrible. He showed her a bird's nest in a willow by a stream. They passed a herd of pronghorn antelope that watched them with calm indifference. Rabbits sprang from under the hooves of their horses with alarming regularity. She was delighted to see a chipmunk, even more taken as a colony of prairie dogs dove into their burrows at the approach of a pair of hawks. But the most fun was a pair of male sage grouse competing for the favors of a female.

"I've never seen birds that could puff up like that," she said.

"They're trying to impress the female."

"How stupid to be impressed by a bag of air."

"I've known some women to be mighty impressed by a windbag, though not one covered with feathers."

Abby saw the gleam in his eye and burst out laughing. The grouse, apparently thinking the laughter was aimed at them, turned and walked away with great dignity. That caused Abby to laugh even harder. "I think we've hurt their feelings."

They rested in the shade of an ancient cottonwood by a stream.

"In a month or two the prairie will be covered with new grass and flowers," Bryce said.

"I thought this was desert."

93

"We get most of our rain in the winter and spring. By the end of the summer, you'll think it's a desert. Some days it's over a hundred degrees. Next January, when it's been below freezing every day for a week, you'll think wistfully back on those one-hundred-degree days."

"Are you sure you're not trying to scare me into going back to St. Louis?"

"No. I'm reconciled to your staying here. As proof, I'm going to teach you how to shoot."

This day wasn't turning out the way Bryce had expected or planned. The words were out of his mouth before he realized what he was saying, yet he knew at once they were true. Maybe he even *hoped* she would stay. Something about Abby had bewitched him, something beyond her looks, beyond the undeniable physical attraction he felt for her. He didn't yet know what it was, but it was like a magnet drawing him closer, holding him tighter. The more he knew about her, the more he wanted to know.

She continued to surprise him. He had expected her to be nervous and awkward around horses. After all, what city girl knew anything about horses except what she could learn from watching them pull wagons and carriages through the streets? He doubted she'd seen a sidesaddle more than three times in her life. Not only did Abby adapt to the sidesaddle quickly, she was at ease with her mount from the first. It took her only a short while to convince the animal she intended to tell him what to do, not the other way around.

What Bryce had expected to be a wholly wasted half hour had turned into a very enjoyable ride that had taken them several miles from the fort. He pleased himself explaining what he'd learned about the plant and animal life that inhabited the plains and foothills. He surprised himself at the pleasure he derived from seeing Abby's enjoyment of this totally alien world.

He'd seen the sage grouse courting ritual before, but he'd never enjoyed it as much as he had while sharing Abby's laughter. Her fascination with the unfamiliar plants and animals, her awe of the mountains that towered in the distance, brought home to him the fact that these sights had been no more familiar to him three years ago than they were to Abby now. How had he missed the excitement of discovery, the joy of seeing things he'd only heard about before, the feeling of awe when every morning he woke up to see soaring mountains that dwarfed anything in Pennsylvania?

Because he'd focused all his efforts on doing his job well and on getting back East, he'd ignored the magnificence of the land. That focus had kept him from realizing he had begun to like what he saw, to feel comfortable in this environment so unlike Philadelphia. It gave him a freedom unlike anything he'd ever been able to enjoy. Odd that it should take Abby, another city dweller, to make him see what lay all around him. Her excitement in discovering something new, seeing something unexpected, fueled his own. He'd even gotten to the point of looking for things he thought would please her. A brazen little chipmunk, as fascinated by them as they were by him, had sent her into peals of laughter.

It was laughter that did it. He'd had no intention of teaching her to shoot—women were much too nervous around weapons. But he found himself looking for some way to prolong their ride. The words were out of his mouth before he had time to give the idea proper consideration. Abby looked so surprised and pleased, he wouldn't have withdrawn the offer even if he'd wanted to.

"I'm flattered you trust me with a weapon," she said.

"I don't. That's why I'm going to teach you how to use one."

The idea had been all right in conception, but he soon discovered the execution caused a lot of problems. There seemed an inordinate amount of body contact required. He couldn't remember this ever happening when he worked with the soldiers.

"We have to dismount," he said. "I can't teach you how to handle a dangerous weapon perched atop a horse that's stamping its foot in impatience or moving about in search of grass." Dismounting required that he help her down from the saddle. That required him to put his hands around her waist while she rested her hands on his shoulders and practically slid down his body on her way to the ground. *That* required that he step back and take a few steadying breaths.

"Let's stand in the shade of these trees," he said. "It will cut the glare and make it easier to see." Too late, he realized the cottonwood grove offered nearly complete concealment on three of its four sides, producing a feeling of intimacy as unexpected as it was unwelcome. He actually felt nervous, a reminder of his schoolboy days.

"Let's start with a pistol," he said. "It's probably the most frequently used weapon in the West." He explained how to load it, how to aim it as an extension of her hand, and how to squeeze rather than jerk the trigger. But when he handed the pistol to Abby, she handled it so badly she nearly dropped it.

"Here, let me show you how to do it," he said.

That was when the touching started. The only way to show her how to hold the gun was to take her hand in his and fold her fingers carefully around it, explaining as he did why she should do it this way and not some other. That took minutes, not seconds. He couldn't stand in front of her, so he stood beside her. He brushed against her shoulder and upper arm several times. By the time he finished he was feeling very warm.

"Now take careful aim and fire at that prickly pear cactus," he said.

"What part of the cactus am I supposed to aim at?" Abby asked.

"It doesn't matter. You won't hit it."

He didn't intend to be cruel, but he was angry at himself. He couldn't remember having any difficulty controlling himself around women in the years since his wife had died. His relationships had always been calm and controlled. It didn't mean they were without passion, but nothing happened until he decided he *wanted* it to happen. He had never been a man to take chances with life. Always know what you're doing, why you're doing it, so you can make sure the results are what you want.

He watched Abby take aim, shift her position, and aim again before walking a couple of steps to the left. He had to smile. If his troops took this long to aim, they'd all be dead. So what was different with Abby? An old military saying sprang to mind: *Know your enemy and you can defeat him.* He didn't consider Abby his enemy, but he didn't like not feeling in control when he was around her.

The sound of the pistol shot interrupted his thoughts. A pink bud shot up into the air and spiraled to the ground.

"I missed it," Abby said.

"No matter. You were lucky to hit anything at all."

"I guess I need more practice." She handed him the pistol with unaccustomed meekness. "Now show me how to use a rifle."

"A pistol is all you need to protect yourself."

"I'm not talking about protecting myself. I've got to

sell rifles. I need to know the differences, the strengths and weaknesses of each kind of gun."

"There are men at the fort better equipped than I am to explain all of that."

"Didn't you use a rifle during the war?"

He decided not to explain that generals made decisions instead of fighting. It made him sound as if he'd hidden behind the courage of other men.

"Let's see what you remember," he said. "Show me how to load the rifle."

Abby remembered his lessons even if she was a bit awkward. With a little practice she'd be able to load a rifle as quickly as any man.

"Most of the time you don't use a rifle for close-up targets," Bryce said. "Unless you're mounted on horseback, you use a sword, pistol, or shotgun. Even on horseback, a pistol is best for short range. It's also easier to use."

"Then why do they make so many rifles?"

"For any target over fifty feet away, you need a rifle. Some rifles are accurate for thousands of yards. That's the only way we can bring down deer, elk, and moose."

"How do I shoot it?" Abby asked.

"You shoot a gun. You fire a rifle."

"Why?"

"No good reason. It's just what we say. Now take the shells out and I'll show you how to hold it, aim, and fire."

This was where it got tricky.

He attempted to show her everything standing at a safe distance, but she moved close to him, touched him as she peered over his shoulder. Giving up, he handed the rifle to her. "Here, you try."

She immediately held the rifle in such a way as to guarantee herself a broken shoulder. There was nothing for him to do but take the stock of the rifle and place it properly against her shoulder.

"My arms aren't long enough," she said.

"They're plenty long. You just aren't used to holding them like this."

He had to show her how to use her left arm to support the rifle. Then he had to show her how to place her finger properly on the trigger. And that was the easy part. After having his hands all over both her arms, he practically had to hold her in an embrace to show her how to line up the target in the sights of the rifle. He wasn't sure how Abby was reacting to his being so close—he thought he could detect a slight change in her voice— but he was so strongly affected he couldn't be sure he was seeing or hearing anything correctly.

Even his muscles refused to cooperate. He couldn't hold the rifle steady. He could tell himself it was because he was holding it through Abby's hands and they weren't steady, but standing behind Abby, his chest touching her back, his arms cradling her in a tighter embrace than some men held their wives, reduced his muscle control to zilch. And increased his respiration and heart rates. His voice sounded unlike himself.

"Can I shoot it?" Abby asked.

"Fire it," he corrected automatically.

"Okay, fire it."

"It would be better to do that at the fort. We have a range for target practice." With those words he stepped away from her. He held out his hand, but Abby didn't give the rifle.

"Why not out here? There's nothing around."

"We don't know that. A whole army of Indians could be hiding out there and you wouldn't see them."

"How? There's nothing there but little bushes," she said, indicating sage and rabbitbush.

"They've spent hundreds of years learning to hide behind those *little bushes*. I'd feel more comfortable back at the fort."

"Will you teach me to hit the center of the target?"

"I thought you just wanted to know how to sell the rifle."

"I do, but it would be fun to learn how to actually hit something."

"What do you want to be able to hit?"

"I don't know. Father used to go deer hunting. Maybe I will, too."

"It takes a while to learn to shoot well."

"I want to try anyway. It's frustrating to spend half an hour listening to you talk about a rifle and not be able to shoot it at least once."

"Okay. Why don't you try to hit that cactus over there?" He pointed to a prickly pear cactus about fifty yards away.

"Is this right?" she asked when she placed the rifle stock against her shoulder.

"Fine. Now squeeze the trigger. Don't jerk it."

He waited while she went through her routine of aiming, changing her position, then aiming again. He was running names through his mind of soldiers who might have the patience to work with her when she fired the rifle, and another bud went spinning into space. "At least you're in the vicinity of the cactus," he said. "With practice you might—"

He didn't get a chance to finish his sentence. Abby fired again and a third bud went flying. Then a fourth, fifth, sixth, and seventh. She turned, a look of disappointment on her face. "I didn't hit it even once."

"You fake!" Bryce exclaimed, realizing he'd been tricked quite thoroughly. "You let me think you were a novice when you're practically a sharpshooter. You intended to hit those buds instead of the cactus."

"How could I do that?" Abby asked, assuming a look of outraged innocence. "I'm a helpless woman from the East. I'm afraid of guns."

"I don't know whether to hug you or turn you across my knee and give you a spanking," Bryce said.

"If I get a vote, I'd choose the first option."

And that was how he ended up with Abby in his arms. Having gone that far, it seemed only logical that he kiss her. Since he'd been trained since birth to be logical, that's what he did.

It wasn't much of a kiss, just a brush of his lips against her forehead. It surprised both of them too much to continue. The important thing was that it had happened at all, that she didn't slap him, and he wanted to do it again. Fortunately, logic came to his aid. If he went any further along this logical course, he'd be in trouble. He made a rapid retreat.

"Congratulations," he said, stepping away from Abby. "That was some of the best shooting I've ever seen."

"Do you congratulate your soldiers like that?"

"Only my women soldiers," he said, answering her smile with one of his own. "Where did you learn to shoot like that?" He didn't care. He just needed something to get his mind off what he'd done.

"I used to tag along with my father every chance I got. That's how I learned to ride and shoot. I got my first rifle when I was seven. We hunted at least twice a week even after we moved to St. Louis. When he started talking about going West, I practiced especially hard so he would take me with him. He didn't, and I stopped shooting until I started seeing Albert. He considered himself a marksman. We used to shoot together. I made sure to lose at least half the time."

"You are a dangerous woman," Bryce said. "Maybe I should warn the Indians and the rustlers."

"I hope you're not angry. You've been so determined to convince me I don't know anything about the West and can never learn, I couldn't help teasing you a little."

"Orman doesn't know how lucky he is you couldn't find the right bullets for that pistol."

"Father never let me touch a pistol or a shotgun."

"You probably won't have time to master every weapon. I expect you'll be fully occupied with your store most of the time."

To his surprise, Abby didn't appear to welcome being reminded of the store. Maybe she was finally realizing she faced a task far beyond her knowledge and experience. Maybe she was even considering going back to St. Louis. He was disconcerted to find himself not only resigned to her staying but actually wanting her not to leave. He wasn't sure why such a crazy attitude had overcome his common sense, but it had.

"I don't suppose the store can take care of itself." Abby sighed. "I'd forgotten how much I used to like riding with my father. We only rode down farm roads, but I always looked forward to it."

"I'm sure you can find some time, but you must never attempt to ride out alone."

"Will you ride with me?"

"I can hardly believe how much I enjoyed it," Abby said, telling Moriah about her ride. "It's not really so scary once you know what's out there and what to expect."

"You can never tell what to expect in a place like this," Moriah said. "Dorrie says there are rattlesnakes."

Abby wanted her sister's full attention, but Moriah moved methodically through the store, straightening piles of shirts and rearranging cans and boxes into attractive displays.

"I didn't see any snakes."

"You don't see them until they strike. Then it's too late."

"Well, I'm sure there's no rattlesnake big enough to attack me while I'm on a horse. I can't wait to ride to the mountains. They're so big, they seem just out of reach. Bryce says they're more than twenty-five miles away."

"It's a good thing you'll be too busy to go in search of the wild beasts that hide in those mountains," Moriah said.

"I'm not interested in wild animals," Abby said, barely resisting the temptation to stamp her foot. "I just want to see the mountains. They look so beautiful covered with snow."

"Dorrie says snow causes floods when it starts to melt. A flood nearly destroyed Denver four years ago."

Abby was thoroughly irritated that she couldn't communicate to Moriah any of the pleasure she'd had in the ride. She couldn't even interest Moriah in the flowers Bryce said would soon burst into bloom.

Resigned, she said, "I think I'll go through the rest of Father's papers. I've got nearly everything straight."

But it didn't take long before she laid the papers aside. She couldn't concentrate with the feeling of excitement continuing to sing in her veins. Maybe that wasn't the right word, but she felt bursts of energy shooting all through her. It was as though she expected something to happen and could barely contain her excitement in anticipation.

But nothing was going to happen except that she would work until it was time to fix dinner. Later in the evening, she and Moriah would return to the store. If they managed to get everything on the newly built shelves, they could open tomorrow. She was pleased with the way the shelves helped display the merchandise, and she was looking forward to receiving customers, but the prospect of receiving their first customers wasn't the reason for her excitement. It clearly originated from her ride. She'd been pleased she remembered how to ride and had quickly adjusted to the sidesaddle. She was even more pleased she felt less afraid, less like a stranger in an ugly and unfriendly land. Maybe most of all she was pleased at the prospect of being able to ride each day. Bryce had offered to assign a soldier to ride with her whenever she wanted.

When she started thinking of Bryce, a smile tugged at Abby's mouth. That bothered her. Any woman would be impressed by a tall, muscular, handsome man in uniform, especially when he was the commander of a whole fort. She'd have to be dead not to feel a glow of satisfaction that he'd taken time from his work to pay attention to her, that he appeared genuinely interested in making sure no harm came to her. For a woman who'd lived in a household of women for fourteen years, it was almost like courting every time she saw him.

She'd depended on his protection as well as his help from the first, when she felt threatened by the unfamiliarity and danger of the West, overwhelmed by the task of running the store and handling the beef contract. She'd needed someone to depend on, even if he was helping more for his benefit than her own. She'd known she was attracted to him, thought he was attracted to her, but there had been something different about this morning.

She'd gone back over their conversation twice without being able to say exactly what it was. Maybe it was more in what *wasn't* said. He'd spent the whole morning with her and never once made her feel she was taking up his valuable time, that he wanted to get this over and get back to his *important* work. He'd made her feel good about her riding. Not once had he acted as if a woman was too helpless to know anything about firearms.

She liked that he didn't try to patronize her or offer her suffocating protection just because she was a woman, that he took for granted she wouldn't fall apart. But none of this, as gratifying as it was, got to the kernel of what had happened out there, why things felt different, as if she expected something good to happen. She liked the feeling, but she needed to know where it was coming from. She didn't want to go around with her head in the clouds, ignoring the real dangers and challenges that surrounded her.

She was determined to succeed. She just wanted to know why she suddenly was certain that she would.

"Is there anybody outside?" Moriah asked.

"It looks like a dozen people," Abby replied after she peeped through the new curtains covering the store window.

"Then you might as well open the door."

Abby was nervous as well as excited to be opening the store to customers for the first time. She hadn't been able to restock the shelves, but all the merchandise was neatly displayed, with prices clearly marked. She'd also placed a piece of paper and pen within easy reach so customers could write down things they'd like to purchase in the store.

For the men she had wine, whiskey, beer, tobacco, canned fruit, and such pragmatic items as shoelaces, combs and soap, hats, boots, pants, and shirts. She also carried buttons, needles and thread, bolts of cloth, and lace. Her immediate objective was to satisfy the needs of the two hundred men and more than a dozen women at the fort. Her ambition was to draw people from the surrounding area because of the quality and variety of her goods.

Dorrie was the first person in the door. "I can't wait to see how people react to what you've done with the store," she said with a bright smile. "I brought every officer's wife at the fort with me."

Abby endured introductions to the seven women. She wanted to know what they thought of the store.

"We're going to have a party to introduce you and your sister," Dorrie said. "They wanted to do it when you came, but I convinced them to let you get settled first."

"We aren't anywhere near settled, but please feel free to wander about the store. I know we're understocked at the moment, but I've set out pen and paper so you can write down any items we don't have that you want us to carry."

"I hope you have canned oysters," one of the older women said. "My husband could eat a can a night if I would let him."

"I'm afraid we're out of oysters right now," Moriah said.

Abby knew this kind of situation could drive a customer from her store. "The man who ran the shop after my father died didn't keep up with the orders as well as he should," she said.

"Bill Spicer is a drunk," the woman declared.

"I expect he ate the oysters himself," another woman said.

"Or gave them to his friends. I don't think people paid for half the things they took."

Abby assured the ladies she would stock their favorite items as quickly as she could. She'd already gotten

Bryce's permission to use the army telegraph to send her orders to Denver. She was expecting the first things to arrive any day.

"I want some candy," a very youthful-looking wife said. "I have a terrible sweet tooth."

That was something else that had apparently disappeared. "I'll order it today," Abby said. But she didn't know if she would get it any time soon. Bill Spicer hadn't bothered paying the wholesalers. Bryce had had to threaten to take the fort's business elsewhere before they would give her credit. She had to pay her back bills and the new ones as quickly as possible. And she had to hire men to haul the goods from Denver.

She could only do all that if the beef herd, all fifty head, arrived on schedule.

Abby spent the next hour talking to the wives, listening attentively to their descriptions of things they'd had back East or remembered seeing in someone's home. She nodded her head and reminded them to write everything down on the paper. It didn't take long before they had filled up two sheets.

"It looks like you're doing a thriving business."

Chapter Eight

There was that strange feeling again, the one that said something wonderful was about to happen. Only now Abby knew what that something wonderful was. She turned to find Bryce smiling down at her. "Actually, I'm doing a thriving business in learning what I don't stock." She gestured to the sheets of paper. "I ought to have a dozen by the end of the day."

"They'll put down things that are useless out here," Bryce said.

"Like a piano?"

"A piano would be useful. Just make sure they pay you for it before you have it shipped."

"Maybe you should be running the store. You know more about everything than I do."

"Only because I've been in the army for fifteen years."

She didn't know a thing about Bryce's past—where he grew up, what his family was like, what he wanted to do when he went back East. Now she wanted to know everything about him, what he was like as a boy, what he used to dream about, why he went into the army, why he hadn't remarried. She knew she ought not to be curious about any of that. It was no way to get Bryce out of her system.

"While I've been living with an aunt who runs a lady's dress shop."

"You can tell them how to dress."

Abby shook her head. "Aunt Emma said I was hopeless. I didn't like any of the fancy clothes her customers bought."

"I think you look just fine the way you are. I never did understand why a woman would want to cover herself up with lots of flowers and lace."

"And this from a man whose dress uniform has enough gold buttons, braid, and cascading plumes to supply at least three modest women!"

Bryce had the grace to laugh. "I didn't design the uniform." He looked around. "Has anyone given you any trouble?"

"Nothing beyond exhausting me with marriage proposals."

"Don't let the enlisted men buy more than one bottle of wine or whiskey at a time. They know the rules, but they'll try to get around you by sending someone else."

"How will I know that?"

"I'll station a man in the store for the time being. He can tell you which ones to watch out for, which you shouldn't trust."

"Thank you. Now I'd better pay attention to my customers or I'm liable to lose them all to Boulder Gap."

"As long as you and your sister run this store personally, I expect you'll have quite enough business. I'll even go so far as to predict you'll begin to attract business from Boulder Gap."

"You're saying we'll be successful because we're

women, not because we do a good job." She wasn't pleased with that.

"I'm saying you're energetic, intelligent, and determined to succeed. You've also worked hard to organize the place and make it look attractive. You'll have a lot more customers because men prefer to look at and be helped by a pretty woman who smiles at them rather than a bewhiskered old man who growls if they stay too long without buying something."

That gave Abby an idea. Despite Bryce's dire predictions, she would ask Dorrie if some other wives would be willing to work in the store. Being completely staffed by women would make it unique. If she was successful, she could expand enough to include a few tables where the men could sit and enjoy their free time. And spend more of their money. And maybe add a space for women to sit and gossip.

"I'll keep that in mind," Abby said.

"While you're at it, keep in mind that every single man at the fort will propose to you at least once a week."

"I guess the only way to stop it is to say yes to one of them."

The easygoing look vanished from Bryce's face. "Don't. I won't give permission."

"Has anyone at the fort heard from the rancher delivering the beef?" Abby asked Zeb when he came into the store.

"I haven't, but there's no such thing as a firm delivery date out here. People get where they're going when they can."

That might be fine for others, but it wasn't for Abby. She had to have the money the Indian agent paid her for the beef to pay the wholesalers in Denver. They'd made it clear they didn't intend to tolerate failure to pay on the designated date. The herd had to arrive on time and without loss.

"Have you heard anything from Hinson?"

"No."

Abby didn't like that. For the first few days Hinson had badgered her to give up the beef contract. He'd tried to convince her by outlining the dangers and difficulties of delivering beef in a territory where thieves operated practically with impunity. When that hadn't worked, he'd offered her money in exchange for the contract. Next, he'd threatened. She was convinced Hinson had found a way to cheat the Indians and make a profit for himself. She was afraid he'd attempt to stop delivery so he'd have an excuse to take the contract from her.

"Where is Colonel McGregor?"

"Out with the new recruits. They come here as green as June apples. It nearly works him to death getting them trained so they won't get themselves killed the first time they go on patrol."

"When will he be back?"

"Not until supper."

Abby took only a moment to make her decision. "I'm going to meet the herd. I've got to know what's happening."

"The herd could be days away."

"I don't have days to wait."

"You can't leave the fort by yourself."

"I don't intend to. I want you to go with me."

Zeb looked alarmed. "I haven't gone on patrol in six months. I'll have saddle sores inside an hour."

"Then I'll ask one of the enlisted men."

"Don't bother," Zeb said, not looking happy. "The colonel will skin me alive if I let you go off with one of them know-nothings."

* * *

"Do you know where to go?" Zeb asked Abby.

"Bryce—I mean, Colonel McGregor—said the La-vater ranch was at the foot of the mountains just south of the Overland Pass," she said, pointing to an area south of the fort. "He said the herd would have had to go north to reach the Indian reservation. Lavater didn't have far to come, so I don't know why he isn't here."

"That's a lot farther than it looks," Zeb said. "The area you're referring to is more than sixty miles away. Herds generally can't make more than fifteen miles a day without walking off the fat."

Abby's spirits sank. She'd expected it to take less than an hour to find the herd. As a last resort she'd hoped to ride to the ranch. She wouldn't have time to ride sixty miles there and back before dark. She didn't like the thought of riding across the plain at night, even with a soldier for an escort. There was no forest to hide people, but there were bands of trees along streambeds, some of them up to a hundred yards deep in places. Smaller trees and bushes dotted the plain. Bryce had said the broken ground near the mountains meant gulches, ravines, and declivities that could hide a band of rustlers or a small herd of fifty steers.

"What's the route they're most likely to take to the reservation?" Abby asked.

"They could follow the foot of the mountains, but that's probably too rough. They could follow one of the creeks so they'd have access to water, but that would take them east rather than north. So I suppose they'd go farther out on the plain to avoid other ranches and plan on reaching a creek at least once a day. There's generally plenty of water in the spring."

"Then let's go."

But Abby didn't feel any of the excitement or the security she felt when she was with Bryce. Maybe it was the fact she knew she could be riding toward danger. She'd brought her rifle. Zeb cast uneasy glances at the weapon from time to time.

"Why don't you go out on patrol?" she asked Zeb.

"I've been a striker for the colonel since his last housekeeper quit and got married."

"What did you do before that?"

"The same as everyone else: drilling, keeping my equipment in order, going on patrols, getting into an occasional fight."

Abby was relieved to know Zeb had experience, but she couldn't stop herself from looking over her shoulder. Already the fort was looking small and distant; already she was feeling exposed to danger.

"How do you find a herd of cows?" she asked Zeb.

"You look for tracks."

"I mean before that. How do you know where to look?"

"You think of where they are most likely to go and look there."

"But there is no place they're 'most likely' to go."

Abby had expected to find a clearly marked path because the stage coach and wagons that had brought her west had followed clear trails. That apparently wasn't the case with cows. She brought her horse to a halt. "The herd will be traveling north."

"Right," Zeb said.

"Which means if we travel west or east, we'll cross their trail."

"If they've gotten this far."

"Let's assume they have. Would I be more likely to hit the trail by riding directly east or west?"

"West."

"Are you sure?"

"As sure as you can be of anything out here. Look,

Miss Pierce, I didn't like being a fighting soldier. I used to take care of a rich man in New York. When he went into the army, I went with him. Once they found out how well I could do as an officer, they never let me near a gun until the war ended. I was tickled pink when the colonel's last housekeeper ran off. I was at his door before her dust settled. I don't even like being on a horse. We should have taken a buggy."

"You can't take a buggy into a ravine."

"A lady shouldn't be wanting to go into a ravine. It's not suitable."

"It's not suitable for a lady to have to chase down stolen cows."

"You're supposed to let your husband take care of stuff like that."

"I don't have a husband."

"Then you should wait until you get one."

Abby was stunned. "Zebulon Beecher—" Zeb winced at the sound of his full name—"you should be ashamed of yourself for acting like women are so helpless they have to wait for a man to take care of them."

"They shouldn't depend on me to take care of them."

"I'm not. I brought my rifle."

"Do you know how to use it?"

"Of course."

"One lesson with the colonel isn't enough when you might come up against cattle rustlers."

"I could kill a rabbit with a rifle before I was ten. *I'll* take care of *you.*" Abby thought for a moment. "I think Hinson is behind this."

"Maybe, but he wouldn't try to steal the herd himself. He'd hire someone else to get shot at so he could prove he was somewhere else."

"I think we ought to go west. I don't see why anybody should bring a herd this far east when it's away from the streams coming out of the mountains. Besides, we'll be going in the direction of the Lavater ranch."

"What do you plan to do if you find the trail?"

"I'll follow it, because it means the cows are on their way to the reservation."

"What if you don't find a trail?"

"Then we'll head toward the ranch. Sooner or later we'll find the herd. Come on, let's go."

The terrain looked more wild and threatening the farther from the fort they rode. She didn't find coyotes friendly animals. They looked far too much like small wolves. Seeing the bones of a buffalo reminded her that even large animals faced death. Even the leaves of the plants looked more gray than green. *Stop being silly*, she told herself. *You're only seeing the dangerous side of everything because Bryce isn't here.* He wasn't going to be at the fort forever. She had to learn to depend on herself.

"Do you think we've gone far enough to have found the trail?" she asked Zeb after they'd ridden for what seemed like an hour. They had pulled into the shade of a cottonwood tree to rest their horses.

"We've gone too far," he said.

That was what she'd been afraid of. They hadn't found the trail because the herd hadn't gotten this far. Just as she started to speak, she heard a sound. "Did you hear that?"

"It's gunfire."

"Someone's after the herd."

"You don't know that. It could be someone out hunting."

"That's not just one gun. It's rustlers," Abby said, slapping her horse on the shoulder with the reins. "I've got to help Lavater."

"How're you going to do that?" Zeb asked, riding after her.

"I won't know until I see what's happening."

Abby discovered she had a great deal more time to come up with a solution than she'd expected. After a mile the gunfire didn't sound much louder than before.

"Sometimes gunfire can be heard for ten miles," Zeb said.

"You're the soldier," Abby said. "What do you suggest we do?"

"Get close enough to see how many there are, then go back for the colonel."

"They would have the cows halfway to Denver by the time Bryce got here."

Something made Zeb look over his shoulder. "Uh-oh!" he said.

"What's wrong?"

"It's the colonel. And he's galloping his horse. He swears at any soldier who gallops his horse across the plain. He says it's a sure way to get killed."

"Then why is he galloping now?" Abby asked, greatly relieved at Bryce's presence.

"Because he's mad as hell. He's probably going to kill one of us. You being a lady means he's going to kill me."

"If he wants to kill anyone, he can kill the rustlers," Abby said, urging her horse into a gallop. The sound of gunfire was growing louder. She suspected Bryce meant to force her to go back to the fort, but she didn't intend to give him the chance. She topped out on a rise of ground that overlooked a wide, shallow canyon carved by a rock-strewn stream. On the far side she could see the herd of cattle and the cowhands defending them. Down below, with their backs to Abby and Zeb, were the rustlers.

"Zeb and I can catch them in a crossfire," Bryce said as he pulled his tired mount to a gravel-spewing stop. "You get back out of sight."

"I can help," Abby said.

"Get back or I'll tie you in your saddle."

Bryce didn't give her a chance to argue. He jumped down from the saddle, grabbed her horse's bridle, turned him around, and gave him a biting slap across his rump with a riding crop that sent him galloping back toward the fort.

It took Abby several hundred yards to convince the ornery beast he wasn't going back to his comfortable stall just yet. By the time she got him turned around, she was too angry to think of danger or Bryce's reaction to her refusal to obey his orders.

The fighting was over by the time she reached the canyon.

"I told you to stay out of sight," Bryce said, still very angry.

"That herd represents my future," she said, even as she flinched at the look in his eyes. "You have no right to tell me what to do."

"You'll soon find I do," he said. "The rustlers have run off. I'm going down to see how the cowhands fared."

"I'm going, too," Abby said.

She wouldn't have been surprised if he ordered her back to the fort on pain of being lashed to the nearest cottonwood. Or cactus. "Bring your horse up between Zeb's and mine," he said after a pause. "Cowhands are usually a pretty rough crowd."

She couldn't imagine what danger cowhands could pose when she was accompanied by two soldiers, but she wasn't willing to push Bryce's temper at the moment. She tried to concentrate on the fact that he was protecting her rather than ordering her around as if she was one of his soldiers. He didn't speak as they rode down into the canyon. Nor did he acknowledge the body of one of the rustlers.

"That's a man we just passed," she said.

"Someone in the patrol will see to him," Zeb said.

"There is no patrol," Abby said.

"There will be," Zeb assured her. "The colonel would never leave without ordering a patrol to follow."

Abby turned to Bryce.

"They ought to be here by the time we've talked to the cowhands."

Two rough-looking men stepped out into the open. Both carried rifles. They waited for Bryce to ride up to them.

"Is this the Lavater outfit?" he asked.

"Who wants to know?" one of the men asked.

"I'm Colonel McGregor, commander of Fort Lookout. I have a patrol following to make sure the beef gets to the Indian reservation."

"You're welcome to what's left of it," the man responded. "Those sons-of-bitches struck us yesterday and ran off half the herd. We can't move because we got two men wounded."

"There's a medic with the patrol. He'll do what he can."

The cowboy cocked his head toward Abby, a sneer on his cracked lips. "Did our fight interrupt your picnic?"

"This is Miss Abigail Pierce," Bryce said. "She holds the contract on that beef. She rode out to see why you were late."

His expression held for a minute before changing to one of curiosity. "You must be from back East," he said.

"I don't see what that has to do with anything," Abby said.

"You will," the cowhand replied, before turning back

to Bryce. "You intending to take these cows to the reservation yourself?"

"I'll detail some men to help you if you want," Bryce said, "but first we're going after the cows they stole."

"They ran them off during the night," the cowhand said. "They shouldn't be too far away." He looked from Abby to Bryce. "You seem to be taking a mighty personal interest in this."

"Any trouble with the Indians becomes a problem for the army," Bryce said.

"The army never worried about us before," the cowhand stated, "and we was robbed every time we set out."

"I was never called on to help," Bryce pointed out. "Baucom accepted the losses as part of doing business. Miss Pierce won't."

"Maybe if Baucom had been pretty enough, he could have asked the army to help him."

"Where are the wounded men?" Abby asked, hoping Bryce wouldn't bristle at the cowhand's insinuation. "Maybe I can help."

"Are you a doc?" the cowhand asked, his tone and stance indicating he thought she was just a pretty female who'd never done anything for herself.

"No, but like every woman, I've helped nurse sick people." The cowhand said nothing. "Maybe we should ask the injured men if they want to reject my help."

"Follow me," the other cowhand said.

Abby found the two men next to the creek under the shade of a peach willow and box elder thicket. One had been shot in the chest, the other in the stomach. Both men had had their wounds bound up with bandages that were dirty and soaked with blood.

"See to Rufus," the man with the stomach wound said. "There's nothing anybody can do for me."

Abby didn't need a doctor to know he was right. "I'll

need some warm water," she said to the second cow-hand.

"We got hot water, but we got nothing for bandages," the boy said.

"I'll use my petticoat." Abby turned to Bryce. "Do you have a knife to cut some strips from my petticoat?"

"In front of these men?" Bryce asked, shocked.

"I'm sure they'll turn away," Abby said impatiently. She would worry about decorum when she was safely back at the fort.

If the situation hadn't been so dire, she would have enjoyed Bryce's discomfort as he approached the task of cutting bandage strips from her petticoat. He couldn't bring himself to raise the hem of her dress, so she did it for him. The ladies in his family must have been very formal to have instilled in him such a rigid sense of decorum. She wondered how he'd ever been able to relax enough to enjoy relations with his wife. Abby was horrified that such a thought would have entered her head. Thank God Bryce couldn't read her mind. She'd have died of embarrassment.

But the thought wouldn't go away. She wasn't experienced at love, but she knew men placed a lot of importance on the physical side of marriage. Her aunt had said if she and Moriah wanted to keep their husbands satisfied and faithful, they had to embrace this need men had and welcome them to their beds. Abby wondered if Bryce's wife had ever welcomed him into her bed.

"I think that's enough," Bryce said, holding up two large pieces of cotton cloth, "but your petticoat is ruined."

"Tear them into strips while I clean this wound."

"I hope that dust cloud is your patrol," the first cowhand said to Bryce. "I'm not up to another fight."

Abby hoped no one would guess she'd never taken

care of such a serious wound, or that the sight of the dirty, bloody bandage caused her stomach to heave. She forced herself to remove the bandage and clean away the caked blood. The wound itself was a small hole with darkened edges.

"You don't have to worry about digging out no bullet," Rufus said. "It came out the back."

The exit wound was much worse, ragged and large. "The army doctor will have something to help prevent infection," she told Rufus. "The best I can do is clean it and apply a fresh bandage."

"You got any whiskey?" the man with the stomach wound asked. "That's about all that can help me now."

"I'm sure the doctor will have something to make you more comfortable."

"How about a bullet to the head?"

Abby did her best to control her shock at the man's suggestion that someone shoot him to put him out of his misery.

"The doctor will have some morphine," Bryce said. "Just hang on for a little longer."

Abby looked to Bryce for guidance, for what to say to this man, but she found no help in his bleak expression. She turned to the approaching patrol, hoping the army doctor would have an answer.

She had expected to see at least a hundred men. She didn't know how the dozen who approached, riding two abreast, could take care of the wounded men, recapture the stolen cows, help deliver the herd to the reservation, and chase down the rustlers.

"Is that all that are coming?" she asked Bryce.

"Yes," he said as he moved toward the young lieutenant who seemed to be in command. Bryce sent the doctor to see to the two wounded men, then gave the lieutenant orders to capture the rustlers and recover the herd. Once they had done that, they were to escort the herd to the reservation. Zeb would stay to help the doctor. As soon as Bryce got back to the fort he would send a military ambulance for the two wounded men. That done, he turned back to Abby.

"Mount up. We're going back. I have a good deal to say to you."

Chapter Nine

"Shouldn't we stay and help?" Abby asked.

"The best way we can help is by getting you back to the fort."

Bryce couldn't decide whether he was more relieved to see that Abby was safe or angry that she could do something so crazy and suffer no consequences to make her understand how dangerous it was.

To keep from thinking of the many grisly fates that could have befallen her during that lonely ride, Bryce had rehearsed what he'd say when he found her. Hearing gunfire, he'd expected to arrive to find Abby and Zeb in a desperate fight with the rustlers. It hardly made him feel any better that she was preparing to catch them in a crossfire.

Now that she was safe and they were headed back to the fort, all the dangers poured into his mind like an onslaught of screaming devils. Did she have any idea of the number of ways she could have been killed by now? Had she given any thought to what the rustlers might have done if they'd captured her? Feeling as if he was about to explode, he realized his feelings were as much a release of tension as an expression of frustration. Before he spoke, he had to calm down. He was a professional soldier. He couldn't lose control.

"How did you know where to find us?" she asked.

"A child could have followed your trail."

"You didn't have to follow me. I was perfectly safe with Zeb."

"Let's stop here for a few minutes," Bryce said, indicating a grove of cottonwood and peach leaf willow.

"What would people think if they found us alone so far from the fort?" Abby's tone was sarcastic.

He put his hands around her waist and lifted her from the saddle before he let himself answer. "I don't know what they might think about you, but they would know the only reason I would be out here would be to rescue a stubborn, hardheaded female from the folly of her own actions."

Abby looked angry, but the fact that she could be angry at being called to book for such a crazy stunt only increased his frustration.

"Did you think I was just trying to scare you when I told you how dangerous it could be out here, or did you think I was trying to make you think I was the big, brave soldier who would take care of the little, helpless woman?"

Abby backed away from him. "I never thought that. I thought—"

"That's the problem. You never thought!"

"I thought enough to realize if I didn't deliver this herd, I'd be ruined."

"While you were thinking of yourself, did you think about anyone else?" Bryce gripped her arms to keep her from turning her back to him. "Not all Indians live on the reservation. We have renegades who roam these plains eager to avenge themselves on any unwary white they can find. They don't discriminate between men and women. We have white men who'd violate you, murder you, and blame it on the Indians. That would cause an uproar in the community and a demand from headquarters that I arrest the guilty parties. That would mean a fight in which many innocent men, white and Indian, would die. And all because you were too stubborn, hardheaded, and know-it-all to do what I told you."

"I didn't—"

"Even if civilians are liars, cheats, thieves, and worse, other civilians think their lives are precious, that their deaths must be avenged. They never think about the soldiers who may die. They're soldiers. It's what they're for. Well, soldiers' lives are precious, too. They have families and friends, hopes and dreams, and I resent it when people carelessly put their lives in jeopardy."

Bryce was certain Abby hadn't thought of things in this light. It took Easterners a while before they really understood they couldn't go about with impunity as they could back home.

"Did you think of how your sister would feel if anything happened to you?" he asked. "She doesn't have your strength, your stubborn will to survive and prosper. She'd be lost without you."

"No." From her expression, Bryce thought that possibility affected her more than anything else he'd said.

"Pamela would be upset, too," he added. "She's never paid much attention to other women at the fort, but she's taken a tremendous liking to you. She talks about you all the time."

"Pamela is a darling child."

"Did you think how I would feel if I found you after some inhuman creature was done with you? Do you have

125

any idea what it does to a man to see a person he likes reduced to such a condition?" His grip tightened on Abby, but she didn't try to get away.

"You don't like me."

He didn't know what caused him to shake her. He'd never done that to a woman before. "I do like you. Why do you think I've tried so hard to keep you alive?"

"You've done everything you could to convince me to go back to St. Louis."

"Because you're safer there. You worry me to death. I never know what you're doing."

"It's not your job to worry about me."

"Haven't you heard a word I've said? What do you think would happen if you were killed? We'd probably have newspapers back East blaring that all Indians should be eradicated. How would you feel knowing your stubbornness might start a war that would cost thousands of lives?"

He realized from her appalled look that he'd said more than he should, revealed more of himself than he wanted. He released her so abruptly she almost fell. He reached out to steady her, but she regained her balance. She looked at him, disbelief and a little fear in her gaze. He forced himself to calm down, to remember he was an experienced officer in command of a fort, not a green recruit facing his first trouble. "I'm responsible for everyone in this area—civilian, solider, and Indian," he said. "I don't have a choice. I have to be worried about everyone."

He thought he could see a bit of relief in her eyes. He didn't want her to take his words the way they'd sounded, like the declaration of some lovesick stripling. She didn't have to know he'd wanted to take her in his arms and hold her tight to reassure himself she was safe.

Bryce didn't know whether to lock her up for her own

safety and his sanity or to admire her courage and independence. He couldn't think of any other woman who after being in the West for barely a week would head off after rustlers armed with nothing more than a rifle and a ten-dollar-a-month striker. Zeb had at least had the sense to tell one of the soldiers what Abby meant to do and charge him to tell the colonel as soon as he returned. That might be the only reason Bryce wouldn't have him flayed alive.

"Why would you do something like this after all I've told you?"

Abby massaged her wrists, glaring defiantly at him. "When will you understand this is my livelihood. I have nowhere to go if I fail. I've got to succeed."

He did understand. What *she* didn't understand was that her efforts to succeed were almost guaranteed to cause trouble. He could take away her license to run the store at the fort, but she was just stubborn enough to move to Boulder Gap and concentrate on the beef contract. It was her ownership of that contract that posed the real danger. It looked as if his best option was to make sure she was able to deliver on the contract.

"How did you know where to find the herd?" That wasn't what he'd expected to ask when he set out after her, but the sooner he got it through his Philadelphia society–conditioned brain that there was nothing ordinary about Abby, that she wouldn't behave the way his mother or any other society woman behaved, the better chance he'd have of keeping her alive. She looked surprised, not sure how to answer him.

"From what you and Zeb told me, I figured the trail was to the west. Going east would be too far out of their way."

"Unless they were trying to avoid the rustlers. But Lavater is too stubborn to do anything sensible like try to avoid trouble. He's a lot like some other people I know."

"You don't have to pretend you're not talking about me. I know what you're thinking, but I didn't have any choice. If I don't pay my bills on time, I'll lose everything."

It had to be hard for a woman who'd never had any real responsibility to suddenly find herself in such a mess. Nevertheless, he had to find some way to make her understand that there were certain dangers she couldn't take lightly.

"You should have asked me to help, instead of taking off on your own."

"This is my problem, not yours."

"I've already explained that anything that happens out here is ultimately my problem."

Abby gave him a steely look. "Do you have authority over civilians?"

"No."

"Then what authority do you have to order me back to the fort?"

He didn't have any, and he suspected she knew it. "When there's danger to people or property, I can exercise absolute authority."

"Since there's no danger, I can go where I want."

"There's always danger to a woman alone. Do you realize if you'd ridden much farther, you wouldn't have been able to return to the fort tonight?" Of course she hadn't. She had no concept of the distances in the West.

"Aren't there ranches, farms, people who live out here?"

"Yes."

"Then I could ask for lodging with one of them for the night."

"That's not always possible."

"Then I'd have slept on the ground like your men."

"If my superiors in Washington found out about that, I could lose my command."

"I wouldn't want you to jeopardize your career."

Sarcasm again, but he resisted the temptation to answer in kind. "Then don't leave the fort without talking to me first."

Abby had always found it difficult to endure lectures. The fact that she was in the wrong made it that much harder. But to have Bryce chide her for deficiencies he'd already taken care of was the last straw. For several moments she was unable to speak without saying something that would later cover her with shame.

"I appreciate your attempts to help me learn and understand how to survive out here," she said when she'd recovered her temper somewhat. "I'm very much aware of my ignorance, but you don't have to rub my nose in it."

"I just want you to understand how dangerous it can be to do anything without thinking."

"I did think. I just didn't know all the things to think about. I would have let Zeb take me back to the fort if I'd realized the extent of the trouble I could cause."

Bryce looked surprised. "I thought I'd have to hog-tie you to keep you from going after that herd."

"I don't make a practice of ignoring danger."

"You have since you've been out here. You haven't taken a single piece of my advice."

"That's because you've just been telling me what I can't do. Advise me how to get done what I need to do and I'll listen to you plenty."

He knew he shouldn't be agreeing to help her, but he couldn't be the one to cause her to fail. She had too much courage; she tried too hard. Maybe if he helped her, she'd soon learn enough to stay alive. There'd be no one to watch her after he was gone.

"Look, Dorrie told me you have to keep the peace to get your post back East, but if the beef doesn't arrive, you'll have a hard time doing that. I have to deliver the beef to have the money to resupply the store. So if you help me, you're helping yourself as well."

"Working together will help both of us," Bryce said, "but if we agree to work together, it will *really* have to be together. You can't rush off after rustlers without talking to me first."

"Okay. We've lost half the herd. What do you suggest I do?"

"Give the patrol a chance to find the cattle. If my men can't, you could see if you can find replacements."

"And if I can't?"

"Put all your effort into getting a full shipment the next month."

"I can't restock the trading post if I can't pay off my creditors."

"Don't try to solve everything at once."

"You can say that because you've got the government behind you. I have no one."

"You've got me. Doesn't that count for something?"

Abby was certain Bryce meant to offer his help in an official way, but the way he said it, the way he *looked* when he said it, invested his offer with a personal meaning.

"It counts for a great deal," Abby said, "but in the end, I must learn to stand on my own two feet."

Bryce wasn't used to a woman who acted and thought like Abby Pierce. He knew exactly what he thought of her as a person. She was honest, forthright, industrious— he could go on enumerating her good qualities, but it added up to her being a person he could admire. He wasn't sure but what he would have preferred a woman he could admire less and who depended on him more.

What did he think of her as a woman? Maybe more to the point, why couldn't he *stop* thinking of her?

There was something about Abby that had gotten its claws into his gut, yet she was as different as night and day from the kind of woman who usually attracted him, from the kind he'd married, from the kind he wanted for his future wife. While he never doubted she was a lady to the core, she was much too forward, too aggressive and energetic, ever to accept, or be accepted into, the society he'd been part of since birth. She would never submit to its restrictions. She'd be ready to scream with frustration inside of a month. He could imagine her running his home efficiently and being a good mother to his children, but she'd most certainly scandalize the very women she needed to impress to help him with his career.

He didn't know why he was thinking like this. Abby didn't like him and he wasn't interested in her in that way. It had to be that she had upset him so badly he wasn't thinking straight. He wasn't used to having a woman at the fort who didn't do what was expected of her. He wasn't used to one whose actions could destroy all his plans for the future. And he wasn't used to having one who was pretty and single staying in his house. He had to get his thoughts under control. Then he had to think of a way to convince Abby to consult him before she did something crazy.

"I agree you've got to learn to stand on your own," Bryce said, "but it will take you a long time to learn everything you need to know. Until then, you shouldn't feel reluctant to ask for help and advice."

Abby smiled at him. It was nothing personal, just amusement. "I have no problem asking for help or advice. The problem is that you and I don't agree on when I need to ask."

That was the crux of the situation neatly stated. "Let's try a compromise. If it concerns the store, talk it out with Moriah. If it involves the fort, the soldiers, anything or anybody *off* the fort, talk to me."

"That doesn't leave room for me to make any decisions on my own."

As far as he was concerned, she shouldn't be making decisions on her own, but he knew she wouldn't like it if he said so. "You don't have to take advice or accept help just because it's offered. Use it to help you know what to expect."

He hoped he'd spoken diplomatically enough to keep her from becoming angry with him. He had no illusions that she would do everything he advised, but at least he would be forewarned. He'd nearly lost control of his temper today when the stableman gave him Zeb's message. His commands, all delivered at a shout, had people moving at a run.

"That sounds reasonable," Abby said. "But," she added before he could breathe a sigh of relief, "it won't work if you insist upon interfering when I don't want you to."

"I won't interfere unless it affects the army's work here."

"But that could be anything."

"You'll have to trust me to know when I can give you your freedom and when I can't."

"That's something else we don't agree on."

"Was it fun chasing rustlers?" Pamela asked. "Are they all dirty and mean-looking? Did they try to shoot you dead? Did they threaten to tie you up and do terrible things to you?"

Supper had proceeded much as it had every other night, but tension lurked beneath the surface.

"Where did you get ideas like that?" Bryce asked his daughter.

"I'm not stupid, Daddy," his daughter said. "Everybody knows being chased by people with guns makes you frown a lot. You always tell me I don't look pretty when I frown. They can't be clean if they never come to the fort to wash. They wouldn't be bad men if they didn't shoot people and take things that didn't belong to them. And you wouldn't have forbidden the women to leave the fort alone if nobody wanted to do terrible things to them."

Abby did her best to keep from smiling, but it was obvious Pamela's common sense approach stunned her father. He apparently still believed his daughter was an innocent child.

"They were very much as you described them," Abby told Pamela, "but they didn't get a chance to do terrible things to me. Your father drove them away."

"Did you shoot any of them?"

"No. We caught them in a crossfire and they ran away."

"They're not very good bad men if they ran away," Pamela said, disgusted.

"You should be glad we were able to scare them off," Abby said. "That way none of the soldiers got hurt."

Pamela looked torn between wanting to keep the soldiers safe and her desire for a more exciting adventure.

"This way the Indians will get their beef," Bryce said.

"And I will get the money to pay my debts," Abby added.

It was clear from Pamela's expression that as admirable and necessary as those two objectives might be, they ranked very low compared to bad men who put up a heroic resistance. For a young girl who'd spent the entire day indoors studying her lessons, excitement was greatly to be desired, even if a few soldiers had to get shot to provide it.

"How did it go in the store today?" Bryce asked Moriah.

"Well enough," Moriah responded with her usual tendency to say less than people wanted to hear.

"Did anyone give you any trouble?" Bryce asked.

"No."

"Daddy said he bet at least fifty men proposed to you," Pamela said.

"I wouldn't consider keeping count of something like that," Moriah said. From her expression one might believe she thought being proposed to was a fault for which she would be blamed.

"Dorrie said she had to drive them off with a stick," Abby said.

"It's all because Zeb told everybody I'm a good cook," Moriah said. "Is any man foolish enough to think a woman would marry him just for the privilege of cooking for him?"

"A lot of men believe that," Bryce said. "There's not a single woman who's come to the fort or Boulder Gap who hasn't married almost as soon as she got off the stage. Very few women are able to make a living for themselves."

"I've been brought up to expect to earn my own living," Moriah said.

Abby was beginning to realize she and Moriah were very fortunate to have been brought up with the knowledge that a woman could survive without a man to provide for her. Their father had always sent money for their support, but Moriah had helped Aunt Emma in her dress shop, and Abby had had her own job. They were used to depending on themselves, making their own decisions.

"I think he considers this habit his soldiers have of proposing to the first woman they meet as something of a joke," Abby said.

"I wouldn't have any less respect for you if you accepted one of them," Bryce said. "There are some very fine men here, but your sister is right."

"I don't consider it at all humorous that these men propose marriage to any unattached female they meet," Moriah said. "I consider it quite tragic."

Abby would have to remember to tell Bryce that Moriah had no sense of humor.

"I'll have the officers speak to the men," Bryce said, "but I'm afraid it won't do much good."

"I expect the best thing to do is to politely refuse and act as though it's of no importance," Abby said.

"Maybe *you* can act as if it's unimportant, but you don't want to get married," Moriah said to her sister. "These men must feel desperate."

"I don't think they're quite desperate," Bryce said, "but they do see marriage as a way to improve their quality of life."

"Why don't you want to get married?" Pamela asked Abby.

Chapter Ten

The question caught Abby by surprise. She hadn't cataloged her reasons. She knew she'd never trust a man again after what had happened in St. Louis. She wouldn't go so far as to say Albert's perfidy broke her heart. So much was happening at the time—her father's death, the scandal about the theft, the loss of her job, the decision to come West—it was difficult to know just how she felt about any one thing. Marriage seemed to hurt everyone. Her father felt rootless when his wife died. Abby felt abandoned when her father wouldn't take her with him. Even her Aunt Emma had warned her to think carefully before marrying. All she could say for certain was that she didn't want to have to depend on a man for her support. No, not just that. She didn't want her happiness, her emotional well-being, to be dependent on anyone else. She didn't want a man's reputation to determine her own. She wanted to be valued for her own achievements, to be seen as a person in her own right, not a reflection of someone else.

"I like my independence," she said to Pamela.

"Don't you want to have babies?"

"That's not a suitable question to ask a guest," Bryce said. "Apologize to Miss Pierce."

"I'm sorry it's not a suitable question," Pamela said, "but I still want to know why you don't want to have babies."

"It's not an apology when you repeat your question," her father said.

"I like children," Abby said to Pamela, "but I'd have to have a husband."

"You can have Daddy. He's not married."

That remark nearly unsettled Abby, but Bryce looked so stricken she immediately felt better. His reaction made her wonder if he might not like her a little more than he wanted to. That thought kindled an unwelcome response in her. Bryce was almost exactly the kind of man she would have wanted for a husband if she hadn't decided she didn't want a husband at all.

"If you can't stop asking personal questions, you'll have to leave the table," Bryce said to Pamela.

"But that wasn't a question, Daddy."

"She's right," Abby said. "But you can't go around offering to give your father to any woman who wants him."

"I don't," Pamela said. "I only want to give him to you."

"I'm afraid you can't do that," Abby said. "Getting married is a complicated thing."

"Why?"

"Lots of reasons," Abby said. "After all, you're talking about living with a man for the rest of your life. He's responsible for taking care of you and supporting your children. Two people have to have a special kind of liking for each other to get married."

"What special kind of liking?" Pamela asked, her brow creased.

"They have to love each other."

Pamela's frown disappeared, to be replaced by a brilliant smile. "Daddy told Zeb he'd love to see you married to a man who'd keep you locked up until you learned how to keep from killing yourself. Is that the kind of love you're talking about?"

"Not at all," Abby said, shooting Bryce a baleful glance. "That is the kind of love that will keep me single."

"I don't understand," Pamela said.

"You will when you get older."

"That's what Daddy says all the time." Her disgust was plain to see.

"One thing you have to learn is not to repeat everything you hear," Bryce said. "It seldom sounds the way it was intended."

"But you told it to Zeb. Why can't I tell it to Miss Abby?"

"You'll understand when you're older," Abby and Bryce said in unison.

"Did your momma say that to you when you were a little girl?" Pamela asked Moriah.

"My mother died when I was five, but I wasn't a very curious child."

"Is it bad to be curious?"

"No, but curiosity can often lead you to ask things that are difficult to answer. Everything is more complicated for adults. If I'd had a choice, I'd never have grown up. I was much happier as a child."

"Daddy says he can't wait for me to grow up. Does that mean he doesn't want me to be happy?"

"Of course he wants you to be happy," Abby said, "but men don't understand little girls. They keep wanting them to grow up because they think that will make everything easier. Of course it doesn't. Men understand women even less."

"I'd rather our dinner conversation be about something we've done during the day," Bryce said, "not issues I consider unsuitable for children."

"Pamela is the one asking the questions," Abby said. "Maybe you're not providing the answers she needs."

"She's seven. How much can she need?"

Bryce sounded angry, but Abby decided he was as much worried he wasn't a good parent as he was uncomfortable. He was used to being in command. Hundreds of men jumped when he spoke. He probably didn't understand why his daughter couldn't do the same.

"Children are naturally curious," Abby said. "They need answers to their questions, but the answers don't have to be complicated."

"I'm aware of the phenomenon of childlike curiosity," Bryce replied with some asperity, "and I make a practice of answering Pamela's questions honestly. It's just that we didn't have these kinds of questions until you came."

"I imagine that's because Pamela has been surrounded by men."

"There are nearly two dozen women at this fort."

"I don't like them, Daddy."

"I think she means she doesn't feel comfortable with them," Abby said, intervening before Bryce could chastise his daughter. "They have their own homes and families. We invaded your home and invited Pamela to be a part of this invasion. She's been a great help in telling us what you like to eat."

"You've been choosing meals because I like them?"

"Why would we cook something we knew you *didn't* like?"

"I never thought about it that way," Bryce confessed

with a vestige of a smile. "Everything tasted so good, I took for granted I'd like anything you chose to cook."

"We only seem like good cooks in comparison to Zeb," Abby said. "As for Pamela's trying to marry you off, did she talk about your marrying any of the female servants you had before Zeb?"

Bryce's expression cleared. "Both of them."

"It's only natural for a little girl to want a woman in the house."

"I like you better than anybody," Pamela said.

"And I like you," Abby said to Pamela. "You're a very special little girl."

"I'm a big girl," Pamela reminded her.

"Big girls know better than to hog the conversation at the table," her father said.

"Miss Abby talked a lot more than I did."

"That's because you asked so many questions."

"You can have my share of the conversation," Moriah said. "I'd rather work."

"Speaking of that," Bryce said, "tell us more about your day at the store."

"We don't have a lot of things people want," Moriah said.

"Don't let them talk you into ordering everything they want," Bryce advised. "Half the time they end up not buying it once it's here."

"You mean having to pay for it makes them sort out their priorities better?" Abby said.

"Something like that," Bryce said. "The men only make sixteen dollars a month, and they're paid in script. By the time you discount the paper fifteen to forty percent, they can't buy much. An industrious laundress can earn close to forty dollars. And she'll get paid in gold or silver. Now you see why every unmarried soldier proposes to you. The officers and their wives will provide most of your custom, but they can be fickle sometimes."

"How do you know so much about what people will buy?" Abby asked.

Bryce smiled. "The officers' wives complain when they have to order things they can't find in the store."

Abby continued to be impressed with the extent of Bryce's knowledge about the fort and everything that happened here. Maybe that was why everything seemed to run smoothly, and the men seemed content. Bryce had a genuine interest in the welfare of his men and their families that extended to the people attached to the fort, even to the Indians on the reservation. Maybe his attempts to control her weren't entirely selfish after all. Maybe he was genuinely worried about her safety. And happiness. After all, he had agreed to let them stay in his house. Maybe she'd have to reevaluate her opinion of Colonel Bryce McGregor.

"Dorrie Spaugh told me very much the same thing," Abby said. "I'm hoping she'll work for us. I think having an all-female staff would help attract customers."

"Probably all the way from Boulder Gap," Bryce said, "but you'll have a problem. As I explained, the officers' wives won't like to have anything to do with the wives of the enlisted men."

"Anyone who works for us will have to treat all customers with equal courtesy," Moriah declared. "Neither Abby nor I will tolerate that sort of snobbishness."

"Maybe we can do something to change things," Abby said.

"The best thing you can do is have a store that provides as wide a range of merchandise as possible. There's no reason for the wives to work making extra money if they have no place to spend it."

"Would you be willing to have a party for the wives so we can meet them?" she asked Bryce.

"Zeb told me Dorrie's already planning a party."

"I mean the enlisted men's wives."

Bryce's hesitation was obvious.

"We'll make all the preparations," Abby assured him.

"That isn't what's causing me concern. There will be some problems with morale among the officers' wives."

"We could do it ourselves, but the message would be much stronger if it came from you."

"That's what worries me. Don't misunderstand, I approve of what you want to do, but not everyone thinks as you or I do. I need some time to consider the best way to do this."

"But you will do it?"

He hesitated again. "All right." A grimly humorous smile appeared. "I do hope your store is a smashing success because I can see you're going to continue to cause a great deal of trouble."

"I won't be selling you any more beef for them Indians," Lavater said to Abby. "It's not worth more than my life. Or the lives of my cowhands."

"How are the wounded men?" She meant to say *man*. The cowhand with the stomach wound had died that night.

"Rufus is a mite better, but he'd be as dead as Tommy if that army doc hadn't showed up."

"Colonel McGregor tells me rustlers don't always attack the herds. I'm sure that next time—"

"There won't be any next time."

"But who will I get to provide the beef?"

"There are lots of ranchers around."

"I don't know who they are."

"I'll give you a list of names."

Once Abby got a look at the list, she felt better. There

were more than a dozen names. She shouldn't have any trouble finding all the beef she needed.

"I want all my money, Mr. Hinson," Abby said.

"Half those cows have been run to death. It practically takes two of them to make one decent beef."

"My contract doesn't say anything about the condition of the cows. It states quite clearly that I'm to receive twenty dollars a head. Fifty head at twenty dollars each comes to a thousand dollars. And I want it in gold."

Lieutenant Collier's patrol had accompanied Lavater's cowhands when he delivered the fifty head to the Indian reservation. There could be no question the contract had been fulfilled. When Hinson hadn't come to her, she'd gone to him. He seemed angry rather than relieved.

She'd been surprised to discover his office was in Boulder Gap, more than thirty miles from the Indian reservation.

"I can only pay you in script," Hinson said.

"The contract says I'm to be paid in gold," Abby pointed out. "I have to pay the rancher in gold. If I had to discount script, I wouldn't make any profit."

"That's not my worry. Besides, I don't have that much gold in the office."

"Then get it. The bank is open. I'll be in town for several more hours."

"It's not safe for you to travel with that much gold. There are thieves more than willing to kill for that much money."

She didn't intend to take the money back to the fort. She meant to deposit it in the Boulder Gap bank so she could pay her creditors. She needed to place a lot of orders to rebuild her stock.

"You have to pay up, so quit stalling," Bryce said.

"I don't have to do anything I don't want," Hinson

snapped. "The army has no authority over me."

"You can ignore me and the Indians, but you can't ignore civilians. If they start complaining that you don't pay them according to their contracts, you'll be replaced."

Abby had asked Bryce to let her handle Hinson, but now she was glad for his help. Many men didn't feel women were of any consequence. A colonel in command of a fort couldn't be so readily ignored.

"As I said, I don't have that much gold in the office," Hinson said.

"I'll take what you have and go with you to the bank to collect the rest," Abby offered.

She could practically read the silent curses in Hinson's eyes. She didn't understand why he was so angry about having to pay out government money. It wasn't as if it was his.

"You have to provide the full fifty head next month, too, or I'll be forced to cancel the contract."

"Baucom told me rustlers always stole part of his herd. I expect to be given every bit as much latitude as you gave him."

Hinson didn't reply but turned and stalked over to the safe. He opened it and started counting out gold coins from a cloth bag.

"That's all I have," he said when he reached seven hundred dollars.

"The bag isn't empty," Abby pointed out.

"I have other obligations," Hinson said.

"Why can't you give me what you have and withdraw the money to pay your other obligations?"

"That's a good question," Bryce said. "I'll be interested to hear your answer."

If looks could kill, Abby would have been struck dead. Hinson counted out the last three hundred.

"There," he practically snarled. "Now get out of my office."

"I can't say it was a pleasure doing business with you," Abby said. She took her money, turned on her heel, and left. "I want to go straight to the bank," she said to Bryce once they were outside. "I've never had so much money."

"You have an armed escort. I think I can get you there safely."

It took less than ten minutes to reach the bank; it took more than an hour for Abby to complete her business there. By the time she was done, she was exhausted but relieved. She'd fulfilled the beef contract and paid her creditors on time, the first steps toward success.

She knew she couldn't have done it without Bryce's help.

"I want to treat you to dinner," she said to Bryce. "Where shall we eat?"

"There's no good place compared to what you and your sister can do."

"I appreciate the compliment, but I'm not cooking tonight."

"Then I guess it has to be Mrs. Clyde's restaurant."

Mrs. Clyde's turned out to be nicer than Bryce had led Abby to expect. It was small—only ten tables covered with red-checked tablecloths—but it looked clean and was reasonably quiet. There was no menu; you ate what Mrs. Clyde cooked that day, or you went somewhere else. Today it was pot roast.

"This is quite good," Abby said when she tasted her first mouthful.

"It's not as good as what you can do."

"How do you know? I haven't cooked pot roast."

"If, when you *do* cook a pot roast, it's not as good as Mrs. Clyde's, I promise I'll apologize to her."

Abby giggled. She was horrified at herself, but it was nevertheless a giggle. "She'll probably think you're crazy."

Bryce grinned. "I'm an army officer. She wouldn't say that."

"My Aunt Emma would."

"I guess that's where you get your sass."

Abby wasn't sure she liked that. "You think I've got sass?"

"Lord, yes. I never met a woman so chock full of it." His expression suddenly changed. "Well, I do know one other, but you're not like her."

Abby wanted to know who, but the change in his expression told her it wasn't a complimentary comparison. "Since my sister and I have to make our own living, I'm thankful I have a good dose of sass."

"What was your life like back in St. Louis?" Bryce asked. "I can't imagine it was anything like what you're doing now."

"We led a quiet, orderly, and predictable existence. Moriah helped Aunt Emma in her dress shop. I did, too, until I got a job in a bank. After supper we used to sit in the parlor talking and sewing. Visiting was mostly reserved for Sunday afternoon. In summer, if we didn't go anywhere, we'd sit on the porch and talk to people as they passed by."

"Why didn't you stay in St. Louis? Working in a bank has to be a lot better than running a store on an army fort."

Abby was tempted to tell Bryce about being accused of embezzlement, but she wasn't sure he would continue to help her if he knew. She hadn't been guilty, so she didn't feel she was hiding anything he needed to know.

"We had taken advantage of my aunt's hospitality long enough. Since our father owned a business, it seemed only logical to take it over after he died."

There was no need to tell him she hadn't had any other choice.

"It's a big transition from St. Louis to an army fort."

"You made the transition from Philadelphia society. I expect that was even more difficult."

"Who told you my family was part of Philadelphia society?"

"Everyone knows. They're all wondering when you'll get your transfer back East."

"Surely there are other things to talk about."

"Not at Fort Lookout. All the women spend half their time talking about you."

"Why? I don't do anything interesting."

"You're a handsome man, successful, wealthy, with a society background. You're single, with a little girl who needs a mother. What could be more fascinating to a cloistered group of women confined to a few thousand square yards of desert a thousand miles beyond the fringes of society?"

Bryce laughed. "It doesn't sound so far-fetched when you put it that way."

"The other topic of conversation is how long it will be before Moriah and I accept one of the many proposals we receive daily."

Chapter Eleven

All sign of goodwill disappeared from Bryce's expression. Abby couldn't decide whether to be flattered or angry at his reaction, but she was sufficiently experienced in the ways of men to recognize signs of jealousy. It seemed Bryce was no more immune to the presence of an attractive, single woman than his equally unmarried soldiers. Since he didn't need a wife to help him achieve a better standard of living, it was quite possible he was attracted to her for herself. She had absolutely nothing against a handsome man finding her attractive.

Since she had no intention of accepting any of the proposals, it didn't make any sense to get angry. It promised to be much more fun to be flattered. Besides, when he wasn't trying to convince her to go back to St. Louis, telling her she didn't know anything about the West, or not wanting her to do anything without talking to him first—which she granted was quite a lot to overlook— she liked him a great deal. Not just the physical kind of liking. The more dangerous kind. She liked *him*.

"You don't have to go all stiff and official-sounding," Abby said. "I have no intention of marrying any of your soldiers. It's just something to talk about other than Indians, who goes on patrol next, or you."

"I'd have thought your store was more than enough to talk about."

"Women don't want to talk business all day. We're much more interested in people. Half the time shopping is just an excuse to socialize."

"I'll never understand women."

"We don't understand men, either."

"I thought women believed they understood men perfectly."

"We learn your habits, what you like and dislike, because that's part of our job, but we don't understand why you're the way you are."

He was smiling again. "You're the first woman I've ever met who's been willing to admit that."

"I don't know why. Admitting you don't understand something is the first step toward understanding it."

"Has anyone ever told you that you sound like a philosopher?"

Abby laughed, pleased. "No, but lots of people have said I talk too much. One or two even said I think too much, but I doubt you'd agree with that."

"I'm not sure I think anyone can think too much, but I do believe you underestimate the dangers around you. You're used to the safety of life in a city."

"I guess I'll just have to depend on you to protect me."

She hadn't anticipated that such a simple sentence offered in jest would cause such a complicated reaction in herself. A small part of her rejected the idea that she needed any man to protect her. But the much stronger feeling was one of pleasure.

"Promise me you won't leave the fort again until you've talked to me," Bryce said.

"I promise, as long as you're at the fort or I have time to wait until you return. Otherwise, I have to do what I think is best."

Bryce leaned back in his chair. "Have you always been this independent?"

"No."

"What caused you to change?"

"Realizing I had no one I could depend on but myself."

"You have a sister and an aunt."

"They have their own lives and responsibilities. Besides, I'm not a child anymore."

"Well, you're a child as far as living in the Colorado Territory is concerned."

Abby smiled. "Are you offering to be my guardian?"

"More like a friendly protector."

Even though Bryce might be developing a personal interest in her, he would be inflexible when it came to anything that affected his job as commander of the fort. Since it was impossible to separate his desire to do a good job from his determination not to let anything interfere with his hoped-for posting back East, she couldn't decide how much of his motivation was professional and how much was personal.

"I would never knowingly do anything that would jeopardize the lives of the soldiers," Abby said.

"I wish more people felt that way."

"I doubt they understand the consequences of their actions."

"They understand. They just don't care. Now we'd better get started if you want to have time to look at those three stores."

"I want to learn everything I can about shopkeeping. I hope to open more stores someday."

After living in St. Louis, Abby didn't think Boulder Gap was much of a town. Its streets were muddy, its buildings rough wood, and its character coarse. Every other building was a saloon that specialized in crooked gambling, excessive drinking, loose women, or all three. It seemed to be populated principally by men who had little or no acquaintance with personal hygiene. The people who appeared to be honest citizens hurried on their way, looking neither left nor right. Abby was glad Bryce had come with her today. The way some men looked at her made her feel queasy. She could understand why Bryce had decreed that no woman should make the trip unaccompanied by her husband. She also found him a great help when it came to looking through the stores. He seemed to know what she should stock and what she should sell only by special order.

"I have Pamela to thank for much of this information," Bryce confessed as they were leaving the last store, a mercantile devoted mainly to supplying miners. "We have very little to talk about during meals except her lessons and what the other families at the fort are doing."

"She's a very bright little girl," Abby said.

"Big girl," Bryce reminded her with what she was certain was the smile of a proud father. "She's seven now."

"And very able to speak her mind."

"Too able. She needs a mother."

Abby felt an instant irritation. "And how would having a mother cause her to speak her mind less?"

"A mother would turn her mind toward the things that concern women, not the matters that concern men. I want my daughter to grow up to be a lady," Bryce said. Since he was occupied leading the horse from the stable where it had spent the day and hitching it to the buggy, Abby couldn't see his expression. He helped her into the

151

buggy, and she opened her parasol to protect her complexion from the sun.

"You'll have to explain that remark," she said once they were underway. "I don't understand why a woman who speaks her mind can't be a lady."

"There's a lot of ugliness in the world," Bryce said. He was too busy guiding his horse through the tangle of wagons, buggies, horses, and pedestrians to face Abby. "A man must deal with all the evil and unpleasantness, but he wants to keep his wife safe from having to face it, from knowing about it, even from knowing about his struggle to provide for his family. He wants to leave her free to create a haven for him where he can revive his spirits, a safe and loving environment in which to bring up his children, and a place that allows him to believe there is good and beauty in the world."

Abby loved the idea of being so valued that a man would do everything he could to protect her, to shield her from the dangers and vicissitudes of the world, that he would look to her and the home she created as a place to find the love and support he needed to build his strength. She knew from experience, however, that men felt this way because they believed women incapable of understanding a man's work. That annoyed her.

"Don't you think a man and woman should share the important decisions in their lives?" she asked.

"Why waste time duplicating effort? It's better if men and women divide the work along the lines of what each is best suited to do."

She might not have objected to that statement if he hadn't included the phrase *what each is best suited to do*. She had worked in the bank long enough to know many men who were so lazy and stupid they retained their positions only because there were no other men available to fill them. Their bosses never thought of giving those jobs to women. Everyone knew females were only good for cooking, cleaning, and taking care of children. Abby admired any woman who could successfully take care of a home, husband, and children, but she resented the implication that women couldn't do anything else. When she'd discovered Albert's embezzling and confronted him with it, he'd refused to believe she could have figured it out on her own.

"I agree that men and women have different spheres of activity to which they're more suited by nature," Abby said, "but I don't agree that a woman can't understand a man's work. How would you like it if I said you weren't fit to rear your daughter because you're a man?"

"I'm not sure I am," Bryce replied. "There are times I'm sure I should have left her with my mother, but she doesn't want to go back and I don't want to give her up."

"You shouldn't give her up. I wish my father had taken me with him when he came West."

She'd always felt her father had left her behind because she was a girl. She was certain he'd never have left a son.

"I worry about her all the time," Bryce said, "about all the things that could happen to her, but I can't imagine a single day without her."

Abby felt most of her irritation at Bryce's attitudes evaporate. Though he had some beliefs she considered old-fashioned, it was hard to be angry with a man who loved his daughter so much he would keep her with him despite any hardships.

"Now you understand why it's so important that I get posted back East," Bryce said. "I want Pamela to have the benefit of having a real lady for a mother."

Abby decided it was a shame some men didn't know

to shut up before they put their foot in their mouth. If her parasol hadn't been so fragile, she'd have been tempted to hit Bryce over the head with it—even at the risk of his losing control of their horse, the buggy ending up on its side, and the two of them being thrown into the brush.

"I'm sure if you look carefully you'll find that, even outside of Philadelphia, there are ladies to be found who will fit your criteria for Pamela's mother."

Not being a stupid man—at least, not all the time—Bryce realized he'd made a serious mistake. "I'm sure there are, but I already know people in Philadelphia."

"Which will naturally make the process of selection faster and easier."

"Possibly," he said somewhat warily, clearly aware he was treading on uncertain ground.

"Don't you consider it important that Pamela like her stepmother?"

"Children don't always like what's best for them. It's more important that her stepmother be a suitable model for her."

Abby could envision Pamela's natural curiosity and high spirits suffocated by a stepmother stuffed full of dignity and moral rectitude. "What about your own feelings for your wife?"

"I hope I will be able to respect and admire her, not just for her beauty and excellent taste and style, but for the quality of her mind and her willingness to put the good of the family before her personal desires."

"You sound as if you're quoting something you read in a book," Abby said with more sarcasm than she intended. "Or as if you're talking about negotiating a business deal."

"A marriage is a lot like a merger, two people coming together to combine their efforts for the good of all."

"Is that how you went about finding your first wife?"

"No, and it was a mistake."

Abby had never heard anyone talk about Bryce's wife and was unprepared to see his expression harden.

"My wife and I had hardly gotten to know each other when I was ordered to take up a position with the Union forces in Kentucky. I only saw her once more before her death."

"What do you mean, you'd hardly gotten to know each other? You knew her well enough to fall in love, didn't you?"

"I married her on impulse. We were totally unsuited to each other."

Abby felt instant empathy. "I didn't know the man I thought I wanted to marry as well as I believed," she said. "I thought he was perfect. Instead he was a petty thief. If it hadn't been for Moriah and my aunt, I don't know what I would have done."

Her confession seemed to have broken down some of Bryce's reserve. He started to tell her about his wife.

"Margaret was beautiful and high-spirited, but I was sure she'd settle down after we married and she had a child. I didn't count on the war separating us almost as soon as we married."

"How did she die?"

"Consumption. The doctors said she didn't take care of herself properly after Pamela was born. She looked frail when I last saw her, but she was full of energy and high spirits. She didn't seem at all unhappy that we hadn't seen each other in more than a year. She encouraged me to return to my duties, but I don't think she was happy being married to a soldier."

"It must have been hard." Men could love a foolish wife just as much as a sensible one.

"It was hard leaving Pamela even though she was only

a baby. That's why I was determined to bring her with me to Fort Lookout."

"Pamela is happier, I'm sure, because you kept her with you."

Bryce's expression lightened. "She's delighted to have the freedom to do just about anything she likes."

"It's not just that," Abby assured him. "She adores you. She talks about you all the time. She's always asking me if I think you'll like this or that. And even though she thinks the Indians are colorful, fascinating, and have been treated very badly, she's angry at them for putting you in danger."

"Pamela is protective of everyone she likes. I sometimes wonder if she's not growing up too fast."

"I think she's a delightful little girl. Big girl," Abby said, correcting herself.

Bryce laughed, then frowned as he glanced at the sky north of them. "I don't like the look of those clouds," he said.

"They're a long way away," Abby said.

"Sudden storms can come up and cause the temperature to drop fifty degrees in less than an hour. We've had patrols trapped in snowstorms before they could get back to the fort."

"Do you think that storm will get here before we can reach the fort?"

"Yes. We need to look for some sort of shelter."

The sky had turned from sunny and blue to lead gray filled with blue-black clouds approaching at a fantastic rate of speed. Shelter that could keep them safe and dry in a raging thunderstorm was probably about as easy to find on the prairie as gold. Bryce pulled the buggy off the trail and made for a belt of cottonwoods, maples, and junipers along a creek. "Let's hope the creek doesn't flood, or we'll be in danger of being washed away."

Abby had learned to be fearful of renegade Indians and lawless white men, but she hadn't yet experienced Mother Nature as an equally formidable enemy.

"I hope there's not much lightning," Bryce said as the buggy bounced wildly over the uneven ground. "Last time we lost several horses."

"I'd appreciate it if you'd wait until *after* the storm has passed to relate all the horrors of previous ones," Abby practically shouted over the increasing wind and the squealing, clattering protests of the buggy and the horse's rigging. "Is it necessary to shake the buggy to pieces, or are you just trying to frighten me?"

"I'm trying to keep you dry," he said. "I'll have a hard time explaining to Moriah why I brought you home drenched."

The first raindrops were so large and driven so hard, they hit Abby's face with almost the force of a physical blow. They barely made it to the shelter of the cotton-woods before the rain started coming down so heavily it obscured the landscape. Bryce put on the brake and jumped down from the buggy. "Let me help you down."

"I don't see how that will help." Abby had to shout to be heard over the sound of the rain pelting the ground and the leaves of the cottonwoods and maples. "The water will start to drip from the leaves any minute now." She tightened her hold on her parasol to keep the wind from ripping it from her grasp.

"The leaves spread the water away from the center of the tree," Bryce said as he opened his saddlebags and took out something that looked like a large folded blanket. "I always carry my rain slicker," he said, unfolding what looked like a voluminous coat. "It will keep most of the rain off us."

"There's only one."

"We're going to share it," he said as he moved to wrap the slicker around both of them. "Until the rain stops, we're going to be as close as lovers."

Chapter Twelve

Before she had time to think, Abby found herself standing with her body pressed between a tree trunk and the very hard, very masculine form of Colonel McGregor. She'd never been this close to any man, not even when Bryce tried to teach her to shoot. After the precipitous, jarring ride across the prairie and the arrival of crashing thunder and flashing lightning that seemed directly over her head, she was completely rattled. Shock and surprise cracked wide her normal control. She could only respond according to instinct, according to her body's natural reaction to a frightening situation and such a close, overwhelming male presence.

"Maybe this parasol of yours will keep some of the water off our heads." Bryce said.

He had rearranged the slicker over his shoulders and brought it together behind her back. That required that he hold her in a tight embrace, her face pressed against his shoulder, her breasts against his chest, her feet squeezed between his boots. No married man could hold his wife in a more intimate embrace.

A flash of lightning and the following crash of thunder were so close she could feel the electricity in the atmosphere. Her first instinct, which she'd yielded to before she was aware of it, was to throw her arms around Bryce and press as close to him as possible. She had never experienced such a storm in her life. Lightning continued to flash all around them, thunder to crash overhead until she could manage no coherent thought except that she had to cling to Bryce for dear life.

When lightning exploded an ancient cottonwood on the other side of the creek and covered the ground with splinters of wood and shredded leaves, she was certain they would die in each other's arms. That image was so powerful, so vivid, she couldn't help wondering what people would say if they found their bodies in an intimate embrace. Did it really matter what others thought? She liked the feel of Bryce's arms around her, the protection of his strength, the comfort of his body shielding her own. It would be so easy to place her life in the capable hands of someone like him.

But she wasn't given time to pursue that thought. As if the thunder and lightning weren't enough to scare her out of her wits, the heavens opened up and hail hurtled down like millions of hard-flung pellets. The noise as it tore the broad, heart-shaped leaves of the cottonwoods was frightening in its volume and intensity.

"Keep your head down," Bryce shouted. "It will stop in a few minutes."

The hail hit the rain slicker with such force she expected to hear Bryce grunt from the impact. Resting his chin on her head and raising his shoulders, he shielded her from the tiny ice balls that came down so fast they soon covered the ground. The small, white pellets bounced continuously, making the ground seem virtually alive.

Then, just as quickly, the hail stopped and enormous drops of rain pounded the ground with nearly equal force. It seemed merely minutes before what had been dry prairie was turned to mud. Soon the dry streambed became a rushing torrent of thick brown water carrying away twigs, sage brush, torn leaves, and small limbs, at surprising speed.

"If it doesn't stop soon, the creek will flood," Bryce said.

The horse was drenched, the sorrel of his coat turned dark brown. He stamped his feet and shook his head to throw off some of the water that poured down on him. The stream continued to rise until it overflowed its banks and covered the low ground in the cottonwood grove.

"Where can we go?" Abby asked as the rain came down unabated.

"We'll stay right where we are," Bryce answered. "This bank is the highest piece of ground for some distance."

Abby didn't know what he meant by *highest ground*. As far as she was concerned the prairie was as flat as Aunt Emma's best platter.

"What if the water reaches the bank?"

"If we get desperate, we can get back in the buggy and head for the fort."

Abby didn't know how. The horse was already standing in a foot of water. They'd be soaked through in minutes, but that was better than being washed away by a flood. "Does this happen often?"

"A few times each year. As soon as the rain stops, the sun will come out. By tomorrow you won't know it even rained."

Looking at the swirling waters in the creek, that was

hard to believe. Yet even now she could seen a strip of blue sky at the far horizon. The storm was moving so quickly she could practically see the strip growing wider. A few minutes later the rain stopped as suddenly as it had started, but they were still surrounded by the swirling, muddy water.

"We'll have to stay here until the creek goes down," Bryce said.

"How long will that take?"

"It depends on how much water the storm dumped upstream."

Now that the rain had stopped and the thunder and lightning had moved away, Abby's position caused her to feel extremely self-conscious. Yet it wasn't possible to move from under the trees because everywhere around them was flooded.

"I shouldn't have stopped here," Bryce said.

"Where else could you have gone?"

"Nowhere. This is the only place."

"Then you didn't have any choice."

That didn't make Abby feel any better. She knew Bryce couldn't have known a storm would blow up so quickly, couldn't have known the creek would flood. It only made sense to make use of the only shelter available. Still, she wished they had raced for the fort. They would be soaked, but at least she wouldn't be locked in Bryce's arms with nowhere to go. One part of her liked the feeling; now that the storm had passed, another part of her panicked.

She'd never been held like this. Her courtship with Albert had been very formal. He'd done little more than gently kiss her good night. As a result, her response to Bryce was unexpected and she didn't know how to handle it. Her body was aroused. There was no other way to describe it. Her breasts were so sensitive they felt almost painful. Heat coursed through her body so she felt none of the cold. Liquid heat pooled in her belly.

Worse still, she could tell Bryce's body had also reacted to their closeness. He was aroused. There could be no mistake about it. He was careful to hold his body stiff and still, but that couldn't hide the change. Nor could he disguise the difference in his breathing. Her head rested on his shoulder. She was aware of every nuance.

There was the feel of his hands on her back. Her skin was so sensitive she became aware of the texture of the cloth against her back. If his fingers didn't move, she might have been able to ignore this, but they were constantly in motion. The longer she stayed in his embrace, the more insistent the panic became.

Finally she couldn't stand it any longer. "I need room to breath," she said, though that wasn't all she needed.

"Water's still dripping from the trees."

"I'll use my parasol."

"It'll barely keep the water off your head."

"That's all right. There's not much water falling now."

"There's enough to get you wet."

She didn't care about water. She would dry. She wasn't certain she would recover so easily from this encounter.

Bryce tipped the parasol to one side and pulled back so he could look her in the eye. "You're afraid of me, aren't you?"

"What makes you think that?" She was afraid of herself.

"For one thing, you're trembling."

"I've never been caught in a thunderstorm with lightning, hail, and flooding. I was scared out of my wits."

"It's gone and you're still shaking. Your eyes are wide with fright."

"If you must know, I'm not used to being so close to

a man, to being held in this fashion. Considering that I barely know you—"

"As commander of the fort, it's my job to keep you safe. You shouldn't be afraid at all."

Fool; he was a man and she a woman. Their bodies understood nothing about rank or social standing.

"I'm not afraid of physical danger"—though she didn't like the look of the floodwaters, and just the roar of them tumbling over rocks and swirling around trees was frightening—"but being held in your arms makes me uneasy." Part of her longed to remain in his embrace, but she refused to listen. It was too dangerous.

"You have to shed Eastern inhibitions when you come West," Bryce said, showing no inclination to release his hold on her even though the dripping from the tree leaves had lessened considerably.

"There are certain standards of behavior that are necessary no matter where you happen to be," Abby said. "You're violating those standards right now."

"I don't want you to get wet. You could catch pneumonia and die. You might slip and fall into the creek. If that happened, it would be virtually impossible to pull you out before you were swept away."

She didn't believe a word he said. "I need room to move about." If she didn't get out of his arms, she didn't know what she would do. Probably kiss him. Just the thought petrified her.

"That could be dangerous. The creek is still rising. I wouldn't want it to carry you away."

"Then put me in the buggy."

The water was knee-high on the horse, but the body of the buggy was well above the rushing torrent. She would be safe from the water *and* from Bryce.

"I'd have to hold you even tighter to carry you to the buggy," Bryce said.

The fact that he seemed to be enjoying this annoyed her. She was sure he wouldn't have treated one of his Philadelphia society women this way. Irritation helped curb her runaway emotions, cool the heat that threatened to consume her body.

"Then I suppose I'd best remain where I am." She tried to assume an aloof attitude, but she was in less control than she thought. She couldn't understand why she should be feeling this way. She'd never felt this way with Albert.

She *wanted* Bryce to hold her close. She was aghast at her own reaction, but her dismay did nothing to change it.

"We do a lot of things differently in the Territories," Bryce said.

She really didn't want to know, but her treacherous tongue asked, "Like what?"

"Women have more independence and men can treat them with more familiarity without being disrespectful."

"How can men be familiar without being disrespectful?"

"A woman can go places by herself, speak to men without being accompanied by her husband. If she's single, she can go to a social, even dance. She's allowed to have men friends without her honor being questioned. She can allow them to steal a kiss without expecting a proposal to follow."

Abby was afraid it was too good to be true. She didn't know much about the rules that operated in high society, but in her social circle women didn't have that kind of freedom. This was *true* independence, the kind she'd never imagined could exist. Some of her aunt's friends thought she'd endangered her reputation just by working in a bank.

"She can do all this and still be respected?"

"A woman of spirit can."

"Do you think I'm a woman of spirit?"

Bryce smiled, but it wasn't a relaxed, genial smile. "There are times I think you have enough spirit for two women."

"Then you think my reputation would withstand going dancing?"

"I can't imagine you dancing any but the most sensible dance."

"Would you still respect me if I let a man kiss me?" She didn't know why she was asking such a foolish question. She had absolutely no intention of letting any man kiss her.

"Yes."

"I don't believe you." She hadn't meant that as a challenge. It was simply too far from her experience to be credible at first.

"Then I'll prove it." He removed her parasol from her grasp, closed it, and dropped it to the ground. Then he kissed her.

Abby's world shattered.

Something told her she'd asked that question for a reason, that this was what she'd wanted. One kiss, and everything inside her turned over and became something else, something absolutely new.

Whereas she'd only tolerated Albert's tentative kisses, she couldn't get enough of Bryce's forceful, demanding lips. Whereas she'd been uncomfortable with Albert's too close physical presence, she found she wanted Bryce to hold her tighter still, to press his body more firmly against her own. Whereas she'd formerly thought of a relationship with a man only in terms of marriage, she was now acutely aware of a desire for a physical relationship. Whereas she'd always thought of her emotional relationship to Albert as love, what she felt for Bryce was pure, unbridled lust.

Horrified at the changes this kiss had wrought in her, Abby tore herself loose from Bryce's embrace. "Stop!" It was practically a cry for help.

"Did I hurt you?" Bryce asked, apparently surprised by her reaction.

Abby hardly knew how to answer. Could it be called hurt when you turned a woman's personality inside out so abruptly she felt a stranger to her own self? Could it be called hurt when it felt as if she'd betrayed everything she believed about herself?

"I guess I haven't been in the West long enough, but I can't accept being kissed by a stranger."

Bryce laughed. "Surely you don't consider me a stranger."

"And I don't see how you can respect me when I can't respect myself."

"You are a beautiful woman, and you deserve to be kissed. I was only giving you your due."

Abby refused to let herself consider what he said. She was still reeling from the discovery that she was an entirely different person from the one she'd thought she was all her life.

"If you were my husband, that would be an acceptable remark. Since you are not, and since I have no intention of acquiring a husband, I would prefer you not think like that."

"I can control what I do but not my thoughts."

Abby was quickly discovering the same truth. Lightning had struck and shattered a tree only a few yards from where she stood. She was standing under a tree that dripped water on her head. The creek had flooded its banks and stranded her on this small bluff, yet all she could think of was the feel of Bryce's lips and the desire to have him kiss her again. Telling herself that she *shouldn't* want that, that she shouldn't even be *thinking* about it did absolutely no good. Her body yearned for his touch. She practically had to grip the tree to keep from pushing herself against him.

"Controlling your actions is enough," Abby said. "Please don't kiss me again."

"Didn't you enjoy it?"

Yes! She'd enjoyed it so much she couldn't think of anything else.

"It's not a question of enjoyment," she said, trying her best to appear as calm as possible. "It's not something I should do. It's not something I want to do."

Liar! At least be honest with yourself.

All right, she did want to do it again, but she wouldn't let herself.

"I enjoyed it," Bryce said.

"Men always enjoy things like that."

"Why shouldn't women also?"

She didn't have a good answer for that. Her aunt had said a wife should try to meet a man's needs, but that she couldn't expect to understand them, that it was something beyond the understanding of most women. Now Abby wondered why that should be so. She couldn't speak for any other woman, but her need was certainly greater than she had imagined. And she understood it too well for her comfort.

"I wouldn't have thought that was possible until just now," Abby said.

"Why do you say that?"

She must be rattled to have made such an admission. She certainly couldn't tell him that his kiss had turned her into a wanton. Maybe that was too strong, but she felt as if she wanted to *be* a wanton. At this moment it seemed the most desirable thing on earth. Abby struggled to control this previously unknown side of herself. She would not allow an act that lasted barely half a minute to wipe away the training and decisions of twenty-four years.

"Several men came calling once I passed my seventeenth birthday, but I only allowed one to kiss me. He never held me the way you did, the way you're still doing."

"He must have been a very tepid fellow. You're better off without him."

"He was a liar and a thief."

"Then you're definitely better off without him."

"Albert wanted to marry me. You don't."

"That doesn't mean we can't kiss again if we want to."

She could feel his arms tighten around her. At the same time she could feel the desire, the *need*, to be kissed filling her up as the thunderstorm had filled the creek, full to overflowing. It did no good to deny it existed. That just caused it to grow stronger. She had a better chance of controlling it if she admitted this was a need that she'd harbored unknown for many years, but a need she would fulfill only when she found the right man. *If* she found the right man. Until then, she would keep her distance.

The problem was that Bryce apparently saw no reason why, since he wasn't married, he shouldn't kiss any woman he wanted.

"I don't want to," she said.

She didn't have to tell herself she was lying.

"I don't believe you," he said. "I can see it in your eyes, feel it in the warmth and tension of your body. Can you deny that you liked it when I kissed you?"

No. She could do many things, but she couldn't do that.

"I was taught it's not wise to give in to temptation just because it's pleasurable."

"So was I, but I've since learned that pleasure is one of the best reasons to give in."

Bryce didn't give her a chance to come up with a rebuttal before he kissed her again.

She tried to feel shocked, violated, insulted, surprised—anything that would allow her to break the kiss and push him away—but nothing worked. Instead she found herself responding to his kiss, rising on her tiptoes to meet him. For a moment she felt no shame, no reluctance, only the need to sink as far into the kiss as she could, to bury herself in the feeling that she was surrounded, embraced, supported, protected by a power that would keep her safe from all danger and heartbreak.

This time it was Bryce who broke the kiss. It made her feel much better to see he didn't look so unaffected this time.

"I admit I enjoyed it," she said.

He seemed to come slowly out of a trance. "I did, too." He sounded surprised.

"However, I'd appreciate it if you wouldn't kiss me again." She ruthlessly stifled the voice inside that screamed in protest. "I don't feel comfortable."

"There's nothing to feel uncomfortable about," Bryce said. "There's nothing wrong with an occasional kiss between two single people who find each other attractive."

Maybe not for him, but the stakes were higher for her. She had discovered a side of herself that was alien. She didn't know if it was real—if it was, why had it remained hidden for so long?—or if it was the outcome of the immediate circumstances. She might be lacking in experience with men, but she knew about the powerful force that pulled men and women together. She just hadn't realized that force lay buried inside her.

"How soon can we start back?" Abby asked. There was nothing more to say about the kiss. She couldn't forget it, but neither would she accept its being the natural thing for her to do. There was no assurance that lust wouldn't turn into emotion, and that would lead to misunderstandings and hurt.

"It shouldn't be much longer. I don't like to drive through floodwater. You never know when a tree branch might be swept into your path."

Abby looked to where lightning had destroyed the cottonwood. A small amount of debris remained on the bluff, but the rest had been swept away by the floodwaters.

"I guess I have a lot to learn about the West," she said aloud. And if Bryce's kiss was any example, not all of it would be unpleasant.

"I wish I'd gotten caught in the storm," Pamela said that evening after her father had regaled her and Moriah with an edited version of the trip home. "Nothing exciting ever happens here."

"You could have had my place," Abby said. "I can't tell you how frightened I was when lightning struck that tree. I was sure I was going to be killed."

"Daddy wouldn't let anything bad happen to you," Pamela said, looking at her father with a childish certainty he could fix anything in her world. "He never lets anything bad happen to people he likes."

"Then he must be a very busy man," Abby said, determined not to blush. "He told me he likes everyone at the fort."

"I didn't mean like that," Pamela said. "I meant—"

"I appreciate your confidence in me," Bryce said to his daughter, "but as I've told you before, the best way

171

to fix trouble is to avoid it in the first place."

Abby could tell from Pamela's disgusted expression that she'd heard that piece of advice too often for her pleasure.

"I would probably have fainted," Moriah said.

"Bryce probably wished I had fainted," Abby said. "Then he could have left me in the buggy and had the rain slicker all to himself."

"I would have jumped on Daddy's horse and raced home," Pamela said, her eyes wide with excitement.

"And been pelted into unconsciousness by two inches of hail," her father said, ruthlessly shattering her image of a heroic ride across the plain with everyone in the fort watching in terror, certain she would be caught but bursting into loud cheers when she dashed into the fort just seconds ahead of a lightning bolt that shattered the gate just after she passed through it.

Abby smiled, because she'd had dreams like that when she was growing up, dreams of what wondrous deeds she'd accomplish when her father sent for her to join him in the wild, uncivilized country he called the West.

But her father had never sent for her. Her dreams had faded and she'd taken a job in a bank. Her dreams changed to visions of success that would attract the attention of a handsome manager who would save her from drudgery by a brilliant promotion only she could handle. That dream had turned into a hope for a perfect marriage with Albert. That hope had died in the ashes left by the conflagration of his betrayal. Sadly, it took her father's death to make possible her childhood dream of going West.

"I would not have been pelted into unconsciousness," Pamela declared. "I'd have put on your helmet."

Bryce was kind enough not to point out that he hadn't taken his helmet with him.

"It was really uncomfortable," Abby said to Pamela. "You wouldn't have liked it at all."

"I don't care if it was uncomfortable," Pamela declared. "Anything would be better than sitting around here listening to Sarah's momma talk about some dance she's planning. We didn't even get wet."

Abby had found it hard to believe the storm had completely bypassed the fort. It had looked big enough to engulf the whole prairie.

"What did you learn from the stores you visited?" Moriah asked Abby.

"Not much, but I have a better idea of what we need to order. Now that I've paid off our creditors, we can replenish our stock. Once we get the money from the next beef shipment, we can order the full line of goods we intend to keep on hand."

They were interrupted by Zeb coming into the room. He approached the colonel and said something so softly Abby couldn't hear it. She could tell from his expression it wasn't good news.

"You'd better tell the ladies," Bryce said. "It's rightly their business."

"What is it?" Abby asked Zeb.

"It's the ranchers you wanted to ask about selling beef to the Indians," Zeb said.

"I hope they all didn't offer to sell. I don't know how I'd decide which to buy from first."

"That won't be a problem because none of them will sell to you."

Chapter Thirteen

"There were fourteen names on the list," Abby said, unable to believe her ears. "Did the soldiers ask everyone?"

"If you want, I can bring one of them in and you can ask him yourself."

"That would be a good idea," Bryce said. Zeb quickly left the room.

Bryce had said it was out of the question for Abby to ride over half the territory by herself. He had sent two soldiers to speak to the ranchers for her. She had been certain she'd have more offers than she could accept.

"I don't understand," Abby said to Bryce. "Did Baucom have trouble getting people to sell to him?"

"The herds were usually attacked, but enough cattle always managed to get through to keep things from turning ugly."

"Who paid for the cows that were lost?"

"I assume the ranchers absorbed the loss. You can understand why they don't want to lose cattle plus get their men shot up."

Abby didn't have any idea how, but she was certain Hinson had somehow managed to profit from the ranchers' trouble.

"These ladies would like a report on your efforts," Bryce said to the young soldier who entered the room in Zeb's wake.

"Me and Frank—that's Private Sturgess, ma'am—we went to every ranch on the list. Some of them was right far way. I thought accommodations here at the fort was pretty bad, but you wouldn't believe what some people live like. Mud and sticks is what I seen in some places. Bugs, too. Why in one place—"

"The ladies don't want a discussion of living conditions," Bryce told the young man. "Confine your report to what the ranchers told you."

"Yes, sir!" the soldier said, obviously disappointed at being unable to relate what he thought was much more interesting information. "Everybody me and Frank asked said they wasn't driving any beef to the Indian reservation. They said you wasn't paying them enough to take that kind of risk. A bunch of them has been shot up these last two months and don't want no part of it."

Abby was floored. She had to find someone who would sell to her. If she didn't, she'd lose the contract. And if she lost her contract, she'd lose the money to stock her store. If she couldn't get stock for the store . . . the consequences fell like dominoes until they spelled ruin.

"I thought western men were supposed to be afraid of nothing," Abby said.

"Those ranchers are afraid of something," the young man said.

"What do you mean?" Bryce asked.

"I got to talking to some of the hands. It was pretty lonely riding all over by myself," he said when Bryce gave him a stern look. "It weren't polite to refuse when they offered me a little refreshment. Anyway," he said, pushing ahead, "one of them said they'd been told anybody trying to deliver cows to the reservation would be met by a vicious gang of rustlers determined to starve out the Indians, and they didn't care how many cowhands they had to kill to do it."

"The government is obligated to feed those poor people," Abby said.

"They said if the government didn't feed the Indians, they'd go on the warpath. Then the army would have to kill them. They said once the army got rid of the Indians, the Territories would be safe for everybody."

Abby turned to Bryce. She was certain he didn't like what he'd heard, but she couldn't tell what he was thinking.

"Maybe I should ask them in person," Abby said.

"Anyone strong enough to threaten fourteen ranchers won't quibble at stopping one woman."

"The Indians have to have something to eat. If they don't—" She didn't want to finish the sentence. Everyone knew what would happen.

"Most of the cows I saw didn't look like they had enough meat on them to feed a family for more than a week," the young man said. "They was skinny as coyotes."

"That's what Texas longhorns look like," Bryce said. "They don't carry much meat, but they're nearly as fast and agile as antelope."

"I saw one ranch that had fat cows."

"Which one was that?" Abby asked.

"I don't know. It wasn't on the list. I was told it was run by a murderer."

"Anything else?" Bryce asked.

"No, sir."

"You did a good job. You're dismissed."

The young man saluted Bryce and left.

Abby felt desperate. As she had done in the past, she turned to Bryce. "What can I do?" she asked.

"I'm not sure yet," he said. "I don't like this business of threatening the ranchers, but I can't force them to sell their beef."

"I have to talk to them," Abby said. She knew that was what she had to do even if getting to the various ranches would be difficult.

"I can't allow you to travel to all those ranches," Bryce said. "It's too dangerous."

"Once they understand starving the Indians would force them to leave their reservation, I'm sure they'll change their minds," Abby said.

"You don't understand how much people out here fear Indians," Bryce said. "Many Indians have been friendly and many more have remained on their reservations, but there have also been attacks and massacres in the past. It's very easy for an unscrupulous person to play on people's fears, especially those who're isolated, like ranchers and farmers. There are also many people who feel all Indians ought to be exterminated."

"Do you think that?" Abby asked, aghast that anyone would advocate the extermination of a whole race.

"What I think isn't the issue. Fear is, and there's more than enough fear on each side to cause a major confrontation."

"Then it's even more important I speak to the ranchers personally," Abby said, her resolve hardening even as she began to consider the difficulties. "I couldn't live with myself if I thought my failure could cause so many people to be killed."

"You can't head off as if this is St. Louis," Moriah

said. "Listen to Colonel McGregor. He knows much more about living out here than we do."

"I'll be perfectly happy to listen to him explain how to do this safely," Abby said, annoyed at her sister's betrayal, "but I won't listen if he tries to talk me out of it. This is much too important for me to back down because of worries about my own safety. I'll have to hire a guide who can protect me."

"Do you have any idea what's involved in your plan?" Bryce asked.

"No, but you can explain it to my guide."

"And who will that be?"

"I obviously haven't had time to find one," she snapped.

"Sarah's father can protect Miss Abby," Pamela said. "Sarah says he's the second bravest man at Fort Lookout."

"I don't want the second bravest," Abby said to Pamela. "Who's the bravest?"

"Daddy," Pamela said, giving Abby a look that said she was seriously offended Abby had to ask.

"I meant other than your father," Abby said, trying to reinstate herself in Pamela's good graces. "He's the commander of the fort. I can't ask him to go with me."

"Why not?" Pamela asked. "Don't you like Daddy?"

"That's not why I couldn't ask him," Abby said, feeling slightly embarrassed at the question. She didn't dare look at Moriah or Bryce. "The commander has to stay at the fort in case there's trouble."

"Daddy took you to Boulder Gap," Pamela pointed out.

"That was for only one day," Abby said.

"Daddy can tell Sarah's daddy what to do."

"Thank you for your suggestions, Pamela," Bryce said, lips quivering with a smile he appeared determined to suppress, "but I think it would be better if you let me run the fort."

"I was just trying to help," Pamela said, obviously affronted. "Miss Abby likes you better than Sarah's daddy."

"Why do you say that?" Bryce asked his daughter.

"She cooks breakfast and supper for you every day."

"So does Miss Moriah," Bryce said. "Do you think she likes me, too?"

"Yes," Pamela said with a brilliant smile. "They both want to marry you."

Moriah looked stunned by Pamela's innocent interpretation of their actions. Bryce looked as if he'd stepped in a cow patty and was horrified at the consequences. Abby was so tickled by their reactions she nearly lost control. "We couldn't very well cook our dinner here and not offer him something," she said, addressing Pamela. "We don't have any money to pay your father for letting us use his extra room, so we're cooking to pay him rent."

"You don't want to marry him?" Pamela asked, disappointed.

"No."

"Do you want to marry him?" she asked Moriah.

"Definitely not," Moriah said, apparently still stupefied by the thought of marriage to a man as big and vital as Bryce.

"Sarah's momma says I can't have a baby brother until some lady marries Daddy. She lets me play with Sarah's baby brother, but I want one of my own."

Abby felt sorry for Pamela. She'd always wanted brothers, too, but she and Moriah had had each other. It must be very hard for Pamela to be an only child. "I'm sure your father will find some nice lady to marry who will give you a baby brother," Abby said.

"Daddy says we have to go back to Philadelphia for him to get married," Pamela said.

"There are lots of nice ladies in Philadelphia," Abby said. "There aren't many here."

"There's you and Miss Moriah."

"You father is not in love with us or we with him."

"Does the lady have to love Daddy before she can marry him?"

"That's a question you should ask your father," Abby said. After that kiss in the cottonwood grove, she wasn't sure what Bryce's requirements were in a wife. If he felt it was all right to bestow his kisses freely now, would he stop once he got married? Many men didn't. They believed a different set of rules applied to men and women, even after marriage.

"I hope any woman who wanted to marry me would love me very much," Bryce told his daughter.

"But how would you know she loved you?"

Abby was anxious to hear how he was going to explain love between a man and woman to a seven-year-old girl. She wondered if he really thought love was important in a marriage. He had told her he would want a wife with beauty, sophistication, and social skills to help him in his career.

"She would tell me," Bryce said.

"But how would you know if it was true?" Pamela asked.

"Maybe I'd ask your grandmother."

That wasn't an answer Abby would like to hear from any man she wanted to marry, but maybe it was an answer that would satisfy Pamela.

"Grandmama says she loves me, but it doesn't feel like it," Pamela said. "It feels better when Miss Abby says it."

It was clear Pamela's answer had unsettled Bryce. She

hoped he didn't think she was trying to work her way
into his daughter's affections to take advantage of him.
"That's because I let you help in the kitchen and lick
the spoon when I'm making a cake," Abby said to Pamela. "I expect your grandmother is more strict."

"Grandmama doesn't cook," Pamela said. "She says
a real lady never sets foot in the kitchen."

Abby was sinking deeper and deeper into a morass
not of her making. Everything she said seemed to end
up being in some way a criticism of Bryce or his family.
At this rate, he'd probably throw them out to sleep on
the parade ground tonight. "Not everyone likes to cook,"
Abby said. "Or has time. I'm sure your grandmother is
extremely busy."

"Grandmama says a lady—"

"It's not really polite to our guests to go on talking
about people they don't know," Bryce said. "Let's talk
about something else."

It didn't take Pamela more than a second to hit on an
equally uncomfortable question. "Are you going to go
to the ranches with Miss Abby?" she asked her father.

"I don't have to worry about that for a couple of
weeks yet," Abby said. "I'm much more interested in
you telling me about the plans for the dance."

Abby gradually relaxed as Pamela excitedly told her
everything she'd learned from Sarah's mother. She had
to visit the ranchers herself, but she needed time to develop her plan so Bryce wouldn't feel he needed to go
with her. She didn't think she could be alone with him
that long without courting disaster.

And giving in to her attraction for Bryce would be a
true disaster.

Chapter Fourteen

"I appreciate your letting us stay with you," Abby said to Bryce, "but Moriah and I are ready to move into the store."

"Who's going to cook for us?" Pamela asked.

"That's a rude and selfish question," Bryce said to his daughter. "Apologize to Miss Abby."

"I apologize," Pamela said, "but please don't make Zeb cook for us again. Daddy will have heartburn."

Despite his daughter's embarrassing remarks, Bryce was aware that Abby's announcement had unsettled him. He'd known from the first that her staying in his house was only temporary. Several times after she'd been particularly troublesome, he'd wondered what he might do to encourage her to move. But over the last few days he'd gradually come to accept her as part of his household.

That in itself was enough reason to want her to leave. It was important that he not make the same mistake he'd made with Margaret: being in love. That had blinded him to faults and made him reluctant to face difficulties. Abby's high jinks kept him on edge nearly every day. He'd been young and foolish when he thought he was in love with Margaret. It had proved to be nothing more than infatuation. He was certain his feelings for Abby were more of the same.

"We survived before Miss Abby and her sister arrived," Bryce said to Pamela. "We'll survive after they leave."

"But I don't want them to leave. I like them."

"They're just moving to the trading post," Bryce said. "They stayed here only until it was ready for them to move in."

"Don't you like them?" Pamela asked.

"Of course I like them, but the trading post is their home."

It appeared his daughter, too, had begun to take their presence for granted. The food did taste better, but it was the atmosphere at meals he enjoyed most. They were no longer a part of the day to suffer through because he needed to eat. He looked forward to the companionship and the lively conversation. Abby might not be sufficiently acquainted with the West to understand its ways, but meals were never boring when she was around. He wasn't in Washington, D.C., now, and he didn't need a sophisticated, well-connected, politically savvy hostess. Abby's sense of community was much more suited to the fort than that of any Philadelphia society belle.

"Sarah's momma says it's not suitable for a lady to live in that store," Pamela said.

"The store is very nice now," Abby said. "Moriah and I are looking forward to having our own rooms."

"Sarah's momma says it's not safe. She says you

never know who might be prowling around at night or what they might do."

"I have a rifle," Abby said.

"Sarah's momma says it's not suitable for a lady to know how to use a rifle."

"Thank you for keeping us informed of Sarah's mother's dictums," Bryce said, "but she's wrong about ladies knowing how to shoot. In Europe even royal ladies know how to shoot. It's considered an admirable accomplishment."

He'd encouraged Pamela to spend time in Sarah's home because he hoped Captain Rodney Mitchell's society-born wife would teach Pamela how to behave when he moved back to Philadelphia, but he hadn't expected her opinions to be leveled at him as criticisms.

"Is Miss Abby going to Europe?" Pamela asked.

"No," Abby said, her lips twitching. "But if learning to shoot is all right for the crowned heads of Europe, I'm sure it's all right for me."

"What's a crowned head?" Pamela asked. "Does it hurt?"

"Only when they lose it," Bryce said, almost at the end of his patience. "And don't ask any more questions," he said, when Pamela opened her mouth again. "You've known from the beginning that Miss Abby and Miss Moriah would move into the store. We talked about what they've done to their rooms every evening."

"I didn't think they'd really leave," Pamela said, pouting. "I thought they liked it here."

"We do," Abby said, "but this is not our home. We've only been visiting."

"Sarah's momma says unmarried ladies need a chaperone," Pamela said to her father. "Can I go live with Miss Abby and be her chaperone?"

"You're too young to be a chaperone."

NAME: _____

ADDRESS: _____

_____

_____

TELEPHONE: _____

E-MAIL: _____

_____ I want to pay by credit card.

__ Visa   __ MasterCard   __ Discover

Account Number: _____

Expiration date: _____

SIGNATURE: _____

Send this form, along with $2.00 shipping and handling for your FREE books, to:

Historical Romance Book Club
20 Academy Street
Norwalk, CT 06850-4032

Or fax (must include credit card information!) to: 610.995.9274. You can also sign up on the Web at www.dorchesterpub.com.

Offer open to residents of the U.S. and Canada only. Canadian residents, please call 1.800.481.9191 for pricing information.

If under 18, a parent or guardian must sign. Terms, prices and conditions subject to change. Subscription subject to acceptance. Dorchester Publishing reserves the right to reject any order or cancel any subscription,

Bryce was amused that Pamela thought she could chaperone a grown woman. On the other hand, he'd always thought he and his daughter were inseparable. It shocked him that Abby had become so important to Pamela that she would leave her father to protect her. He hadn't realized she needed a mother figure so badly.

He liked Abby and didn't want her to leave, either. Rather than disturb his life, she'd made it flow more smoothly. His life at home, that is. Outside of his house, her presence was something else entirely. Yet that didn't change the fact that he'd miss her. Abby had a presence that was impossible to ignore. Things were different when she was around. They were better, though he couldn't always say why.

"You'll be able to visit them whenever you like if you promise not to cause them any trouble," Bryce said to his daughter.

"I never cause trouble," Pamela said, incensed. "Miss Abby says she doesn't know how she could get supper on the table without me."

That remark caused memories to materialize in Bryce's mind with startling vividness. Margaret could never prepare a meal without the assistance of a cook, who generally ended up banishing her mistress from the kitchen. It was the same with the housekeeper. Bryce could remember more than one disaster. He'd almost been relieved when the war broke out and he could leave Margaret to his mother. Then Margaret had died, and Bryce had never stopped feeling guilty for not being brokenhearted.

"I'm sure you were a great help," Bryce said to his daughter. "Maybe you can help Zeb."

"Zeb doesn't want me in the kitchen. He says I get into things."

"Men don't understand about women and their kitchens," Abby said. "You can come over to the store and help us cook sometimes."

"Why can't you cook here?"

"Because I'm sure they're tired of cooking for five people," Bryce said. "Now stop badgering them."

"Am I badgering you?" Pamela asked Abby.

"Moriah and I want to move into the store," Abby said. "We've been looking forward to having our own home. I've enjoyed staying with you and your father, but we really want to go."

Bryce wouldn't tell Pamela he'd been thinking of suggesting that Abby and her sister stay permanently in his house. Sarah's mother was right; it wasn't proper for two women to live unchaperoned with nearly two hundred single men around. Not that he and Zeb weren't single as well, but he had his position as commander of the fort to protect him from gossip, though he wondered if it was sufficient to protect him from himself. It didn't matter. The presence of Pamela, as well as Moriah, would guarantee that he and Abby would never be alone long enough for the opportunity—or the need—to overtake him. His daughter really was a perfect chaperone.

The very fact that he was having these thoughts was the best possible argument for Abby's departure. Maybe he'd been a widower too long. Or his position allowed him little chance to satisfy his physical needs. Or having Abby so close all the time was a temptation he couldn't ignore. He'd started to think that maybe he could let himself go, indulge in a little harmless romancing. Despite what she said, Abby was attracted to him as much as he was to her. She valued her independence, but she was also a woman with a woman's needs. Maybe they felt the same way.

What was wrong with him? Even if Abby had been willing to indulge in an affair, even if they'd had the opportunity to do so, he was an idiot even to think about it. He might have been able to do so safely with some other woman, but with Abby it was the same as committing suicide. Once he started, he wouldn't be able to stop. There was something about her that kept pulling at him, trying to draw him in, tempting him. He couldn't blame it on Abby. She'd been careful to keep her distance. He was the one who kept stepping over the line, who couldn't keep his hands off her, who might find himself enslaved by her hazel eyes. He was the one in danger of becoming a willing slave. If he'd had any sense, he would have put every carpenter at the fort on the job of getting the trading post ready so the sisters could have moved out of his house almost immediately.

Now he'd come to enjoy her being here so much he doubted if he'd be able to put her out of his mind. One more reason to hope his family could hasten his reappointment. His mother kept writing that she had several eminently suitable candidates anxious to meet him, women who came from wealthy families with the necessary connections to promote his career, who knew how to run a household, who were willing to provide him with children. That was what he needed for his career. What he needed for Pamela. But a small voice whispered it wasn't what he wanted for himself.

"When do you want to move?" Bryce asked Abby. "It's too late tonight."

"Tomorrow morning," Abby said. "That'll give us plenty of time to carry all our things back to the trading post."

"There's no need for you to do that with so many able-bodied men about," Bryce said. "I'll get Lieutenant Collier to send a few over."

"We don't want to impose," Moriah said.

"Thank you," Abby said. "I'd rather not be required

to drag my trunk across the parade ground." She turned to Moriah. "We've accepted so much help already, there's no point in getting cold feet now."

"I'm not getting cold feet," Moriah said. "I don't want strangers in my bedroom."

"They've been in there for weeks," Abby said.

"I wasn't living there then. It'll be different now."

"Just tell the men where you want them to leave things," Bryce said. "I'll make sure they know not to go into your bedchamber."

"*Bedchamber* is a little grand for our living quarters," Abby said with a laugh. "I just hope we can keep from feeling that we live in the cellars."

"I like the thick walls and the lack of windows," Moriah said. "It makes me feel safe."

"Having two hundred soldiers surrounding me makes me feel safe," Abby said.

"Daddy makes me feel safe," Pamela said.

"Your father makes everyone feel safe," Abby said.

The smile she directed at Pamela, then turned on Bryce, caused him to feel he was facing something very dangerous, something so close it could grab him at any minute. It was his duty to protect the owner of the trading post, whether it was Abby Pierce or some withered old man who cussed and chewed tobacco, but he should have recognized his growing emotional attachment. Well, he had now and was determined to fight back. He couldn't afford to make another mistake.

"Maybe we shouldn't have tried to move in one day," Abby said to Moriah as she dropped into a chair. "I'm exhausted."

"What did you expect after working in the store all day? I told you I could take care of it."

Abby was delighted with the appearance of their living quarters. The four rooms—parlor, kitchen, and two bedrooms—were small, but they were clean and neat. The walls had been whitewashed, so it didn't feel so much as if they were living in a cave. Bryce had found them new mattresses for their beds. They hadn't been able to salvage much of their father's furniture, but chairs, tables, dressers, and various other items women at the fort decided they didn't want any longer provided Abby and Moriah with all the furnishings their small rooms could hold. Dorrie promised pictures for the walls.

"There are three reasons why I couldn't let you do everything yourself," Abby said. "First, you had as much work to do as I did. Second, you couldn't take care of everything by yourself, not with getting proposed to at least once a half hour. Third, I couldn't let you receive all the proposals. I'd become unbearably jealous."

"You know proposals don't bother me. I don't even hear them."

"Not even when someone asks you for the second time?"

"Especially not then."

Abby was sure her sister heard the proposals, but Moriah would go on talking as though nothing had been said. Abby couldn't do that. Though she wasn't interested in any of the dozens of men who proposed to her, she couldn't bring herself to ignore them. She knew they didn't love her and didn't expect her to love them in return. She also knew they were only proposing because a wife would make their lives easier, but she still felt sorry for them. They were away from home and family for years at a time—in some cases for the rest of their lives. They had very little feminine company of any kind. They worked hard and risked their lives for people who, according to Bryce, rarely showed gratitude. She couldn't blame them for wanting wives even if their motives were mostly selfish. She did her best to make them realize her refusal wasn't personal. She wanted them to understand that she didn't intend to marry anyone. Ever.

"You're too nice," Moriah said. "By the time you finish talking to them, they're half convinced they're in love with you. It's much kinder to ignore them completely. I don't raise any false hopes."

"I don't think they have any hopes at all. Bryce has made it absolutely clear he won't grant anyone permission to marry."

Abby knew she ought to get up and help Moriah with supper, but she didn't want to move just yet. "Don't fix anything for me," she said. "I'm not hungry."

"You always say that when you're upset," Moriah said without looking up from her work. "You need to eat."

"I'm not upset. I'm just too tired to move." Abby looked at her sister. "I suppose you think I'm upset because I can't find anyone to agree to make the next beef shipment to the reservation."

She didn't intend to worry about it just yet. Bryce had said he would speak to some of the ranchers. It was as much in his interest to make sure the beef got to the reservation as it was in hers. She was sure the ranchers' refusal stemmed from their prejudice against working with women. She didn't understand why they should care who paid them, but she was certain she could overcome that problem once they got to know her.

"I wasn't thinking of the contract," Moriah said. "I was talking about the colonel."

Abby snapped to attention. "What do you mean?"

"Everyone knows you're sweet on him."

"Everyone *can't* know because I'm not."

Moriah didn't say anything, but the lengthening silence annoyed Abby.

"You know I have no intention of getting married," Abby said, irritated. "Albert completely destroyed my faith in men. And if he hadn't, I certainly wouldn't be fool enough to think any respectable man would want a wife who's suspected of being an embezzler."

"You were cleared."

"I was not cleared. They just couldn't find any evidence to arrest me. I'm sure they're still looking."

"The colonel doesn't know any of that."

"I know it, and that's enough. What makes you think I'm sweet on Bryce?"

Moriah shrugged her shoulders, irritating Abby further.

"You can't think I'm sweet on him just because I've agreed to let him help us. It makes sense to let him do the things we can't do for ourselves. It's in his best interest to make sure the Indians get their beef. He's said that several times. You've heard him yourself."

Moriah continued to work in silence.

"He hasn't done anything for me he didn't do for you as well," Abby told her unresponsive sister. "I might think you were sweet on him."

"No, you couldn't."

No, not with Moriah trying to turn down his help at every opportunity and scowling nearly every time she set eyes on him. From the way she behaved, you'd think Moriah was the one who'd been betrayed.

"Why do you think I'm sweet on Bryce?" Abby asked again.

"You always use his Christian name. I never do."

"You don't call any man by his Christian name, not even men you've known all your life."

"It's not proper."

"I don't see why not. Bryce isn't much older than I

am. I'm not one of his soldiers, who's obliged to recognize his rank."

She had tried to address him as she would any other formal acquaintance, but she found herself thinking of him as Bryce. Before long that was what she called him. It just seemed the natural thing to do. When you saw someone every day, you just naturally got past the point of using formal titles.

"You spend a lot of time with him," Moriah said.

"I don't have much choice, things being in the muddle they are and neither one of us knowing how to get them straightened out."

"I haven't asked for his help."

"You don't want to stay here. Failure would give you a perfect excuse to go back to St. Louis."

"I've made no secret of the fact that I dislike this place and think it's unsuitable for decent females, but I don't want to fail."

Abby was surprised by her sister's sudden show of feeling. It was unusual for Moriah to show any kind of deep emotion.

"I'm sorry. That was unfair of me. You work as hard as I do, but you got me upset with your remarks about Bryce."

Moriah stirred the contents of a pot, then turned to Abby. "You act different when he's around. I can see it in your eyes, in the way you suddenly become more energetic. I can even hear it in your voice." She turned back to her cooking. "Dorrie was commenting on it just the other day."

"If I act that way, I'm sure it's only because I'm grateful he's helping us. For goodness sake, Moriah, he's given us carpenters to make this whole trading post over, detailed men to help us practically every day, and made it possible for us to get credit for the store. Not to mention letting us stay in his house until this place was fit to inhabit."

"I haven't forgotten any of that, and I'm grateful, but I don't hang on his every word, nor do I look at him as if he's the most wonderful man in the world."

"Do I do that?" Abby asked, aghast.

"Yes."

"You must be mistaken."

"Ask Dorrie."

"Dorrie sees romance every time one of the soldiers proposes to one of us. I'm sure our staying in Bryce's house has her thinking we're practically married already."

"She was hoping the colonel would fall in love with you."

"Why? She knows the kind of wife he wants. She's the one who told us."

"She says none of the officers want him to get that promotion. They say he runs the best fort in the West and takes the best care of his men. They're afraid of getting someone like that Lieutenant Colonel George Custer they say is going to be court-martialed. He's so awful his officers hate him, but General Sheridan likes him, so he can get away with anything."

"Where did you hear all this?" Abby asked, amazed her sister knew anything outside of what they needed to restock the store shelves.

"I hear the men talking. They like to chat when they buy something to eat."

Abby had instituted her idea of cooking for the soldiers. It kept them very busy, but the food was responsible for most of their profits so far.

"I asked Dorrie," Moriah continued. "She said it was true."

Abby could hardly believe her actions had become a

topic of conversation at the fort. Even less could she understand why anyone thought she wanted to marry Bryce. Or that he would consider marrying her.

"You can tell them there's no possibility Bryce will ask me to marry him. Or that I would accept if he did," she hastened to add. "I'm sorry if they're worried about getting a bad commander, but Bryce wanted to get a post back East before we arrived."

"They were hoping you could change his mind."

"Moriah, *you* aren't hoping I'll marry Bryce, are you?"

Moriah didn't look up from her cooking. "I believed you when you said you didn't want to get married. However, if you've changed your mind, and if we're going to stay here, it would be much more comfortable if you married the colonel."

"Moriah Evangeline Pierce!" Abby exclaimed. "I never thought I'd hear those words coming out of your mouth."

Moriah stopped stirring her pot and looked at Abby. "It only makes sense, if you're going to be married, to marry to your greatest advantage. And if you can never love any man, why does it matter whom you marry?"

Abby would never have believed Moriah would say such things if she hadn't heard it for herself.

"First, I don't love Bryce and he doesn't love me. Second, I don't want to get married. Third, he wants a society wife who can help him with his career. But assuming all that weren't true, I would never marry a man I didn't love. I can't believe you'd think I would."

"Dorrie says a woman has to think of her future."

"This store is my future," Abby said. She had become so agitated she didn't feel tired any longer. "Move over. I'll help with the cooking."

But when Abby went to bed, she found being exhausted wasn't enough to make her fall asleep. After lying awake for hours thinking about what Moriah had said, she gave up and got out of bed. She went into the parlor. Rather than light a lamp, she sat in the dark, staring out of the small window, trying to figure out her true feelings.

She was attracted to Bryce. She'd been surprised and dismayed at the strength of this attraction, but she hadn't worried about it. She didn't plan to marry and he would soon go back East. That would be the end of it. When she considered the matter in that light, it didn't seem so momentous that she'd let Bryce hold her and kiss her, or that she'd enjoyed it and wanted more. She told herself she couldn't control her body or the wishes of her silly heart, but she could control her actions. All that had changed now that she was the subject of gossip.

She moved restlessly about the room. Not yet familiar with the arrangement of the furniture, she bumped into a table, mumbled a curse that would have turned her Aunt Emma's cheeks pink, but didn't light a lamp. That would bring Moriah out of her room, and she was in no mood for company.

It was hard not to like Bryce, even if he had done his best to get her to go back to St. Louis. Maybe it was because he'd been willing to help whenever he could, had encouraged rather than belittled her efforts. Maybe it was because he'd actually been kind. He had expressed regret that she wouldn't be staying in his house any longer. She suspected he was reluctant to go back to eating Zeb's cooking, but he'd been kind enough to say he and Pamela were sorry to lose the pleasure of her company.

She plopped down on a lumpy sofa. She missed the pleasure of his company, too. Talking to Bryce provided her with something beyond the usual female subjects of households, husbands, and children to discuss. She supposed she would have felt different if she'd had a husband, a household, and children to worry about, but she didn't, and right now such conversation made her unhappily aware of her loneliness. She liked her independence, but she was discovering it didn't answer all her needs.

She didn't understand that. She'd never felt lonely before. She'd always had Moriah, Aunt Emma, and plenty of friends. If the loneliness started after Albert's defection or her father's death, why should it have taken her so long to realize it? Did it have to do only with Bryce and Pamela—was something deep within her being nourished by them?

There were many things that didn't make sense. Just seeing him made the day seem a little brighter. His smile or a few kind words had the power to make even the greatest fears or obstacles seem unimportant. Just being around him made her feel happier even when she was arguing with him. She thought of him a hundred times a day. He seemed a natural and permanent part of her life. She knew he said he was going back East, but somehow she'd managed to put that out of her mind.

All of this, even though she'd convinced herself she would never marry, that she didn't want a husband, that she wanted to be independent, to have complete control of her life. Was she crazy? Didn't she know she wanted it all?

She got up and started pacing again. Aunt Emma told her frequently that she couldn't have her cake and eat it, too. The trouble was, she couldn't decide whether she wanted to have her cake and be independent, or eat her cake and have a family. She'd been certain of what she wanted when she left St. Louis. Now she wasn't so sure.

A great feeling of sadness swept over her, a feeling

of loss. A hot anger at Albert. He'd caused her to lose her belief in love, her trust in men. He'd made it impossible for her to marry Bryce even if he asked her because she was filled with a terrible fear that any man she married would betray her love. If it happened a second time, it would destroy her. She couldn't take the risk.

Abby suddenly became aware of small, scraping sounds. She'd assumed it was a mouse they hadn't managed to trap. She'd been so deep in thought she hadn't realized that it didn't sound like a mouse. Someone was in the store. Abby wasn't worried about her safety. The door into their quarters was stout and bolted shut, but they couldn't afford to have anything stolen. Her impulse was to wake Moriah, but if there was danger, she didn't want to expose her sister. If there wasn't, there was no need to disturb her sleep.

Abby went to the gun rack and took down a small carbine. It was already loaded. Bryce had said an empty gun was no gun at all. Being careful to make no noise, she eased open the well-oiled bolt on the door, turned the handle, and opened the door a crack.

At first she saw only the shadowy interior lit by moonlight coming through the barred windows, but she could definitely hear movement. She couldn't see anyone, but she knew someone was there. It was impossible to light a lamp. She didn't have enough hands. Besides, the lamp would blind her to any movement in the shadows while making her whereabouts plain to the thief. Neither could she call for help without giving him a chance to get away. She had only one choice.

"I know you're in there," she said. "I've got a rifle. Light the lamp so I can see you."

The room exploded with the sound of a pistol shot in close quarters, the sound of a bullet burying itself in the wood of the thick door. Afterward Abby could never understand why she'd remained so calm. Remembering what Bryce had said, she aimed her rifle at the spot where she'd seen the flash of the pistol and pulled the trigger. She was rewarded by a scream of agony and the sound of a body falling against one of the counters.

Chapter Fifteen

Bryce had been restless all evening. Unable to stay cooped up inside, he was on the porch when he heard the first muffled shot. His first thought was that someone had accidentally discharged a weapon inside one of the barracks. He had gotten to his feet when he heard the second shot. One shot could be accidental; two couldn't. He knew exactly where the sounds had come from.

The trading post.

Abby and Moriah were alone. He raced inside, grabbed his pistol holster, and was outside running across the parade ground within seconds. The ground seemed much too small when he drilled his troops, especially the cavalry unit, but tonight it seemed a mile across. The trading post had been built on the perimeter across the fort from the army buildings because it was used by civilians, and Bryce needed to keep intrusive traffic to a minimum. Tonight he wished he'd done just the opposite. Before he reached the trading post, he saw lights come on in barracks and officers' houses.

The door to the trading post was unlocked. Bryce rushed in to see Abby holding a lantern, looking at something on the floor. Moriah stood next to her sister, her arms around her shoulders. A carbine rifle lay across the counter next to her.

"What happened?" he asked. "Who fired those shots?"

Abby looked up, her face ravaged by horror. "I killed a man," she said. "I killed a man," she repeated, as though the reality had not yet sunk in.

"What man? Where?"

"Bill Spicer," Moriah said, pointing to an area of the floor out of Bryce's range of vision. "He broke in and Abby shot him."

"I didn't mean to kill him," Abby said. She appeared to be in shock.

Bryce holstered his pistol and rounded the counter blocking his view. Bill Spicer lay on the floor, a bullet hole right where his heart would be. A pistol lay on the floor nearby.

"What was he doing here?" Bryce asked.

"Trying to rob the store, I expect," Moriah said.

Lieutenant Collier entered the store at a run. "What happened?"

"Miss Pierce shot a thief," Bryce said, indicating Spicer's body.

"I heard two shots," Collier said. "Was one Spicer's?"

"The first one," Abby said. "It struck the door." She didn't appear to have the energy to point out the hole, with the bullet still buried in it.

"He must have been a bad shot," Collier said, "with you standing in the doorway with the light behind you."

"I didn't light the lamp," Abby said. "I knew it would blind me."

"You mean you did this in the dark?" Collier asked in amazement. "Damned fine shooting. Remind me to knock next time I want a new pair of socks." More soldiers poured into the store.

"Have the men remove the body," Bryce said to Collier. "We can turn it over to the civil authorities tomorrow." He crossed to Abby's side. "How are you feeling?"

"She's feeling shocked and stunned," Moriah snapped. "How would you feel if you'd been shot at? I forget," she said, before Bryce could answer, "you get shot at all the time. I don't imagine it bothers you, but it's never happened to my sister before. As for killing a man—"

"There's no reason to be angry at Bryce," Abby managed to say.

"I'm sure you were hoping only to scare him off." Bryce put his arm around Abby. "You need to sit down. Maybe your sister will fix you some hot milk."

"She'd be better off with a slug of whiskey," Collier suggested.

"My sister's not in the habit of indulging in spirits," Moriah said.

"I don't imagine she's in the habit of shooting thieves, either," the unblinking Collier responded.

Bryce ignored both of them and guided Abby into her parlor and eased her down on the couch. "Do you have any brandy in the store?" he asked Moriah.

"Yes, but—"

"Bring me a bottle and a glass."

"I told you, my sister doesn't drink spirits."

"I'm just trying to help her over the shock," Bryce said, impatient with Moriah's resistance.

Moriah didn't move, but Collier arrived carrying a bottle.

"Where're the glasses?" he asked Moriah.

When she didn't answer, he opened cabinets until he

found one. He poured an inch of brandy and handed it to Bryce. "I'll put the body in the stable. Do you need anything else?"

"Have some men check around the post. I want to know if anyone else came with him."

"I think you're a mighty brave lady to face a worthless bum like Spicer by yourself," Collier said to Abby. "Any one of my sisters would have screamed and fainted dead away."

"That's what I feel like doing right now," Abby said.

"You go right ahead if you feel like it. The colonel's got a good hold on you." With that piece of cheerful advice, Collier took himself off, thereby sparing Bryce the necessity of ordering him to leave before his mouth got them both in trouble. Bryce raised the glass to Abby's lips.

"It smells awfully strong," Abby said doubtfully.

"Just take a sip. Hold it in your mouth a moment, then swallow."

Abby took the glass and warily lifted it to her lips. She took a tiny sip, held it in her mouth for a moment, then swallowed. Her eyes grew a little wide and her mouth opened in surprise, but all she said was, "That wasn't as bad as I expected."

"Good. Now keep taking tiny sips while Moriah tells me what happened."

"I was asleep," Moriah said. "The first shot woke me. I rushed in here to find Abby standing just where you found her, staring at Spicer's body."

"Has Spicer been around the store recently?"

"We haven't seen him since Abby said she wouldn't pay him until he gave her the rest of the money the store had taken in."

"Have you heard any rumors about him threatening to get his money back on his own?"

"No. I'd forgotten all about him."

Bryce felt uneasy. Spicer was no-good, lazy, and loud-mouthed, but he'd never heard of Spicer being angry at Abby or threatening revenge. Maybe he was just breaking in to get liquor. What surprised Bryce most was that Spicer had shot at Abby. He'd never known the man to carry a gun. But he supposed a man would take unusual risks when he thought he could get his hands on money or free liquor.

"Are you feeling any better?" Bryce asked Abby.

She nodded.

"Good. Now drink the rest of your brandy."

Only then was Bryce surprised to realize Moriah was looking at him with an expression that was either anger or severe disapproval. One trouble with his marriage had been that he couldn't read his wife's moods. Apparently he wasn't any better with Moriah. He supposed she disliked his sitting with his arm around Abby almost as much as she disapproved of the brandy, but he didn't intend to move. He'd seen soldiers go into shock the first time they killed an enemy. He was certain the shock would be even greater for Abby.

"Both of you are coming back to my house," he said to Moriah

"We've just moved in here."

"I doubt either of you would get any sleep if you stayed here. I'm not certain Spicer was alone. I'll have Collier set guards on the post for the rest of the night. Tomorrow morning we'll decide what to do next."

"This is our home," Moriah said. "We have to live here."

"Fine, but you'll stay in my house until we figure out how Spicer got in and if anyone else knows his secret."

Moriah didn't look at all pleased, but after a slight

hesitation she left the parlor. "Are you feeling better?" Bryce asked Abby.

"A little."

She still looked pale and completely unlike her usual energetic, decisive self. She'd drunk half the brandy.

Bryce didn't find it a hardship to continue sitting next to Abby, his arm around her. He'd been thinking about her all evening. It had started even before each mouthful of Zeb's supper reminded him that Abby and Moriah were no longer staying in his spare bedroom. He missed the feeling of expectation that greeted him after a long day. He missed Pamela running to meet him with a hug and kiss, excitedly telling him what Abby and Moriah were preparing for supper and how she'd been allowed to help.

He missed the animated conversations at dinner, discussions that ranged from trapping and gold mining in the Rocky Mountains to the latest style of dress in St. Louis to discussing the pros and cons of where to establish the trading post's line of credit. He missed lingering at the table while Zeb cleaned up, enjoying his coffee and brandy, unwinding from his day. The evenings had had a way of helping him forget he was stationed at an outpost of civilization, a point where two ways of life collided, a conflict in which it was preordained that only one could survive.

As much as he loved his daughter and enjoyed being with her, he missed the companionship of an adult who could understand the strain of his work, the worry of a father for his child, the pitfalls of a stressful career. He missed female companionship, that special something no man could provide, no matter how close the friendship, no matter how many shared experiences.

The sound of a burp scattered his thoughts.

"Sorry," Abby said. "It's the brandy."

"It's all that sipping," Bryce said, amused at her embarrassment. "You get air in your stomach."

"Next time I'll swallow it in one gulp."

"Let's hope there won't be a next time."

Abby picked up the brandy bottle, which Collier had set on a table next to her. "I think it's unfair for men to keep this to themselves. I might like a little more."

Bryce took the bottle from Abby. "You've had enough for your first time. Brandy can sneak up on you."

"You drink more after dinner."

"I'm used to it, and I'm twice your size. It takes twice as much to achieve the same effect."

"I hadn't thought of that."

"If you're still feeling the need for something to buck you up when we get back to the house, I'll let you have a sip or two more."

"Get back to what house? I'm already home."

"Bryce has decided we have to go back to his house," Moriah said as she entered the parlor. "I've packed only what we'll need for tonight."

"I want to stay here," Abby announced.

"It's not safe," Bryce said. "We don't know if there was anyone with Spicer and we don't know what he was after."

"He was alone," Abby said. "I'm sure he was after money."

"I expect you're right," Bryce said, "but how did he get in? The door was barred from the inside."

"I don't know."

"You can't stay here until we find out. Do you feel able to walk, or do you want me to carry you?"

"You will not carry my sister across the parade ground," Moriah said, a look of horror on her face.

"I can walk," Abby said. "I'm feeling fine."

Bryce wouldn't have minded carrying Abby, but he knew it would be impossible to stop the gossip that action would cause. "On the way over you can explain exactly what happened," Bryce said to Abby.

But Abby's explanation didn't answer Bryce's two questions: How did Spicer get in and why did he try to shoot her?

Pamela met them at the front door. "I knew you'd come back," she said, practically dancing with happiness.

"We're only here until it's safe to go back," Abby said.

"You're safe here," Pamela said.

"That's why I brought them back," Bryce said. "Now get back into bed. You shouldn't be up."

"Everybody's up," Pamela said. "They thought it was an attack."

"It was only two shots," Bryce said. "That's hardly an attack."

"It sounded like one," Pamela insisted.

"Well, since you're up, you can help us get ready for bed," Abby said. "We've kept your father up much too late. I'm sure he's exhausted."

"Daddy never gets tired," Pamela said. "He's indyfa . . . indyfat . . . table" she added. "I never can say that word."

"Do you mean indefatigable?" Abby asked.

"That's it!" Pamela said, delighted. "Sarah's momma says he's indyfa . . . well, you know what I mean."

"Apparently the Fort Lookout oracle has spoken," Abby said, grinning at Bryce. "I hope you're able to live up to it."

"Nowhere near it," Bryce said.

"Then we'll go to bed before your secret is exposed,"

Abby said. "You'd better show us the way," she said to Pamela. "I'm not sure I remember."

Pamela headed off, followed by Moriah, whose disapproval was apparent by her silence.

"Thank you for your concern," Abby said to Bryce. "And for the brandy. Now I think I'd better follow Pamela. I'm feeling very tired and a little light-headed. I may truly have forgotten how to find my way."

Bryce watched her go, aware of an unfamiliar set of emotions at work inside him. He had the odd but good feeling that suddenly everything was all right, now that Abby was back in his house, that the sight of her disappearing up the stairs on her way to bed was the way things ought to be. Some unidentified tension inside him eased. He felt relief, knowing she was safe, but there was something more fundamental going on, something he'd never had the opportunity—or the need—to identify.

He had no trouble understanding one set of emotions. They mostly boiled down to fear. Fear that he was becoming too attached to Abby for his own good. Certainty that Pamela was.

Then there was the other set, the set that compared her to the kind of wife he needed for his career, found her wanting, and didn't seem to care very much. The set that said his family, especially his mother, would call him a fool for allowing someone like Abby to cross his threshold, much less spend weeks sleeping in his spare bedroom. The set that said if he thought as much about his promotion as he did about his work at the fort, he probably would have had his promotion by now.

Then there was the set that said he ought to put it all out of his mind until tomorrow, that he ought to get himself a cigar and a glass of brandy and enjoy it on the front porch.

Bryce liked the last set best of all.

*   *   *

Dorrie came hurrying from the store into the parlor of the trading post. "There's a man outside who wants to see you. He says he heard you need somebody to deliver beef to the Indian reservation."

"Thank goodness," Abby said, getting up from her desk. "I was beginning to get desperate."

Dorrie clutched Abby's arm. "You can't see him."

"Why not?" Abby asked.

"He's a killer."

Abby blinked. "How do you know?"

"Everyone knows. He was convicted and sent to prison."

"Whom did he kill? And why?"

Abby didn't know why she was asking such questions. The fact that the man was a killer ought to be enough for her, but she also had to find someone who would deliver this month's shipment of beef to the reservation.

"It happened before the war," Dorrie said. "My husband says all his ranch hands are killers, too."

Abby had never been called on to face a killer before, but the situation didn't feel quite as perilous as it sounded. The killing might have been a tragic mistake, a crime of passion, even an accident, she told herself. Whatever the facts, the man had paid his debt to society and was now the owner of a ranch. Abby didn't feel he should be punished for the rest of his life for what could have been the result of a youthful inability to make the correct decision. Besides, there were several soldiers in the store.

"I'll talk to him," Abby said to Dorrie. "I owe him that much courtesy for coming to see me."

"I'll warn Moriah to stand near the guns."

Abby couldn't suppress a smile. "Moriah would faint before she'd touch a gun. I'll be perfectly safe." She walked out into the trading post. "Where is he?"

"Over there, looking at the new rifles. You think he wants to buy some? I don't think murderers ought to be allowed to have guns."

"Then they'd be at the mercy of anyone else who did. Do you think that would be fair?"

"I guess not," Dorrie said, clearly not convinced in her heart, regardless of what her brain might tell her.

"What's his name?"

"Tibbott. Russ Tibbolt. I think you ought to send for Colonel McGregor."

"The beef contract is my responsibility. I'll deal with it myself." She crossed the room to where the guns were displayed. "Mr. Tibbolt?"

The man who turned to face her was nothing like what she expected. About the same height as Bryce, he was built along more slender, even lankier lines, which made it easier to see the evidence of muscles in his shoulders and arms. Much to her surprise, he was handsome, neat, and clean-shaven. She didn't know why she expected a killer to be ugly, slovenly, even dirty.

"I'm Abigail Pierce. I understand you wanted to talk to me about my beef contract."

"I hear you need someone to deliver fifty head of beef to the Indian reservation," he said, coming right to the point. "I can, but it'll cost you fourteen dollars a head on delivery."

"I've been getting them for eight."

"You don't have anybody to deliver your beef," he said. "I could have asked even more, and you'd have had to pay it if you wanted to keep the contract." His eyes were cold, his expression neutral, his stance relaxed and casual. He had her over a barrel and he knew it.

"If you're going to rob me by upping your price, why

don't you just withhold your beef, let me fail, then bid for the contract yourself?"

"Most people cheat the Indians. You don't. Besides, I don't have enough beef to fulfill the contract myself on a regular basis. My neighbors don't like me and won't sell me as much as a maverick calf. I'm sure your assistant has told you I'm a killer and an ex-con. I have to pay my hands higher wages than most. That makes it more expensive for me to be in business. Fourteen dollars seems reasonable. You get half the profit and I get the other."

He might be a killer, but he was also a cold, hard businessman.

"There's the added risk of delivering the beef. Someone doesn't want you to succeed. I expect they'll try to stop me."

"I'll speak to Bryce . . . Colonel McGregor. I'm sure he'll send some men with you."

"Thanks, but my men can handle it. You just worry about who you're going to get to deliver beef the next month." He turned to leave.

"Don't you want a signed agreement?" Abby asked.

"No, ma'am. I trust you," he said over his shoulder.

"I've never seen anyone so rude and abrupt," Dorrie exclaimed after he left.

"If he can deliver the beef, I don't care how he acts," Abby said. Her profit had been reduced, but she had another month of breathing space.

"I don't know why I never thought you'd have parties at an army fort," Abby said to Dorrie and her husband. "I guess I thought you'd be off fighting all the time."

"We have parties to keep from going crazy," Dorrie said. "There's nothing to do in a place like this."

That might be true for the wives of the officers, but

it wasn't true for Abby. It seemed she and Moriah never had enough time to do all the work necessary to run the trading post. She couldn't imagine how her father had managed alone. Abby and Moriah had moved back to their quarters after two nights. Pamela had cried, but it couldn't be helped. Abby had been beginning to like staying there far too much.

"Where did you ever find a band?"

"There are always men who can play at any fort," Dorrie's husband said. "They're happy to do it for the extra money."

The orchestra was a grab bag of the available players and instruments—a fiddle, two trumpets, a trombone, a flute, and a piano one of the wives had had shipped from Denver. Abby thought the ensemble was more suited to play marches than dance tunes. The trumpet players were two of the fort buglers. They played like it, too.

"I'm sorry Colonel McGregor couldn't be here," Dorrie said. "He's a marvelous dancer."

"The ladies stand in line to dance with him," Dorrie's husband said.

"That's because the rest of you can't keep from stepping on our toes. Our slippers don't give us much protection."

Dorrie wore embroidered silk, slippers. Abby couldn't afford anything so pretty or fragile.

"Lieutenant Collier seems to be an adequate substitute," Abby said.

"He dances well enough," Dorrie said. "But he's not as tall or as handsome as the colonel."

"Nor as rich and socially prominent," her husband finished for her. "The things a woman looks for in a man."

"That's not all we want," Dorrie said.

But Abby was sure Bryce was superior in that department, too.

"I brought you some punch," Pamela announced. She was coming toward Abby with slow, deliberate steps to keep from spilling the liquid that sloshed dangerously close to the rim of the cup. "Sarah's momma said I couldn't have any. She said it was a wine cup."

Abby rescued the cup from Pamela. "That was very thoughtful of you."

"I wish Daddy was here. It's no fun without him."

"I'm sure Abby thinks so," Dorrie said with a wink.

That had been happening more and more since the break-in at the store. Apparently Collier had made it his business to tell everyone how worried Bryce had been about her, how he'd sat next to her on the sofa, his arm around her, forcing her to sip brandy until she could regain control of her feelings. There was no hiding the fact that he'd brought her back to his house or posted sentries at the trading post. Abby kept telling everyone he was just as worried about Moriah as about her, but no one appeared to believe her.

And Moriah didn't help matters by muttering *Stuff and nonsense!* She'd been less communicative than ever, more diligent in her work, as if she was determined to live in her own little world. Abby had done her best to talk her sister into coming to the dance tonight, but she'd refused point blank. Even telling Moriah the party was for both of them proved futile.

"If they want to see me, they can come to the store," Moriah had said.

Abby had looked forward to the gathering. She hadn't been to a party in so long she'd almost forgotten what it was like. She was looking forward to dancing with handsome men and forgetting her troubles for at least a few hours. Bryce's being called away at the last minute was a disappointment, but she was determined to show everyone she could enjoy the party without him. As much as she liked Bryce, as much as she enjoyed his company, as much as she might wish their relationship could grow into something more meaningful, she knew there was no future in it. She had made her up mind to enjoy his friendship while it lasted, to take advantage of his help as long as it was offered, but with the understanding that it would end soon.

"We'll all have to get along without the colonel when he goes back East," Abby said, "so we might as well get in a little practice now."

"Nobody wants him to go," Dorrie said. "I know I shouldn't do anything so mean, but I keep praying he won't get his promotion."

"Who's getting a promotion?" a voice behind Abby asked.

"Daddy!" Pamela exclaimed excitedly.

Chapter Sixteen

Abby felt her breath catch in her throat. She forced herself to wait a moment before turning around to face Bryce.

"I thought you were miles away," Dorrie said.

"It was a false alarm," Bryce replied. "A farmer saw Indians crossing his land and was sure they'd come to murder him and his family. He didn't know his homestead sat astride a major travel route from the winter campgrounds—or care that it was on reservation land. Is all the dancing over?"

"Not at all," Dorrie said. "We won't stop for hours yet."

"Lieutenant Collier said he was going to steal all the ladies from you," Pamela said to her father. "I told him you'd put him in jail if he stole even one."

Pamela wasn't happy when everyone laughed.

"I'm here to make sure he doesn't," Bryce said. "And I'll begin by stealing Abby away from him."

"He never stole Abby," Pamela announced. "She said she didn't want to dance."

"I hope you've changed your mind," Bryce said to Abby.

"You ought to dance with the other ladies first," Abby said.

"You're the only unattached female in the room," Dorrie pointed out, "plus being the guest of honor."

"In that case it would be downright rude not to dance with you," Bryce said.

Abby was acutely aware that many eyes around the room watched everything Bryce did. She was also aware that many would attach undue meaning to the fact that he'd managed to get back from a patrol in time for the dance, something that had never been a priority with him before. And that he had chosen Abby as his first partner.

"I'm honored," Abby said.

"Sarah's momma says the man is supposed to say he's honored," Pamela informed them. "The lady is supposed to smile, say 'Thank you,' and offer him her hand."

"I don't know what we'd do without Sarah's mother to tell us how to behave," Dorrie muttered between clenched teeth.

"You've got to do it right," Pamela prompted.

Bryce grinned and executed a half bow. "I'm honored, milady."

"Thank you, kind sir," Abby said, extending her hand.

"Did we do that right?" Bryce asked Pamela.

"You did it perfectly," Dorrie said impatiently. "Now start dancing before she remembers something else Sarah's mother said."

As nervous as Abby was about dancing with Bryce with everyone watching her, she couldn't repress a smile. "I didn't know Pamela was so interested in manners," she said to Bryce.

"She wasn't until I suggested she ask Sarah's mother how she should behave."

"I think it's sweet."

"You wouldn't think so if you'd grown up encumbered by so many rules it took you years to learn them all. One of the reasons I joined the army was to get away from all that."

"The army has even more rules."

"They're to make everything work better, to help the soldiers survive."

"I expect society developed its rules for the same reason."

"I'm sure you're right, but after spending half the day in the saddle on a senseless errand, I don't have the patience to discuss it. Let's dance and forget society and homesteaders."

This wasn't the first time Bryce had put his arms around her, but it seemed momentous tonight. She didn't know whether it was the whispers she'd been hearing or the fact that he was holding her in public. Whatever the reason, her skin was exquisitely sensitive to his touch. A physical desire for him descended on her like a wall of floodwater, drenching her with desire and washing away nearly all her control.

"Maybe you should write some instructions that can be handed out to new settlers when they arrive," she said, determined to take her mind off her body's reaction to Bryce's nearness, desperate to keep anyone from guessing how powerfully his holding her in his arms affected her.

"I don't want to talk about it tonight. I just want to enjoy dancing with you."

She wanted to talk about *anything* rather than think about dancing with him.

"A rancher walked into the store today and offered to supply the beef for the reservation this month. I can't tell you how relieved I am."

"I'm glad the ranchers finally gave in. Which one was it?"

"Russ Tibbolt."

Bryce stiffened. "He's an ex-con. He served time for murder."

"Dorrie told me, but I don't care about that as long as he delivers the beef."

Bryce pulled back far enough to look her in the eye. "You've got to be careful. You don't know what a man like Tibbolt might do."

"I don't have to see him again except to pay him. Besides, if he's paid his debt to society, I don't see why I shouldn't do business with him as well as anyone else."

"Let me know when he comes for his money. I'd like to be there."

He'd pulled her close again. Knowing he was determined to protect her caused the physical attraction to leap up another notch. Much more and she'd have to leave before she did something scandalous.

Like what? Cover his face with kisses? Throw him on the floor and attack him?

Abby couldn't believe these thoughts had entered her mind. It was as if another woman had taken over her body, was supplying ideas that kept flying about like a plague of demons. This wasn't the real Abby. She'd never even thought anything like this about Albert, and she'd thought she was in love with him.

Could she be in love with Bryce?

Of course not. Her emotions were still raw from Albert's betrayal. It was only natural she would lean on a strong and capable man, would feel attracted to him when he showed an interest in her. The fact that he was extremely handsome and understanding only made the attraction more inevitable.

But such a natural tendency could be dangerous. It would be all too easy to start reading more into his actions, his intentions, his smiles than was really there. He was helping her because her failure could damage his career. As for his interest in her—the kisses—well, she was pretty and, with the exception of Moriah, the only single woman around. It was almost inevitable that he would show an interest in her.

She needed a distraction to help her get over Albert, time to establish her business on a firm footing so she would never again be dependent on anyone. As long as she could keep that in mind, there was no reason she couldn't relax and enjoy Bryce's attentions. As long as she kept her heart uninvolved, she could endure the physical attraction. His interest was born of this particular time, place, and set of circumstances. She had to keep reminding herself it wouldn't translate to any other place.

She had been so deep in thought she hadn't realized the music had ended and Bryce was leading her off the floor.

"You're preoccupied tonight," he said. "Is something wrong at the store?"

"No." She couldn't tell him that her thoughts had been entirely of him. "Still, there's a lot to think about."

He smiled, and her legs threatened to go out from under her. "There's always a lot to think about, but it's good to put it out of your mind every so often and think of something else entirely."

"What should I think about? Everything causes some sort of problem."

"Then don't think about anything except tonight. It's a nice party, the food is good, the company pleasant, and you're dancing with a man who thinks you're the most captivating woman here. That ought to give you at least a few happy thoughts."

More like several dozen. Abby had a sinking feeling her heart wasn't managing to say uninvolved.

"Don't let anyone hear you say that. You have no idea the kind of rumors it could start."

"Are you afraid of rumors?"

"I am when they're untrue. I've been the victim of them before."

"You never told me about that."

"It's something I'm trying to forget. I'd like some punch," she said when they rejoined Dorrie and her husband. "I'm thirsty."

She insisted Bryce dance with the officers' wives. She wanted to head off any gossip about the two of them. It wouldn't be possible to put an end to the whispers, not when she and Moriah were the only two single women at the fort, but she was determined not to give them more fuel. She also allowed herself to be led out on the floor by several enlisted men.

She turned down a marriage proposal from each of them.

"All these proposals could turn a woman's head," she confided to Bryce.

"You're the most beautiful woman here tonight," he said.

Abby hoped she wasn't blushing. "Well, it's time for me to go home," she said. "I have a store to run. I can't let Moriah do all the work just because I spent half the night dancing."

Bryce was waiting for her when she finished thanking all the hostesses.

"You don't have to walk me back," she said.

"I've been in the saddle all day and I'm tired. Besides, you're the only single woman present. Someone has to see you safely home."

"You could organize a patrol from among the enlisted men," Dorrie said, mischief in her smiling eyes.

"They'd probably knock Abby down in their struggles to see who got to walk next to her," Bryce said. "She'll be safer with me."

Abby wasn't sure. Six enlisted men posed no danger to her. One colonel did. An involuntary shiver ran through Abby when the night air hit her.

"Cold?" Bryce asked.

"A little." The room had become hot from the proximity of so many bodies and the lamps it took to light the room.

"Let me put my overcoat around you."

"Won't you be cold?"

"The army doesn't know how to make uniforms out of anything except wool. If I wore this over my uniform, I'd perspire."

The overcoat was so heavy, Abby almost asked him to take it back. However, the night air had become quite cool and she appreciated the warmth.

Once her eyes became accustomed to the night, she could see everything with remarkable clarity. The moonlight had tinted the fort, surrounding plains, and mountains silver.

"Are you and your sister comfortable sleeping at the trading post?" Bryce asked.

"Why shouldn't we be?"

"Having that much liquor in one place tempts people to break in. Your father slept with a shotgun at his bedside."

"I have my rifle."

"You shouldn't have to do that. I'd feel better if you were still using my spare bedroom."

"We trespassed on your hospitality long enough."

"I didn't think of it as trespassing. It was a pleasure for Pamela and me to have you."

Abby laughed. "Is Pamela still complaining about Zeb's cooking?"

"Yes, but that's not what I'm talking about. We'd have enjoyed having you stay with us even if you didn't cook. Pamela adores you. And I think you're rather special, too."

"I enjoyed it, too," Abby said, determined not to let him know how much, "but the trading post is our home. There's no reason for us to stay anywhere else."

"Not even for your safety?"

"You've put a guard on us at night. How much safer can we be?"

"You'd be safer sleeping in my spare bedroom."

Why did he keep doing this? If he just wanted someone to eat dinner with, he could come right out and ask. Moriah would probably fuss, but Abby would enjoy eating with him and Pamela a couple of times a week. She stopped in the middle of the parade ground and turned to Bryce.

"Staying in your house would only cause gossip."

"Why?"

"Don't pretend to be dense. You're single. So am I. Your attention and help have caused people to wonder about our relationship. If I were to stay in your house—especially since there's no need now—people would be certain something was going on."

"Not with Moriah there, too."

"Even with Moriah. They'd suppose she was encouraging me to try to entrap the most eligible man at the fort."

"But everyone knows I'm not looking for a wife."

"They might think I'd settle for a more informal relationship. A man's reputation can survive something like that. A woman's can't." She turned back toward the trading post.

"If I find anyone questioning your reputation, even in a whisper, I'll transfer him to the worst fort in the West."

Abby was touched that Bryce was so concerned about her reputation, but he had to know punishing people would only make things worse.

"Thank you," she said, "but I'm happier where I am."

"I'm not."

She turned to him again. "Why not? Everyone knows you intend to choose a wife from your own social circle."

"Just because a woman will make a perfect wife doesn't mean she's the woman you love."

Abby knew Bryce wasn't in love with her—she didn't want him to be—but her pulse quickened. He wouldn't have mentioned love if his feelings for her weren't very strong. She wanted him to like her—she really wanted more than liking—but she didn't know what else she wanted. And even if she did, she didn't know if she should reach for it. It could be dangerous to both their plans for the future.

"Don't you want to love your wife?"

"It's more important that a couple have the same goals, the same willingness to sacrifice to achieve them."

"I know love can blind you to faults and shortcomings, make you see what you want to see rather than what's really there, but I couldn't marry a man I didn't love. I'd rather remain alone. You're not in love with me."

"I didn't say I was, but just because you don't fall in

love doesn't mean you can't hold someone in deep affection."

Abby turned toward the trading post. "Deep affection is for friends of the same sex. Between a man and a woman it can only cause pain."

"Not if both hold each other in deep affection," Bryce said.

"What are you asking of me?"

"I find you very attractive and I like you very much. I want to spend more time with you, time when you're not in the store and I'm not dealing with my responsibilities. I want to get to know you better. I have a very difficult time standing here talking to you without touching you. Will you let me see you more?"

"Yes," Abby said, casting caution to the winds.

"When?"

"I don't know. I can't neglect my work. That would be unfair to Moriah."

"I can delegate someone to help her."

"It would be better if I could get one of the wives to help her."

"You won't take a long time to do it, will you?"

"No."

"Will you let me know as soon as you're free?"

"Yes."

Abby didn't understand why she was getting more depressed with every word. She was a grown woman with the natural needs and desires of a grown woman. She was an independent businesswoman, so she had no one to answer to, no one to set up rules for her to follow. There was no reason to be upset, angry, or hurt.

So why did she want to cry?

"I'm glad I was able to get back for the party tonight," Bryce said. "I would have hated to miss dancing with you."

"I don't dance that well."

"It's not the dance. It's the dancer."

They had reached the porch of the trading post. Abby was about to pull the rope that was attached to a bell in their living quarters so Moriah would unbar the door. Her sister didn't like being in the post alone with the front door open.

Bryce reached for Abby's hand. "Don't go in just yet. You don't have to worry about gossip. No one can see us."

Abby wasn't sure about that, but she didn't want the evening to end just yet. She liked being with Bryce. Over the last several days she'd come to realize that only work kept him from being constantly in her thoughts. Bryce slipped his arms around her waist and pulled her close.

"Have I told you I think you're beautiful?"

"Yes, but I never told you I think you're handsome."

"Do you?"

"You know you are. Every woman at the fort thinks so."

"I'm not concerned about every woman, just you."

He pulled her so close, their lips were only inches apart. She felt the warmth of his breath on her cheek. Her body was growing too warm for the overcoat. When he slipped his other arm around her waist, the overcoat slid off her shoulders. It fell to the ground almost unnoticed as his lips met hers in a passionate kiss.

Abby thought she had gotten used to her response to Bryce's touch, but now it seemed to be stronger than ever. Her body strained to meet him, to press itself against him, to draw warmth and strength from him. She seemed to want to burrow inside of him until she became part of him. Her arms wound around Bryce's neck, pulled him down closer to her, binding him to her with all her strength. She rose on her tiptoes to be closer still, to return his kiss with equal fervor.

Bryce's first kiss had been a shock and a revelation, one she'd since dreamed about many times. She'd never believed such an expression between two people could be proper, but now she didn't care. Nothing in her life had had the power to make her feel so alive, so full of energy, so *wanted*.

Though she understood in her mind why her father had never wanted his daughters to join him, she'd never been able to overcome the feeling that she was somehow inadequate, that she didn't measure up, that she was unwanted. Albert hadn't been able to banish that fear. But being in Bryce's strong embrace, being kissed with nearly savage energy, made her feel she was so important this man would move heaven and earth for her.

She *needed* to feel wanted.

Bryce deepened their kiss, drawing her to him as if she belonged to him. His tongue invaded her mouth like a swaggering conqueror, vanquishing all before him as though it was his divine right. She fought to hold her own against him, yet didn't mind being overpowered, overwhelmed, overcome. The magnitude of her defeat was at the same time a measure of the depth of his desire for her. Her weakness was at the same time her strength. The joy of her surrender was immense.

Bryce broke their kiss with such suddenness she felt all her support had been withdrawn at once, that she was plummeting through space with nothing to break her fall. She felt weak, limp in his embrace.

She wondered why neither Albert nor any of the other men she'd known had attempted to kiss her as Bryce had. She wondered why just being with Bryce had affected her more powerfully than all the times she'd spent in the company of men who said they liked her.

She wondered why Bryce could make her question her decision never to be married, never to allow herself to fall in love. She wondered why his kisses made her realize she had never loved Albert even though she'd thought she wanted to marry him. Bryce made her question everything about her relationships with men, past and present.

But all the questions were pointless; Bryce would be leaving soon.

"It's no wonder the men propose to you over and over again," Bryce said, sounding breathless. "You're enough to make a man forget his responsibilities."

Maybe some men, but not Bryce. Whatever his feelings might be, he didn't let them rule his head. He never lost sight of his ultimate goal.

"You're just saying that to make me feel better," Abby said. "Any woman would like to feel she had that kind of power over her man."

But a woman of conscience, a woman of character, would never exercise it.

"Sometimes I get the feeling you're more dangerous to me than any outlaw or rogue Indian. You make me want to do things I shouldn't." He leaned back so he could look into her eyes. "Sometimes I feel as if you must be a witch."

"No supernatural powers here," Abby said, thinking that the men in her life had turned their backs on her without difficulty. "You're just vulnerable because you're a single man, I'm a single woman, and we're momentarily trapped at this fort with no commitments to anyone else. Once you're back in the East you'll scratch your head trying to remember what it was you found so interesting about me."

"I don't have to do that. I already know."

Abby didn't want to know. This was a casual relationship, one that would end when Bryce left the fort. If it was to leave no scars, they would need to keep their importance to each other on a physical level. Verbalizing their feelings would only cause pain.

"Then let it be your secret," Abby said. "I'm told men like to keep their women guessing."

"It's the other way around. Besides, it's no secret. Any man who meets you would feel the same."

"You can tell me about my eyes, my skin, my teeth." These were all superficial things that wouldn't touch her heart.

"I'd rather talk about your soul, your spirit, your strength of character."

"Don't!"

Bryce seemed surprised by her reaction. "I thought women liked to be loved for more than their physical beauty."

"We're not talking about love. Besides, every woman likes to be told she's beautiful."

"That's not what draws a man to a woman for more than a short time. Hair turns gray, skin dries and shrivels, teeth may decay, and eyes can go blind. But that's all on the surface. It's what's inside that counts."

"It's time for me to go in. Moriah will be worried. And you have to get up early for the first drill."

"I've directed drill more than once without sleep."

"Bryce, you're going to choose a wife for practical purposes. There's no point in thinking about my inner qualities."

"But that's what makes you so special. A man could very easily love you forever."

Something inside Abby snapped and a sob tore loose from her throat.

Chapter Seventeen

"I can't do this," she cried. "I thought I could, but I can't."

"Can't do what?" Bryce asked, apparently confused and worried by her sudden outburst.

But Abby couldn't tell him. How did you tell a man you couldn't pursue a casual relationship because you'd suddenly discovered you were in danger of falling in love with him? She might have been able to if he hadn't started talking about inner qualities that could make a man love her forever. Didn't he know that every woman longed to believe a man loved her for her inner beauty, that age would increase and deepen rather than wear down the strength and intensity of his love?

She reached for the rope and pulled hard. She had to get away from Bryce.

"What did I say to upset you?" Bryce asked.

"Nothing. I'm just tired. I've been under a lot of strain since I got here. I guess it's bothering me."

"You didn't seem on the verge of tears just moments ago."

She pulled on the rope again. "It comes on without warning." She pulled the rope again, praying Moriah would hurry.

"I can't leave you like this."

"Men get drunk when things bother them. Women cry." She heard the bar being lifted and the key inserted in the lock. She practically fell into Moriah's arms.

"What's wrong?" Moriah asked as soon as she got a look at Abby. "What did he do to you?"

"Nothing," Abby said, hoping to reassure her sister. "I'm just tired."

Moriah looked from one of them to the other, her expression far from friendly. "I appreciate your seeing my sister safely home," she said to Bryce. "Good night." She closed the door in his face, then led her sister inside.

"Tell me what happened," she said. "And don't leave anything out."

Bryce remained standing on the porch, trying to figure out what had just happened.

Sometimes Abby seemed like two people. One was a hardheaded businesswoman determined to succeed. She didn't mind asking for help or going against convention. She was strong, resourceful, and knew exactly what she wanted. She made decisions based on practical reasons, not emotional ones. She seemed determined to live her life without husband or family. She regarded the soldiers' repeated proposals with humor, understood the difficult life they led, and didn't blame them for wanting to make it easier.

Then there was the Abby who responded eagerly to his kisses, much more eagerly than he would have expected. It wouldn't have surprised him if she'd slapped him the first time he kissed her, even refused to speak to him afterward. That same Abby had reappeared tonight to enjoy being held in his arms, to enjoy his compliments. The way she'd responded to his kiss had led him to believe she was opening the door to a closer relationship.

Then she'd slammed it abruptly, leaving him with no clue as to what had caused the sudden change. He was equally puzzled by her insistence that he confine his compliments to her physical appearance. He knew women wanted to be thought beautiful, but Abby wasn't a person who valued the external over the internal. She discounted her physical appearance. Though she dressed well, she never wore anything out of the ordinary.

None of this made sense. Maybe he'd ask Dorrie. She could be flighty, but she was bound to know more about this sort of thing than he did. Besides, he had to figure out what the changes in his own feelings for Abby signified.

He had grown up in a society where marriages were contracted for social and financial reasons far more often than for love. Some people, his mother being one of them, considered love dangerous to the stability of a marriage. They said love was irrational, temporary, and the cause of much self-destructive behavior in men and women. They believed respect, common goals, and similar backgrounds formed the basis for the most successful marriages. Bryce had married for love, and it had been a disaster. He had every intention of choosing his next bride for practical reasons. He hadn't thought his attraction to Abby threatened that intention until tonight.

He'd recognized his physical attraction to Abby from the beginning. The fact that she was the first attractive single woman to come within his orbit had made it easier to accept the unanticipated strength of his feeling for her.

Tonight, however, he'd realized the things that appealed to him most about Abby had very little to do with the superficial. Yes, he enjoyed her cooking, but it was the impulse behind her offer to prepare his meals that was important. He was glad of her friendship with Pamela, but it was the enjoyment she got out of letting Pamela help that was important. The same was true of her insistence that the Indians get all the beef they were promised and get it on time, her continuing effort to make sure the store carried as much as possible of what the people at the fort wanted, her friendship with wives of officers as well as enlisted men. Maybe most telling was the fact that he'd forgotten he'd ever wanted her to go back to St. Louis.

Something very profound had changed in his thinking, and he'd better figure out what and why before he did something he would regret.

Abby didn't know the man who walked into the store, but he wasn't one of the soldiers. She hoped he was a rancher or homesteader. She wanted to build her clientele among the civilians in the area.

"I'm Abby Pierce," she said, introducing herself to him. "I'm one of the owners of the trading post. Can I help you find anything?"

"I'm just looking," the man said. "I usually buy what I need in Boulder Gap, but this place is about an hour closer."

"We're in the process of restocking the store," Abby said. "If you don't see something you want, write it down. We're keeping a list so we can serve our customers better."

"Sounds like a good idea."

"We're hoping to serve the civilian community as well as the army," Abby said.

"What about the Indians?"

Since they weren't supposed to leave the reservation, Abby had assumed that market was closed to her. "I was under the impression the Indian agent handed out what goods and supplies they needed each month."

"I wouldn't be too sure. I heard Russ Tibbolt and his boys were attacked by Indians two days ago while they were driving a herd to the reservation."

"That doesn't make any sense," Abby said. "Why should they try to steal what was already theirs?"

"Maybe they weren't so sure the agent was going to hand it over."

Abby didn't trust Hinson, but she was sure he'd never try to steal the beef. "What happened to Tibbolt and his men?"

"I don't know, but what chance could he have against a lot of Indians? There were only four of them with the herd."

Abby untied her apron, jerked it over her head, and threw it atop a pile of shirts. "Come with me," she said to the man. "I want you to tell Colonel McGregor what you know."

She practically had to drag the man across the parade ground to Bryce's office. He was worried Bryce would somehow hold him responsible for the attack. Abby listened while Bryce questioned the man. He didn't say anything beyond what he'd already told her, but when asked to give his opinion of what might have happened, he said he figured Tibbolt and his men were probably dead. Bryce sent a message to Lieutenant Collier to put together a troop of thirty men to be ready to ride within the hour.

"You'll have to show us where the attack took place," Bryce said to the man.

"I want to get home. The wife will be worried. She don't like being left alone, especially not when there's Indians about."

"I'll send a couple of soldiers to stay with your family until you can return," Bryce said. "Just tell us how to find your place."

"Do you think Tibbolt and his men are dead?" Abby asked after the man had left to give directions to the soldiers who were being sent to his house.

"I don't know," Bryce replied, already making preparations to lead the patrol. "It would depend on how many Indians attacked, whether Tibbolt had good, dependable men, and how determined the Indians were to steal the beef."

"He said maybe the Indians didn't think Hinson was going to give it to them. Do you think he could be selling what he's supposed to give the Indians?"

"Anything is possible. I won't know until I see for myself."

"If Hinson is stealing, you've got to stop him."

"I told you, I have no authority over him or the Indians. I'm only allowed to get involved when something goes wrong."

"But that's too late."

"I know that, and the army knows that, but we can't convince the men in Washington. You'd better get back to the store. I've got to get ready to ride."

"I'll do no such thing. I'm going with you."

The last thing Bryce wanted was to have Abby go with him, but she had made it clear she was prepared to ride out on her own if necessary. He couldn't let that happen. If the Indians killed a white woman, everyone within a hundred miles would be demanding that the army wipe out the Indians. They wouldn't make any distinction between rogue braves and the men, women, and children who lived peacefully on the reservation. Bryce admired Abby's courage and spunk, but at times he wished she hadn't been so liberally endowed with those traits.

"This looks about where it was," the man said when they rode into an area where the ground fell away on either side of the trail. "You could hide I don't know how many Indians in there and no one would see them until it was too late."

"Have the men spread out and see what they can find," Bryce said to Collier.

"You'll find a lot of blood if the amount of shooting was anything to go by," the man said. "Went on for half a day."

That made Bryce feel better. If the attack had been over quickly, he would have assumed the Indians had killed all the men and made off with the beeves. The longer the fight, the more chance Tibbolt and his men had survived.

"How could Indians hide here?" Abby asked, looking into the ravines on either side of the trail.

"Indians are masters at hiding in places you and I would find impossible. Besides, the herd itself might have served to screen their attack."

"What will you do if you find bodies?" Abby asked.

"There won't be any. Tibbolt or his men would have buried their dead, and the Indians would have carried theirs away."

After asking the man a few more questions, Bryce allowed him to go home. Abby was nervous and upset by the time Lieutenant Collier and his men returned.

"We found a lot of cartridge shells, especially where

Tibbolt's men would have been holed up," Collier said. "Apparently he was prepared for trouble."

"Any signs of blood?" Bryce asked.

"Not there, but we found plenty of it elsewhere. It looks like Tibbolt's men may have been too tough for the Indians to handle."

"Did you find any footprints?" Bryce asked.

"Lots of them. Some hoofprints, too."

"Unshod?"

"Yes."

There went his last hope there was another explanation for this attack. "Show me," Bryce said.

Collier led him to a deep gully with a sandy bottom. Several horses had been left there. Bryce beckoned to the Indian scout who rode with him. "What can you tell me about these footprints?"

"Six horses," the man said after several minutes of careful study.

Bryce had expected more.

"Not Indian ponies," the scout said.

"How can you tell?" Bryce asked.

"Look," the scout said, pointing to perfectly preserved hoofprints in the damp sand. "Nail holes in hoof. Shoes been pulled off."

Bryce got down on his hands and knees to study the footprints. He wouldn't have noticed it himself wouldn't have been able to see it if the sand hadn't been wet when the attack took place, but there were barely discernable mounds of sand in the hoofprints that showed that at some time at least several of the horses had been shod and the nails pulled out. Bryce breathed a sigh of relief. If the scout was right, white men disguised as Indians had attacked Tibbolt and his men. He would have to go to the reservation.

"Mount up."

235

"What are you going to do now?" Abby asked.

"We're going to the reservation."

"I'm coming, too."

"I figured you were," Bryce said.

Abby didn't know what she'd expected the Indian reservation to look like, but what she found shocked her. There were no wooden structures, though one soldier at the fort said he'd seen the wood the government purchased for the Indians. There was no schoolhouse, no hospital, no warehouse where supplies could be kept. The Indians all appeared to live in their own tepees amid the squalor and filth that came from a large number of people and animals living in the same location for an extended period of time. She saw only a few children, all without clothing. Everything they had appeared to be old and tattered, mended, or broken beyond repair. She saw a few old women but no men.

"I thought the government had promised to take care of these people," Abby said to Bryce.

"It did. They receive supplies each month."

"What kind of supplies?"

"Clothes, beef, dry goods, farm implements, seed, animals, everything they need to be able to give up their traditional life."

"These people can't have been getting enough to eat," Abby said. "Look. You can see those children's ribs."

"I've seen their dogs on the plains hunting for prairie dogs and other rodents," Lieutenant Collier remarked. "They look like living skeletons."

"Why isn't Hinson's office here instead of in Boulder Gap?" Abby asked.

"He's allowed to have his office wherever he likes," Bryce said.

"Look," Collier said, pointing to a place in the distance where Abby could see men riding around a corral shooting arrows into, and rifles at, cattle. It appeared that most of the women and children were gathered nearby.

"It looks like the beef arrived," Bryce said.

"What are they doing?" Abby asked.

"They're pretending to hunt the cows as they would buffalo," Bryce explained. "They ride around shooting until they're all dead. Then they strip the carcasses and feast. They'll probably eat everything in a couple of weeks and then have nothing until the next shipment arrives."

"Why doesn't someone explain that they ought to kill one or two at a time? That way they won't have to eat it all to keep it from spoiling."

"I think they're too hungry to wait," Bryce said.

Abby was surprised to see Russ Tibbolt and three other men who looked like cowhands with the Indians at the corral.

"I see you survived the attack," Bryce said after he'd dismounted and introduced himself and Collier.

"Did any of your men get hurt?" Abby asked.

"Just a graze that doesn't amount to much," Tibbolt said.

"Did you lose any cows?" Bryce asked.

"One killed by a stray bullet," Tibbolt said. "We butchered it and brought in the meat. They ate every scrap of it last night."

Abby looked to where the Indians had stopped shooting at the cows. They all appeared to be dead. "Couldn't you convince them to kill just a few at a time?"

"My job was to get the beef here. It's no concern of mine what they do with it."

"About the Indians that attacked you—" Bryce said.

"They weren't Indians," Tibbolt said.

"How can you be sure?" Abby asked.

"I know how they live. I know how they fight. Those weren't Indians."

"Our scout agrees with you," Bryce said. "He says someone had recently pulled shoes off those horses."

"I'd say you've got someone who doesn't want the Indians to get their beef," Tibbolt said.

"Or doesn't want me to have the contract," Abby said.

"Looks like you've got a problem," Tibbolt said to Bryce.

"It's not my problem. The Bureau of Indian Affairs is under the Department of the Interior. The army has no authority here."

"It'll be your responsibility if the Indians leave the reservation," Tibbolt said. "If they're starving—and they look pretty damned close to it to me—they'll leave it sooner or later."

"Come with me," Bryce said to Tibbolt. "I want to talk to the chief."

"You speak their language?" Tibbolt asked.

"No, but we have a scout who can translate."

Abby followed as they went in search of the chief, who turned out to be a handsome man, younger than Abby had expected, with a broad, sturdy body. He didn't look happy to see the soldiers. He had a heated conversation with the scout before he translated for Bryce.

It turned out the chief was angry his braves had been accused of attacking Tibbolt. He said none of them had left the reservation, even though they hadn't seen the agent in more than three months and hadn't received their monthly supplies since last summer. He said his people were hungry, had no warm clothes, and had no implements or seed for the crops they were supposed to plant to provide them with food. He said if it hadn't been for the beef, his people would have starved. He complained about the ranchers who continued to graze their cows on reservation land, homesteaders who settled near the best water. He wanted to know why the Great White Father in Washington had continued to break all his promises, yet expected the Indians to stay on their reservation, to wait patiently for supplies that never came, and never raise a hand against a white man no matter what he did.

Bryce promised to talk to the agent. He assured the chief he didn't believe they had attacked Tibbolt. He said if the chief heard anything about white men disguised as Indians, he was to send a message to the fort, but under no circumstances was he to leave the reservation.

"You've got to force Hinson to give the Indians the supplies promised to them," Abby said to Bryce when he'd finished speaking to the chief.

"I told you, I have no authority over him," Bryce said. He was just as frustrated and angry as Abby over the situation. "The army has asked repeatedly for authority over the Indian Bureau, but Congress continues to deny it."

"Then what can we do?"

"I'll speak to Hinson, but it will be more effective to file a written complaint against him. It will be slow, but it might trigger an investigation, even his removal."

"He's a brutal, selfish man. I'm not surprised he's able to ignore the Indians. Well, now at least they have beef."

"You'll have to find someone else to deliver next month's supplies," Tibbolt said. "Even if I had the beef to sell, I wouldn't put my boys through the danger of delivering another herd so soon. I don't know who's out to stop you, but I expect they're the reason no one else will take on your deliveries."

"Could you buy beef from one of the ranchers, then sell it to me?" Abby asked Tibbolt.

"Ma'am, I served time for killing a man who was well liked. When they see me coming, most of those ranchers meet me with a rifle and a promise to use it if I set foot on their property."

"I'll think of something," Abby said.

Three days later Abby still hadn't thought of a solution. Moriah came from the store into the parlor where Abby was working at her desk. One of the army carpenters had finished cutting out a window and Abby was enjoying the sunlight.

"You ought to give up the contract," Moriah said. "Let someone else worry about it."

"I can't, not when the beef is all the Indians have. Bryce said the government promised to supply everything they needed. He says the money has been appropriated. It's promised in the budget, but it's not getting to the Indians."

"I imagine Hinson is selling everything he can," Dorrie said.

"He's got to be," Abby said. "The chief said they hadn't received anything since last summer."

"With all the mining going on, there's a market for everything," Dorrie said.

"I know," Abby said. "I wasn't impressed with the stores I saw in Boulder Gap. They're all run by men, but it's women who buy half the goods sold. I could steal half their customers in a year if I had the money to set up the kind of store I want to."

"We've got enough to do running this store," Moriah said.

"I don't want to be stuck running this store for the rest of my life," Abby said. "I want to expand, to grow. One day I'd like to open a store in Denver."

"Gosh," Dorrie said. "You'd have to be awfully clever to do that."

"I am clever."

"And brave."

"Bryce says I'm brave, too."

"I'd be more likely to say foolhardy," her sister said. "You've got no business riding all over, especially not to an Indian reservation."

"My husband says the Indians are an abomination," Dorrie said. "He says no decent human could live like that."

"They wouldn't have to if they received the supplies the government promised them," Abby said, her anger rising. "I've a good mind to write another letter to Washington."

"I think three are enough," Moriah said.

"It would have been better if you'd signed one of them," Abby told her sister.

"I didn't see the reservation."

"I told you what it was like."

"I won't put my name to something I haven't seen for myself."

Abby had accepted her sister's decision and hadn't pressed her, but it would be better if more civilians would write. Bryce told her most people were afraid of the Indians and wanted them gone.

Bryce had written, but he said Congress thought the army wanted responsibility for the Indians so it could increase its control of the West. Consequently, most members of Congress ignored the army's complaints about the way the Indian Bureau was handling the problem.

"Taking the Indians' part may make the ranchers and farmers angry enough to boycott the store," Dorrie said.

"I don't see why," Abby said. "The Indians were guaranteed those supplies so they could stay on their reservation and not be a danger to anyone. If they don't get them, they have to leave to find food. I don't see why everyone isn't clamoring for the government to give the Indians everything they could possibly need."

"No one likes the Indians," Dorrie said. "Most people wouldn't care if they all died."

"Well, I care," Abby said, trying to hold back her anger. It wasn't fair to get angry at Dorrie just because she said things Abby didn't like. She had to learn to present her views in a manner that would encourage people to listen to what she said, not make them so angry they ignored her opinions.

"What do you care about?" Bryce asked, entering the store and bringing the sunshine in with him.

Chapter Eighteen

"About the Indians," Abby told him.

She wished he hadn't come. Ever since the party, she'd been careful not to be alone with him. Her admission of weakness had led to the collapse of all her defenses. A little more encouragement and she'd be completely in love with Bryce McGregor. Since he was only interested in indulging in a brief flirtation until he got his new appointment, her only chance to keep a tight rein on her rebellious heart was to stay away from him.

But within the limited confines of the fort, it was impossible to avoid seeing him several times a day. And even when she didn't see him, she had to listen to people talk about him. It seemed no one talked about anyone else. They discussed what he did during the day, what he *didn't* do during the day, the orders he gave, and the orders he *should* have given. The men discussed the problems in the area and what they thought Bryce was planning to do about them. They speculated on who would take Bryce's place and how that commander's orders would agree or conflict with what Bryce had been doing.

The women preferred to speculate on the wisdom of his decision to bring Pamela West with him, what kind of woman he'd marry, and whether he'd want more children. The prevailing opinion was that he'd want at least one son. Abby didn't know what they'd talk about after he left. They'd probably die of boredom.

"What are you doing here?" she asked Bryce. "Zeb was just here this morning."

"I came to ask you to look in on Pamela. She's not feeling well."

"Have you taken her to the doctor?"

"She's heard people call him 'the butcher' so often, she really believes he amputates all his patients' arms and legs."

"You ought to horsewhip the person who told her such rubbish."

"I'd like to, but that won't help me now."

"I don't know anything about children's illnesses. Why don't you ask Sarah's mother?"

"I suggested that, but she wants you. She says she won't talk to anyone else."

"Can you help Moriah until I get back?" Abby asked Dorrie.

"I can handle the store without help," Moriah said.

"I know you can. I doubt Father could have done any better."

The last thing she wanted was to go anywhere with Bryce. He only had to come into her line of vision and she couldn't think straight. All her arguments why she shouldn't be attracted to him lost their meaning. Her promise to herself that she would devote her life to making her store a dramatic success turned into a deadening weight around her neck. She could think of no reason why she should fight her desire to give in to the ever-more-powerful longing to feel someone loved her, even if for only a short time.

Telling herself she was a weak fool, Abby stiffened her backbone and clenched her fists. She would concentrate on Pamela. It was safe to love Pamela.

"Tell me what's been happening," Abby said as they walked across the parade ground, her stride matching Bryce's. The faster they got to the house, the less time there would be for temptation to rear its head.

"Not a lot that I can see. She doesn't have spots, she's not sick to her stomach, and she doesn't have a raging fever."

Since she didn't sound seriously ill, Abby didn't feel quite so helpless. "She must have complained of something."

"She moped about the house saying she didn't feel well. I wasn't too worried until she refused to eat supper. Pamela complains about Zeb's cooking, but she always has a good appetite."

"What was she doing when you left?"

"Lying on her bed balled up in a knot. Anytime I tried to go near her, she pushed me away and asked for you."

Abby hoped Pamela wasn't faking an illness to get her to move back into the house, but she wouldn't put it past the child. She was a very bright little girl, and she still wanted Abby and Moriah to live in her father's extra bedroom.

"How is she?" Bryce asked Zeb when they entered the house.

"She's started crying," Zeb said. "She says her ear hurts."

"Poor thing. She probably has an earache," Abby said. "I used to get them when I was a child. Sometimes I would cry all night."

Abby could tell from the horrified look on Bryce's face that he didn't know what to do with a child who might cry all night.

"I could be wrong," Abby said. "Let's hope so."

She found Pamela curled up against her pillows, her thumb in her mouth, her eyes closed. An occasional sob escaped her. Abby eased herself down on the bed and put her hand on Pamela's shoulder.

"Your father tells me you're not feeling well."

Pamela's eyes flew open. "Miss Abby!" she cried and threw herself into Abby's arms. She tried to talk, but she was crying so hard Abby couldn't understand what she said. She just held her close until she stopped crying.

"Now tell me what's wrong," Abby said.

"My ear hurts something awful," Pamela said, starting to cry again. "Please make it stop."

"When did it start hurting?"

"It's been hurting all day, but it didn't make me cry until Daddy tried to make me eat supper."

"I thought you'd feel better if you ate something," Bryce said. He sat down on the bed next to Abby. He kept patting Pamela's leg as if he didn't know what to do but couldn't stand to do nothing.

"It hurt to chew," Pamela said.

"Why didn't you tell me?" Bryce asked.

"Sarah's momma says a colonel's daughter can't cry, that she has to be brave no matter what."

Abby was beginning to think it was time Pamela spent less time at Sarah's house. "It's all right to cry when you hurt," she said. "It's Nature's way of telling you something is wrong."

"Can you make it go away?" Pamela asked.

"Not right now, but I can do something that will help you feel better." Abby started to get up, but Pamela's arms tightened around her.

"I don't want you to go."

"I'm not leaving. I'm just going downstairs."

"I don't want you to go. It doesn't hurt as much when you're here."

Abby could remember feeling the same way when she'd had an earache and had gone to sleep in Aunt Emma's arms. There was something about being held that made everything seem better.

Unbidden, her thoughts flew to the times Bryce had held her in his arms and how wonderful it had felt. Ashamed to be selfishly thinking of herself instead of the sick child, Abby wrenched her thoughts away from memories of Bryce's embrace. "Tell Zeb I need him to do something for me," Abby said to Bryce.

"What is it? I'll be happy to do it."

"I want him to roast an onion."

Bryce looked at her as if she'd lost her mind. "Why would you want him to do that? Pamela hates onions. Both of us do."

"I don't want her to eat it," Abby said. "I'm going to wrap it up and put it next to her ear. The heat will ease the pain."

"I'm not sure we have an onion. Would a stone do?"

"I've never heard of anyone using anything but an onion."

"If the stone doesn't work, I'll have Zeb ask around until he finds an onion. We'll have that stone ready in two shakes of a lamb's tail," her father said.

"Have you ever seen a lamb shake its tail?" Pamela asked Abby after her father had left the room.

"No, I don't think so," Abby replied, amused by the question.

"Then I don't suppose you know if it shakes its tail very fast."

Abby warned herself not to laugh. "No, I don't. Why do you want to know?"

"The faster it shakes its tail, the sooner Daddy will be back."

Abby had forgotten how literal children could be. She was certain there was no lamb in the world that took as long to shake its tail as it would take to heat a stone through. Abby put a pillow behind her back and moved next to Pamela. "We can sit here together until he comes back," she said. "Tell me what you did today."

"I haven't been feeling well," Pamela said.

Abby tightened her arms around Pamela and listened while the child told her in painstaking detail of the onset of her earache. Bryce came back while Pamela was still describing her morning. He settled on the foot of the bed, mouthing to Abby that Zeb had a stone buried in the coals in the stove and would bring it up as soon as it was hot.

"Sit over here," Pamela said to her father, pointing to the spot right next to her and opposite Abby.

Bryce settled next to his daughter, moving his left hand behind her until it rested on Abby's shoulder. Abby felt a surge of emotion go through her that threatened to destroy her calm. She had spent days avoiding being in the same room with him and now they were sitting practically side by side, touching, and she couldn't move away. She could only hope he would soon get bored and go downstairs to work. But Pamela reached out for her father's other hand, gripped it hard, and pulled it across her stomach until she was enfolded in a double embrace. Bryce settled back to listen to his daughter's recital.

Despite Abby's efforts to concentrate on what Pamela was saying, she was acutely aware of Bryce's touch. Nor could she drive the picture from her mind of the three of them sitting together on the bed like a loving family.

Abby knew then that her talk of never getting married and devoting herself to the store was merely the result of being hurt.

This was what she wanted.

Almost from the moment she'd arrived at the fort her actions had belied her words. She had turned to Bryce from the very beginning, depended on him, asked him for help and advice. She'd told herself she wouldn't need to depend on him, even see him, once she learned all she needed to know to manage her store. Maybe she'd believed it, but she'd been wrong. While she was turning to him for help, she was also learning he was a very different kind of man from Albert. The fact that he meant to look for a wife in Philadelphia hadn't been able to stop her from realizing he was everything Albert wasn't.

And everything she'd ever wanted.

Now she came face to face with the realization that she was in love with a man who was out of her reach. Worse, she was forced to concentrate on his daughter while trying not to think about him. It would have been so much easier if Pamela had called for Moriah.

"What makes my ear hurt so much?" Pamela asked. Tears had brought her recital to an end.

"I don't know, but it will soon go away," Abby said. "My earaches were always gone in the morning. Have you ever had an earache before?"

"I don't think so."

Bryce shrugged his shoulders, so Abby figured she hadn't. It wasn't something you forgot easily.

"Did it hurt a lot when you had an earache?" Pamela asked.

"Yes."

"Did you cry?"

"Yes. My Aunt Emma used to hold me until I fell asleep."

"Will you hold me?"

"Of course I will."

Pamela had started to cry again. "I'll go see if Zeb has the stone warm yet," Abby said.

Pamela's grip tightened. "No," she cried. "You stay. I want Daddy to go."

Abby could see it hurt Bryce to have his daughter prefer her comfort to his, but he didn't hesitate.

"Why didn't you want your father to stay with you?" Abby asked as soon as Bryce had left the room.

"Sarah's momma said mommas are supposed to stay with sick children. She says daddies don't know what to do."

Abby was certain Sarah's mother had only the best of intentions, but she needed to stop trying to be a substitute mother. "Maybe some daddies don't know what to do," Abby said, "but your father would very much like to stay with you until you feel better. Didn't you like having him hold you while you told me about getting sick?"

Pamela nodded.

"You've got a very special daddy. He brought you to live with him rather than leaving you back East with your grandmother."

"Grandmama said he shouldn't take me to a desert where savages ran around naked and killed people."

"Your father wanted you with him because he loves you very much. No one in the world loves you more than he does. Next time, ask him to stay with you."

"Can't you both stay?"

Abby wanted to say she would stay as long as Pamela needed her, but she knew she couldn't make false promises to this child. She was obviously reaching out for a mother figure, first by quoting everything Sarah's mother said and now by wanting Abby to stay with her. Pamela was liable to interpret any promise to stay as a promise to stay forever. Even if she didn't, Abby knew it would be wrong to let Pamela become too attached to her. Her father would remarry before long, and it was important that she be able to think of his new wife as her mother. It wouldn't help if she'd already put Abby in that position.

"I can stay with you tonight," Abby said, "but I have to go back to the store in the morning."

"Can't Miss Moriah take care of the store?"

"Don't you want your father to stay with you?"

"Yes, but I want you, too."

"I'm sorry, darling, but I can't stay all the time."

"Don't you love me? I love you."

The look of entreaty in Pamela's eyes almost brought Abby to tears. The child needed a mother, yet Abby could never be that mother. Pamela had yet to learn that love could hurt as well as make you happy. It wasn't a lesson Abby wanted the child to learn at her hands.

"Of course I love you. Everyone at the fort loves you. But your father is going to get married when he goes back to Philadelphia. That lady will be your mother. You'll want to love her more than anyone."

"You could marry Daddy. Then you'd be my momma. I love you more than anybody."

The situation was only getting more complicated. Most likely Bryce wouldn't appreciate her speaking for him, but she didn't see any other choice.

"I can't marry your daddy because I'm not going to Philadelphia. I'm going to stay here."

"I don't want to go to Philadelphia. Grandmama doesn't like me."

"I'm sure your grandmother loves you very much. She

just wants you to learn to behave like a little lady."

"That's what Sarah's momma says."

Well, at least the woman had got one thing right. "Your daddy wants to go back to Philadelphia," Abby told Pamela. "He will have a nicer job, and you can live in a nice house with a real cook." The sound of boot heels in the hall let her know Bryce had returned.

"One warm stone carefully wrapped," he said, handing it to Abby. "Zeb roasted an onion, but I doubt Pamela could stand the smell. I know I couldn't. I'd rather have an earache."

"You wouldn't if you'd ever had one," Abby said. The stone was much heavier than an onion and considerably harder. She'd have to find a way to keep it next to Pamela's ear without binding it to her head.

"I need one of the pillows from the extra bedroom," she said to Bryce.

"What are you going to do?" Pamela asked.

"Make a nest in the pillow so you can lay your head next to the stone. The warmth from it will make your ear feel better."

Bryce returned with the pillow. It took only a moment for Abby to settle the stone in the middle.

"Now lay your head next to it," Abby said to Pamela. "Does that feel better?"

"It still hurts an awful lot."

"Give it a little time."

"Are you going to leave now?"

"No. I said I'd stay all night if you needed me."

"I want you to stay." Pamela held out her hand to her father. "Daddy, too."

"Wild horses couldn't drag me away from my big girl," Bryce said. He sat down next to his daughter in much the same position as before.

"Sarah's momma says wild horses are dangerous, but

Sarah's daddy says he likes wild horses because they have spirit. He said I had spirit, too. Do you think I have spirit?"

"Lots and lots," Bryce said. "You've got almost as much spirit as Miss Abby."

"Sarah's daddy says Miss Abby is a Tartar. When I asked what it meant, he said it was a good thing, but Sarah's momma frowned. Why did she frown?"

Abby frowned herself. "I expect she thought he shouldn't have said that to you," she said. "It's probably something your grandmother wouldn't like."

"Why?"

"Being a Tartar out here may be a good thing, but I'm not sure it would be so good in Philadelphia."

"Why?"

Abby hadn't been around children enough to remember that *why* was their favorite word.

"Let's save that until tomorrow," Bryce said. "If Abby answers everything tonight, you'll never have time to go to sleep."

Abby was grateful Bryce had stepped in. She adored Pamela and enjoyed being with her, but she had a lot to learn about what it meant to have a seven-year-old around all the time. It caused her to like Bryce still more for keeping his daughter with him. No one would have criticized him if he'd left her with her grandmother.

Though it was impossible for him to be with her all the time, he spent several hours with her every day. He made a point to eat breakfast and supper with her, as well as be home in the evening. The depth of his commitment to his daughter only made him more worthy of love in her eyes.

"Do I have to go to sleep?" Pamela asked.

"Your ear won't hurt as much when you're asleep,"

Abby said. "Keep it next to the stone. The heat will make it feel better."

Pamela must have been exhausted, and the heat from the stone must have made her ear hurt less because it didn't take more than a few minutes before her eyes closed and she fell asleep. Abby adjusted her position to be more comfortable.

"You can go home now," Bryce whispered softly. "You don't have to stay."

"I promised Pamela I'd stay all night if she wanted. I can't go back on that now."

"How will you get any sleep?"

"I'll sleep right here."

"Why don't you lie down in the extra bedroom?"

"She wants me here."

Bryce said nothing for a few moments. Then he whispered still softer, "I want you here, too."

But he only wanted her as long as it was convenient. Abby knew she couldn't accept that.

Bryce eased himself up from the bed before his cramp became something it would take him the better part of a day to work out. He needed to put more oil in the lamp before it guttered and charred the wick. His stocking feet made no noise on the bare boards of the bedroom floor. He picked up the lantern and turned to leave the room, but the sight of Abby and Pamela asleep in each other's arms mesmerized him.

He would never understand what it was about sleep that could turn looking at a child or wife into a heart-wrenching experience, but seeing Abby and Pamela was an epiphany rather than simply a moving sight. He knew without a doubt this was how things ought to be. He didn't know why he hadn't understood before.

Neither did he understand why Abby thought she

didn't want a family of her own. She had undoubtedly been hurt by someone, but everyone got hurt sooner or later. People got over it and moved on, rather than allowing one bad experience to ruin every chance for happiness. He'd never asked Abby about her past. Maybe telling someone else would help her put it behind her. It was obvious she loved Pamela.

Bryce knew the kind of wife he needed for his career. His experience with Margaret had proved to him that marrying for love could be dangerous. How could one tell true love from fascination, infatuation, or lust so strong it felt like a passionate and lasting love? His physical needs weren't so strong that they blinded him to everything else. Pamela had needs that were equally important. And Abby was the perfect person who could fulfill them.

She wasn't the perfect person to fulfill his career needs, but he was beginning to suspect she was the only person who could ever fulfill his personal ones. Giving in to those needs would mean turning his whole life—his career, his family's expectations, and everything else—upside down. He didn't know if he could do that. He didn't know if he *wanted* to do that.

He left the room on silent footsteps.

But as he moved down the hall, down the steps, and to the kitchen, he couldn't get the picture of Abby and Pamela out of his mind. If Margaret had ever comforted her child through the night, he didn't know about it. She hadn't wanted the discomfort of bearing a child or the responsibility of caring for it. His mother said women had children out of duty, that one of the advantages of wealth was to be able to hire someone else to take care of them.

His mother had never understood why he wanted Pamela with him. He hadn't been sure himself in the beginning. He'd been away most of his daughter's life. He hardly knew her. He just knew he couldn't leave her to grow up without a mother or father. Maybe he'd resented the fact that he'd been brought up by maids and nannies.

He found the kitchen dark. Zeb had gone to bed. Bryce set down his lamp, lit the one Zeb had used, which still had plenty of oil, and blew out his own. He turned and retraced his steps.

The sight of Abby and Pamela together struck with even greater force than before. He had a visceral feeling that this was something he had to have if he was ever to be happy. That realization caused him to look at his life as he'd never done before. He'd been taught to judge his happiness by his professional success, the contributions he could make to society, to his country. Because of his privileged birth, he'd been taught his duty was greater than that of ordinary men. He was not to think of himself. Duty came before everything.

Abby had changed that.

Even though he'd done his best to convince her to go back to St. Louis, he'd been attracted to her from the first. He'd begun by thinking he was only looking out for his own interests, but somewhere during the last weeks that had changed to wanting to look out for Abby. He had fooled himself into thinking he wasn't personally involved. Now he knew better. The question was what he was going to do about it.

He didn't know. He'd only just realized he wanted far more from Abby than a love affair. He didn't yet know what compromises he would be willing to make. He didn't know whether she would be willing to make any at all. She had seemed determined to keep men out of her life. And then there was his conscience. He'd been taught his duty was to serve his country before anything else. Could he live with himself if he turned his back on that duty? Did he believe it *was* his duty?

Hell! He'd thought he had his life all figured out. Then a stubborn woman from South Carolina by way of St. Louis had come into it and upset everything. Grant had said Southerners were a stubborn lot who would stick to their beliefs no matter what it cost them. He wondered if Abby really believed she could never trust a man again.

"What are you thinking?"

The sound of Abby's voice startled Bryce. "I thought you were asleep."

"I woke up when you went downstairs. I've been watching you stand there, looking at us. What were you thinking?"

Chapter Nineteen

Bryce wasn't ready to let anyone know what he'd been thinking. He still had more questions than he had answers.

"I was thinking it was extremely kind of you to give up your night's rest for my daughter."

"After all you've done for me, it was the least I could do in return."

So she thought it was a duty, the repayment of a debt. Bryce felt disappointed; the excitement inside him cooled. He felt foolish for having considered turning his life upside down for a woman whose feelings hadn't changed. This night hadn't been an epiphany for her, but simply something she did out of duty, perhaps out of friendship as well. He wanted to leave the room, to hide. It felt as if his thoughts had somehow been exposed to her view and she'd rejected them. He was embarrassed he could be gullible enough to consider changing his life for a woman.

No, gullible was the wrong word, because it implied

Abby was somehow at fault. She'd never vacillated from the position she'd laid out when he first met her. He was the one who'd changed. He was the one who was simpleminded enough to think all could be changed for love. Stupid to make the same mistake twice. What made him think he knew what love was this time? Maybe his epiphany was nothing more than the natural feeling of inadequacy a father experienced when he couldn't comfort his daughter and his thankfulness to a woman who could.

"I appreciate what you've done, but I don't want you to think it's your duty."

"I don't," Abby said, looking a little surprised. "I'm very fond of Pamela. I had earaches myself. I know how much they hurt."

"She seems to be sleeping peacefully now."

"You ought to lie down," Abby said. "You have a full day ahead of you tomorrow."

"I'll stay."

"Then you'd better settle down and stop talking. We're liable to wake her."

Bryce settled down next to his daughter, his arm around her, his fingertips touching Abby. That seemed like a metaphor for their relationship. Nothing more substantial, nothing more enduring.

Yet something within him had changed. After tonight he could never view Abby or himself in the same light again. He was certain his life would never be complete without her.

"You could stay with Pamela again tonight if you want," Moriah said to Abby as they got ready for bed. "Now that Colonel McGregor has a guard on duty, I don't mind sleeping here by myself."

It annoyed Abby that Moriah continued to refer to

Bryce by his title. She'd done her best to make her sister understand their relationship was purely friendship. As for Pamela, no woman could ignore a sick child calling her name. Neither meant Abby wasn't capable of controlling any foolish tendency to become romantically interested in her father.

"She's much better today. Practically well, in fact." Abby had come back to the trading post after breakfast, but she'd checked on Pamela three times during the day, the last time after supper.

"Her father ought to get married. That child needs a mother."

"He plans to do so as soon as he gets back East. With his looks and family connections, I'm sure it won't take long."

"What happens if he doesn't get posted back East?" Moriah asked. "Dorrie says promotions are practically impossible to get since the end of the war."

"Bryce's family is wealthy. They have important connections."

"This young colonel we've been hearing so much about, George Custer, is a personal favorite of General Sheridan, but he's stationed in the Dakotas."

"From what I've heard Bryce say, he's a bad officer and ought to be relieved of his command. Maybe they've sent him to the Dakotas to get him out of the way."

"Custer's not the issue. The promotion is. Dorrie says no one is getting them."

"Fortunately we don't have to worry about that."

"I think we do," Moriah said, looking directly at her sister. "If he doesn't leave soon, you're going to fall hopelessly in love with him."

It was useless to deny what Abby knew to be the truth, but there was no point in letting Moriah know it was already too late. "It wouldn't matter if I did fall in love with Bryce. I'm not what he's looking for in a wife."

"I'm not interested in him. It's you I'm worried about. I don't want you hurt."

"Bryce can't hurt me unless I let him. I'm not going to talk about him anymore. I'm so sleepy I can hardly keep my eyes open."

"You should have taken a nap."

"I left you alone too much as it was. Don't fret. I'll be fine as soon as I get a good night's sleep. Start thinking about when you want some time off."

"I don't need any time off. I'm your sister, Abby. You don't have to try to make up for every minute you're out of the store."

"I feel guilty leaving you alone so often."

"I don't like leaving the store. I'm comfortable here."

"Everyone says you're a brilliant saleswoman, better than Father ever was."

"That's nonsense," Moriah said, brushing the compliment aside. "I just happen to like what I do."

"As well as be very good at it." In her own quiet way, Moriah had learned more about the people at the fort than Abby. Some of the soldiers had even started asking her for advice. Moriah always declined, but that seemed only to encourage them. Abby wished her sister weren't so reclusive, but that was past praying for. She gave her a hug and a kiss. "Have I told you lately how much I love you? I couldn't have done this without you."

"You can do anything you set your mind to," Moriah said, her voice brusque. "You don't need me. And you don't need Colonel McGregor."

"Forget Bryce," Abby said, striving to keep the irritation from her voice. She picked up her lamp. "Now I'm going to bed for what I hope is a dreamless sleep. See you in the morning."

Sleep, however, was reluctant to fold Abby in its embrace. She knew she was in love with Bryce. She couldn't change that, so it didn't make sense to deny it. How was she to protect her heart when Bryce left?

Pamela's future worried her just as much. She fell asleep worrying about how she would be treated by a stepmother who might not love her and a grandmother who didn't understand her. She finally dreamed that Bryce's house had caught fire and there was no one to rescue Pamela. She was hanging out an upstairs window calling Abby's name.

"Abby! Abby! Wake up."

Abby fought her way to wakefulness to find Moriah bending over her. Abby must have called out in her dream and wakened her sister, but Moriah spoke before Abby could.

"The store's on fire!"

"No," Abby said, sitting up in bed, trying hard to clear the cobwebs of sleep from her mind. "I was just dreaming about a fire. I'm sorry I called out, but—"

"You're not dreaming," Moriah said, dragging her sister to her feet. "Smell the smoke."

Abby had waked enough to distinguish reality from her dream. The rank smell of smoke was very real. "The store!" she cried. "We've got to save the store or we'll be ruined."

Without stopping to put anything over her gown, Abby rushed from her bedroom into the parlor. She could see smoke coming from under the door. She unlocked the door and threw it open. Flames covered half the store. She could see piles of clothing burning, hear cans and bottles explode in the heat. She didn't know where to begin, but if she didn't do something soon, they'd lose the trading post and everything in it, including their living quarters.

"Grab anything you can to beat out the flames or smother them," Abby said to Moriah.

"You can't go in there. The fire's too hot."

"I have to, or we'll lose everything." Abby grabbed one of the heavy wool blankets folded neatly on a shelf behind the counter and began to beat the flames. It didn't take her long to realize she wasn't making any progress. It took her even less time to discover why. She smelled kerosene. Someone had soaked the merchandise with the extremely flammable fluid.

"We can't stop this by ourselves," Abby shouted to her sister. "Go for help."

"I can't leave you."

"Go!" Abby screamed.

Abby didn't know whether she sent Moriah for help because she thought they could save the store or because she didn't want her to see the destruction of their dream of independence. She attacked the fire with renewed fury, cursing the man who'd set it, hoping she found out who he was so she could have the pleasure of killing him herself.

She struggled on, oblivious to the smoke, the heat, and the danger. Only when she was on the verge of giving up did she hear someone pounding on the door and shouting for her to open it. A wall of flame separated her from the exit, but her only hope of saving the store was to open that door.

"Wake up, Daddy. There's a fire in Miss Abby's store."

"It's just a dream," Bryce said, dragged unwillingly from a deep sleep. He hadn't slept much the previous night and was dead tired.

"It's not a dream," Pamela insisted. "I can see it."

"It's probably just a light."

"I saw a man climb in the window. Then he climbed

263

out again. I saw him strike a match and throw it in the window. That's when I saw the fire."

Bryce was fully awake now. He threw back the covers and hurried to the window. Pulling back the curtain, he saw a bright light coming from the trading post.

"Run downstairs and wake Zeb. Tell him to get as many people as possible over to the store with buckets, wet blankets, shovels, axes, anything they can lay their hands on."

"What are you going to do?"

"I'm going to the store as soon as I can get some clothes on. Now hurry."

It seemed to Bryce his clothes had rebelled against him. Even putting on his pants seemed to require thought, whereas before he'd done it automatically. Finally he managed to shove his feet into his boots and snatch up a pair of gloves. As he raced across the parade ground for the second time in recent weeks, he decided he ought to include foot racing as part of the men's fitness regime. He arrived to find some men pounding on the door.

"Use your ax to break it down," he directed. "Break out the windows."

"That'll just make the fire burn hotter," one man said.

"That's a chance we'll have to take. We can't stop it standing out here."

Before anyone could lay an ax to the door, it opened and Abby stumbled out. Bryce managed to catch her before her body hit the ground.

"Is she dead?" somebody asked.

"Just fainted." He hoped he was right. The fire had singed her hair and eyebrows. Blisters covered her face, arms, and hands. If he hadn't known who she was, he might not have recognized her. "Put out that fire," he ordered as he picked Abby up and carried her away from the building.

He didn't need to stay to help. The men could do just as well without him. Someone had to take care of Abby.

Pamela was waiting at the door when he returned.

"Is she dead?" she asked, tears glistening in her eyes.

"No. She fainted. Run upstairs and turn back the bed."

"Is she going to stay with us?"

"For as long as it takes her to get well."

"Can I sit up with her?" Pamela asked, running ahead of her father.

"If she wants you to." Bryce had dreamed of holding Abby in his arms, but this price was too high.

"She doesn't look alive," Pamela said when he laid her on the bed.

Abby groaned.

"She is. Now go tell Zeb I want him immediately."

By the time Pamela returned with Zeb, who'd had the forethought to bring hot water and an emergency medical kit, Bryce had managed to get Abby into bed and under the covers. Though it wasn't cold, she was trembling from shock.

"Is she all right?" Zeb asked.

"I think so," Bryce said. "She seems to have nothing worse than some bad burns on her fingers."

"The fire burned her hair," Pamela pointed out.

"It'll grow back," Bryce said.

Abby tried to talk, but she couldn't choke out a word he could understand.

"Give me some water," Bryce said.

"I'll get it," Pamela said. She dashed from the room and came back seconds later, bringing the water from her own bedside table. Bryce poured some into a glass, which he handed to Pamela.

"Hold that while I sit her up."

Putting his arm around Abby, he lifted her into a sitting position, then took the glass from Pamela and held it to Abby's lips.

"Let me hold it," he said when she tried to take it from him. "You burned your fingers."

"Key," Abby managed to say after draining the contents of the glass. "I burned them on the key when I unlocked the door." Her voice rasped from the smoke she'd inhaled.

"Let me look at your hand," Bryce said.

Abby held out her hand for his inspection. The pads of two fingers and the thumb on her right hand were badly blistered. "The first thing to do is put some salve on the burns and bandage them," he said. It didn't take long, but Abby's reaction told him the burns were very painful. "Now you need to rest."

"I can't sleep until I know about the fire. Where is Moriah?"

"I'll send Zeb to look for her. I expect she'll be able to tell you how much damage the store suffered. Tell her to come prepared to stay here," Bryce told Zeb.

"Do you know how the fire started?" Bryce asked.

"No."

"Pamela saw a man throw a match inside. This is the second time someone has broken into the store. You and your sister are staying here until I find out who did it and can make sure it won't happen again. Don't argue. That's an order. Anyone who disobeys that order will be under arrest."

"Does that include me?" Abby asked.

"It most particularly includes you," Bryce said. "You're the one most likely to disobey it."

"You can't hold me here against my will."

"Stop being so stubborn and let me take care of you.

That's the least I can do after you took such good care of Pamela."

"I'll stay tonight, but that's all."

Bryce was certain smoke would make it impossible for her to return to the trading post for several days. "Good. Now I want you to tell me exactly what happened."

Abby didn't tell him anything he hadn't already guessed. At first he hadn't believed Spicer's break-in was connected with the attempts to stop delivery of the beef, but the fire changed that. Someone was trying to drive Abby and her sister from Fort Lookout.

She had finished by the time Moriah arrived.

"Thank goodness you're safe," Abby said. "What happened to the store?"

"The structure wasn't damaged much," Moriah said, "but we lost about half of the merchandise. Someone soaked everything with kerosene."

"I need to see what can be saved," Abby said.

"You can do that tomorrow," Bryce said. "Right now I want you sound asleep in fifteen minutes. There's nothing more you can do tonight. You can do your work much better tomorrow if you're rested."

"How can I rest knowing our store is half destroyed?"

"The same way I rest knowing my men will go into battle the next day. Now, are you going to sleep?"

"Yes, sir, Colonel, sir," Abby said. She executed a mock salute. "Anything you say, sir!"

Bryce repressed a smile. "Go to sleep before I decide to put you under lock and key. Come on, Pamela."

"Will Miss Abby and Miss Moriah be here in the morning?" Pamela asked when her father put her back in bed.

"If I have anything to say about it, they'll be here every morning for weeks and weeks."

Pamela broke into a huge smile. "Thank you, Daddy." She took her father's hand and held it to her cheek. "I love you very much."

"I love you, too," Bryce told his daughter.

"Do you love Miss Abby? Sarah's momma said if you married Abby, she would be my momma. Please, Daddy, marry Miss Abby."

Bryce had already decided that was what he wanted, but he wondered if Abby wanted to marry him.

Abby did her best to be optimistic, but seeing the virtual destruction of everything she'd worked so hard to achieve nearly caused her to burst into tears.

"It'll take a while for the smoke and kerosene fumes to clear," Bryce said. "You won't be able to work in there for a couple of days. That'll give the men time to clean up."

"I can't stand around doing nothing."

She hadn't slept well. Only Moriah's steady breathing had kept her from getting up and pacing the room. She felt caged, unable to do anything to fix her situation. She knew it was pointless to attempt to do anything before daylight, but thoughts of ruin kept her too on edge to sleep. She'd barely managed to restrain herself long enough to choke down some breakfast, yet viewing the mess that had once been her store made her wonder why she'd bothered.

"There's plenty to do," Bryce said. "You can start with an inventory of what was in the store and make up orders to replace everything. When you get back in the store, you can cross off anything that can be salvaged."

"Where am I going to find the money to pay for it?"

"Credit," Bryce said.

Bryce's complacent attitude was about to drive her into a screaming fit. Having something to occupy her mind wasn't enough. She wanted to know who had done this. She wanted someone she could punish.

"You can't stay here for a while," Bryce said. "Why don't you and your sister pack what you'll need for a few days?"

"That part of the post isn't damaged," Abby pointed out.

"Collier says the whole place reeks of smoke. It won't be safe to breathe the air for several days."

Abby didn't want to agree with Bryce. She wanted to strike out at someone, anyone, to work off some of her frustration. She was so angry she forgot the pain in her fingers. Moriah had broken the blisters and put fresh salve and bandages on them this morning. She'd covered her head in a cap to hide her burned hair, but she couldn't hide her singed eyebrows and eyelashes, or the red spots where heat had burned her face, shoulders, and arms.

"Come on, Moriah," Abby said, turning her back on the store. "I can't stand looking at it when I can't do anything to fix it. Let's get what we need and go back to Bryce's house."

"Zeb will be glad to help you," Bryce said.

"I will, too," Pamela said, beaming. "I want you to stay forever."

"Thank you," Abby said, trying to smile, "but it won't be necessary. I know what I have to do to salvage the situation. I'll use the money from the beef sales to pay for repairs to the store."

"You don't have anyone scheduled to deliver beef this month," Bryce reminded her.

"I know. That's why tomorrow I'm going to start going from ranch to ranch until I talk someone into agreeing to sell me the beef I need."

"You can't do that," Bryce said. "I forbid it."

Chapter Twenty

Abby could hardly believe what Bryce had said even though she had heard the words herself. Maybe he'd let being in control of two hundred men and their families go to his head, but he'd soon learn he had no authority over her. Maybe it was her fault for letting him become so involved in her life, for spending too many nights under his roof, but this was one of the reasons she had no intention of marrying. Aunt Emma had warned Abby and Moriah to be wary of controlling men. And who would be more controlling than a man whose job was to control everyone around him, a man for whom control had probably become so habitual he wasn't even aware of it? By now he probably considered it his God-given right.

She would set him right on that score. He had the authority to take away her contract to operate a trading post at Fort Lookout, but he didn't have the authority to control her actions as an individual citizen. If she wanted to ride all the way to Denver by herself, he couldn't stop her.

"You can't forbid me to do anything as long as I don't do it on government property. And not one single rancher lives at the fort."

"You're not strong enough to make that kind of ride," Bryce said. "You've worn yourself down working and worrying about the store. Now you've got blisters on your fingers and burns on your arms and face. You can't even hold reins in your hands, and you're talking about riding hundreds of miles and spending several nights in a tent. Assuming you had the strength, you don't have a tent or any of the equipment you'd need to cook your meals."

Abby's anger cooled considerably. He was worried about her safety rather than trying to exercise his authority.

"I don't plan to ride out this afternoon," she said, "but I can't wait long. I need the money to pay for rebuilding the store. That doesn't begin to touch what it will cost to stock it."

"The trading post is army property," Bryce said. "We'll take care of the repairs, just as we did cleaning it up and building new shelves."

She felt stupid not knowing that, but it was an enormous relief to know she only had to come up with the money to replace the ruined merchandise. "That doesn't change the fact that I have no money."

"We can talk about that when you're feeling better," Bryce said. "I have to work. I'll see you when you get to the house."

"Can I help you pack?" Pamela asked.

"Sure," Abby said. "With my hand bandaged like this, I need all the help I can get." Abby had hoped she would

271

find the fumes and smoke weren't as strong as Bryce said, but they were worse. She could hardly keep from coughing. "We'd better grab a few things and run," she said to Pamela.

"I want you to take everything," Pamela said. "I want you to stay in our house forever."

That was the last thing Abby needed to hear. Despite her determination to remain single, and despite her periodic irritation at Bryce's high-handed manner, it was a great temptation. She could repeat to herself all the reasons she had for not marrying, but she would always come up with reasons why they didn't apply to Bryce. What ultimately stopped her was his decision to wait until he got back East to look for a bride.

"I can't stay in your father's house forever," Abby told Pamela.

"Why not?"

"It's not my house. This is."

"It's burned," Pamela pointed out. "It stinks, too."

"I know, but it won't after it's fixed."

"Don't you *want* to stay with us?"

That was a much harder question to answer. "I like you very much," Abby said, choosing her words carefully, "but grown ladies can't live in a man's house unless they get married first."

"I'll ask Daddy to marry you," Pamela said, breaking into a smile and clapping her hands together. "That will make everything all right."

"You can't ask your father such a thing," Abby exclaimed, aghast.

"Why not? Daddy likes you. He told me so."

"Liking someone and wanting to marry them are two different things."

"Sarah's momma says if a man likes a lady, he ought to ask her to marry him."

Abby decided it would be a good idea for Bryce to forbid Pamela to ever again set foot in Sarah's house. "Sarah's mother is talking about a different kind of like. Your father likes me as a friend, the way you like Sarah. It's not the same as when a man and woman like each other and want to get married. Your daddy and I are just friends."

"Sarah's momma said if you married Daddy you'd be my momma."

"That's true, but—"

"Sarah's momma said it was very important for any woman who married Daddy to like me. Don't you like me?"

"Of course I do."

"If you like Daddy and you like me, why don't you want to be my momma?"

Abby could feel the ground sinking under her feet. She was certain Pamela would repeat the whole conversation to Bryce. She was also certain she would get some very important parts wrong, or leave them out, and Bryce would have no idea what Abby had really said.

"I don't know how to explain it to you, but even though I like you and your daddy very much, I can't marry him and be your mother. People have to love each other to want to get married. That's a very special kind of like that can only happen between a man and a woman."

"But I love you."

From bad to worse. Abby wondered why she'd ever thought she could be a mother when she couldn't explain something so ordinary as love to a child. She had to give Bryce a lot of credit for being able to handle situations like this. If he didn't send Pamela over to Sarah's mother for another indoctrination session, that is.

"I love you, too," Abby said, "but that's not the same as a man and a woman loving each other and wanting to get married. Now no more questions. I need to pack quickly."

Abby kept Pamela's attention engaged by asking her what clothes she thought Abby ought to take, but she couldn't derail her own thoughts so easily. Pamela's questions had raised the lid of a Pandora's box. Now that the questions had been voiced, Abby couldn't ignore the answers.

Yes, she did want to be Pamela's mother. Yes, she did want to marry Bryce. Yes, she did want to move into his house.

But admitting she'd fallen in love with Bryce didn't change any of the hard realities. He didn't love her and he didn't want to marry her. The sooner he went back East, the better.

"You asked Abby what?" Bryce tried to speak calmly to his daughter, but he was afraid it came out as a shout.

"I asked her if she'd marry you and be my momma, but she said you didn't love her. I love Miss Abby. Why don't you?"

"Your loving Abby and wanting her to be your mother is not the same as my loving Abby and wanting her to marry me."

"That's what she said, but I don't understand."

The question flummoxed Bryce. What his daughter didn't understand was that it didn't matter what he felt for Abby. She didn't love him and she didn't want to marry him. He had to put a stop to Pamela's imaginings. He was deeply sorry Pamela had grown to love a woman who didn't want to be her mother. He was just as sorry Abby didn't feel anything more than a physical attraction for him.

"I'm not sure I can explain it so you'll understand it, either," Bryce said. "Abby and her sister are going to stay here and run the store in the trading post. You and I will soon move to Philadelphia."

"I don't want to go to Philadelphia. I want to stay here. Don't you like it here?"

Yes, he did. More than he had expected. He'd taken for granted that he wanted to go back to Philadelphia and Washington, D.C., because that was the natural way to pursue the career he'd envisioned for himself. But recently he'd begun to realize it was his family's dream, not his. Though he found the situation on the frontier frustrating, he also found it challenging. He liked being his own boss. He preferred being active to sitting behind a desk. And though the plains couldn't compare to the beauty of the Pennsylvania woodlands, Pennsylvania had nothing to compare to the majesty of the Rocky Mountains.

Since Margaret's death, his family had been telling him he had to marry again because he needed a wife to help in his career and to be a mother to Pamela. But recently he'd realized he wasn't anxious to leave Fort Lookout. That feeling had grown stronger after Abby arrived.

"I do like it here," Bryce told his daughter, "but I have to go where the army sends me."

"Are they sending you to Philadelphia?"

Blaming everything on the army would probably satisfy Pamela, but Bryce didn't make a practice of lying to anyone. He certainly wasn't going to begin with his daughter.

"No, but Grandmother has been trying to get the army to give me a job back East."

"Will she stop if you tell her you don't want to go there?"

He doubted it. His mother had always believed she knew what was best for everyone. A desire to rebel against his mother's control had been part of the reason he'd married Margaret. He wasn't foolish enough to do that again, but neither would he ask his mother's approval before he chose a wife.

"Grandmother wants us back East so she can see you more often."

"If she comes here, she can see me all the time."

Bryce smiled at the notion of his mother living at Fort Lookout. "Grandmother wouldn't want to leave Granddaddy and all your uncles, aunts, and cousins. And they couldn't all come out here," Bryce said, answering what he was certain would be his daughter's next question.

"Miss Abby said she would stay with us until her house stopped stinking. Can you make it stink for a very long time?"

Bryce picked up his daughter and sat her on his lap. "You can't make Miss Abby stay with us."

"Sarah's momma said if you married Miss Abby, she would have to live in our house forever. Please, will you marry her?"

"Miss Abby doesn't love me."

"Miss Abby said everyone at the fort loves you."

"Miss Abby means they don't want a new commander. That's not the same as Abby loving me enough to marry me."

"If I loved her enough, would she marry you?"

The look on his daughter's face was enough to break Bryce's heart. The one thing she wanted more than anything else in the world and he couldn't give it to her. "It's not enough for you to love Abby. She would have to love me, and I would have to love her."

"Do you love her?"

"No." He was telling the truth, wasn't he? He liked her a lot, wanted to be with her, dreamed of making love to her, but that wasn't love, was it? It wasn't the crazy kind of passion he'd felt for Margaret. Falling in love with her had been like being in a daze and discovering after it wore off that he didn't feel the way he'd thought.

"Why not?" Pamela asked.

"There's not always a reason. It just happens. Or it doesn't. You can't make yourself fall in love."

But could you stop yourself from falling in love? Did lining up all the reasons why you shouldn't love someone make any real difference in the end? Knowing why he should keep his feelings for Abby under tight control hadn't stopped them from growing stronger. Was it true love this time, or was he doing what he'd done with Margaret? If Abby ever decided to marry, she'd make a good wife and mother, but what about him? Would his feelings for his wife remain constant, grow stronger? He couldn't say. He'd failed in his one attempt.

But he wanted another chance, and he meant to have it even it if entailed changing his plans.

"You don't have to go with me," Abby said for the two dozenth time. "I can take Orman and the boys with me."

"No." His refusal was blunt and clearly not up for discussion.

After Orman, Hobie, and Larson had sobered up, they'd been so apologetic about trying to attack Abby and her sister, Abby had felt guilty about keeping them in prison. She'd convinced Bryce to let them out each day to work for her, but Bryce would never let them be alone with her without at least one soldier present to guard her.

"Any one of your soldiers would do just as well," Abby said.

"I like to believe I'm more capable than an ordinary soldier," Bryce said. "Besides, things are so quiet nobody will notice I'm gone."

Abby's efforts to convince Bryce to let one of the enlisted men accompany her on her trip were rooted in her fear of being alone with him for more than a few minutes. Thinking of being alone with him for several days was causing her to break out in a cold sweat.

"Daddy's the bravest man in the whole fort," Pamela said. "Don't you want him to protect you?"

"You must learn not to put people on the spot by asking them personal questions," Bryce told his daughter. "I want to talk to the ranchers, too," he said to Abby. "I'd like to know who's causing trouble with the Indians. I might even send a small patrol out to do some reconnaissance."

"That means he's going to spy on people," Pamela helpfully informed Abby. "I wish I could go. I've always wanted to be a spy."

"I would prefer you not tell people I'm spying on them," Bryce said to his daughter. "I'm collecting information, trying to find out what people are saying, what they're doing, how they're feeling."

Abby didn't know who was putting pressure on the ranchers. Hinson needed the beef deliveries if he was to keep his job. Baucom had told her he didn't want the contract, so why weren't the ranchers willing to sell to her?

"I don't have no steers to sell," the rancher said, making no attempt to hide his contempt. "I don't want no dealings with no woman."

"This is a business arrangement, Mr. Oliver," Abby said. "It shouldn't matter to you that I'm a woman."

"Don't be a damned fool," Oliver replied. "Of course it matters."

"Don't call Miss Pierce a fool," Bryce said.

"I'll speak any way I please," Oliver said.

"Then you'll spend the next month in my jail."

"You can't do that," the man blustered. "I'm an honest citizen. The army's supposed to protect me."

"The army's supposed to protect Miss Pierce, too."

"I ain't done nothing wrong."

"What about the hides of stolen beef buried in the sand by your creek?"

"You won't find any such thing on my place."

"I can by morning," Bryce said with a pleasant smile, "even the body of a man you murdered for his money."

Oliver, clearly furious Bryce would threaten him with crimes he hadn't committed, might not believe Bryce could produce cowhides and a body that didn't exist, but he was reluctant to test that opinion.

"I ain't selling nothing to no woman," he said. "She should be home taking care of her husband and having babies. Business is a man's job."

"I've got no beef to sell," Mr. Bright said.

"We saw steers as we rode in," Abby said.

"Sure, I got steers, but I don't have any to sell."

"The government needs to keep its promise to supply the Indians with food as long as they stay on the reservation," Bryce said. "Miss Pierce holds the contract."

"I know who she is, and I know what she wants the beef for, but I'm not selling."

"Why not?" Abby asked.

"There's been threats," Bright said.

"From whom?" Bryce asked.

"Don't rightly know, and I don't want to find out."

"You don't have to cave in to threats," Bryce said.

"Who's going to protect me and my family if they're real?"

"You should speak to the sheriff in Boulder Gap, but the army will protect you if necessary."

"You going to sit up at night to see nobody shoots through a lighted window? You going to station troops in every ravine and behind every tree to see nobody tries to dry gulch me when I'm away from the house?"

"You've got to stay to supper," Elma Carr said to Abby. "You can't eat sitting out there in the dust."

"I don't want to impose," Abby said. "I just wanted to ask your husband about selling me some beef."

Mrs. Carr averted her gaze. "He'll be in for supper. Since you have to wait, you might as well join us. He'll want to talk to the colonel. He's been some worried about Indians attacking our cows."

Abby didn't make any comment. This was the seventh ranch they'd visited in three days. It was also the seventh time they'd heard about trouble with the Indians leaving the reservation. Nothing really serious, just a butchered steer and some tense encounters, not enough to call out the army. But since the army had so obligingly come to call, the ranchers were ready to pour their troubles into Bryce's ear.

Bryce had fulfilled his promise to accompany Abby with a small patrol under Lieutenant Collier. Abby had yet to spend the night in the tent Bryce had brought for her, but she was determined to refuse if Mrs. Carr offered her a bed for the night. The ranch house was much too small to accommodate guests. She wasn't even certain Mr. Carr had enough beef to sell. She wouldn't have stopped once she saw how small the house was, but Bryce wanted to talk to every rancher. He didn't need to know what they had to say. He'd heard it already. He said it was more important to assure them that he didn't believe there was any real danger.

Abby could tell Mrs. Carr craved female company. She had five children—all boys who helped their father run the ranch. Despite her protests, Abby helped Mrs. Carr get the meal on the table.

"You've got more than enough to do taking care of six men without having two guests drop in on you unexpectedly," Abby told her.

"It's a lot easier with two sets of hands," Mrs. Carr admitted when they had put the last of the food on the table.

"You ought to get one of those boys to help you," Abby said, surveying the five sturdy young men who settled down at the table with their father.

"Doing woman's work would shame them," Mrs. Carr said.

"Men cook at the other ranches. I've seen them."

"It's all right when there's no woman about."

Abby shouldn't have been surprised. Men where just the same in St. Louis.

"Dig in," Mr. Carr said to Abby and Bryce once they'd said the blessing. "If you don't watch out, these boys will eat it up from under you." He spoke with a good deal of pride. Abby thought it must be nice for a man to have so many fine sons, but it had to be lonely for a woman without any daughters. And that didn't begin to touch on the amount of work she had to do. Abby made a mental note never to marry a rancher.

There wasn't much talk at first. It seemed eating was serious business for the Carr men. Abby was sure they were on their best behavior, but that didn't stop them from reaching for what they wanted even if it was halfway down the table. In what seemed like a remarkably short time, the bowls and platters were all empty, the apple pie had vanished down seven throats, and there was nothing to do but settle back over hot, black coffee.

"Let me help you clean up," Abby said to Mrs. Carr.

"I appreciate the offer, but you've helped enough already," Mrs. Carr said. "You sit right here and enjoy your coffee."

Abby was tired. It had been a long and disappointing day. Besides, she wanted a chance to convince Mr. Carr to sell his beef to her.

"I supposed you're here wanting beef for your Indians," Carr said to Abby after he'd taken several swallows from his cup.

"Yes," Abby said. "As you know—"

"I don't have enough steers to sell you fifty head," he said, "but I wouldn't if I did. I won't do nothing to help those Indians."

"The government has promised to feed them as long as they stay on the reservation," Bryce said. "Now that we've taken away their land and killed the buffalo so cattle can have the grass, they have no way to provide for themselves."

"Yeah, they do," Carr said. "They got stealing from ranchers and settlers. And when they can't do it without nobody seeing them, they don't mind killing."

"Have any of your cows been stolen or any of your boys been hurt?" Bryce asked.

"Can't tell about the cows until roundup," Carr said, "but they daren't touch one of my boys. They know they'd have the whole bunch of us down on 'em in a flash."

Abby didn't imagine a large group of Indians would be afraid of six men.

"The army ought to be protecting ranchers and farmers," Carr said to Bryce, "not them damned redskins."

"I'm trying to protect everyone," Bryce said. "The

United States Government doesn't want anybody killed."

"Then get rid of them redskins," Carr said.

Around the room Abby saw affirming looks on the faces of the five boys. Mrs. Carr's thoughts weren't so easy to read, but Abby was sure she'd want to be rid of anyone who would threaten her family. What mother could feel otherwise?

"The government has given them land of their own," Bryce said. "They have just as much right as you to live peacefully and support their families."

"I'm telling you, they're not living peaceful," Carr said, banging his clenched fist on the table for emphasis. "They're out there raping and killing and stealing just like they always did. They're savages. This country won't be safe for decent people until they're got rid of."

Abby could barely control her disgust and anger. Indians had raped, killed, and stolen in the past, but so had white men. Even then she couldn't understand anyone's desire to exterminate a whole race of people. She was glad Carr didn't have enough steers to sell. She wasn't sure she could have forced herself to take them.

"Did you get rain from the thunderstorm?" Bryce asked to change the subject.

Abby was grateful they'd been able to reach the Carr ranch when they saw the storm approaching. It looked like it could be just as violent as the one that had stranded them in the cottonwood grove.

"Damned storm passed right by us," Carr said. "We didn't get a drop, and I could sure use it. I'll never get used to clouds dumping water in one canyon and skipping another. It was never like that back in Ohio. Carson, across the ridge, nearly had his bunkhouse washed away last spring. I warned him about building too close to a creek, but he wouldn't listen. Damn fool Yankees think they know everything."

Abby forced herself to listen with feigned interest to Bryce and Carr discuss grazing conditions. She was relieved when Bryce said it was time to leave.

"I hope you don't mind if my men set up camp on the creek about a mile from here," he said to Carr.

"Glad to have you. Maybe it will convince those murdering savages to rob somebody else."

"You can't spend the night in an army camp," Mrs. Carr said to Abby. "You'll have to stay with us."

"Thank you, but giving us supper was more than generous," Abby said. "The colonel has brought a tent for me. I'll be perfectly fine."

"The boys can sleep outside," Mr. Carr said. "The ground won't hurt them none."

Abby was certain it wouldn't, but she doubted they'd appreciate being moved out of their beds.

"Thank you, but there's no reason for anyone to sleep on the ground when I already have a bed."

It didn't take them long to say their good-byes and ride toward the place Bryce had chosen for the camp. Abby hoped Lieutenant Collier had had time to get everything set up. She'd spent a lot of time in the saddle during these last three days, and exhaustion had finally caught up with her. Every part of her body ached. She would have loved to be able to soak in a long, hot bath, but she'd have to wait until she returned to the fort. In the meantime she hoped the camp bed was soft. The bed she'd slept in last night had smelled of unwashed bodies and was as hard as any plot of ground the Carr boys might have had to sleep on.

Abby began to grow uneasy when they found no camp. "Maybe Lieutenant Collier decided to camp somewhere else."

"If he did, he'll send someone to show us where to go."

That turned out to be the case. The creek that left Mr. Carr's canyon joined with the that of his neighbor about a mile from the ranch house. The rainstorm had caused the creek to leave its banks.

"It flooded the whole camp just after we'd set up," the soldier told Bryce. "We came damned near to losing all the equipment and half the packhorses."

"Watch your language," Bryce warned. "A lady is present."

"Sorry, ma'am," the soldier said, flushing red and looking very much like the teenager he probably was, "but it came up so fast it scared me half to death. First there was nothing but some rain up in those hills. Next thing I knew, there's a wall of water three feet high coming straight at us out of that canyon faster than a horse can run. I nearly embarrassed myself."

"Soldier!" Bryce barked.

"Sorry, ma'am," he said, turning redder than ever.

"Don't apologize," Abby said, trying not to laugh. "I got caught in a flood recently myself. I know exactly how you felt."

The soldier looked relieved, but Bryce ordered him to stop talking and show the way to the new camp. It wasn't far, but Abby was glad to see it was on high ground well away from the creek. She'd heard too much about floods lately.

"I understand you had a little excitement this afternoon," Bryce said to Lieutenant Collier when they reached camp.

"You could say that," the young man said. He looked harassed.

"Did you lose anything?"

"None of the animals, though I don't know how one mule survived. I guess he's too mean to die."

"I hope he wasn't carrying any important equipment."

"That's just it. He was carrying Miss Pierce's tent. It got washed away. The only tent left is yours."

Chapter Twenty-one

Abby looked at Bryce, and he looked at her. Then they both turned to the Lieutenant.

"You brought only two tents?" Bryce asked.

"We brought six, but the others got washed away, too. We can look for them tomorrow once the floodwaters recede, but we've got only the one for tonight."

Abby didn't know what to do. It seemed selfish to have a tent to herself when the men had to sleep outside on the ground. Yet she knew she wouldn't get a wink of sleep if she slept outside. Just knowing she was within reach of any wild animal that ventured by would keep her awake.

"Miss Pierce ought to stay at the ranch house," Collier said.

"I'll take her back now," Bryce said.

"They have only two bedrooms," Abby said. "All those boys will have to sleep outside, and it might rain again."

"You could ride back to the fort," Collier suggested.

Abby looked toward Bryce.

"We couldn't reach it until nearly midnight. It would take us half of tomorrow just to get back to where we are now."

"If the men can sleep out, so can I," Abby said.

"You'll have my tent," Bryce said.

"Where will you sleep?"

"With the men."

"It's my fault you're out here in the first place," Abby said. "I should be the one to sleep out."

"I apologize for pulling rank, but I'm the commander. I decide who will do what."

"You can't order me around. I'm a civilian."

"As long as you're part of an army operation, you're as much under my command as these men."

Abby had always believed marriage put women too much under the power of men. She hadn't realized military rules were even more confining.

"If you give me a couple of men, I could go back to the fort," she said.

"The troop isn't large enough to split."

Bryce had blocked her at every turn.

"I'll agree to sleep in the tent if you will, too," Abby said to Bryce.

"It would ruin your reputation," Bryce said.

"I can't believe even a libertine would attack a woman with ten soldiers only yards away."

Bryce's smile appeared to be trying to break through. "You do like getting your own way, don't you?"

"Doesn't everyone?"

"I expect so, but I've never met anyone who made it a crusade."

"I'm just doing what I must to earn a living."

"Your *earning a living* has kept me busier than the Indians or the rustlers combined."

"I didn't ask you to follow me everywhere I went."

"No, but since you won't take my advice about where not to go and what not to do, I'm forced to do what I can to protect you. Do we have a cot for Miss Pierce?" Bryce asked Collier.

"Yes."

"I don't need a cot," Abby said

"The ground is still wet from the rain," Bryce pointed out.

"Then you'll get wet," she said to Bryce.

"I'll spread my rain slicker on the ground."

She'd forgotten he carried a rain slicker in his saddlebags.

Abby was uncomfortable for the rest of the evening. She had nothing to do but watch while the soldiers put up the one tent. Bryce insisted it be set up a little distance from the rest of the troops to give her privacy. He wanted to set up a watch, but Abby refused to be responsible for any soldiers being dragged from their beds in the middle of the night. She said if Bryce couldn't protect her while sleeping in the same tent, the fort needed a new commander.

Getting ready for bed would be easy. She would sleep in her chemise. The storm had turned the creek muddy, so there was no place to wash her face or brush her teeth. Her preparations devolved to removing her shoes and brushing her hair.

"Is that cot comfortable enough for you?" Bryce asked from the opened flap. He hadn't set foot inside the tent.

The canvas cot felt as hard as a rock. "It's fine."

"You'll need a blanket. It can get very cold at night, especially after a rain."

"Do the men have enough blankets?"

"I'm sure they do."

Bryce probably assumed the men could sleep with

nothing over them while she needed several blankets to keep warm. She felt guilty enough already without knowing she had deprived anyone of his blanket. "I'd like to see for myself."

"You don't trust me?"

"I believe you're generally truthful, but I'm sure there are times when you give me the answer you think I ought to have rather than the one that is strictly accurate."

Bryce smiled. "In other words, you don't trust me."

"Not entirely." She turned to Lieutenant Collier. "Do all of the men have blankets?"

"Yes, ma'am."

"Do they have enough to keep them warm?"

"Yes, ma'am."

"There's no use trying to fool her," Bryce said to the lieutenant. "She's going to find out anyway. I expect the only blanket any man has is his saddle cloth. They'll use their saddles for pillows and their rain slickers to keep warm."

"Is that so?" she asked the lieutenant.

"No, ma'am." He looked pleased with himself. "I instructed the men to bring their bedrolls. Having a tent overhead won't keep a man dry, but his bedroll will."

"Good thinking," Bryce told the young lieutenant. "I knew there was a reason I picked you to lead the patrol."

"You picked me because all the other officers have wives," Collier said with a cheeky grin. "They don't like it when he sends their husbands out unless there's real trouble," he explained to Abby. "That's why lowly officers like me get these details." He suddenly looked embarrassed at something. Bryce laughed.

"And here I was thinking your smooth tongue would make you a general before you turned thirty," Bryce said.

"What's wrong?" Abby asked.

"Just an army joke," Bryce said. "You'd better make sure your men have taken advantage of your excellent planning," Bryce said to the lieutenant, who quickly took his leave.

"He said something he shouldn't, didn't he?" Abby asked.

"It was nothing important. It's time for bed."

Abby wasn't ready to go to bed just yet. She was too anxious about sharing the tent with Bryce. That didn't make any sense because she was certain he wouldn't so much as touch her hand without her consent. Maybe she was agitated because of what she *wanted* him to do.

Until she'd arrived at Fort Lookout, she'd behaved in a circumspect manner her entire life. Neither her thoughts nor her body had betrayed her. Now she wanted what she couldn't have, what she shouldn't want.

Why was she having such a difficult time over a man who didn't want to be involved with her any more than she wanted to be involved with him? But that was the problem: She *did* want to be involved him, and she believed he wanted to be involved with her.

"I'm too restless to go to bed yet," she said to Bryce. "I'll take a short walk."

"You can't go by yourself."

"With this much moonlight, it's practically like day."

"Nevertheless, you can never tell what kind of danger might lurk in the shadows."

"Maybe one of the soldiers wouldn't mind going with me."

"I'll go," Bryce said.

"You're the commander. Your duty is to the men."

"Lieutenant Collier is in charge of the men. I have no responsibility at the moment other than to make sure you're safe."

"I thought you were always responsible for your men."

"I'm the commander. I can make my own rules."

"What would General Sheridan think if he heard that?"

"He'd probably ask why I hadn't sent you back to St. Louis yet."

"I'd tell him I refused to go."

"Not one refuses General Sheridan, not even stubborn civilian women."

"Then I'm glad you're here instead of him." That came out sounding like something she didn't intend to say.

"So am I."

She refused to let herself think of what he might mean by that. He might be strongly attracted to her, but he intended to go back East to look for a wife. There was no middle ground there.

"When I first got here, I couldn't understand why people wanted to move out here," she said as she started walking away from the camp. "It seemed too hot or cold, too wet or dry, and filled with hostile Indians."

"And what have you decided?" Bryce asked, falling into step with her.

"That most of them came for the wrong reasons. They want land, space, freedom, but they wanted it to be like it was back East. By concentrating on how it differs from back East, they miss the challenges that excite people brave enough to try hard things, new things."

"It's a harsh land," Bryce said, "but it has a majesty, a grandeur unmatched in the East. Seeing the snow-capped mountains in winter is worth the hot, dry summers."

"You don't sound like a man who can't wait to go back East."

"I just appreciate what the West has to offer. The mountains are not only beautiful in the winter, they're cool and inviting in the summer. You've never tasted water until you've drunk from a sparkling mountain stream or eaten fresh fish until you've tasted trout pulled from the water and put straight into the pan. In the spring the prairie is an endless, waving ocean of grass and flowers. What I find most extraordinary is the sense of limitless space. You can see for miles in all directions. In the mountains you can see peaks stretching far into the distance. At night the sky is endless, the canopy of stars beyond counting. Here, look up now. Have you ever seen anything like that before?"

"I never paid much attention to the sky before."

"I guess people in cities don't. Their minds are as rigidly confined as their bodies."

"Do you like it here?" she asked.

"I was sure I wouldn't when I received my assignment, but I've grown to like it very much."

Much to her surprise, she had, too. She wondered what Moriah would think of that.

They'd walked well away from the camp by now. Beyond them the swollen creek carried its burden of silt and debris to unknown destinations. She wondered whether Lieutenant Collier would ever find the other tents. She shivered.

"Are you cold?"

"A little." She thought it was more nerves than the temperature.

"Let me give you my coat."

"No. You'd be cold and I'd be hot."

"Then I'll put my arm around you."

Not giving her an opportunity to object, he stepped behind her, leaned her back against him, and closed his arms around her. She felt engulfed. "Is that better?"

Not trusting her voice, she nodded.

Why was this happening to her? She didn't trust men. She didn't want to get married. She didn't want to be controlled by anyone. She wanted to build her own life, to be independent. She had come West to escape men, not to find one.

Well, she *hadn't* found one, because Bryce didn't want her the way she wanted him.

"There's something about looking at the sky at night that has a way of making your troubles seem awfully small," Bryce said.

"Mine seem gigantic."

"That's because you're too close to them. When I look at the sky and see how enormous it is, I realize my part of the world is so small as to be insignificant. That makes my problems feel small, too."

If staring at the sky could do that for Abby, she vowed she'd build an observation deck on the store. Moriah would think she was nuts, but anything for peace of mind.

"Maybe when I get my life as well ordered as yours, my problems won't seem so big."

Bryce turned her around in the circle of his arms. "You don't have to worry. I'll take care of you."

It was hard to think with her body pressed against his. She could feel the hard power of his thighs, the warmth of his embrace, the comfort of his arms. She could also feel the heat pouring from his body into hers. It took all her concentration to keep her mind on what he was saying. She didn't like feeling she was facing her problems alone, but she didn't expect Bryce to solve them for her. He wouldn't always be here. She had to learn to stand on her own two feet.

"Thank you for the offer, but the store is the way I will support myself, so it's my responsibility."

"Don't get your back up. I just want you to know I'll be here if you need help."

"That's not what *take care of you* means where I come from."

"What does in mean in St. Louis?"

Abby was having difficulty understanding just how Bryce saw his relationship with women. She had been born into a rigid social structure where the lines of acceptable behavior were clearly drawn. A man's relationship with a woman was intended to lead to marriage or he kept his distance. Friendship could exist between men and women who'd grown up together, but it faded after marriage. Except for a kiss on the hand or possibly a welcoming kiss on the cheek, physical contact was not allowed. Apparently society people behaved differently.

He didn't appear to be any more than moderately attracted to her, but her physical attraction to him was almost too strong for her to control. She had never considered making love to any man except her husband, yet she'd thought about making love to Bryce. And it petrified her.

"Where I come from it means you're in love and you want to get married," she said.

Bryce looked taken aback. "That's quite a mouthful."

"Which is why people don't say it unless they mean it." It was obvious from his alarm that he hadn't meant his words that way. "We'd better get back before Lieutenant Collier sends a search party for us."

"He knows I won't get lost."

"Tomorrow will be another long day. I'm tired. I'm not used to riding so much." She started back without waiting for him. She would have enough trouble sleeping in the same tent with him. The situation wouldn't be made easier if she let him kiss her. She shouldn't have let him hold her. She could still feel his arms around her. She would probably feel them all night.

"I'll let you get ready first," Bryce said.

Abby ducked inside the tent. She felt uneasy yet excited. And she didn't feel the least bit cold. Rather, she felt too warm.

It's knowing you're going to be sleeping in the same tent as Bryce.

Why had she done it? Could it be just that she felt guilty for taking Bryce's tent? She couldn't be sure, but some impulse had caused her to refuse to drive Bryce from his tent. She was stuck with that decision now, so there was no point thinking about it anymore. She took off her dress, folded it up, and lay down on the cot. It felt as hard as the ground. She turned over to get more comfortable and ended up on the ground.

"Are you all right?" Bryce asked. Apparently he hadn't gone far.

"I just fell out of the cot," she said, half laughing, half angry with herself.

"Be careful to stay in the middle when you turn over."

How could she do that when she was asleep? She set the cot up and got back in, but turning over nearly dumped her on the ground again. She'd never survive the night. She folded the cot and spread her blanket on the ground. It was a little hard, but not uncomfortable. It would be better to put up with the discomfort for one night than worry all night about falling.

"You can come in," she called to Bryce.

"Why aren't you using the cot?" Bryce asked when he entered.

"Because I feel safer on the ground. You can use it."

"Not if you sleep on the ground."

"There's no reason for both of us to sleep on the ground."

"If my commander ever found out I slept on a cot while a lady slept on the ground, I'd lose my rank."

"Even though it's my choice?"

"Even then."

"That's stupid."

"Probably, but that's the way things work. Do you have enough blankets?"

"Stop worrying about me and go to sleep."

Abby was acutely aware of every sound Bryce made. She couldn't see anything after he closed the flap, but he was so close she could reach out and touch him if she wanted. She *wanted*, but she wouldn't let herself. She kept reminding herself that she'd decided the love and passion she felt weren't enough. There had to be love and passion and commitment on his part, but that wasn't going to happen so it was more than past time she stopped thinking about making love with him.

But she couldn't stop with him only inches away. Somehow in the dark, the future she tried so hard not to think about seemed possible. Here in this tent, in the dark, miles away from all the problems that beset their lives, she felt free of restraint. Something about being around Bryce made her feel that wasn't all bad. In the back of her head an insidious little voice kept whispering that her life would be better than ever if she would only give in and let Bryce make love to her.

"Are you asleep?"

Abby knew she should remain quiet. Bryce couldn't have anything new to tell her. Still, she couldn't pretend sleep. She had to know what he wanted to say.

Bryce knew she hadn't had time to fall asleep. Her breathing was still too rapid, too heavy. He shouldn't have waited until now to talk to her, but they hadn't had any time alone since they'd left the fort.

And all that time he'd been thinking. He'd thought

about Abby. And himself. And Pamela. He'd thought of his future, the plans he'd made, the expectations of his family, of the army. Yesterday he'd realized what he wanted had changed without his being aware of it, and Abby was the reason. It had taken him the best part of a day to work out what the changes meant. Now he thought he knew.

"I'm still awake," Abby said.

The tension in Bryce's body eased. He'd crossed the first hurdle, but he wasn't sure where to start.

"We got off on the wrong foot in the beginning, didn't we?"

"I wouldn't say that. I wanted to make my store a success. You didn't want trouble to keep you from being posted back East. We soon realized all we had to do was work together."

"I came to realize more than that."

She wasn't going to make this easy. He was certain she liked him. He felt it every time she made an extra effort to stay away from him. He felt it when she was willing to sleep in a smoky trading post rather than spend a few more nights in his house. He felt it every time she looked at him, then turned away.

"You can't be truly interested in me," Abby said. "You've been dogging my footsteps only to make certain I didn't do anything to cause trouble. You're waiting until you go home to look for a wife. You told me you were going to pick one out for your career, not for love."

"I've changed my mind."

"About what?"

"Choosing a wife for the job, not for love."

"Why?"

"Because I've fallen in love."

Chapter Twenty-two

Abby didn't make a sound. She couldn't.

"Don't you want to know who I've fallen in love with?"

"No."

"Why not?"

"Because I think you've confused love with something else."

"I didn't recognize it at first. I thought it was a purely physical attraction for a pretty woman."

"And when did you realize it was something more?"

Abby held her breath. She didn't want Bryce to go on. She was afraid to believe that he had truly changed his mind.

"Yesterday."

She'd expected him to say the night she sat up with Pamela. Or the fire. Some men tended to fall in love with women they rescued.

"What changed your mind?"

"It was a lot of things. But if I had to point to one, I would say it was your courage."

"I'm not courageous."

"And your determination."

"You mean stubbornness."

A rustling of the bedroll and Bryce's hand touching her arm told her he had closed the space that separated them. She wanted to pull her hand away, but some impulse caused her to reach for him. Apparently her brain still hadn't overcome her heart's hope that Bryce could love her.

"Stubbornness can be good," Bryce said. "In you it is."

"That's not what you said at first."

"I was wrong. I was too busy thinking about myself. When you told me you didn't want a relationship, something in me wouldn't give up. I knew I wanted you. When I saw you with Pamela, I knew I needed you."

He wanted a mother for his daughter, a wife for his career, but did he want a lover for himself? She would like to be Pamela's mother. She wouldn't mind helping him with his career once she learned what to do, but he would have to want her for himself. He would have to love her.

"Tell me why you think you need me," Abby said.

"Because I can't stop thinking about you. I can't stop wanting you."

That was good, but it wasn't good enough. Maybe he couldn't stop thinking about her, wanting her, because she was the only woman present and he'd been without a woman for a long time. She wanted to be the only woman he wanted regardless of the number he had to choose from.

"You've even made me question what I want to do with my life."

That sounded much more promising. "How do you mean?"

"I realized that while I might like to go back East, I enjoy the work I'm doing now."

"You mean you'd give up a Washington, D.C., appointment?"

"If that's what it takes to make you consider marrying me."

"You don't have to give up anything to make me consider marrying you," Abby said. "You only have to love me."

Bryce covered the rest of the distance between them. His arms went around Abby and his lips met hers in a passionate kiss. She didn't know how they found each other so easily in the dark, but it didn't matter. They *had* found each other.

"I love you more than I thought I could love anyone," he said. "I was afraid to let myself fall in love because I made such a mistake the first time. I married despite knowing there were a dozen reasons why I shouldn't. But this is different. I can think of more than a dozen good reasons why I *should* love you."

Abby thought of all the reasons she had for never marrying, and suddenly they didn't seem very important. She'd probably come up with them as a defense against getting hurt again. When she'd fallen in love with Bryce, she'd used them as weapons to keep herself from letting down the final barriers. Now that he said he loved her, her resistance collapsed.

She loved him so desperately she wondered how she had found the strength to keep him at a distance. She couldn't have loved Albert, because what she'd felt for him had never caused her to be on the brink of casting aside nearly everything she believed just to be with him. She knew without even thinking she'd do whatever, go wherever Bryce wanted as long as he loved her.

Abby returned Bryce's kisses eagerly. She'd waited so long for this, dreamed about it so frequently, told herself it would never happen, that the release of all restraint induced a kind of euphoria. She felt deliriously happy.

"I fell in love with you weeks ago," she said, after breaking their kiss. "I didn't want to trust a man that much ever again. Whenever my resolve started to weaken, I would tell myself you wanted a socialite for a wife."

"That's what my family wants. I tried to make myself believe an arranged marriage was better than one based on love, but you ruined that theory forever."

Abby allowed him to nestle her in the curve of his arm. "How did I do that? I've caused you nothing but trouble."

"I think that's why I fell in love with you. You never gave up. You refused to let anything stand in the way of your success. Yet as determined as you were to keep me at a distance, you always had time for Pamela."

"She's a darling girl."

"She's a terror, and you know it. I live in fear of what will come out of her mouth next."

"I think she's sweet. She asked me if I'd marry you so I could be her mother."

"What did you tell her?"

"What I told you; that I couldn't marry anyone who didn't love me."

"What are you going to tell her now?"

"I'll let you tell her. Besides, you might change your mind when you see me in the daylight. My eyebrows still haven't grown out."

"I never loved you more than when you fell into my arms that night."

"You must be besotted."

"Completely."

He laid her down and leaned over her. "I wish I could see you now, but I don't need light to be able to see your face. Your image never leaves my mind."

Abby pulled him down so she could kiss him. "Your image is always with me, too. I thought I'd never love anyone but Albert, but I can't even remember what he looks like."

"Good. If you ever showed him to me, I'd want to murder him for what he did to you."

She realized now it wasn't knowing Albert didn't love her that had hurt so badly. It was knowing he'd lied about her, tried to get her in trouble just because she wouldn't lie for him. He'd ruined her reputation out of spite.

"I've thought about him for the last time," Abby said. "Now it's up to you to make sure I never have reason to think of him or any other man again."

"That's a challenge I can't resist," Bryce said.

If anyone had told Abby that one day she'd be sleeping in a tent on the plains in the Colorado Territory being kissed by the man she loved with a dozen soldiers sleeping no more than fifty yards away, she'd have sworn it couldn't be. She felt giddy at the improbability of it all. Surely she'd wake up and find she'd dreamed the whole thing.

But the feel of Bryce's lips was too unmistakable, the pressure of his chest against her breasts too stimulating, the knowledge that the man she loved loved her in return too stupefying for her to have remained asleep. She had to be awake. This had to be real.

Throwing caution to the winds, Abby threw her head after her heart.

This wasn't the first time Bryce had held Abby in his

arms and kissed her, but never before had she allowed herself to concentrate on the exquisite feeling. Now she was free to wallow in it, to enjoy every second, every sensation, every shred of happiness. This wonderful man belonged to her and she to him. She could do this every night for the rest of her life.

Knowing that only made Abby more hungry to experience everything she could right now. Having given him free rein, she realized she'd been missing more than she guessed. Such as Bryce kissing her shoulders. That sent shivers up and down her spine. It had such a delicious feeling of decadence, even naughtiness. Abby had been circumspect her whole life and still ended up suspected of a crime. Never again would she hold back. She wanted everything regardless of the cost.

She wanted it when Bryce's tongue invaded her mouth, searching for the sweetness. Her arms tightened and she clung to him, her own tongue forcing its way into his mouth, engaging in a sensuous dance of invitation. She had never felt such a need to be close to anyone, to belong to him, to be part of him. And for him to belong to her, to be part of her. It was as though their lovemaking was a dance to signify the commingling of their spirits, the mating of their souls, the joining of their lives.

She wanted it just as much when Bryce kissed the tops of her breasts. It was an intimacy she'd never shared with any man, not even in her dreams. It was so much more meaningful that she was now sharing it with Bryce, welcoming him, holding his head hard against her. Just the feel of Bryce's chest pressed against her breasts stirred sensations in her belly. His kisses had turned those same sensations into spirals of warmth that caused her to move against him, to know instinctively there was more, much more.

She thought she'd found it when Bryce reached inside her chemise and cupped her breast, but she learned almost immediately she was wrong. When he stroked her nipple with the tip of his finger, she moaned with delight. When he kissed her nipple, she writhed with pleasure. When he took her nipple into his mouth and sucked it gently, she thought she'd rise off the ground in ecstasy. Shivers arced through her body like sparks from a Fourth of July firecracker, leaving trails in their wake that slowly turned to heat. When he nipped gently at her nipple, she gasped in shock and pleasure.

She offered no objection when he slipped her chemise off her shoulders and down to her waist. She wanted to give her body to him. He was teaching her things she'd never known were possible. Not even Aunt Emma's hints had helped her imagine the glorious things that could happen when a man and a woman fell in love and gave themselves to each other. Maybe not every man knew what Bryce knew. If not, it was a great shame so many women had no idea how beautiful giving yourself to a man could be.

And she was giving herself to Bryce. There would be no hesitation, no stopping, no wondering if she was doing the right thing. She loved him, he loved her, and she wanted them to be together in every way possible.

She reached up and took his face in her hands. With her fingertips she traced the outline of his strong jaw, felt the roughness of his beard, the softness of his full lips, the thickness of his hair. She pulled his head down and took his mouth in a slow, languorous kiss. She'd never thought of Bryce as soft in any way, but his lips were like warm, moist velvet. As the kiss deepened in intensity, she felt his heat pour into her and spread throughout her body. Unlike the languid warmth that pooled in her belly, this heat burned its way through her like a fire, consuming her.

Her breathing became quick and shallow. Her body arched toward him, moved against him. His hands slid down her sides, leaving her skin deliriously sensitive to touch. All her senses were heightened until she felt she was a mass of nerve endings, aware of textures for the first time in her life.

She was acutely aware the first moment Bryce's hand touched her thigh. Immediately her skin burned from his touch, heat spiraling out in rapidly expanding circles. It increased tenfold when his hand moved between her legs. Her body stiffened, the muscles clamped into place when he entered her.

"I won't hurt you," he whispered.

"I know," she said, trying to relax her muscles. Bryce's fingers touched a spot that sent a shock through her unlike anything else she'd ever experienced. Every muscle in her body turned rigid, her breath stopped. Then just as suddenly she went limp and her breathing started up at twice the speed.

Her body took on a life of its own. She couldn't even control simple movements. The spot Bryce had found sent bone-numbing pleasure radiating throughout her body, shattering her thoughts completely. She could only react to the increasing power of the sensations that held her in their thrall. Her body rose off the ground, pushed itself against Bryce's hand trying to drive him deeper inside her. The harsh sound of her breathing was broken intermittently by moans that grew more feverish. She was approaching an edge, an abyss, a point where she could endure no more.

She tried to call out to Bryce, but her own moans of pleasure stifled her protests. She tried to push him away only to have her arms wrap themselves around him and pull him closer. She tried to throw up a wall to hold back the tide, but the flood doubled in size and then exploded, carrying her up and away, overwhelmed by ecstasy.

Before she could recover herself, Bryce moved above her and she felt him enter her, stretching her until she was certain she could stretch no more. Almost immediately his movement within her brought a resurgence of the sensations that had so recently robbed her of all ability to think or act. Abby welcomed the feeling of being joined with Bryce, sensing she was no longer an individual but part of a larger whole. She let the sensations wash over her, lift her out of herself, take her to the edge of ecstasy that she truly shared with the man she loved. Without knowing it, this was what she'd been waiting for, what she'd lived for. She embraced the climax that carried them into oblivion together.

Abby could hardly wait to reach the fort. They had decided their return from their trip to the ranches wasn't a good time to announce their new relationship, but trying to act as if nothing had changed between them was about the hardest thing Abby had ever done. A hundred times a day she impulsively turned to Bryce, a comment on her lips that would have made their relationship unmistakable. She practically had to tie her hands to her sides to keep from reaching out to touch him every time he came near. The frustration grew so great, she felt like screaming.

The last two days had been a disappointing series of visits to ranchers who said they didn't have any beef to sell, didn't want to work with a woman, refused to sell beef to the Indians, or simply didn't want to expose their hands to the danger of attack. One of them named Parker said he'd sell his beef to Abby, but only if she could pay cash up front.

Lieutenant Collier had recovered the lost tents, but Abby had spent her last night as the guest of a rancher. She lay in her comfortable bed wide awake, wishing she could share a bedroll with Bryce. She kept telling herself to be patient, that they would soon be able to tell everyone of their love.

She had never been part of what is generally called society, certainly not the society into which Bryce had been born, but she'd been brought up well and had no fear of being unable to be a wife Bryce could be proud of. She would be a good mother to Pamela and the children she hoped to have, but she had some significant questions when it came to helping him in his career. There would be a great deal to learn and she would meet many powerful people, but it wasn't those challenges that concerned her. It was giving up her independence.

She liked working with Moriah in the store. It had given Moriah something important to do, brought out a side of her that had been hidden, given her confidence. Abby liked feeling they provided an essential service to the community. People depended on the store to improve the quality of their lives. And then there were the Indians. It was important they continue to receive the beef they needed to survive.

She couldn't forget the people who were trying to drive her out, who had rustled her beef, attacked her, burned her store, maybe even murdered her father. She couldn't let them defeat her.

Nor could she give up this man, no matter what the cost. There had to be some compromise, some way she could have the best of everything.

"You glad to be home?" Bryce asked as they approached the fort.

"Yes," Abby said. "I had no idea how tiring it was to ride a horse all day. I thought the horse did all the work."

Bryce laughed. "That's why horseback riding is considered good exercise."

The fort seemed so peaceful lying quietly under the afternoon sun, it was hard to realize tensions were so high that war between Indians and ranchers and homesteaders could break out any minute.

"It seems so quiet," Abby said to Bryce.

"That's the way I like it. The men find it unbearably boring, but I prefer boredom to getting shot at."

She had listened to the men talk about their experiences during the recent war. It sounded horribly brutal. She couldn't imagine why any man would want to fight if he could avoid it. Descriptions of what Indians sometimes did to their victims were even more shocking.

Their entry into the fort caused only mild interest. None of the men in the patrol were married, and there had been no fighting to talk about. Abby expected the only person to show any real excitement would be Pamela.

"I'll come over tonight to talk about what's to be done about the beef contract," Abby said to Bryce.

"I want you to come with me now."

"After being gone for five days, Pamela deserves to have you all to herself. She'll be full of questions."

"Not as many as she will have tonight. You sure you want to wait?"

"Yes. Moriah will be waiting to hear the results of our trip."

"I'm sorry we don't have any good news to tell her."

Even though they would be separated only by a parade ground, Abby wanted to kiss him good-bye. It felt unnatural just to ride off as if nothing had changed. Bryce got down and helped her dismount.

"One of the men will take your saddlebags to the trading post after they've unsaddled the horses," he said. He kept his hands on her waist a moment longer. "See you tonight," he said. "Come early," he added in a whisper.

Refusing to stand there staring after Bryce like a lovesick female, Abby turned toward the trading post, telling herself not to look back. She'd be seeing him soon enough.

The store was busy when she entered. Moriah, Dorrie, and another woman were all serving customers. Even in time of peace, soldiers always needed something. Moriah looked up when Abby entered, but her expression didn't change. The only difference Abby could see was in her eyes. Moriah seemed to relax; the lines at the corners of her eyes smoothed out. That was about as much as Moriah would do to show she was glad Abby was back safely.

Dorrie was just the opposite. "Abby!" she shrieked in a shrill voice. "You're back."

Immediately everyone in the store looked up. "We're all back," Abby said. "We had a very uneventful trip."

"It's been quiet as a tomb here," Dorrie said. "I was hoping you at least would have something exciting to tell us."

"Nothing. Everyone's still getting ready for the spring roundup."

Moriah finished with her customer and followed Abby into the back. "Did you find anybody to deliver the beef?" she asked.

"No, but—"

"I didn't think you would. Someone is determined we won't succeed with that contract. I think we ought to give it up."

"When did you come to that conclusion?"

"While you were gone. I didn't like the idea of you

being out there. I can't see any reason for you to keep risking your life because of this contract."

"I wasn't out there alone. I had Bryce and a patrol led by Lieutenant Collier."

"Less than a dozen men. You said there were hundreds of men on the reservation."

"I don't want to talk about that now," Abby said. "I have something to tell you." She couldn't help grinning. She was bursting to tell her news.

"What?" Moriah asked.

"Bryce and I are in love," Abby announced, practically dancing with excitement. She took both of Moriah's hands and held them tightly. "He told me two nights ago."

"You said you didn't love him," Moriah said. There was no smile in her eyes.

"I kept saying that because I hoped I could make myself believe it, but I knew weeks ago I was in love with him. I just never thought there was a chance for us."

"And what makes you think there is now?"

"I just told you. He loves me."

"How do you know?"

"He told me. He said the words. *I love you.*"

"How do you know he's telling the truth?"

Abby hadn't expected her sister to be thrilled, but she hadn't expected her to be almost angry either.

"I can tell," Abby said.

"You were wrong about Albert."

"That's part of the reason I can be so sure now. This is nothing like it was with Albert."

"He could be telling you he loves you so you'll become his mistress."

"Moriah! I can't believe you'd say a thing like that, not after all the help he's given us."

"He's a handsome man, rich and successful. I'm sure

he's used to women falling all over him, some willing to do anything to please him. He's been out here for years without a wife. Something like that could drive a man to say things he doesn't mean."

"Have you been talking to Dorrie?"

"Why would Dorrie say something like that?"

"I don't know. Why would you?"

"Because I'm worried about you. I know you as well as anyone can. You're a beautiful woman, single, and beguiling. Men have always liked you. I didn't expect anything different from him, but you were so adamant you weren't going to get married, that you could never trust another man, I thought your interest in him was mostly to show you could attract someone even better than Albert."

"I'm fully aware of how superior Bryce is to Albert. When I think back, I can't imagine what I saw in him."

"He was handsome and attentive, but he wasn't the only man to show an interest in you."

"He was extremely good at building up my ego."

"Are you certain the colonel isn't catching you on the rebound?"

"Positive. I did my best not to fall in love with him, and I'm sure he did his best not to fall in love with me. After all, we thought we wanted very different things."

"What do you want now?"

"We haven't had a chance to talk about it. I wanted to tell you first. And I thought he ought to tell Pamela before it becomes public knowledge."

"You'd better sit down and make sure you want the same things before you say anything to anyone."

"Why?"

"Because he wants a fancy job in Washington, D.C. A wife with money and the right connections would be a powerful boost to his career."

312

"Bryce said that he loves me so much, it's changed what he wants out of life. Don't you think that's significant?"

"It'll be significant if he actually does it. Have you thought about Pamela?"

"Of course I have. I adore Pamela. I'd love to be her mother."

"How will you get along with his family? We're perfectly respectable, but we're just nice people whose father managed a trading post on an army camp."

"I can't believe my ears. What has gotten into you?"

"Are you willing to give up the store, your independence? You'll have to go to so many social events, you won't have time for your children. You'll spend more time with your dressmaker than with them. Oh, I forgot: Our aunt is a dressmaker. Maybe you can take her to Philadelphia with you. Ask your mother-in-law to recommend her to all her friends. It ought to do your reputation loads of good for people to know your aunt makes dresses for senators' wives."

"Don't be ridiculous."

"Ridiculous, am I? How do you suppose people are going to react when they find out you were accused of embezzling?"

"I was never charged. Besides, how would they find out?"

"That sort of thing always comes out. Have you told Bryce?"

"I haven't had a chance yet."

"Why have you waited so long?"

"Until he said he loved me, there was no reason to tell him."

"Well, there is now."

They were interrupted by a knock on the door.

"Come in."

Dorrie entered, her face white. "Bryce is out front," she said. "He's here with a man who says you are wanted for embezzlement."

Chapter Twenty-three

When Abby saw Bryce's expression, the bottom fell out of her world. It wasn't belief or disbelief. Not even anger or confusion. She could have dealt with those. It was the hurt, the look that said he didn't understand why she hadn't been open and honest with him, a look that said he would have believed her, supported her if she'd told him everything, a look that said he wondered what else she might be hiding from him. An unfair accusation had ruined her life in St. Louis. Now it was threatening to do the same thing here.

Abby hadn't given in to despair in St. Louis and she wasn't about to do so now. She'd deal with this man, dispose of his accusation, then she'd talk to Bryce.

"I don't know where you got your information," Abby said to the man, "but it's wrong."

"Let's go into your office so we can discuss this privately," the man said.

"You've already made the accusation where everyone

can hear," Abby said. "I'd rather everyone heard why you're wrong."

The man looked around at the several attentive and curious faces. "I would strongly advise you against it."

"I don't take advice from a man who makes unfounded accusations. I demand to know the reason for your presence and for making such a statement without proof. What is your name? I intend to lodge a complaint with your employer."

"My name is William Bennett. I'm a lawyer representing three firms who've given you credit. I'm here to tell you they want your accounts paid in full immediately. If you don't, I'll close down the store and seize all the merchandise against your debt."

"You can't demand that anyone pay an account immediately," Bryce said. "You must allow a period of time to make the payments."

"I'm not authorized to do that."

"It doesn't matter," Bryce said. "You have to do it or I'll have you escorted out of the fort."

"You can't do that."

"You'll find I can. As Miss Pierce has already mentioned, you haven't offered any proof to back up your accusation."

"I don't need proof. It was in the newspapers that Abigail Pierce was accused of being an accomplice in an embezzling scheme."

"It was also in the papers that the investigation turned up no proof that I ever had any involvement in Albert's scheme and that no charges were ever brought against me," Abby said. "Consequently, your statement that I'm *wanted* for embezzlement is a lie."

"A slip of the tongue," Mr. Bennett said. He offered no apology for having made the statement.

"A man in your profession should know a *slip of the*

tongue can sometimes hang a man," Bryce said.

"This isn't a hanging matter," Bennett said, somewhat defiantly, Abby thought.

"If you destroy Miss Pierce's ability to make a living, it's plenty serious."

"All my clients want is the money owed them."

"They will be paid according to the terms of our agreement," Abby said.

"In light of the police investigation of Miss Abigail Pierce, my clients have withdrawn their agreement," Bennett said.

"Please tell your clients they'll get their money," Abby said.

"How?" Bennett asked, his manner rude and scornful. "If you sold everything in here, you wouldn't have enough to pay your debts."

"That statement shows you know nothing about the retail value of goods," Abby said. "I suggest you stick to making false accusations. At least you're competent at that." She was pleased to see Bennett turn red. She was relieved to see a trace of a smile on Bryce's lips.

"I'm competent enough to tell you that as of now you will not be allowed to purchase any goods, *even if you pay for them in cash*, until you've settled your present debt in its entirety."

"Have you any other messages to deliver?"

"As soon as the judge reaches Denver, we'll have a judgment against you. Then we'll see about whom you can keep off the fort," Bennett said, turning to Bryce.

Bryce didn't answer, just smiled in a way that said he wasn't impressed.

"Then don't come back until you have such an order," Abby said. "Be sure to tell your clients that they will get their money."

"They'll get it, all right," Bennett said. "I'll make sure of that."

He left in a foul humor. Abby guessed he'd expected to scare her so badly, she'd give him every cent she could lay her hands on.

"I know you're wondering what happened back in St. Louis."

"You don't have to explain," Bryce said.

"Yes, I do. This is my home. I can't live here with people thinking I might be guilty of embezzlement."

"No one believes that," Dorrie said.

"You'd wonder," Abby said. She took a deep breath. "I was seeing a man named Albert Guy. He and I worked for the same bank. He had asked me to marry him. In the meantime, I stumbled on evidence he had been embezzling money from the bank. When I faced him with it, he said he'd been doing it for us, so we could start our marriage on a solid financial footing. I told him I couldn't marry him knowing we were depending on stolen money to make it possible. I told him to give the money back. He was furious with me, said he couldn't, that it would be too dangerous. I told him I didn't care, that he had to give it back. Then he told me he didn't have it, that he'd already spent it for a house. I knew he hadn't done any such thing, and I told him if he didn't give it back, I'd report him. I also told him that I couldn't marry him, knowing he was a thief.

"I gave him two weeks to give everything back. As it turned out, someone else found the same evidence and informed on him, but he blamed me. To get back at me, he told the police I was his accomplice. Since everyone knew he'd asked me to marry him, I suppose the police figured that was logical. In any case, they investigated me for several months. They went through every piece of paper I ever handled and found absolutely no evidence I'd had anything to do with the embezzlement. I didn't even have access to the accounts involved. But Albert told them that even though he'd done the actual embezzling, I'd been the one to come up with the idea and tell him how to do it. He said I'd spent part of the money on clothes. That caused the police to investigate my Aunt Emma, because she makes women's clothes. It also involved Moriah, because she worked for Aunt Emma.

"Even though the police could find no proof, everyone seemed to believe I couldn't be practically engaged to Albert and not be a party to what he'd done. I lost my job at the bank and was unable to get another one. It was clear I had no future in St. Louis. The scandal also caused my aunt's business to suffer. That terrible year was capped off by our father's death and the end of the allowance that my sister and I had depended on for our living. It was then that I decided to move to the Colorado Territory and start fresh. You know everything that's happened since."

"What a horrible thing to happen," Dorrie exclaimed. "And to be treated so badly by people you thought were your friends."

Abby murmured something, but she was looking at Bryce, waiting anxiously to know what he was going to say, what he thought.

"I'll make sure Bennett leaves the fort," he said to Abby, "and make sure everyone understands he's not allowed anywhere near you. Pamela wanted me to remind you that we're expecting you and Moriah for supper tonight. She's excited about playing hostess."

Abby desperately wanted to call out to Bryce, to bring him back so she could explain why she hadn't told him about St. Louis, but though his expression had remained neutral, she could tell he was upset. She didn't know whether it was at Bennett or at her.

Moriah pulled Abby from the store and closed the door. "We can't go to supper at the colonel's tonight."

"Of course we can," Abby said. "Staying away would practically be an admission of guilt."

"And you can't marry him."

"Why not?" Abby asked, angry Moriah was always throwing up barriers between herself and Bryce.

"Because your reputation will follow you wherever you go. Can you imagine his mother being willing to welcome a suspected felon into the family? Something like that would be enough to ruin his career."

"There was never any evidence against me," Abby said, desperate to make that point.

"It won't matter. Just the suspicion will be enough."

"His family can't be that bad."

"Do you remember how the Pinckney family reacted when their son married an actress? They disinherited him and refused to have him in the house again. And they didn't have any high social position to protect. I expect the McGregors would rather he remain buried in the Territories than face that sort of scandal."

Abby had been trying to tell herself none of this would mean anything to Bryce, that he would believe her, would still love her, but she couldn't deny that the scandal could be detrimental to his career.

"Do you think he's going to break it off?" Abby asked.

"No. I think you ought to be the one to release him from his promises."

"He hasn't made any."

"That will make it easier. It's hard to regret losing what you never had."

It was obvious Moriah had never been in love. Just

knowing Bryce didn't love her any longer would be the most devastating blow she could imagine.

"I've got to get back to the store," Moriah said. "Take the rest of the afternoon to get settled and have a bath. We can talk later."

"We're going to have supper with Bryce and Pamela," Abby said. "There are things that have to be said, things that have to be straightened out."

"I don't agree, but I'll stand by you no matter what you do."

Abby embraced her sister, doing all she could to fight back the tears that threatened. "I never doubted you. You've never once failed to have implicit faith in me."

"I know your soul, and I know it's pure."

Abby hoped Bryce had an equal faith in her integrity. She closed the door behind Moriah and sank down into a chair at the table. She had a lot to think about before seeing Bryce again.

Pamela met Abby and Moriah at the door when they arrived. "Daddy isn't ready yet," she said, practically dancing with excitement. "He said I was to act as hostess until he finished dressing."

"We're not early, are we?" Abby asked.

"You're six minutes late," Pamela said.

Abby bent down to give Pamela a hug. She hoped the child didn't see the tears in her eyes or ask why she was crying. "You'll make a marvelous hostess for your father when you grow up."

"That's what Sarah's momma told him, but he said he didn't want me to waste my time at dreary old political gatherings. He said he wanted me to meet a nice boy, get married, and have lots of grandchildren for him to spoil. Would you like coffee?" Pamela said, apparently remembering her role as hostess.

"No, thank you," Abby said. "I'll wait to have mine with dinner."

"Me, too," Moriah said.

"Zeb is cooking supper. Daddy says he still can't cook half as good as you and Miss Moriah, but he's been much better since you came."

Abby found it more difficult to keep the tears from her eyes. She turned away from Pamela. "Did you set the table?"

"Yes, but Zeb helped."

"You both did a beautiful job."

"We did it just like you showed me," she said proudly. "Daddy said I can do it when we go back to Philadelphia."

It seemed there was no safe topic. Abby wondered if it would have been easier to see Bryce alone. Zeb entered with glasses and wine.

"Could I offer you ladies something to drink?" he asked.

"No, thank you," Abby and Moriah said in unison. "Pamela was just telling us Bryce said she could set the table when he goes back to Philadelphia," Abby added.

"She'll be getting her chance a lot sooner than any of us expected," Zeb said, his smile disappearing. "The colonel got his papers today. He can head back East tomorrow if he wants."

The strength left Abby's limbs, and she sank down on the couch. She had hoped to have time to come up with a solution to her dilemma, but it was too late now. Bryce had the promotion he and his family had been working for ever since the war ended. He wouldn't want to wait. He had probably already regretted falling in love with her. He was a gentleman and would never have thrown her over publicly, but no one except Moriah knew. He could hurry back to Philadelphia and no one would ever know.

And she had to let him. If he didn't want to, she had to make him. Moriah was right. Marrying her would ruin his career. She couldn't live with that knowledge. His family would blame her. She knew he would defend her, but that would drive a wedge between him and his family. She would have to tell him before he said anything to Pamela.

Thinking of Pamela made Abby want to cry all over again. She had grown to love the little girl; her quick intelligence, her outgoing personality. The child deserved a mother who was more interested in her than in Bryce's career, one who would spend time with her, answer her endless questions. In Philadelphia Bryce would probably have even less time to spend with her than he did now.

"Are you all right, miss?"

"What?"

"You've been staring off into space," Zeb said. "I don't think you've heard a word I've said."

"Sorry. Trying to figure out what to do about the store and the beef contract is driving me to distraction."

"I'm sure it is, miss. I'd ask the colonel if I was you. He's real good at solving problems."

"Now that he'll be leaving for Washington, D.C., I guess I'd better get used to solving my problems myself."

"What problems do you have now?"

Abby turned to see Bryce entering the room. Just the sight of him caused her resolve to weaken so badly it almost gave way entirely. His smile had the power to banish all the clouds of fear and despair, even resentment and anger. She could banish all thought of past injustices. He looked so handsome in his uniform, she felt weak at the knees. Any woman would give her right arm to be married to such a man. She couldn't possibly give him up.

He was a good man who took great care of those who depended on him, took his responsibilities seriously, considered public service an honor rather than a chance to enrich himself. Which was exactly why she had to give him up.

"The same old things," she said, forcing herself to return his smile, "but there'll be plenty of time to talk about that later." Bryce looked as though he would reach out and take her hands. She couldn't allow that. Her resolve could never withstand his touch. "I think I will have some coffee now," she said, turning to Zeb. "It smells awfully good." She picked up a cup and saucer and held it out for him to pour the coffee.

"He still hasn't learned to make it as well as you," Bryce said.

"I'm sure he will. He learns quickly."

"Thank you, miss," Zeb said.

"We'll get a chance to decide when we have dinner. Pamela tells me she insisted he serve only your favorite dishes, the ones you showed him how to make."

"Which I do think was a mistake," Zeb said. "There's no way I'm going to cook her favorite dishes better than she does herself."

"I'm sure you did very well," Abby said, moving toward Moriah and Pamela. She felt exposed to too much danger, being so close to Bryce. She cast around frantically for something to talk about, but she couldn't think of any subject that wouldn't lead to his having to reveal his plans for the future. She had to speak to him, but she wanted to get him by himself first.

"How did Sarah's father do in your absence?" she

asked. "Did he show himself ready to have his own command?"

That topic lasted until Zeb called them to the table. After that, the subject was food. Pamela insisted upon asking Abby and Moriah's opinions of each dish. She then queried her father before favoring Zeb with the collected opinions of what he could do to make the dish even better next time. Zeb, who'd begun the meal looking nervous and afraid of failure, soon looked harried from trying to remember everything Pamela said. Abby finally rescued the poor man by telling Pamela she'd write everything down and give the instructions to Zeb so he wouldn't have to try to remember all the details.

"Thank you, miss," Zeb said, clearly grateful.

"Everything is really very good," Moriah said. "You've done quite well."

Everyone knew that was a real sign of success. Moriah didn't give compliments often. Zeb was pouring the after-dinner coffee when Bryce said he had an announcement to make.

"Could I speak with you first?" Abby asked.

"All right. What did you want to tell me?"

She could think of no other way but to be bold. "I need to speak with you alone for a moment. Would you mind if Moriah took Pamela for a short walk?"

Everyone knew immediately that something important was about to happen.

"I want to stay," Pamela said.

"I promise we'll tell you everything when you get back," Abby said. "No secrets. I just have some ideas I want to discuss with your father before I decide what to do."

Pamela didn't look happy at being sent away, but the promise of later disclosure served to mollify her somewhat.

"Miss Moriah and I will talk secrets," she said, tossing her head in challenge.

"You have to tell me your secrets if I tell you mine," Abby said.

"All right, but they'd better be good."

As soon as they left, Bryce took Abby in his arms and kissed her before she could stop him. Being unable to prevent the kiss, she saw no reason why she shouldn't take an equal part in it. It was some moments before she and Bryce stepped back from each other.

"That's what I want to talk to you about," Abby said.

Bryce laughed. "You want me to kiss you again?"

"No." Abby stepped back. "I don't want you to move until I've finished."

A frown crossed Bryce's face. "What's happened? Did that lawyer come back? I gave orders—"

"No, he didn't come back. I know we haven't talked since we got back from visiting the ranches, but—"

"I was going to tell everyone after dinner."

"That's why I wanted to talk to you. We made no promises and no decisions. I think it's best that we leave it that way."

"What are you talking about? I love you. I want to—"

"Are you sure? Couldn't it be just that you and I have been thrown together in a situation foreign to both of us? You became involved because of my ignorance. You're a young man, healthy, attractive. I'm one of only two women available. If you'd had hundreds to choose from, would you have ever noticed me?"

"Are you trying to say you don't love me?"

She ought to. That was what she'd planned to do, but she couldn't make herself say the words. She wasn't any good at lying.

"I should have told you about St. Louis before now, but I had no idea your interest in me was more than a desire to be helpful. If I'd ever believed there was any chance of a stronger attachment, I'd have told you, and you'd have known any relationship between us is impossible."

"You said the police never had any charges against you. I know you could never be a party to an embezzlement."

"I could be lying. You told me people came West to get away from their past mistakes. How do you know I'm not doing exactly that?"

"You could never lie. You're much too concerned with the welfare of other people. That's part of the reason you're so upset about this beef contract. You're worried about the Indians."

"Then you can understand why I can't marry you. I know you haven't asked me and maybe didn't intend to, but I couldn't in any case."

Bryce's smile of amused concern vanished, to be replaced by a look she hadn't seen before. It was a look of steely determination that would brook no opposition. "Who's been talking to you? What did they say? If it was Sarah's mother, I'll—"

"No one said anything. I've known all along I wasn't suited for a society life in Philadelphia or politics in Washington, D.C. I would have told you so if I'd had any notion what would happen."

"You could have told me two nights ago."

"Why? You told me you loved me. You didn't ask me to marry you."

"You knew that was what I meant."

"I hoped, but I didn't know."

"If you hoped, then why—"

"I wouldn't be the first woman to hope for what I couldn't have. Maybe I thought I could learn the rules of society, even learn how to meet famous and powerful people without stammering."

"You can do anything you put your mind to. You've proved that."

"But once that lawyer said I was wanted for embezzlement in St. Louis, I knew any future for us together was impossible. Having a wife suspected of a crime would ruin your career."

"But you weren't charged."

"That won't make any difference. I was investigated. The only reason I wasn't arrested is that they couldn't find any evidence against me. People think I was involved, that at least I knew what Albert was doing and approved of it."

"But you told him you'd turn him in if he didn't return the money."

"If I'd been the one to turn him in, they might have believed me. When I didn't, it was only my word against his."

"I don't care about that."

"I do. I won't be responsible for ruining your career."

"I can quit the army, not go into politics."

"No! This is what you've wanted all your life. Zeb told me you got notice of your promotion today, that you can leave as soon as you like. You said Sarah's father wanted to see if he could handle his own command, so you've got someone to take over until the army finds someone to replace you. There's no reason for you to wait. You and Pamela can leave tomorrow."

"I love you, Abby Pierce. I want to marry you."

"You think you do. Maybe you *really* do," she said, when he began to protest, "but you've been stuck out here with no one to look at but me. After nearly three years, any unattached female would look good. You don't know how you'll feel once you're back in Philadelphia."

"I know enough not to tell a woman I love her unless I'm sure. No matter where I go, my feelings for you won't change."

"I hope they will," Abby said. She took a big breath. "You have to go back East without me."

Chapter Twenty-four

Bryce couldn't understand how Abby could think he would change his mind. He'd accepted her explanation without question because he knew she wasn't a thief. He wasn't a fool. He knew such a thing might cause trouble sometime in the future, but he wasn't about to let Abby suffer for something she didn't do. Leaving without her was out of the question. He wanted everyone in Philadelphia, especially his mother, to know right from the start that he had a woman he loved and intended to marry. No political marriage for him. He wanted love, and this time he knew he'd got it right.

He took her in his arms despite her resistance. "I'm not leaving Fort Lookout without you. I'd like for us to be married in Philadelphia with all my family and friends gathered around, but where it happens isn't important."

"It's much too soon to make decisions like that. We haven't talked about any of this. We've only known for two days that we care for each other."

"Days and hours don't matter. Even if I'd only known for a minute, I'd be just as certain as I am now." He didn't understand her hesitation.

"I can't be sure of my mind quite as quickly," Abby said. "There's a lot to consider. Your career, your family, Pamela—"

"Pamela loves you. She'll be ecstatic when I tell her."

"You can't tell her."

"Why not?"

"Because I haven't made up my mind what I want to do yet."

"It sounds as if you're saying you don't love me."

"Saying I love you when we're alone in a tent is one thing. Saying I love you with the whole world watching, is another. Maybe you're sure of yourself, but I'm not sure I want to be a social or political wife." She struggled to break his embrace, but he wouldn't release her.

"You don't have to."

"Then there's your family to consider. I'm not what they wanted."

"They'll love you."

"No, they won't, and you know it. But it's not just your family, your career, or my uncertainties. I've got to figure out what to do about the store and my debts."

"I'll pay them for you."

"I won't let you do that. Moriah would never agree, either."

"Have you asked her?"

"I don't have to. She hasn't wanted me to accept your help from the beginning."

Bryce realized he was handling the situation very badly. He had been in a position of command for so long, he had a tendency to forget that not everyone had to do what he wanted. He had to listen to what Abby said. Afterward he could figure out how to solve the problem. He released her. "All right. Tell me what you want to do."

Abby backed away, looking relieved, not nearly so desperate.

"First, you ought to leave without me. You need to have time to decide what you want to do with your life. Maybe you want to make some changes in your plans, maybe you don't, but you need to decide without any outside pressure."

"What will you do while you wait?"

"Save the store."

"How do you plan to do that?"

"I've got to pay off my debts. Those people don't care whether I committed a crime as long as they get their money. I'll have it if I can deliver the beef to the reservation one more time."

"How are you going to do that when no rancher is willing to make the drive?"

"I only know one way." She hesitated. "I have to buy the beef and deliver it myself."

Bryce's first reaction was to tell her she was crazy and forbid her even to think of such a solution, but he'd learned that forbidding Abby to do one thing could cause her to do something even more foolhardy. He'd protected her so well, she didn't fully realize the extent of the danger she could be in.

"Do you have enough money?"

"If I bargain well."

"Do you have a crew?"

"I plan to ask Orman, Hobie, and Larson."

He'd been against her hiring those rowdies to freight her merchandise from Denver, but he had to admit they'd been well-behaved since they went to work for Abby. Obviously she had seen something in them he hadn't, but that didn't mean he was comfortable leaving her alone with them for a couple of nights.

"You don't have a herd."

"Parker will sell to me. He told me when we were there. He just doesn't want to expose his hands to unnecessary danger."

"But you don't mind exposing yourself."

"You told me Western men are very respectful of a good woman."

Abby had obviously thought everything through and come up with what she considered was one solution to all their problems.

"This has all come up too fast for either one of us to have had sufficient time to think about it. I know you believe you have a solution, but surely with time we can think of something less dangerous."

"But it solves everything."

"Except what to do about the beef contract next month."

"I can do the same thing."

"That sounds like a good idea, but why don't you wait a few days to give us time to see if we can find another solution? The beef isn't due on the reservation yet." Abby looked stubborn, so he didn't push it any further. "Come here," he said, holding his hand out to her. "At least we don't have to keep our love a secret from ourselves."

She seemed reluctant, started to say something, but Moriah and Pamela chose that moment to return.

"Miss Moriah and I have two secrets," Pamela announced proudly. "Which one do you want to hear first?"

Two nights later Abby waited under the porch until the guard Bryce had posted passed her in his circuit of the trading post. Bryce thought he'd talked her out of buying the herd and delivering it herself, but it was the only solution that wouldn't require her becoming even more indebted to him. She was certain if he lent her the money to pay off her creditors, he'd cancel the loan when he got to Philadelphia. She had to forget him. Owing him a debt of gratitude of such magnitude would make that impossible.

Actually, it would be impossible to forget him under any circumstances.

How did you forget the only man you'd ever truly loved? It was impossible when he was also the most handsome, the finest, the most honorable man you knew. It was impossible when you believed he loved you. It was impossible when you loved him enough to give him up. But there was no point in going over all that again.

Bryce told her it was crazy to think of trying to deliver the herd herself. Dorrie told her the same thing. Moriah refused to discuss it, but no one had come up with a better idea, though Bryce had spent most of last evening proposing and discarding several possibilities. This was the only one that could work. Maybe after this he would realize she was much too independent, much too strong-minded to be his wife. Maybe he would be relieved to go back to Philadelphia without her.

The guard disappeared around the corner. Moving quickly, she picked up her skirts and ran along the edge of the fort until she was around the wall and out in the open. She breathed a sigh of relief when she saw the men waiting for her.

"I still wish you hadn't told the colonel what we was doing," Orman said. "He don't like it when people goes against his orders."

"I'm the one going against his orders, not you," Abby said.

"That's as may be, but it's us that will end up with

our necks in a noose if anything happens to you."

"Nothing's going to happen. That's why you're here," Abby said. "Now stop complaining and help me into the saddle."

"I don't like you being out here with us," Larson said. "People will talk."

"They're going to talk about me in any case, so you let *me* worry about it. You concentrate on getting the beef to the Indians."

"I don't know why you're so worried about them Indians," Orman said. "They gets along just fine by themselves."

"No one leaves them alone anymore," Abby said, "but I can't pretend my primary concern is the Indians. I need the money the Indian agent will pay me to settle my credit debts before I can buy anything else for the store. Now let's not talk anymore. I want to be at the Parker ranch by dawn."

They made the ride in near silence. Orman and Larson rode on either side of Abby, with Hobie bringing up the rear. They reached the ranch just as Parker and his hands were getting up from the breakfast table.

"I told you I wasn't driving a herd to them Indians," Parker said when he saw Abby.

"I'm not asking you to drive a herd anywhere," Abby said. "I want to buy fifty head from you. I'll take responsibility for getting them to the reservation."

"Does the colonel know about this?" Parker asked.

"Yes."

"And what did he say?"

"He told me not to do it," Abby said, "but he doesn't have the authority to keep me from conducting any business I choose as long as it's not at the fort."

"I expect he'll come after you."

"He doesn't know I've left. I need fifty of your fattest

steers. I'm willing to pay seven dollars a head for them."

"I wouldn't sell them for less than ten."

"I don't have five hundred dollars."

"Then I'll sell them to the miners. They'll pay me eight."

"If someone else doesn't beat you to it."

"Okay, nine dollars."

"Seven."

"Nine."

"I'll pay you cash."

"When?"

"Now. I've got it with me."

"How about eight dollars?"

"How soon can you round them up?"

"I can have them ready by noon."

"If you have them ready for us to drive by noon, I'll pay you eight dollars. Any later and it's seven."

Parker's gaze hardened. "Are you sure you mean to do this?" He looked at the men with her. "These men ain't cowhands."

"You get the steers here by noon and let me worry about everything else."

Parker grinned slowly. "You're one stubborn lady."

"I don't see anyone trying to spoil me," Abby shot back.

"I don't think anybody'd dare. Mount up, you lazy sons-a-bitches!" Parker shouted to his hands. "The lady wants her beef ready to roll by noon. Tell your men to lend a hand. They might learn a few things that will help them on the trip. You can visit with the wife while we're gone. Ask her to pack a few things that'd be easy to cook over an open fire."

Abby passed an uneventful morning listening to Mrs. Parker complain about the difficulties of ranch life. She thought the western plains offered no comparison to her parents' home in Michigan, but she admitted her husband was much happier.

"Give a man space to roam about unhindered and he doesn't want for more as long as he's got a full stomach and a soft bed to sleep in. My husband didn't like working for anybody else. Couldn't go back to it now."

Abby wondered how Bryce would respond to taking orders after three years of being the one to give them. She scolded herself for letting her thoughts run back to Bryce. She'd vowed to begin putting him out of her mind, but she wondered if she'd ever be able to do it.

"You ever driven cows before?" Mrs. Parker asked.

"No. My father won the contract before he died. I didn't have any choice but to keep it."

"Nobody's ever wanted it but Baucom," Mrs. Parker said. "There's always an attack. My husband says he never delivered as much as half of what he ought."

"Baucom told me he didn't want it anymore, that it was too much trouble."

"That's queer," Mrs. Parker said. "He's the one who convinced my husband it wasn't safe to attempt a delivery."

"When was that?"

"I don't remember exactly, but it was after he lost the contract. I think it was some time after you came. Seems to me I remember my husband saying Baucom expected to get the contract again after your father died."

Mrs. Parker shifted abruptly to asking Abby what experience she had cooking over an open fire. Since Abby had none, she spent the next hour getting advice on every topic from how to build the fire to where to find fuel and water. Abby was relieved when the men arrived with the cows.

"Your men don't know much about cows," Parker said to Abby as she counted out the money.

"They only need to know enough to get them to the reservation."

"I hope they're better with guns."

"Why do you say that?"

"You know you're going to be attacked."

Abby wondered if she was crazy to be delivering the herd herself. Everyone had advised her against it. But since there was no possibility of a future with Bryce, it was her only way to support herself. She couldn't imagine herself falling in love with anyone else.

"We're armed," she said, indicating her rifle. "I'll take my chances."

"Stay in the open as much as you can during the day," Parker advised. "When you camp at night, make sure you find a place that protects your back. And stay well back from the campfire."

"You're making me nervous," Abby said.

"I'd feel better if I could make you give up. I feel guilty for selling you these steers."

"I know the risks and I'm willing to take them."

"Do you know how to get to the reservation?"

"There's a clear trail."

"Don't follow it. Head about ten miles to the south. It's rougher country and the grass isn't so good, but you may slip by anybody trying to waylay you. I've already talked to your men. I also exchanged your horses for some experienced cow ponies. Army horses don't know nothing about working cows."

Abby wanted to be on her way. The sooner she got started, the sooner this would be over. "Thanks for your advice and the horses. Are we ready to go?" she asked Orman.

"As ready as we'll ever be."

"Then let's get started."

Abby had never been on a cattle drive before, but it

took her less than ten minutes to know she never wanted to do it again. Parker said once the steers started moving, they'd gradually line up behind a leader and stay pretty much in that order for the rest of the drive. They didn't do that at first. Steers kept trying to break away from the herd to get back to their usual feeding grounds. If Parker and his hands hadn't helped, they would never have gotten the herd on the trail without losing half of it.

After about an hour the cows had settled down and started to sort themselves out. Now the trouble was handling the herd. She didn't know the trail so Orman had to take over leading. Hobie rode the left flank and Larson rode drag. That left her to ride the right flank. That was fine until a steer broke ranks and headed for a grassy ravine. Her cow pony started after him so quickly, Abby was almost thrown out of the saddle. She held on for dear life while the pony galloped to head off the steer. She managed to get the reins in her hands when the pony got around the steer and hazed him back to the herd. The steer made one more attempt to escape, but the pony used his shoulder to crowd him back to the trail. Giving up, the steer trotted docilely back to his place in the line.

"Good job," Hobie shouted across the line of steers. "You'd make a good cowhand."

Abby was sure her smile was sickly. "The horse gets all the credit. It was all I could do to stay in the saddle."

The herd finally formed a line of no more than two abreast, but by late afternoon she was exhausted, covered with sweat and dust, and hated the sight of cows. She might never eat beef again. But her ordeal was far from over. With evening came the need to find a bedding ground for the herd and get them settled while she tried to cook something edible.

The men took care of the herd while Abby wrestled

339

with finding enough fuel to build a fire in the open and cooking a stew without getting ash in the pot, getting burned by flying embers when the wind started up, or catching her dress on fire. By the time the stew was done, she wasn't hungry. She practically had to force herself to drink some coffee, which turned out to be too strong from sitting over the fire so long.

"Best coffee I've had in months," Orman said.

"Stew's great, too," Larson said, eating hungrily.

He was covered with dust from riding drag. She could see the outline of where he'd pulled his handkerchief over his nose and mouth. Hobie was still with the herd. He'd eat as soon as Orman replaced him.

Abby had seated herself gingerly on a small boulder. Her bottom was sore, and the muscles in her back and arms were so stiff and knotted from her long day in the saddle, she could hardly bend over. She didn't look forward to sleeping on the unforgiving, rock-strewn ground. That would be adding insult to injury.

"Do you think we can reach the reservation tomorrow?" she asked.

"If we get an early start," Orman said.

"Cows is always up early," Larson said.

Cows! She didn't understand why people called steers cows. She'd discovered it didn't matter if they were cows, calves, steers, or bulls. As far as Westerners were concerned, they were cows. And why would anyone want to spend his life hanging around these ornery, dangerous beasts anyway. They liked living in country that was too hot it the summer, too cold in the winter, and too dry all the time. It was filled with rocks, dust, and more thorny plants than any decent country ought to have. There were practically no trees, no rivers, and no roads. If you didn't become best friends with your horse and know how to use a rifle in your sleep, you could die and no one would ever find you.

If that was what she *really* thought, why did she like living here so much? Why would she want to stay even if her name were cleared and she could go back to St. Louis? When had she decided the land was beautiful rather than a barren and forbidding desert?

She didn't know, because in the beginning her attention had been focused on all the wrong things. She had concentrated on getting the store running, delivering on her contract, establishing a way to make a living. She had decided to learn as much as possible about living in the West, not because she liked it or thought it was beautiful and challenging, but because it would help her manage her store more profitably. She wanted to learn more about the people, about their hopes and dreams, so she could stock her shelves properly never expecting she would come to like them for themselves. She'd assumed she would have gone back East if she'd had the chance.

Then she'd fallen in love with Bryce and realized she didn't want to leave. What a time to discover she actually liked sagebrush!

She didn't understand how the thought of him leaving could hurt so much when it had been less than a week since he'd said he loved her. She didn't understand how such a short period of hope could overwhelm months of truly believing she didn't want to fall in love or marry. Obviously she'd been fooling herself. Her reaction was understandable, but it was stupid and self-deceiving. It was also the sign of a weak character, and Abby did *not* have a weak character.

She'd made some mistakes, and she'd paid for them. Her heart was broken, but she would learn to live with it. She would put all thoughts of Bryce McGregor behind her and start over.

"You going to bed down next to the fire?" Hobie asked.

She'd been so deep in thought, she hadn't realized he and Orman had exchanged places.

"Parker said we ought to sit well back from the fire. I suppose that means we ought to sleep well back from it, too."

"It can get mighty cold out here at night."

"I'll be all right. Maybe we ought to move farther back now."

"Why?"

"Because anyone sneaking up on us in the dark can pick us off like pigeons in a shooting gallery," Larson said.

"Indians never attack at night."

"It wasn't Indians that attacked the last herd," Abby said.

"As long as they was pretending to be Indians, they have to try to act like them, don't they?" Hobie said.

"Maybe," Abby replied. "They could be depending on people hating Indians so much, they'll believe anything against them."

She tried to stand up and nearly fell.

"You all right?" Hobie asked.

"Just stiff from so long in the saddle," Abby told him, regaining her balance. "I've never ridden so much in my life."

"Nor chased cows, I bet," Larson said.

"You can be certain I've never chased cows."

She moved her arms and legs to work out some of the stiffness. She was almost afraid to go to bed. Her muscles might be so stiff in the morning she wouldn't be able to move. She was exhausted, but she wasn't sleepy. She was certain someone meant to attack them, but she didn't know when, where, or how many.

She couldn't help wishing Bryce were here. He knew all about ambushes and how to fight. He knew the best places to make a stand, which strategy to employ, how to use his forces to the best advantage, and dozens of other things she didn't know about but that were essential to surviving a gunfight with rustlers. Why did she think she could do this by herself? Why hadn't she tried to talk Bryce into helping her? He would have, even though he didn't approve of her plan.

She was doing this because it was the only way she could pay her debts. She hadn't asked Bryce to help her because she had to learn to get along by herself. And now was the best possible time to start. If she was lucky, Bryce would be gone when she got back. It would be hard not seeing him, but it wouldn't be half as hard as having to say goodbye.

"Have you worked out a schedule for night guard?" Abby asked Hobie.

"Yes."

"When is it my turn?"

"You don't have no turn."

"I'm just as responsible for this herd as anyone else," Abby said, "so I'll take my turn. Put my name in the rotation and call me when it's my turn."

"Yes, ma'am," Hobie said.

It took Abby some time to find a spot that was not too far from the fire, offered some concealment, and was level and reasonably free of rocks. She had laid out her bedroll and slipped her tired and stiff body inside it when she heard the sound of approaching hoofbeats. Her apprehension eased somewhat when she realized it was only one horse, but she sat up on her bedroll and reached for her rifle.

"Do you hear someone coming?" she called to the men.

"Yeah," Hobie replied.

"Stay in the shadows until we know who it is and what he wants," she said.

"I got my rifle ready," Hobie said.

But as Abby heard the hoofbeats coming steadily closer, she wondered if this might be a ruse to get them so focused on one man, the rest of the attackers could approach unnoticed.

"Keep your eyes open," she said. "Someone could be sneaking up behind us."

"I'm watching," Hobie said.

"Me, too," Larson added.

Abby listened intently for any sound of men approaching under cover, but she kept her rifle pointed in the direction of the rider whose outline was barely perceptible in the dark night.

"Come to the fire if you're a friend," Hobie said. "But know I've got my rifle aimed at your heart."

The rider slowed his horse to a walk, then dismounted. A moment later Bryce walked into the ring of light around the campfire.

Chapter Twenty-five

"What are you doing here?" Abby asked

Bryce felt the muscles in his shoulders relax when he saw Abby emerge from the shadows. For the last several hours he had harangued his horse about the insanity of women, their incredible stubbornness, their inability to recognize danger, and the stupidity of men who ran after them. But he forgot everything the moment Abby stumbled into view. He only remembered he loved her, and she appeared to have been hurt. He rushed forward to put his arms around her, to support her, to hold her steady.

"What's wrong with you?"

"Nothing."

She tried to push him away, but he held her still more tightly. "You can barely walk."

"I'm stiff from being in the saddle so long."

He wanted to tell her that if she'd listened to him she wouldn't have been in the saddle at all, she wouldn't be stiff, and neither of them would be out on the prairie in the middle of the night. Instead, he said, "I'll massage some of the kinks out or you won't be able to move in the morning."

"What are you doing here?" Hobie asked. He approached the campfire with his rifle aimed at Bryce. "Why aren't you wearing your uniform?"

Bryce ignored Hobie. "Why didn't you tell me what you were going to do?" he asked Abby.

"You'd have tried to stop me."

"You can't do this by yourself. What if rustlers attack?"

"We're armed and ready."

Abby had no idea what being prepared for a gunfight really meant.

"She's got us to take care of her," Hobie said.

"Now she's got me, too," Bryce said. He had to admit the three men had served Abby well since she had persuaded him to let them out of jail, but he still didn't trust them.

"We don't need your help," Hobie said.

"I'm not asking you," Bryce said.

"You can't boss nobody around without no uniform."

"I've momentarily given up my command," Bryce said to Abby. "Making sure you're safe is my personal responsibility."

"You're not responsible for me, Bryce."

"Since when is a man not responsible for the woman he intends to marry?"

"You're not going to marry me."

"Have you stopped loving me? Have you decided you don't want to be Pamela's mother? Have you decided you don't want to have my children?"

He hadn't meant to hit her so hard, but those questions had plagued him from the moment Moriah appeared at breakfast to tell him Abby had disappeared during the night. Moriah had been the one to tell him she was sure Abby had gone to buy beef from Parker. Parker had told Bryce he'd advised Abby to drop about ten miles below the trail. He'd probably still be looking for them if he hadn't spotted the campfire. Apparently Hobie and his friends didn't realize such a big fire could be seen for miles.

"We've been through all of that," Abby said.

"Maybe you've been through it, but I'm still waiting for an answer." Abby tried to move from the circle of his arms, but he wouldn't release her. "Have you?"

"You know I haven't," she flung at him.

"What about Pamela, other children?"

"I haven't changed my mind about anything." She looked up at him, her eyes bright in the firelight. He suspected she was crying.

"Then why didn't you let me help you?"

"Because you'd have refused to let me go, and we both knew this was the only solution. You know I can't be the kind of wife you need. I'll give you stubborn children who will flout your wishes, and I'll tell Pamela to forget everything Sarah's mother told her."

Bryce didn't know whether to laugh from relief or shake Abby for practically scaring the life out of him. And all during this interminable, horrible day he'd been worried she didn't love him.

"You're exactly the kind of wife I want and need. I want stubborn children as long as they're yours, and I've been telling Pamela for weeks to ignore Sarah's mother. Now that we've cleared that up, we can discuss how soon we're going to be married."

"If you think I'd marry you knowing I'd destroy your career and drive you from your family, you're the one who's crazy."

"So you've decided you love me enough to give me up for my own good. Is that it?"

She didn't answer.

"Don't you think you ought to leave that decision to me? It's my career and my family."

"You've been out here so long, you've forgotten what it's like back East. Once you get back, you'll start to think differently."

"Abigail Pierce, if you think I'm too stupid to be your husband, then say so."

"I don't think you're stupid."

"You must. I'm thirty-two years old, a widower, and the father of an incredible daughter. I've fought in a war, commanded a fort, survived growing up in Philadelphia society and my father's career in Washington, D.C. I remember exactly what life back East is like, and I know exactly what I want and what I'm willing to do to get it. If having you for my wife means changing my plans, I'll change them."

It was clear from Abby's expression that she didn't believe him.

"Don't you think I thought of all this before I said a word to you? I was afraid you wouldn't marry me because you didn't want to go back East, didn't want to have anything to do with Philadelphia society, didn't want to have to cope with the Washington political arena, didn't want to take on another's woman's daughter. When I found you and Pamela loved each other, I knew the rest didn't matter."

Abby wanted to believe Bryce so much, she was shaking from the strain of keeping her hopes within bounds. Could any man love her enough to give up so much? It didn't seem possible. Her father hadn't loved her enough to take her with him. Why should she think Bryce could love her enough to change his plans for her?

You fool, he loves you enough to have taken off his uniform and come after you. What more proof can you want?

She knew she didn't need any more proof, but she was frightened. If she gave in now, she'd give in completely. But she'd been deserted so many times—by her mother, her father, the man she thought she loved—it was hard to believe it wouldn't happen again. Still, it was difficult to doubt Bryce's sincerity.

"Do you really mean that?"

"Yes."

"What will you do?"

"What would you like me to do?"

She had no idea. No one had ever asked her a question like that. "I don't know. What do you want to do?"

"I've taken my plans for granted for a long time. I'm not sure."

"Sounds to me like you two ain't never met before," Hobie said. "How about you sleep on it so me and Larson can get some shut-eye."

"Put me in the night watch rotation," Bryce said.

"You don't have to do this," Abby said.

"Of course I do. Now, where is your bedroll? I want you to lie down so I can work on these stiff muscles."

Abby knew she ought to resist, but she was too tired. Besides, it was what she wanted more than anything else in the world. Tomorrow would be time enough to wonder if Bryce knew what he was saying. Tonight she wanted to believe he loved her enough to give up everything for her.

Even if she couldn't let him do it.

"What were you doing sleeping in the bushes?" Bryce asked.

"Parker said I was to sleep away from the campfire. I've never slept in the open before. I felt better with

something around me, even if it was only a few bushes."
Settling back down on the bedroll reminded her of how
much her body hurt. She didn't know if she could ever
get to sleep.

"Lie on your stomach," Bryce said. "I'll start with
your shoulders."

Abby was certain if she ever lay down, she would
never get up again. She anticipated pleasure from
Bryce's hand on her back, but the muscles screamed in
protest. She groaned involuntarily.

"It takes a while to get used to being in the saddle all
day," Bryce said. "You shouldn't try to do it all at once."

"Don't scold me. I feel miserable already."

"Just relax and try to go to sleep."

Abby was certain she'd never be able to sleep with
Bryce's hands on her back, but exhaustion set in as soon
as her muscles began to relax.

"You sure that's something a gentleman ought do to
a lady?" Hobie asked.

"Not normally," Bryce admitted, "but these are unusual circumstances."

"How's that?" Larson asked, suspicious.

"First, the lady isn't used to riding. She's extremely
tired after being in the saddle all day and night, and her
muscles are so tight and stiff she can't sleep. If she's
going to be able to ride tomorrow, she needs as much
sleep as possible."

"Still don't seem right for you to be touching her in
ways that would get me thrown in jail."

"It's all right because you two are watching to make
sure I don't do anything improper."

"Looks to me like you're already improper," Hobie
said.

"What are we supposed to do if we don't like what's
happening?" Larson asked.

"You're not supposed to do anything unless Miss Pierce has a complaint," Bryce said.

"You got a complaint, miss?" Hobie asked.

"No." Abby thought her voice sounded suspiciously weak.

"You don't have to be afraid to speak up," Hobie said. "There's three of us if you need help."

Abby couldn't help being amused at how the tables had turned. Living in the West wasn't very comfortable or predictable, but it sure wasn't boring. If Aunt Emma could see her now, she'd swear Abby ought to be fainting from shock. Instead, Abby was wondering why no one had ever told her how delightful it could be to have the man you loved gently massage your body, even if he was limited to the parts Hobie and Larson thought were acceptable.

"Does this feel better?" Bryce asked. "You'd better say yes," he whispered, "or your watchdogs will start drawing cards to see who shoots me."

"It feels wonderful," Abby said loud enough for Hobie and Larson to hear. "I think the army should institute massages for all soldiers when they've spent the day in the saddle."

"It's not quite the same," Bryce whispered.

"You think other women would like something like that?" Hobie asked.

"They would if they feel like I do right now," Abby said.

"I believe they're considering it as a courting technique," Bryce whispered.

Abby chuckled, but she was losing interest in the conversation. Eyes closed, head resting on her hands, she felt fatigue settling on her like a heavy fog, clouding her brain and making the voices seem indistinct and far away. She didn't have to worry. Bryce was here. Everything would be all right.

"Abby, wake up."

Abby tried to shove away the hand on her shoulder. She felt drugged, so deep in sleep she was certain she couldn't wake up if she tried. Even her eyelids felt too heavy to open. The effort to flex her fingers depleted her scant supply of energy.

"You've got to wake up. We can't stay here. The rustlers are closing in."

Abby's body fought to remain asleep, but something in the back of her brain screamed a warning she couldn't ignore. Abby opened her eyes to see Bryce's face only inches away.

"There are at least a half dozen men working their way through the brush right now," he said. "I've already told the boys to fall back to a better defensive position. We've got to get there before the rustlers reach the campfire and find no one here."

For a moment Abby was fearful her body wouldn't move, but Bryce took her hands and pulled her to her feet. He folded up her bedroll and picked up her rifle while she tried to wake up enough to walk without falling over her own feet.

"How did they find us?"

"You have to learn not to build a campfire that can be seen for miles."

"The boys were afraid I would be cold."

"It's better to be cold and alive."

Abby was sufficiently awake to agree with that aphorism.

"Keep your head down," Bryce said as he led Abby past the still-glowing ashes of the campfire. "They might be able to see you against the skyline."

Abby followed Bryce for what felt like a mile before he dropped into a dry wash. The sand made walking more tiring, but she no longer stumbled over rocks or caught her skirt on thorns. Hobie and Larson had already taken up positions behind some rocks. Bryce positioned her between them and behind a large cottonwood.

"Stay there and keep your head down," he said. "I'll tell you when to shoot."

"Where's Orman?"

"He's with the cows. We can't take the chance that they'll make off with your herd and leave us looking like fools."

"You were asleep. How did you know they were coming?"

"I didn't go to sleep. They only had this one night, so I figured they would attack as soon as they could find you."

"You think the same people are behind all the attacks?"

"Yes. I think the attacks when Baucom had the contract were faked. I never heard of any of his men getting hurt, but he consistently lost half the consignment. After he lost the contract, cowboys started getting shot."

"Baucom told me he was glad to get rid of the contract, that it was too dangerous."

"He lied."

"Then—"

"Hinson and Baucom are in this together. I expect they found a way to share the money they made on the missing cattle, but I can't prove it."

Abby didn't know why she hadn't seen that herself. "You think they were behind the fire?"

"I think they'd do anything they could to drive you out of business so you'd have to give up the contract."

"Enough to kill me?"

"I'm afraid so."

Despite Bryce's warnings, Abby had never considered herself in real physical danger. Not that she doubted Bryce when he told her what *could* happen. It was just that things like that didn't happen among civilized people. She'd been prepared to believe Indians would do terrible things. Everyone knew they were uneducated savages, but she had believed white men were too civilized to kill indiscriminately for the sake of money. Now she'd learned the Indians had honored their bargains while the white men, from the politicians on down, had cheated on theirs. Maybe Albert wasn't so different. Maybe Bryce was unique, a man of honor and integrity who would give up his career for what he thought was right, for the woman he loved.

And she was that woman.

"They're coming," Larson whispered. "I just saw one of them stand up."

"That's careless," Bryce said. "They must think we're all asleep. Don't anyone fire until I give the signal."

"Why not just kill them now?" Larson asked. "That's what they planned to do to us."

The stark reality of what it meant to live in the West became even more clear to Abby. There was no effective police force or code of behavior to protect the helpless. One had to be willing to fight for the right to be free. Men killed and expected to get away with it.

"Keep your voice down," Bryce said. "They're getting close."

"You should have brought the army with you," Hobie said. "Your troops could have shot up the whole lot of them."

"Rustling is not the army's concern unless the Indians are doing it," Bryce said.

Abby didn't understand that, but then, she didn't understand why the army had no control over the white men who cheated the Indians but were expected to protect these very same men from the Indians.

"That's an Indian out there," Hobie said.

"I expect they're white men dressed up as Indians."

"Let's kill us one and see," Larson said.

Abby remembered the shock she'd felt when she realized she'd killed Spicer and felt sick to her stomach. "I don't want to kill anyone," she said to Bryce.

"All you have to do is fire in their direction," Bryce said. "We've got a pretty good position. Larson and Hobie can guard our flanks while you and I blunt a frontal attack."

Abby found herself growing more and more nervous. She didn't like waiting, especially when she didn't know what was going to happen. Worse, she was feeling guilty. What if something happened to Bryce? He wouldn't be here if it weren't for her. When she'd made up her mind to drive the herd herself against his advice, she hadn't expected him to follow after her.

But she should have known better. In the back of her mind she'd probably thought he would come after her to protect her. Worse still, she'd probably counted on it. How could she have done something so awful, so underhanded? How could she face Pamela if anything happened to her father because of her own selfishness?

"You shouldn't be here," she said, turning to Bryce. "This isn't your fight."

"I'm here because I love you. How could I be anywhere else?"

"You could be with your daughter. She doesn't need you getting shot because of me. You could both be on your way East."

"I'd just as soon he didn't go anywhere right now,"

Larson said. "I think they just discovered the camp is deserted."

"The embers are still warm, so they'll know we're on to them," Bryce said.

The four of them were so quiet, Abby could hear herself breathe. She could also detect the sound of someone moving through the brush.

"Any moment now," Bryce whispered.

For Abby the whole night was taking on a surreal aspect. It was impossible to believe that she, Abigail Pierce, reared on a South Carolina farm and in a quiet household in St. Louis, could be crouching in a dry streambed in the middle of the night, rifle in hand, ready to take part in a gun battle with people who were willing to kill her to steal her cows.

But even as she decided she must be going crazy, she saw Bryce take careful aim. He had been brought up in a wealthy Philadelphia household, no doubt protected from all the unpleasantness of the world, taught all the rules of gentlemanly behavior. Yet here he was calmly preparing to do battle. Even though it was hard to fathom, it obviously was possible to be caught up in this world without losing her sanity.

But when the first rifle shot shattered the quiet of the night, she was no longer sure.

"Aim for the flash of light," Bryce said, "but keep under cover. They'll be doing the same."

It seemed to Abby that flashes of light came from all directions. The sound of rifles exploding into the night slammed into her ears like a physical force, bounced about in her head as if they'd taken on solid weight. She felt as though madness were all around her.

"Keep an eye out for our flanks," he warned Larson and Hobie.

"I'm worried about my back," Hobie said.

"Orman is covering us."

"I thought he was watching the herd," Abby said.

Abby still found it difficult to believe she was in a life-and-death struggle, but the sound of bullets smashing into the sand, rocks, and tree trunks was rapidly convincing her. She wasn't willing to accept defeat at the hands of some thieving men who were cowardly enough to attack a woman at night. That made them even more despicable than Albert. She aimed her rifle at a gun flash and squeezed the trigger.

The sound of a man screaming in agony made Abby's blood run cold. She looked around to make sure Bryce was still safe, that neither Larson nor Hobie had been hit. Her body sagged with relief when she saw all were safe.

"Who got that one?" Larson asked.

"The colonel," Hobie said. "Now pay attention. We can't depend on him to save all our hides."

Abby realized that applied to her as well. These men were in danger because of her. It didn't matter that she'd paid them. She had to do her part to make sure they came out of this alive. She aimed, fired, and was rewarded by a loud yelp.

"Congratulations," Bryce said. "I think you grazed one."

A bullet smashed into the trunk of the cottonwood she was hiding behind and sprayed her hair and clothes with pieces of bark and wood fibers.

"Get down!" Bryce shouted.

She raised her head long enough to fire at another flash, then dropped back into the bottom of the streambed.

"Stay here and keep them busy," Bryce said. "I'm going to try to get behind them."

"You can't go out there by yourself," Abby said.

"No one knows we're here," Bryce said. "In a protracted gun battle, they've got the advantage. They could keep us pinned down until we exhaust our ammunition."

Abby realized she'd subconsciously expected help. She couldn't imagine being anywhere so isolated that a gunfight could take place without anyone else hearing it. She started to argue with Bryce, but he was already running down the dry streambed. Moments later he disappeared into the dark.

Abby didn't know what force impelled her to action, but she leapt to her feet and followed him.

She couldn't catch Bryce. He moved too swiftly through the brush. It was all she could do to keep him in view. From time to time she lost sight of him—her skirts were a real problem—but she refused to be stopped. It wasn't long before Bryce had gone far enough around the attackers' flank to circle back. Realizing she was behind them now and unlikely to be seen or heard because of the gunfire, she moved more swiftly to get closer to Bryce.

Up ahead Bryce slowed, then stood up. He appeared to be trying to locate the positions of the people below. If the rustlers found themselves caught in a crossfire, they'd be sure to run. With two guns in front and two guns behind, even the larger force of rustlers would feel they were too exposed to carry on the fight.

Bryce raised his rifle, appearing to be waiting to make sure of his target. She raised her rifle, too, ready to give supporting fire.

That was when she saw a man rise up out of the brush behind Bryce, his rifle pointed at Bryce's back.

Chapter Twenty-six

That man was Luther Hinson.

Abby couldn't believe how calm she felt. She didn't have to stifle the impulse to scream, to shout a warning at Bryce, to panic or faint. She calmly swung her rifle around, took quick aim, and fired.

She couldn't tell if she'd seriously injured Hinson, but he dropped his rifle. Bryce whirled to see who'd saved his life. He couldn't see her face in the dark, but it was impossible to mistake her silhouette. Abby didn't know what he might have said to her, for at that moment a bullet smashed into the rocky ground close to her feet.

"Get down!" Bryce shouted. "They know we're behind them now."

It seemed the number of attackers had doubled. Bullets crashed into the ground all around her. Abby found a small depression and flung herself into it, but Bryce was firing at the men below. Not willing to be useless, she crawled several feet, then fired.

"Keep up a steady fire," Bryce said. "They're trying to escape."

Less than a minute later the firing stopped.

"They're gone," Bryce said. He quickly covered the distance between them, swept Abby up into his arms, and kissed her soundly. Abby knew she shouldn't allow him to continue thinking he could give up his career for her, but she couldn't resist these few moment in his embrace. After being afraid he might be hurt, she needed reassurance that her folly hadn't brought him any harm.

"Are you all right?" Bryce asked.

"Except for a skinned knee and shattered nerves, I'm fine," Abby said in a shaky voice. "What's in a little gunfight to upset a girl?"

Bryce chuckled. "Nothing if that *girl* is Abby Pierce. Let's check on Hinson."

But Hinson had vanished. A shattered rifle left on the ground showed what Abby had hit.

"Do you think they'll come back?" Abby asked.

"I don't know. Right now all I care about is that you're safe."

"We need to make sure the others aren't hurt."

All three men were unharmed.

"Let's have some breakfast and get these cows on the move," Bryce said. "The sooner we reach the reservation, the sooner I can have my woman to myself."

They finished breakfast and were on the move at dawn. Thirty minutes later they saw Lieutenant Collier and a detachment of soldiers coming toward them. Bryce and Abby rode forward to meet them.

"I caught these men running away about an hour ago," Collier said, grinning at Bryce. "You wouldn't happen to know what set them off, would you?"

Abby saw several men she didn't know, but her gaze settled on two she did. Luther Hinson sat astride his horse glaring at her, his left hand wrapped in a bandage covered with blood.

"Seems someone shot him through the hand," Collier said.

"Abby did when he tried to shoot me in the back."

Ray Baucom's arm was in a sling. "Who got this one?" Collier asked.

"Abby again," Bryce said. "I heard a yell after one of her shots."

"Ma'am, I sure am glad I'm on your side," Collier said, considerably impressed by her marksmanship.

"It was pure luck," Abby said.

"I considered turning them over to the local sheriff," Collier said, "but attacking the commander of a United States fort makes this a military matter. Seems the commander wasn't wearing his uniform, so the scallywags wouldn't know they were putting their necks in the army's noose."

Collier was grinning. If Abby hadn't been so in love with Bryce, she'd have given him a hug and a kiss on the spot.

"In that case I suggest you lock them up until the commander can put his uniform back on and decide what to do with them," Bryce said.

"You got nothing on me," Hinson said.

"Nothing but rustling, attempted murder, arson, and cheating the Indians of nearly everything the government has given them."

"You can't prove anything."

"I can swear you were going to shoot Bryce in the back," Abby said.

"Being caught with rustlers pretty much makes you one of them," Bryce said. "Then there's the matter of the fire at the trading post. My daughter saw you throw a match through the window. That fire could have killed both Abby and her sister."

"No court is going to believe a kid," Hinson said.

"How about Abner Pierce's death? We have a witness who says it wasn't an accident, that the two of you killed him."

"You can't have a witness," Hinson said, "because we didn't do it."

"He saw you stop the wagon," Bryce said. "While Baucom talked to Abner, you came up behind him, hit him over the head so hard you killed him, then tried to make it look like an accident. You didn't contact me because you knew I'd realize Abner would never lose control of a wagon. You'll both hang."

"Hinson didn't mean to kill him," Baucom said. "We were just going to make him hand over the contract."

"Shut up, you fool," Hinson said.

"Hinson said it was better that he was dead, that he'd never have given up the contract."

Hinson tried to attack Baucom, but the soldiers wrestled him to the ground.

"I'm not going to be hanged for something you did," Baucom yelled at Hinson.

"Lock them up," Bryce said.

"Where did you find a witness?" Abby asked.

"I didn't. I was bluffing."

"But how did you know what happened?"

"I guessed Hinson was the brains behind the scheme to steal the beef and murder your father. Baucom was just greedy. He pretended not to want the beef contract to deflect suspicion from himself, but I suspected he'd draw the line at murder." He turned to Lieutenant Collier. "I'll see you in a couple of days."

"Where are you going to be?"

Bryce winked at Abby. "Working under cover."

* * *

Bryce had insisted Abby and Moriah have supper with him their first night back at the fort. He said she was too tired to worry about cooking and Moriah deserved a break after having the store all to herself for so long. Much to Abby's surprise, Moriah made no objection. Abby felt bad that Zeb had worked so hard to make sure everything was just right because she had been too nervous to eat more than a few bites. She'd spent the evening wondering what Bryce was going to say.

She knew the time had come when Zeb put brandy and coffee on the table and left. Pamela had been bouncing in her seat all evening as if she had a secret it was nearly impossible to keep to herself. Bryce had kept up a steady flow of conversation, smiling, even joking, but there was an underlying solemnity to his tone that made Abby uneasy. Despite the show he was putting on, he was on edge.

"I expect this is going to be the most important evening of my life," Bryce said after Pamela had very carefully poured coffee for Abby and Moriah. "I'm not at all sure things are going the way I want." He picked up an envelope and passed it to Abby. "There's a telegram inside. It was waiting for me when I got back today."

"Why are you giving it to me?" Abby asked.

"Because it's about you."

Abby knew without asking that it was from the police in St. Louis. Who else would go to the expense of sending a telegraph message about her? And the only reason she could imagine for sending such a message was that they'd finally found some evidence they could use against her. Her heart felt like lead in her chest. Why had she ever thought she loved Albert? Why hadn't she turned him in the moment she found out what he'd done instead of giving him two weeks to return the money?

"Go ahead and open it," Bryce said. "You must know what it says."

"Have you read it?" she asked.

"Yes. It was addressed to me."

"You might as well tell me what it says."

"You don't want to read it for yourself?"

"I expect I'll have plenty of time for that."

"If you're sure."

Abby nodded.

"It's from the chief of police. It says Albert Guy has admitted he lied when he implicated you. He says you had no part in the embezzlement, and that once you found out what he'd done, you gave him two weeks to return the money before you reported him. In a nutshell, you are completely cleared of all suspicion. The chief promised to send a newspaper clipping of the story."

"I knew it all the time," Pamela crowed. "I knew you'd never do anything wrong."

Abby looked up at Bryce, hardly able to believe her ears.

"I knew it, too," he said. "Some people simply can't do anything wrong. They don't know how."

Abby knew she was smiling even though her eyes were filling with tears of relief and happiness. "You said I did the wrong things all the time."

"I only said that when you didn't follow my advice. But so far you've managed to bring off everything you've attempted."

"I couldn't have without your help."

"I'd like to believe that, but I'm not so sure." His smile remained, but it seemed fixed and stiff. "I have a second envelope here," he said as he passed it to Abby, "but you don't have to open it. You either send it to Washington or you tear it up."

"What is it?"

"It's my acceptance of the promotion."

"Why give it to me?"

"Because what you do with it will determine what I do. You see, Pamela and I had a discussion this afternoon. Well, it was hardly a discussion. We were in agreement before we even started. We took a vote and it was unanimous."

"What are you talking about?"

"We voted to invite you to become a member of our family. I want you to be my wife."

"And I want you to be my momma," Pamela said.

"Bryce, I've already told you—"

"I asked Moriah her opinion of what you said. And she said—"

"I said you were lying to yourself," Moriah said. "You've been in love with the colonel for weeks. It's stupid to keep denying it."

"I don't deny it," Abby said, feeling cornered. "What I said was I wasn't the best wife for Bryce. I'd come between him and his family, and I'd probably blight his career."

"Pamela and I took another vote," Bryce said. "You want to tell her what we decided, Pamela?"

"We don't have to go to Philadelphia if you don't want to. We can stay right here. Daddy can keep on telling people what to do, and I can learn to ride and shoot a rifle like you."

"You can't do that," Abby protested. "I couldn't stand it if I knew I was in the way of your career."

"We took another vote. It was also unanimous. Actually, we took a lot of votes and they were all unanimous. We're not going anywhere without you. If you stay, we'll stay. If you leave, we'll follow you. We can't be happy unless you're with us."

"Sarah's momma says my new momma would have to love me. Do you still love me?"

"Of course I do."

"I want to marry you," Bryce said. "Not just for Pamela. For myself. I'll do anything I can to convince you to say yes."

"For God's sake, Abby, put the man out of his misery," Moriah said. "Tell him you want to marry him."

"Don't be stupid," Abby snapped. "Of course I want to marry him, but I don't want to ruin his life."

"Then tell him you'll be happy to go wherever he goes and support him in any career he chooses. You can, you know. You don't have to worry about St. Louis anymore."

"I thought you didn't want me to fall in love with him."

"I didn't, but it was obvious you were crazy about him. Besides, as men go, he seems fairly decent."

From Moriah that was high praise.

Abby's heart beat so rapidly she felt breathless. It looked as if she could have everything she'd dreamed of. All she had to do was say yes. She looked from Bryce to Pamela and back to Bryce. Poor dear, he looked almost white with tension. She could understand why Pamela was so anxious for her to marry her father, but it was hard to believe a man as strong and self-sufficient as Bryce could possibly look as though he would fall all to pieces if she refused him.

She looked at the envelope in her hand. He had placed his future in her hands. She could tear it up, and they would stay here. She would be sure of her place at the fort and secure in the knowledge that she could handle the job of wife of a fort commander. After the last three months, she felt she had conquered the hardest part. She had the strength to become a woman of the West. She could learn to feel at home here.

Or she could send the envelope off, and pack her bags for Philadelphia. She would have to face his family, prove she was more worthy to be his wife than some socialite picked for her pedigree and family connections. She would also have to face the world of Washington politics. She didn't know anyone in government, had no idea what happened or what role she could play. Going back East would be a difficult task, probably one she would never fully master.

But she knew whatever she did, or chose not to do, Bryce would continue to love her. That was all that mattered. She handed the envelope back to him.

"I'll go wherever you go," she said.

"We're going to stay here!" Pamela squealed with happiness, jumped down from her chair, and threw herself into Abby's arms. But even as she hugged the little girl to her bosom, Abby's eyes were on Bryce. His reaction was far more restrained than his daughter's, but for Abby it was what counted most. She could tell how worried he'd been that she would refuse him, how relieved he was she hadn't, how happy she'd made him.

She knew because she saw tears cause his eyes to glisten with happiness. She'd never tell him what she'd seen, but she'd carry the memory in her heart always.

Author's Note

No man was ever more caught in the middle than the Indian agent. Appointed by the federal government to live among the Indians, he dispensed annuities that often did not arrive on time. Singlehandedly, he was supposed to restrain the legions of traders who cheated the Indians and illegally sold them whiskey. He was expected to teach the Indian how to farm in areas that were often too arid for agriculture—and where, in any case, the government often supplied the wrong kinds of farm implements. It was also the agent's job to keep white settlers off Indian land. But in this capacity, too, he was practically powerless, since the government steadily undermined his role by giving in to the demands of land-hungry pioneers. For all this he was paid less than a village postmaster. Not surprisingly, most agents were ineffective or plain dishonest, and the few who were committed to the job ultimately failed.

For every good agent, there were many more corrupt ones. Samuel Colley, a Cheyenne agent, had his son join him on the reservation. The young man arrived with about 30 cows to his name, and presumably following the example of his father, amassed a small fortune of $25,000 within two years by selling goods that rightfully belonged to the Indians. At another reservation a new agent arrived in 1869 to take up his post and found that his predecessor had not been seen for a month. There was no money, and there were $14,000 worth of unpaid bills. None of the annuities promised to the Indians in return for their land had been distributed to them in four years.

Willian Barnhart, the agent at the Umatilla Reservation, had to be replaced for killing an Indian. His successor, Timothy Davenport, was surprised to find a salaried school-teacher but no school. This enterprising fellow had been acting as a private secretary to Barnhart; he openly admitted to Davenport "the place of agent at Umatilla is worth $4,000 a year." An agent's salary was $1,500.

The above excerpt was taken from *THE OLD WEST: The Indians* (Time-Life Books, 1973, p. 169).

WYOMING
Wildfire

Leigh Greenwood

With the inheritance of half her uncle's Wyoming spread, Sybil Cameron feels she's gained her independence at last. Then she meeets her partner, Burch Randall–a man who believes a woman has no business running a ranch. She vows to keep her cool no matter what. Yet as Burch's muscular arms close around her, a deliciously hot feeling courses through her body.

To Burch, Sybil is a wild filly: spirited, headstrong, and in need of a man's brand. But he soon learns this is one woman not to be tamed. In fact, he finds he glories in her passionate abandon, revels in her raw courage, and wants only to take her and set the prairie ablaze in a Wyoming wildfire.

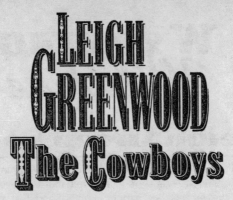

LEIGH GREENWOOD
The Cowboys

The freedom of the range, the bawling of the longhorns, the lonesome night watch beneath a vast, starry sky–they got into a man's blood until he knew there was nothing better than the life of a cowboy . . . except the love of a good woman.

___Jake	4593-1	$5.99 US/$6.99 CAN
___Ward	4299-1	$5.99 US/$7.99 CAN
___Buck	4592-3	$5.99 US/$6.99 CAN
___Chet	4594-X	$5.99 US/$6.99 CAN
___Sean	4490-0	$5.99 US/$6.99 CAN
___Pete	4562-1	$5.99 US/$6.99 CAN
___Drew	4714-4	$5.99 US/$6.99 CAN
___Luke	4804-3	$5.99 US/$6.99 CAN
___Matt	4877-9	$5.99 US/$7.99 CAN

Wild Desire

Phoebe Conn

Nineteen-year-old Eliza has run the Trinity Star Ranch since she was a mere child. Though she is every inch a lady, she has no trouble standing up to any man. That includes the tough-looking drifter she finds camping on Bendalin land. Little did she dream that Jonathan Blair was the friend who'd saved her uncle's life on the battlefield, or that his dark good looks and brash seduction will tempt her to forget both the rules of deportment and the duty she owes her family.

Jonathan takes what he wants from life. And he wants Eliza. Though she is already engaged to be married and far outclasses him, he will let nothing stand in his way.

I Do

MIMI RISER

"Florrie or Dorie—'tis such a wee dif'rence. Dinna ye fear, lassie, Alan'll still wed ye," declares Angus MacAllister, chief of the Texas branch of the Clan MacAllister. And with these words, the mixed-up mayhem begins. When Dorcas Jeffries offers to temporarily stand in for the bride in a ridiculously archaic arranged marriage, she never imagines she will find herself imprisoned in an adobe castle or being rescued by the very man she is trying to escape. She is sure her intended bridegroom will be the worst of an incorrigible lot. But what do you say to a part Comanche Highlander whose strong arms and dark eyes make you too breathless to argue? What else but "I do"?
